The father of monsters

Season of the Runer Book IV

Abigail Linhardt

ACKNOWLEDGMENTS

I'd like to acknowledge my editor J.H. Flemming for her patience and amazing comments and edits. She always finds several little holes that need patching and makes my manuscript stronger.

I'd like to thank K.N. Nguyen for beta reading for me and asking all the right questions to get me to see the flaws in the early drafts. Thanks for reading for me.

Lastly, and as always, thanks to my narrator Aaron. He's been patient with me and always encourages me with his praise of the books. Thanks for giving my words a voice once again.

SEASON OF THE RUNER
BOOK IV
THE FATHER OF MONSTERS

ABIGAIL LINHARDT

I dedicate all the effort and time spent on this book to my family. To my brothers who game with me and my sisters who don't let me become a stranger.

Chapter 1

The Scholar

The wind of Alika blew gently, warmed by the afternoon sun as it wafted through the soft, gauzy shroud. An archway opened up onto a large, round balcony overlooking the city below. The bright, sapphire rivers cut through the red and gold structures, offering quick transport to the caravans, merchants, and others who depended on its quick currents.

Allowing the river to carry the colorful river boats, the current pulled them south towards Mysir and the ruby throne of the Dynast Pharaoh. Massive bronze wheels along the shores pulled the boats and ferries back up the river in the opposite direction, allowing for easy travel in both directions. Every river in Alika offered more than water and good fishing: they were the lifeblood of the country, how the people moved quickly from one end to the other. The Three Rivers ran out from the center, an eternally gurgling natural spring large enough to set the ship of every pharaoh of Alika in and still have room to navigate. To the east of the spring in Mysir, the Cradle watched over the most luscious jungles of Alika. To the southeast, the Dynast Pharaoh's gold and ruby palace glittered like a newly forged khopesh in a field of gold and emerald.

Abigor Sharar didn't raise his face to take in the last rays of the day's sun as he focused on the Dynast palace. Even miles away, it was visible over the hills, jungles, and river. The Cradle, that great golden orb where the salty water was turned to clean, fresh water was hidden behind the mountains. The salt taken from the Alikan rivers was priceless, containing magical properties beyond any herb or crystal he'd encountered yet. But the Alikans and their theocracy guarded it, only allowing the Order of Temples and Prophets and the Dynast Pharaoh to handle the precious salt. Taking in the sheer magnitude of The Cradle made Sharar sigh in satisfaction. He'd long ago found a friendship with the young Masahk Dynast Pharaoh. It had been his longest trial, and now, all those years of research might finally pay off.

Sharar tilted his golden telescope to focus on the back of the Dynast Palace. Despite his new lenses, he couldn't make out much over the distance. One day, he hoped to develop a lens so powerful, he could spy on the moon the Alikans worshiped. He could almost spot the scales in Mysir's square: the symbols of the moon and sun and their prime gods, Krah and Ashmalia. Krah was a lion-type Masahk, and Ashmalia was some sort of hawk-type. But he had more pressing matters than stargazing like a magi through a telescope. One of those matters lay two floors below his feet. The reason he'd built this estate on Alika, far from his home. He pulled back from the telescope, his mind wandering to darker places now. Being so close to the one thing he wanted to hide from the world always made research difficult.

"Your spirit fades with the setting sun," a melancholy, rough voice said behind him. "It sets even now."

Sharar sighed quietly in frustration, pretending to adjust the gears and dials on his telescope. The damn djinn had a way of reading his emotions, which he'd never found a way to hide from.

"I thought I told you to leave me for tonight," Sharar replied easily. "What good is a slave that constantly disobeys its master's orders?" He looked up, feeling the djinn wouldn't leave. Turning, he faced him.

The djinn appeared in his spiritual form: he had the sharp features of an Al'Myrahn man, but his skin was pale, almost like frost and ice. A light mist hovered over his flesh, like the melting of snow. His hair, swept up into a long ponytail, glowed bright white, like his eyes, and hovered in waves around his shoulders. Sharar had long been unsatisfied with the djinn. Where other djinns were monsters who haunted and terrorized dwellings, often fighting to possess their victims, this one merely existed, forever melancholy. It had all the same powers the others did. So what did it matter?

"I have done all you asked," the djinn replied. He raised his hands, showing the spectral, icy shackles that hung from his wrists. "I cannot deny you."

Sharar smiled and scoffed gently. "Not this conversation again, demon. I have made two wishes already. You cannot convince me to free you with the last. I made that quite clear the day I found you. The more wishes you grant, the stronger you become."

"I am not so old as my bound brethren," the djinn tried again.

Sharar clicked his tongue. "No, making more wishes works in your favor, not mine. I only have one left. It will destroy you, so I know how desperate you are to escape me. I won't do it. Not yet."

"Why not wish to know where the Mahit'Onomicon is?" the djinn asked. "That's what you seek, is it not?"

Sharar shook his head, almost grinning. "The way in which wishes must be asked is too much of a riddle, demon. I won't give you the chance to foil my plan of devouring you, just to let you go to the next moronic fool who will wish for wine, women, and gold." He made a sound of disgust. "I made the mistake of throwing one wish out of desperation. I won't do it again. I must rely on myself."

The djinn didn't reply to this.

Sharar paced the length of his balcony, looking out over Gypsu. "They're moving pieces I have not found yet, but I am close.

Sheikh Sahir has sent me invaluable information." He stopped pacing. "Any word?"

The djinn shook his head.

"It's been too long," he murmured, pushing a few loose strands of his deep, black hair back under his headscarf. "I need a distraction." He turned sharply to face the djinn. "Fetch me a girl. An Al'Myrahn, if you can. I need the exertion."

ع

WHILE THE DJINN WAS OUT, Sharar left his study and descended to the basement, where his darker experiments took place. He had left behind much in Hatal, and had made a note to have the remainder of his devices sent to his estate in Alika. He hoped that soon he'd have need of it. He examined a few notes he'd taken some months ago when he'd last visited the Dynast Pharaoh. The young Masahk ruler of Alika was ignorant and eager to make his mark on the ancient dynasty of his family. Easily molded. But the Vizier, a jackal Masahk named Nasor, was wary of Sharar, and had blockaded all of his attempts to dig deeper into any leads he had.

He shoved the scrolls aside on a table and moved to inspect the black box of a Runer he'd acquired. He took out the vial of sulfates and held them up to a flame, letting the light be cut on the prismatic ingredient inside. He turned it, making specs of rainbow dance over his face and the pillar the light hung from. Ever since cutting Tzarik open, he'd thought he'd been closer to divulging the ingredients. He'd had a Runer comrade given to him by Sahir some years ago now, but that damned man wouldn't let the secrets of the runes out, either. But he didn't care about that Runer's blood. No. Tzarik's was better. Tzarik's held the answer.

Sharar gripped the vial and his eyes shot to the huge, chained metal doors at the back of the dungeon. No, what lay beyond that room couldn't read his thoughts. Then why did he feel the need to apologize?

Growling, he shoved the sulfates away and left the dreary basement. When he reemerged, the djinn was just coming in the door, a young girl struggling against his grip. The djinn had disguised himself as an Al'Myrahn man before fetching the girl. To anyone in Alika, he looked like the servant of the scholar. The girl's kohl tracked down her face in dark streaks. When her golden eyes landed on Sharar, she stopped struggling, panting for breath.

"I've heard of you," she said in a beautiful voice. "The other girls talk about you. Please, don't take me. I'll do anything you want if you let me go."

Sharar smiled darkly. He moved towards the alabaster stairs that led to his bedchambers, signaling the djinn to bring her. "Sabi, you will forget all I do to you once you are paid."

Inside his elaborate bedroom, he went to a golden chest with three locks on it. One was a rolling dial of symbols, another took a key, and the last slid into position to open. He reached in and pulled out a thimble-sized ruby. He held it out to the girl.

"What's your name?" he asked.

Her eyes rounded upon seeing the gem. She stammered timidly. "Zahra."

With her captivated, the djinn let her go, bowed, and backed out the door, locking it behind him. Zahra turned, gasping at the sound of the lock. Sharar loved the fear in her eyes. It made everything he was about to do ten times more enjoyable. If something as base as this could be enjoyable. But he'd found ways to make it so.

"I don't care," Zahra whimpered. "Anika told me about you before she…" She gulped, clasping her hands over her chest.

Sharar took in her appearance, moving behind her. She wore little more than a gauzy white dress laced and decorated with cheap golden satin. Her little slippers were well worn. Her hair was her best feature: clean, silkier than Xian fabric, and thick. He ran his hand from her scalp all the way down to the ends, which hung below her backside. He let his hand move along the bottom of her thighs, waiting for a reaction. When she gave none, he moved close, pressing himself into her, and brought both his hands around to her stomach.

She tensed, making a small, panicked grunt. Her hands quickly went to work out of habit, running up and down his lean fore-arms. They caressed a brand there. Zahra looked down, taking in the handprint-shaped brand.

"What is this?" she murmured. "Like a demon took hold of you."

Sharar laughed lightly through his nose. "You've heard stories of me. A demon *has* taken hold of me."

Leaning into her neck, taking in the amber scent of her hair, he let one hand trail down between her thighs and the other grip the ample flesh of her breast. Her heart thudded against her ribs under his hand, and he noted her breathing: ragged, dry. She was thirsty. Her stomach growled loudly.

"Please," she tried again, eyes shut tightly. She bit her bottom lip as he found her most tender spot. "Stop."

"No," he growled.

ℤ

LYING ON HIS BACK, looking up into the veils and silks over his bed, Sharar contemplated the last three hours. Zahra had begged him to stop, but he hadn't. She'd cried out in pain when he'd tormented her with flails and whip-like reeds. But moments later, she'd gasped in forced pleasure as he'd driven himself into her. She'd gripped his shoulders so tightly at one point that he now had bruises on his skin. Then, when he'd choked her as he'd finished his pleasure, she'd begged for mercy.

Sex was mundane. He'd decided that long ago, but the way

people spoke of it, he thought he must be misunderstanding something about it. It was base animal behavior—beneath him. He'd tried to elevate the act by studying torture and pleasure, but very few, even those who said they enjoyed such a thing, seemed to desire it as he did. He raised his hand above his face, taking in Zahra's blood coating his palms. What didn't he understand?

Zahra shook next to him, sobbing softly and clutching the cotton sheets to her bruised, battered body. Sharar kicked her towards the edge of the bed with his bare foot. She gasped, but moved.

"Food is on the table," he told her. "Eat and drink."

She hesitated a minute, head snapping to the table near a set of beautifully ornamental floor-to-ceiling windows facing the west. A golden carafe of red wine waited on the round table, surrounded by a pile of grapes, cheese, oranges, and dark bread. He could practically hear her salivating.

"Eat," he commanded again. "It's not a trick."

He liked how her golden eyes glanced at him over her bruised shoulder, questioning. He'd done this for the last three hours: promised pleasure, then given pain instead. When she didn't move, he shoved her out of the bed and spread out on it, sighing. She hit the marble floor hard, but bolted up and ran to the table. He strained his head up to watch her. Zahra devoured a chunk of cheese and choked on it, chasing it with a gulp of wine straight from the carafe, foregoing the golden goblet. The wine dribbled down her chest and mingled with blood from cuts on her thighs. He noted how the pain from the alcohol in her wounds didn't stop her from continuing to drink.

She reached for a glass pitcher of clear Alikan water, downing that next. Then she shoved a half dozen grapes in her mouth before savagely biting at the bread. She sank to her knees, still bruised from him shoving her earlier, and ate like an animal at a trough. He reimagined her eyes looking up at him from that position. He winced in disappointment. Even remembering it gave him no pleasure.

Sharar slid off the bed, holding the sheets around his middle, and moved in front of the full-length gilded mirror. He turned his head, admiring his lean neck and defined shoulders. Zahra's hands had left bruises on them, matching the brand on his arm from his djinn. He'd never been a physical man, not like Tzarik or other men. But he'd also made sure to tone his body to perfection, to never end up like his old master at the seminary. The man had been so corpulent that he had four servants to carry him around the grounds. In fact, Sharar could not remember a time he'd seen the man walking. He had claimed that one need not be of a strong body if the mind was strong. Sharar didn't believe him.

He was about to turn away from the mirror when his eyes landed on a scar just below his bottom rib. The scar faded and reappeared depending on how inflamed it was. Being two years old, he expected it to be little more than a white mark on his bronze flesh, but sometimes, it came back in full force. It wasn't a normal scar; he'd been stabbed by a small sigiled blade wielded by a Wushito master.

The Xian master had stabbed him when he'd tried to run, leaving the mysterious crypt on their continent closed. But ShanBao had been stronger than he'd thought. The man had grappled him, stabbed him, and dragged him up the steps to the temple where the crypt was hidden. He remembered the feeling of the ghostly cold metal inside him. The wound had hurt, but more than that were the horrifying visions that came with the sigiled blade. The cursed visions often haunted his nightmares. The blade carried some sort of dark magic he hadn't been able to define yet. Because of that, the wound festered sometimes, opening up afresh and wracking him with pain and terror.

Behind him, the sound of the door unlocking and opening

made Zahra jump and curl in on her self, covering her nakedness. The djinn stood in the doorway.

"A letter, sira," the djinn said softly, entering and handing it to Sharar.

Sharar took it, recognizing the sloppy handwriting of Sheikh Sahir from Moshav. He tore it open and began to read.

Behind him, Zahra cringed under the table, eyes on his servant. The djinn took up her dress from the floor and walked it to her without looking at her. Confused and grateful, she took it, dressing quickly.

"Do you need me tonight?" she asked Sharar.

His eyes sped over the words. Sahir said he had urgent news. Things that could not be written down. He had sent Amir—the Runer long in Sahir and Sharar's pay—his way after posting the letter. The letter informed him that Sahir had instructed Amir to wait at the ports of Gypsu. Amir would find Sharar, then follow him home. Sahir had not felt comfortable putting Sharar's Alikan address in the letter. Sharar had worked with Amir before, but realized he'd never met the hunter at his estate on Alika. They'd always met somewhere else and Sharar had led him there. He'd met Amir often at his estate in Hatal. It was for the best that Sahir hadn't put the location in the letter, lest it fall into another person's hands, as it seemed another of his letters had.

"No," he replied to Zahra, folding the letter up. "You are free to go. Take the ruby."

He moved to pick up his clothes and started to dress. The djinn fetched the ruby for Zahra, handing it to her wordlessly. She took it and licked her lips, contemplating. "Are you leaving town?"

Curious, Sharar glanced at her over his shoulder, using the mirror before him. Did she want to come back, unlike the others? Was Zahra swayed by the wine, food, and generous pay? It was exhausting finding a new girl every time the urge came to him.

"No," he said. "My family is here."

Zahra's brows went up in shock and her mouth popped open. She looked around. "You have a wife?" she asked, scared.

"Oh, you are kind, Zahra. No woman would have me forever. Surely you can see why. I have no wife."

His wound twinged. No, not now. He slowed as he dressed, listening to his body. He went pale, clammy, and swallowed carefully. "My son is here. Now, go."

The girl nodded, eyeing the table, no doubt wondering if she could take some food for herself for the night. When she didn't move, Sharar turned, intending to shout at her to just take it and leave when his wound ignited. The sudden, piercing hot pain shot through his ribs, up his chest, and around his stomach. His guts turned in sudden sickness. He clasped his hand over his wound and stumbled backward. The djinn moved to save him from crashing into the mirror, catching him. Sharar panted, praying the pain would subside. Sweat immediately beaded on his brow and he couldn't stop another loud groan of mounting pain.

Zahra snatched the carafe and a silk napkin off the table and ran to him. The djinn knelt, cradling him as the pain grew more than ever before. Sharar threw his head back in a silent cry, pressing madly into the wound. Zahra submerged the cloth into the wine, then shoved it into his mouth before he bit down. A large swallow of the wine flowed from the cloth down his throat. The soft buzz of the alcohol helped ease his pain. Zahra did it three more times until the agony finally began to wane. Her hand quivered as she stroked his temple soothingly, her fingers in his damp hair.

Panting in relief, he pulled the cloth from his mouth, his jaw aching. Never had it hurt that much before. Or so suddenly. Perhaps it grew worse the longer it went untreated. But he didn't dare approach a Xian who might know how to treat the malignant wound. They knew who he was on that continent.

"What is this?" Zahra asked, pulling his hand away to look at the freshly bleeding, blackening knife wound.

Sharar gathered his breath. "I'm a cursed man, Zahra. Leave."

She glared at him, shoving him so he rolled out of the djinn's grasp. She gathered up handfuls of food, shoved more down her front, took the ruby, and fled out the bedroom door.

Sharar lay on the cold floor, curling in on himself. He'd get her back. She'd seen him in pain. He'd make sure she didn't remember it when she returned for more food, drink, and gemstones. Her pain would be far worse.

Pushing himself up, he stumbled to his ornate, roll-top desk and pulled out the ships' schedules for the docks. Sahir had sent the letter the day before Amir had left Moshav. The Runer would arrive the next night on the passenger ship from Al'Myrah.

Another pulse from his heart sent one last pang to his wound. Pulling his hand away, he examined the black blood on his palm. His hand shook.

"I wish I could heal you," the djinn said in a stony tone that made Sharar not believe his words. "But that magic is equal to my own. Demonic, from a god."

Yes, he knew. They'd discussed the wound many times. There was no cure for his impending fate. But perhaps there could be some relief. He made a mental note to ask Amir to try the Runer healing on him once he arrived. He'd need his strength for whatever news Amir brought him from Al'Myrah. He needed to be ready to move.

Chapter 2

A New Trial

Spring burned hot on Al'Myrah. After the frozen air of Caerwren and the wet rains of Xia, Sybal had almost forgotten. Even a month into the new season, the sun of the east beat down on the golden dunes. The last time she'd experienced the fickle Al'Myrahn springs bringing their freezing rain and cold nights into scorching afternoons, she had been the heiress of a diamond mine. The spring on Xia had driven Tzarik mad. She'd enjoyed the rain then as it came warm. The rain at night on Al'Myrah was rare, but when it did come, as it had three times since leaving Moshav, Signar howled like a wounded wolf.

Sybal woke early to observe the horizon. The sun was already up, baking her pleasantly. They had entered Bagdula's borders several days ago, so she knew they were closer to Hatal than Moshav now. A few villages and settlements speckled the provinces, but the barren parts of the desert felt endless. She checked her waterskin to find it almost gone. They had no food, either. Signar ate more than both of them put together, and had depleted their meager supplies quickly. She told herself that boys his age ate ravenously. She remembered when Abdul had hit sixteen. Her mother, Freja, had thought he'd eat them out of house and home. Signar, being a wild wolf, was far worse.

She moved the animal skin tarp aside to peek in at him. He

slept in his human form, curled up in the corner. His long, yellow hair was a mess, tangled in the old braids and gold adornments he'd had in his long tresses when they'd left Caerwren. Over the days of their travel, he'd quieted down significantly. He'd howled at the night sounds of Al'Myrah for several nights. Sybal remembered the frozen, silent nights on Caerwren too well. But he calmed in other ways. He'd learned to nod or shake his head to communicate just enough when he was calm. However, just when she'd thought they'd made progress, he'd had a terrifying fit of rage.

Tzarik moaned on the other side of the wagon cage. She hurried over, seeing him trying to wrap his wounds around his middle.

"Let me," she said, kneeling in front of him and taking the bandage. She raised his arms over his head and motioned for him to hold them there. She inspected the massive bite marks around his stomach and ribs. "They need cleaned a little," she sighed, agitated.

She rummaged in his pack, looking for any medicinal herbs. She was out. Finding a few dried leaves, she halted. "This is all you have left," she said seriously, looking up at him. "We need to find a city. Mahal is the closest city in Bagdula. It's near the border—"

"And what about him?" Tzarik cut in.

The damned wolf. All he cared about was the stupid boy. Sybal ground her teeth, looking away. She didn't want him to see the rage in her eyes.

"This was him," she said, gently touching the wound on his stomach. "Tzarik, he could have killed you. He had you in his jaws." The memory flashed before her eyes in a red haze.

She didn't know what he had been doing in the boy's cage. She'd fed Signar that night, given him water. There was no reason for Tzarik to go near him. When he had, he'd approached the boy, his hand out. At first, she'd thought Signar would let Tzarik touch him, but then he'd snapped like he always did. He'd shifted instantly into his wolf form and attacked. Signar had whipped his head around faster than either of them could move and had clamped down on Tzarik's middle. She remembered seeing Tzarik being shaken in his great lupine maw like a rabbit. His scream of pain, and no doubt shock, had burned in her ears. For his aggression, Sybal had given Signar another scar to go with the one over his face, which she'd bestowed on him during the fight for the bridge in Northica. This one had landed on his chest. But it had saved Tzarik.

"He's made progress since we left Caerwren," Tzarik argued weakly.

Sybal crushed the leaves and went back to wrapping the bandage. Artiah only worked so well on Vaeson bites they found out. "I won't deny he has," she said, giving in to try to reconcile their constant argument. They needed to be on the same side. "But you cannot deny we need to find a city. We have no water, no food. And..."

Just as she was about to bring up the hunt, her left hand tingled. She took a deep breath and flexed her fingers, then squeezed them hard.

"I feel it, too," he agreed. "But we cannot leave him. We'll have to hunt in shifts. Alone."

"I can manage," she quipped.

He lowered one arm, gently touching her face. "I know you can."

She smiled and blushed, looking away. "I'll find you something easy. A ghoul, or maybe you can banish a nest of saam-abras."

Tzarik made a face. "Saam-abras? They give leprosy. That's the last thing I need right now." He reached for his waterskin once she finished binding his entire torso. She noted how he tipped it, only to find it empty, and tried to hide his concern from her.

"I'll go into Mahal," she said, standing up. "I don't want you to travel more than we have to. I'll take whatever money we have left and see what I can get. In the meantime, set a trap for a rat or something. I'm starving."

Tzarik grunted and stood up, moving to the cage. He wrapped his fingers around the bars, looking in. Sybal eyed him carefully, making sure the ravenous, hungry maw of a giant wolf didn't snap out, taking his hand off. Instead, the long, thin, pale fingers of the boy slipped out, touching Tzarik's hand. Taken aback, she moved to see into the slit of the tarp. Signar crouched inside, reaching towards Tzarik cautiously, testing the contact.

His emerald eyes flashed to Sybal and he scurried out of sight.

Tzarik sighed. "Let's move."

SYBAL MARCHED SILENTLY beside the cage for several hours. The front right wheel squeaked now, and the back left wobbled precariously. If she'd seen these things, she knew Tzarik had. In the distance, rippling under the river of heat waves coming off the sand, Mahal came over the dunes. About a mile out from it, a tiny village spread out, surrounded by sheep. Sybal noted the rock formation nearby and a cluster of green trees and bushes.

"Tzarik, water," she said, pointing.

He gave her a leery glance but headed to the village anyway. If they didn't ask, the answer was always no. A few shepherds outside the village spotted them. Two of them turned to face them, crooks in their hands, and stood shoulder to shoulder. Sybal spotted the well behind them. They stopped the horses and scanned the men.

"We don't want a fight," she whispered, seeing Tzarik's eyes feast on the rocky walls of the well. "Mahal is just beyond. Let's go around."

Inside the cage, Signar coughed, choking. She glanced inside.

He lay on his side, panting in the heat. His lips bled from chapped cracks. She gathered her courage. Knowing she'd regret it, she strode forward.

"Let us pass," she said to the shepherds. "We are heading for Mahal. We don't want any trouble."

One of the shepherds took two steps towards her, crook posed for a fight. "What are two Runers carrying in such a large wagon?" he asked. "We've not seen a Runer in some months."

"Have you need of one?" she asked hopefully.

One of the other shepherds nudged the first and whispered to him, brazenly pointing to Sybal.

Impossible, she thought. *They cannot still remember me on this continent.* It had been nearly three years since Ala'Nar.

"The lady Runer," the second said. "The murderer."

"Shit," she mumbled, turning back to Tzarik. "We go around. They know who I am."

He looked like he might argue, despite having to lean against the horse and holding his side in pain. "Can we fill our skins?" he called to the shepherds. "Please. We have no water and we've been traveling for days."

The shepherds squared up, gripping their crooks hard. One smiled darkly. "Come and take it, Runer. If you can. I've been needing some sport."

"Stop it," Sybal snapped at him. She shoved past Tzarik to the cage. "He can have what's left of mine." She lifted the tarp and pulled the cork out of her skin.

Signar looked up at her. He didn't move.

"Come here," she snapped in Caerwren. "We have to keep moving." Her left hand tingled. At her tone, Signar recoiled, whimpering. Growling, she shoved the skin into Tzarik's chest and marched back to the horses. "Make him drink." She took the reins in her hand and forced them onward, making a large circle around the village.

She didn't look back, but a few minutes later, she heard Tzarik softly whispering praise to the boy in Al'Myrahn. Gritting her teeth, she led them around the village to the borders of Mahal.

Being a smaller city, Mahal didn't have the walls Bagdula or Hatal had. But a patrol of city guards did walk the perimeter every mile or so. Caravans filed in and out all across the city. The temple in the center could be heard even on the borders. Sybal led them to a spot outside that looked like it was often frequented by travelers. Fire pits dotted the space every few yards, and an abandon clay cup lay near a circle of rocks that blocked the hot wind.

"Stay here," she ordered Tzarik. She held her hand out and he tossed her his coin purse. It was very light. "I'll be back before the moon is high. Sleep if you can." She checked the setting sun to time herself, then turned to march into the city, but stopped and rounded on Tzarik. "Do *not* open that cage. I don't care if he convulses from dehydration and vomits blood. Do you understand?"

Tzarik pulled a face at her tone, but nodded. He moved to one of the abandoned fire pits and began collecting debris to make a fire. "Bring back something to drink," he called to her. "Something besides water."

ᛒ

MAHAL HAD QUIETED down since the sun set, but a few people still moved about the sandy streets for late night business. The public houses began to light up and throw their doors wide open for the wary merchants, farmers, and travelers who wanted entertainment, drink, and food. Sybal passed a few, tempted to just spend the money on a room for herself and a hot bath.

The bathing room she'd experienced on Xia pleasantly haunted her dreams. Scented oils, brightly colored soaps...a comb for her hair. These things seemed like distant memories. Like fantasies she'd never see again. Deciding it wouldn't hurt to look into one of the houses, she stood outside one with particularly wide front doors. The smell of cooking meat, fresh barrels of ale, and hookah smoke almost made her pass out from desire. Her mouth watered.

The people inside cheered as a young man sang a high, impressive note to announce his presence to entertain them. She watched him, allowing herself to be taken in by his golden voice and the ridiculously colorful outfit he wore. Sashes around his hips were covered in bells to draw attention. She listened for a few moments before deciding he was not as good a singer as Vicdan. And not near as handsome. He worked the women and a few men as if he were, but she could see they wouldn't be taken in by his lack of charm. She'd met Vicdan in a place like this, where they had worked together to steal a new wheel fiddle for him. She smiled faintly at the memory.

Your sword has been idle for too long.

Sybal jumped, gasping. The voice had come back. Every other night or so, it whispered to her. Though it spoke with Freja's tone, she told herself it was not her mother. How could it be?

Listen to me, Sybal, my darling, it said sweetly. *Don't shut me out. This is a gift from beyond death. I've missed you.*

Sybal frowned, aggressively wiping at the tears that came to her eyes, and continued down the street. "Leave me be, please," she begged. "Even if you are my mother, speaking to the dead is heresy. It's not right."

Always the good and righteous girl, the voice said. *Praying to the east, going to temple, living by the laws of the mihals. There is more than one god, Sybal. I can show you.*

"I know," she grunted, sweeping the street with her eyes to find a shop or a notice board. She needed water, a hunt, and then food. "But I chose my god long ago."

Faithful.

"Talking to yourself?" a kind voice said behind her.

Sybal turned to see a witch outside a small shop snuggly set between a stable and a blacksmith. The woman looked to be from Bahratt. She gathered up baskets of herbs from a table outside her shop.

"I have an herb for that," she smiled, her eyes sparkling like the golden ring in her nose.

"Are you a witch?" Sybal asked, approaching her.

The woman nodded. "I'm closing up, but if you need something and have coin, I won't tell you no." She eyed Sybal up and down. "A lady Runer. Fascinating. Never seen one. You need something for the hunt? Dragon's wort, black root, smoke crystals?"

"Do you have something for...sleep?" Sybal asked, inspecting the fragrant cuttings before her. "Deep sleep."

"Having trouble nodding off?" the woman asked, motioning for Sybal to follow her inside. "I just take a few swallows of arak. Sends me right off."

"Something stronger," Sybal pressed. "Something for a creature...the size of a horse with the strength of a wolf."

The witch put her hand on her hip. Her other hand went for a bundle of tiny white flowers on a spiny twig, but she hesitated. "It's none of my business, but are you planning on killing someone?"

Sybal shook her head. "I'm a Runer, witch. I don't kill people."

"So, it's a monster?"

She nodded.

The witch still looked concerned, but lifted a handful of sprigs and began to wrap them into a bundle. "This is harmala," she explained. "There are seeds on these branches. That's what you want. They need to be powdered. You have a mortar and pestle?"

Sybal nodded again.

The witch then picked up another plant, a simple one with heart-shaped green leaves. "Kava. These two are fine on their own, but mixed..." She took a steadying breath. "They can induce what the healers call a dead sleep, when the brain is alive and the creature breathes, but they are more dead than alive. It's very strong. You only need a little, even for the size of creature you speak of. Give it a pinch like this." She showed Sybal with two fingers and her thumb. "No more if you want it to live. It will be in this dead sleep for six to eight hours. Due to the nature of the herbs, when the thing awakens, it will be severely dehydrated. If you wish it to live, give it water right away."

"Thank you," Sybal said eagerly. "It is necessary for the hunt. Where is the nearest notice board?"

The witch pointed south. "Outside the hall of justice. One bronze piece." She held her hand out.

Sybal tossed the witch the coin and took up the herbs. She wanted to hunt with Tzarik, but he'd never leave Signar. She would give the boy food laced with the herbs, explain to Tzarik, then they could hunt together. With the coin from a good hunt that required two Runers, they could rent a room in a public house. Together.

Tzarik stood just outside the bars, watching Signar sleep. The moon had started its crawl up the sky almost an hour ago. Sybal would be back soon, and hopefully with two patents for hunts and some water. They needed that hunt finished and coin in their purses by the next night or they'd all die of hunger. A gazelle had danced past, tempting him, but he'd missed his shot and didn't want to waste the energy to even retrieve the arrow.

Signar whined in his sleep, flinching away from harm only he could see in his nightmares. Tzarik slowly slipped his arm through the bars and moved his hand towards Signar, but couldn't reach him.

"Whatever you're remembering in your dreams, it should have never happened to you," he said softly. "No one deserves to be treated as we have. And by the people the gods gave us to. We couldn't choose our parents or the ways in which we were conceived. But we're alive now, and that's worth fighting for."

He moved around to the back of the cage and slipped under the tarp, unlocking the door. It opened with a rusty squeak, but Signar didn't wake. Tzarik walked softly up to him and crouched next to him. "Not long ago, I wished I was dead. But that was wrong. Being alive, even suffering, is better than giving up. Because we have a chance to save ourselves."

Slowly, he laid his hand against Signar's head. He needed the boy to know he would never harm him. That he was safe. Tzarik had thought Azar was his savior, someone who would never hurt him. He'd been wrong. If Signar understood that Tzarik would protect him with his life, then maybe he could master his outbursts. Besides that, Signar deserved to be safe. He'd unjustly borne the abuse from his entire clan his whole life.

Signar's nose twitched and his eyes opened. Tzarik held his ground. The boy might be able to be subdued. But the wolf inside him could not. Signar spotted Tzarik and flinched, rolling away to cower in a corner. He clapped his hands over his head and pulled his knees up to his chest. He still only wore the brown, animal-skin leggings they'd taken him in.

"I won't harm you," Tzarik reassured him. Even now, with only the boy there and no sign of the wolf, Tzarik knew he'd made progress.

The boy tried to lick his bleeding lips, but his mouth was too dry. He whimpered and turned his eyes up to the moon as if begging it for water.

Satisfied, Tzarik stood up.

"What are you doing?" Sybal screamed from behind him. She pulled her scimitar from its sheath and dashed toward him.

The sudden movement ignited the frenzy in Signar. His eyes locked onto Sybal and he growled. Before Tzarik could move, the boy leapt, transforming into the golden wolf in midair. Sybal made it to Tzarik just in time and drew halat. The wolf hit the barrier and yelped. Sybal gripped Tzarik's arm and tossed him behind her, facing Signar.

"Back off," Sybal barked to the wolf. He snarled, showing his teeth, and licked his lips. She took a furious step forward, fist raised.

"Sybal, don't!" Tzarik called.

Her fist connected with Signar's nose, hard. The wolf yelped and stumbled to the floor of the cage, a boy once again. He crumpled in a heap, holding his bleeding nose and crying. Sybal yelled at him again, forcing him to back away. He scurried around her, sobbing into his hands, and crouched behind Tzarik. The sight of Tzarik between her and Signar hit something inside her. She exhaled hard, eyes wide.

Tzarik yanked her from the cage and slammed the door closed, locking it. Rage at her boiled in him, mixing with the pure adrenaline from the near fight.

"He wasn't going to hurt me," he growled at her, stomping back to the fire. "He fears you, is terrified of you. Isn't that enough? He knows you're the one who gave him that scar on his face. He remembers, Sybal."

"I told you not to go into the cage while I was gone," she shot back. "You've lost all the blood we can afford to let you lose. Artiah is hardly working on the Vaeson bite because you're starving, thirsty, and exhausted. I have to keep you safe."

She marched to her pack, pulled out the last piece of meat they had, and tossed it to Signar. The boy leapt on it, eating it raw.

Tzarik panted, having trouble getting his breath back as his wound throbbed. He knew she cared about him. Wanted to protect him. "I took him to tame him," he reminded her. "I know he understands me when I speak to him."

He tracked her mad pacing with his eyes.

"What is it?" he asked. "You're carrying tension in your hips."

She stopped and gave him a sidelong glance over her shoulder. Yes, he'd been looking at her backside while she stomped around the fire. He'd noticed the stiffness where normally her hips had a gentle, elegant sway. Telling her this, and seeing she realized what he'd been looking at, put her a little at ease. She scoffed through her nose, hiding a smile.

She joined him at the fireside, handing him her waterskin. It was full. Grateful, he took it and filled his mouth, holding the cool well water there before swallowing. Never had water tasted so good.

"I found this," she said, calmly taking a scroll out of her hip satchel.

He took it. With his newfound skills, thanks to Vicdan, he read the patents. It called for a Runer to come and investigate a haunting at an old mining estate.

"It mentions chains," he mumbled, reading it again to make sure he'd understood.

"An abu Al'salasel, maybe," Sybal offered, taking a small drink.

Tzarik tried to keep his tone even as he spoke. "It would take both of us. We can't hunt this."

"Yes, we can," she replied eagerly. She pulled a clay jar from her satchel next. She popped the large cork out and showed him a tan powder. "It's a mixture of herbs. It induces sleep. We hide the cage behind the estate. I looked it over. He will sleep for hours."

"Poison him?" Tzarik challenged her, aghast.

She groaned and shook her head. "It's not unlike a sleeping draught for a child's nightmares. Tzarik, look at the pay."

She unrolled the patents again. The sum was substantial. Enough to get them to the docks in Hatal and even pay for passage on a ship to Alika. It had to be a serious haunt. It was tempting, but he couldn't leave Signar.

"What if someone finds him?" he asked. "He'll be afraid. He could change, hurt someone."

"He won't," she argued. "He'll be passed out. He won't hurt anyone."

She said the final words through gritted teeth. He couldn't fathom why she hated the boy so much. Perhaps it was a facade to keep feelings for him at bay.

Perhaps if he gave in, let her have this, she'd be willing to trust him. Help him.

Chapter 3
Master of the Dead

The tiny peninsula stuck out of the western side of Alika towards Porsh. The Black Sea's waves rolled in the night, turning white in the moonlight as they crested. Tarkan didn't care for the nightly beauty. He'd come to Alika after days on Porsh to find one thing, and the quest had been fruitless so far. Makan Alu'Ekmet lay half buried on the peninsula, the brother city to Makan Almyat on Al'Myrah. A small place the necromancers took as their own before Tarkan was even born. The death cult of Alika had kept Makan Alu'Ekmet alive for some time after Porsh was destroyed. Being ancient and only a century abandoned, Tarkan hoped to find clues to point him to the Mahit'Onomicon, or something that might help in a few other endeavors he'd been chasing since escaping the Deep. Before him, the necromancers had been ambitious, not the frightened, traveling tribes they were once Ishmael destroyed their country.

Ishmael. His father had been a strong Necro'Khan, and had left behind five spells of his own. Tarkan had not had such a fruitless journey to Porsh; he'd found the spells, and the ambition to try them drove him to Makan Alu'Ekmet. Ishmael had one powerful, unrealized experiment...

The tombs of Makan Alu'Ekmet were his first stop in his search. He needed a fleshy body to ease the pain in his throat. Though partly healed, the burning scars still got inflamed and took his voice. He slipped between the black onyx pyramids, hoping one had been opened and robbed to give him easy access to the secrets inside. To his luck, he found one gate torn from its hinges and lying open. He spotted footprints going in and out with the unmistakable line of a chest being dragged out over the grave-yard's gate. If this wealthy family had been buried like others on Alika, their most valuable gems were inside the sarcophagi with them. Hopefully, the grave robbers had opened those as well.

Inside the small pyramid, the only light came from the open doorway. But it was enough for Tarkan. He scanned the entryway and found three sarcophagi before him. They were all opened with the utmost disrespect, shattered stone littering the floor. The embalming of the Alikans was unmatched. The history of the immortal Masahk who originated from Alika had led to the desire to preserve corpses forever.

Tarkan leaned over a sarcophagus and found a woman inside. Her black skin made it almost impossible to see her inside the darkness. Which also meant her flesh was almost entirely intact. Good. He needed her throat. Gripping her neck, he gargled out his own penned verses for a new spell. The words vanished into the air and his flesh crawled. Not in the pleasant way it did when using the five spells of necromancy. Almost like they burned, knowing he spoke heresy. His own spell.

Rather than taking on another's wounds, as the spell originally did, he gave his wounds to her. His throat opened and air filled his lungs more easily. He gasped, loving the cold wind inside him at last. When he was sure all his injuries now lay upon the woman's corpse, he let go. As he did, he swore the blue, cat-like eye of his god watched him. The wreath of dark tendrils snapped in anger. He sensed Nephron spread his four black wings, threatening to fly down from the celestial world to punish him.

"Yes," he said, able to speak at last. "I know you see me. After giving me this throne, I defy you. But now, *you* must have faith in me. I will give back tenfold what I have taken." He ran his hand down his neck, feeling for the missing inflammation.

He glanced around the tomb. "Show me your secrets," he whispered, looking at the etchings on the wall. "What were you hiding here?"

Every tribe of necromancers, every faction of the death cult, had their secrets. Things they kept hidden even from other Apostles. When he was able to create his own spell, he knew the others must have done so before him. The five spells were just the beginning. Even Ishmael had secret research, ideas he'd never seen come to fruition. He'd been to his father's house already and had taken his scrolls. The idea of giving away his wounds had come from there, along with something he thought might never work: something Ishmael had been working on and waited for in his deep sleep. But that would have to wait. Sahir had told Tarkan that the Dynast Pharaoh believed Sharar to be the Father of Monsters, the man able to read the Mahit'Onomicon. So he'd come to Alika to track Sharar down and find out what he knew. Did Sharar believe the book lay buried somewhere on Alika?

Humming in disappointment, he moved out to the streets of Makan Alu'Ekmet. He had eternity to search, but he'd rather not take that long. Especially with Sharar sleeping on the same shores, making his way to the Dynast Pharaoh as well. Ishmael hadn't disclosed where he'd hidden the Mahit'Onomicon. Tarkan trusted Sharar to find it, but he had to be powerful enough to take it from him.

The night turned to a scalding day, which brought on a cold

evening. He'd walked miles, never stopping. His horse, being a risen creature, did not need rest, water, or food. His waterskins were filled with blood, but did not satisfy like flesh. Finding living sentients willing to give up flesh had not been easy. It made him too known. Twice, he'd risen a wild dog and made it attack unsuspecting farmers. He'd devoured their flesh moments before they died. But even that was risky.

On the second night, he cast the spell on another corpse near the center of the city to relieve his pain. The full moon above lit up the square. So much sand had blown in over the years that the Temple of Apostles looked like it leaned into a dune. Makan Alu'Ekmet had been a place of experimental necromancy, thanks to the Alikan cult. He hoped something inspiring waited inside. The necromancers of Makan Alu'Ekmet were not like his family or those who followed Ishmael. They were the tribe who'd broken from Porsh, apposing Ishmael. He'd known two of them in his lifetime, Ashkan and his wife, Elahel. They'd renounced their tribe and joined him and his then-apprentice, Shiva. But they were different from every other tribe of necromancers in one specific way...

Something moved to Tarkan's left. He froze, halfway across the square. It could be nothing, but no sentient in their right mind would enter Makan Alu'Ekmet. And never alone. Then he felt eyes on him from one of the lower towers of the temple windows. He was surrounded. Spreading his hands, he felt for some dead to raise. Bodies swarmed under the sands, ready to obey him.

To his left, a man ran at him, a black staff in hand. He recognized the robes of a master of Apostles, a leader among the necromancers in the temple. Confused, he slipped out of the way of the attack and pulled up a few risen from the sand to surround himself. The robed man attacked again in a jerky motion. Half his flesh had rotted off his face.

Risen? he asked himself. He sent his own at the master, fending him off just long enough to scan the other buildings. Another necromancer lurked among the dead.

As his risen warriors defended him, something else came up from behind him, coming out of the temple: the enormous, half-decayed corpse of a griffin. Its fur and feathers hung off in a grotesque array. The comb-like ears on its falcon head were filled with holes. The monster snapped at Tarkan, forcing him to leap out of the way and land hard on the ground. The griffin screamed and unfurled its partially decayed wings.

Hissing the well-known spell, Tarkan wavered only a little, since not much blood had been spilt inside Makan Alu'Ekmet. Cursing, he ran, ripping risen up from the ground as he did. The griffin charged at him, leapt overhead, and landed before him, forcing him back the way he'd come.

He dashed down the street to the square where more undead battled. Then he spotted the culprit. Standing in the doorway of the temple was the form of a man in black robes not unlike his own. The hood obscured his face, but Tarkan knew the man looked at him. Composing himself, he marched back into the square, protected by his risen. The other necromancer raised his hands, calling the griffin. The beast ran, barreling towards Tarkan.

Tarkan smiled. "I am master of the dead."

He shouted, commanding the risen beast to obey him. Tarkan shot his left hand out to the new assailant, stopping the griffin in its tracks. Once he knew he had it in his grasp, he slowly turned his head towards his nemesis.

"Show yourself, brother," he commanded. Already his throat burned again, swelling. With his other hand, he waved and whis-pered the spell to summon risen, ending with his own command, and took control of every standing corpse. He made them all face the other necromancer. He was master of the dead. He could command even another necromancer's risen.

The man took a step backwards in shock. "So it's true," he said.

"Tarkan. You have ascended like your father before you. Ishmael would be proud."

He removed his hood slowly, showing his unmarked face. His bright green eyes almost glowed in the dark like Tarkan's blue ones. His black hair hung lank below his shoulders. The skin on his face pulled tight over his skull, showing he had not consumed in a long time.

"Ashkan, Bone-Scriven," Tarkan said, partly surprised. "One of House Nashira, traitors to Porsh. Twice a traitor?" he asked. "You once traveled beside me. You and Elahel. You no longer stain your skin."

"Traitors to our tribe," Ashkan corrected. "After we left you, there was no reason to hide our tribal ways under the staining ink, falsifying the scriptures on our flesh. It felt like heresy. Bone-Scriven hiding among Flesh-Scriven necromancers." He shook his head. "Perhaps we were cowards then. We should have never left House Nashira. Elahel knew that. But that's why you killed her."

"Bone-Scriven are cowards," Tarkan shot back. "That's why I took her life. Scriven bones hide from mortal eyes."

"The agony outweighs the cowardice," Ashkan replied savagely.

Ashkan whispered a quick spell and vanished, wavering from sight. Realizing he was blood-walking, Tarkan spread his risen out, fanning over the area.

"Ashkan, you cannot hide from me," he called. "I've been looking for you. Why are you here, hiding away amongst the desolate and dead?"

Tarkan slowly moved, trying to pull away from any fight that might ensue. He might be able to take control of any risen, but if he couldn't see it, know it was there, Ashkan could attack. He half reached out, trying to find another beast that might lurk under the sand.

"Why have you been hunting me?" Ashkan's voice asked,

echoing around the entire square. "I watched you as you looked for me. With little Zeva."

"Do not say her name," Tarkan hissed, sending a handful of risen to rush an area he thought he caught a glimpse of Ashkan's cloak in. "We are both alone now, brother. Why have you greeted me so?"

A risen exploded up from the sand, stabbing at Tarkan. The thing's rusty spear grazed his side. He panted, taking control of it, too. His throat swelled, cutting off his air. He gasped, willing the wound to stay on the body he'd put it on.

Having enough, Tarkan called the Deep to him. Ashkan could vanish in this world, walking over spilled blood. But Tarkan could vanish entirely. Pulling it open, blood whipping from his pores in ribbon-like waves, he slipped inside the Deep. Opening the Deep without the Blood Path took its toll, but he needed to risk it in this fight.

As he suspected, Ashkan came into full view. White as a ghost, a skeleton in robes, he moved around the square, raising bodies outside of it. They moved inward—even though the structures were not visible in the Deep—and came to overwhelm him. The other necromancer stopped, noticing Tarkan had vanished entirely. Ashkan had always been a strong necromancer. Ishmael had said being Bone-Scriven made them weak cowards. But Ishmael had been wrong.

Slipping back out from the Deep, Tarkan pulled a giant, dead cobra from the sand and commanded it to strike where Ashkan had been. The snake flared its decomposing hood, rising several yards above Tarkan's head before snapping forward. Ashkan cried out before he turned visible. He rolled away from the attack and scrambled to his feet. Before he could run, Tarkan commanded the snake to seize him. It lunged again, catching his left foot in its boney mouth.

Ashkan flailed against it for just a moment more before giving in to submission.

"Ninety years," Tarkan hissed, his throat searing. He motioned over one of the risen and grabbed its throat, giving it his wounds. "Ninety years you walked with me and Shiva. Why do you strike out against me now, brother? I know you searched for the book. We all have. But none had the courage to do what it took to ascend. I have. You cannot hope to overpower me now."

Ashkan pulled futilely on his trapped leg. He looked up at Tarkan with his green eyes. "I knew it would be you. You have nothing to fear from the Bone-Scriven. We have been scattered since Ishmael. You know this. Our people are in hiding. We are weak." He took a breath. "I should not have brought the risen against you now."

Tarkan looked with mild jealousy at his mark-less face. But he did not envy the agony of becoming Bone-Scriven. It was a sacrifice they made to stay hidden. The green eyes in their eastern faces made the lowly sentients pause, but since they were not the blue of the necromancers or Runers, they showed little suspicion.

"There have been almost no new Bone-Scriven Apostles," Ashkan said, wincing in pain. "We have no hope of surviving."

"As it should be for traitors of the scriptures," Tarkan mused. He commanded the snake to jerk its head once, pulling a pained groan from his fellow necromancer.

"How?" Ashkan gasped, head down to hide his pained expression from Tarkan. "How did you ascend?"

The question cooled Tarkan, making him halt his next command. He'd not spoken about it in weeks. He'd never been alone this long.

"Have you been guarding Makan Alu'Ekmet all this time?" he asked Ashkan. "Protecting the necrotic wisdom hidden here from lone Porshains?"

"I have," Ashkan replied. "Though I destroyed the scrolls."

"Destroyed?" Tarkan growled. He wrenched his hand back, commanding the snake to toss Ashkan across the square.

The necromancer, thin and frail as he was, rolled until he hit a stone pillar hard. He sat up, but Tarkan's risen surrounded him. He ordered one to raise a spear, preparing to kill Ashkan and pin him to the pillar.

"Father's spells spoke of this place," Tarkan growled. "I journeyed to Porsh only to be directed to Alika, Ashkan."

"Tell me how you did it," Ashkan cried over him. "Tell me how you became so powerful."

Tarkan stayed the risen. "I am not powerful yet. I was going to hunt for such knowledge amongst the scrolls in the catacombs of Makan Alu'Ekmet. Why, Ashkan?"

Ashkan stood up, leaning against the stone for support. "Because I knew it would be you. I wanted to find you, to walk by your side again, as I once did. To be your apprentice once again."

"Then why did you attack me?"

Ashkan bowed his head. "I was afraid. Porshains have lived in fear, leaderless, for too long. A century of hiding. Not now. I have read things within the scrolls no necromancer has ever tried before. Things to make our god, Nephron, fear us. Spells we can learn to show our enslaved brothers in Mysir, to make them follow us."

"The slaves in Mysir are Porshain," Tarkan countered. "Not necromancers."

"But they could be," Ashkan said. "They deserve to partake of the power our country discovered and was destroyed for. Willing Apostles. You have nothing to fear, Necro'Khan."

Tarkan walked through the horde of risen. "You could not have ascended, Ashkan. You had nothing to give up." He swallowed hard. "Zeva knew no amount of sacrificed souls would make Nephron bless me as he has. Make my heart into ruby."

Ashkan's expression changed, his green eyes filling with sympathy. "He wanted her?"

Praying he wouldn't regret his choice, Tarkan told Ashkan what had happened on Caerwren. He didn't spare any details, even describing his humiliating submission to the mad Red Reks. How he'd fought Zeva on her choice to become Scriven and then an Apostle. Then, how he'd pulled Kjarton-Reks from the Deep.

"Runers can exorcise spirits?" Ashkan asked when Tarkan explained how he'd put the Reks' spirit into the Runer.

"A locking script," Tarkan explained. "I wasn't sure it would work, but I had a theory. He must have broken the script; the spirit of the Reks left him. I met him in battle on the Bridge of Tier'Morlan, where he turned Zeva against me."

"Did she escape?" Ashkan asked once Tarkan finished his story.

He shook his head. "The Vorlamir hunted me fiercely. I ran and ran, but the Deep is still his domain. When I finally escaped, I didn't know where she was."

She was gone. The Runers, having turned her against him, had let her die. Zeva was gone.

His throat burned, and he gagged, gripping his neck. The returning pain made him double over. Ashkan caught him, holding him steady.

"I never hated you, brother," Ashkan said. "I saw the future of the necromancers in you. Spare me and let me walk with you, as I once did. Tell me what you want to know and I will divulge the secrets I read in the scrolls."

"I don't have much time," Tarkan gasped. "There is a man..." He coughed. "A man who seeks the Mahit'Onomicon. He is here already. He possesses a djinn, and will become a sorcerer, if he is not one already."

"What man?" Ashkan asked.

"The one who imprisoned me, who hurt Zeva to force me to do his bidding. We cannot let him take the book. Already he made one wish to control the beasts and monsters of the map. The Dynast Pharaoh, compelled by this man, has nearly been swayed to questing for the hiding place of the book. The Overseer prophesied such a man to the Pharaoh, saying he would be the one to read the book, to rule with it. The man they call the Father of Monsters."

Ashkan understood. "A djinn cannot raise the dead nor control the risen. He must be hunting for another necromancer."

"He hunts for me," Tarkan acknowledged. "He does not know I have ascended. But he will."

"Brother," Ashkan said, "I can see you are unwell. Spare me. Let me walk with you, and together, we will find this man and the Mahit'Onomicon. You have nothing to fear from me. I cannot hope to stand against you now."

Ashkan was right; Tarkan was at least more powerful than any other necromancer on the map. But he knew all too well that necromancers were stronger in numbers.

"Very well," Tarkan said solemnly. "You shall be my first Apostle."

Chapter 4

Unbound Djinn

Sybal watched Tzarik hesitantly give Signar the water tainted with the herbal mixture. He kept mumbling apologies as the boy ravenously drank swallow after swallow. She tightened the leather cords around the animal-skin tarp so the searching fingers of the wind would not lift the flaps once they had him hidden out of sight. The less Signar could see, the better chance he had at suppressing his wolf. She wasn't sure the sheikh who owned the plantation and mine would let them store the large wagon cage on his property, but knowing the price he offered to remove the haunt helped ease her mind.

Tzarik led the horses into the city, and they navigated in silence. The eyes of the people turned to watch them when they realized what the two travelers were. Most whispered and pointed, but a few spat at them, and others mumbled curses as they passed.

They hate those who protect them, the voice said sadly to Sybal. *They should die upon your blade in the name of the god whose sulfates flow in your veins.*

Sybal flinched, rubbing her eyes fiercely with the palm of her hand as if she could rub the voice away. *I do not know that god,* she replied. *Layth'asad, the lion of Al'Myrah, is my god.*

Do you not know the tower in the north? Freja asked her daughter. *Or have the stories of the Silent Tower melted on your golden sands?*

Sybal tried to ignore the voice. Hearing her mother speak to her so intimately made her wild with a mysterious rage. It could not be Freja. But what if the Deep had left some mark on her, or a connection to the dead?

Her sulfates ran, telling her that eyes looked hard at her. She glanced sideways to find Tzarik watching her. She tried to ignore him, looking ahead. She took out the patents and checked the name and address again. The one who had ordered the patents was called Sheikh Lirahl. The back of his grand estate faced the east and spanned several pastures of sheep, fields of wheat, and a few tunnels underneath, where some semi-rare gems were mined. The west side faced into the city just outside his gates. Sybal offered the patents to the guards at the gate, and she and Tzarik removed their cowls to show their blue eyes and pale veins under dark skin. Convinced they were Runers, the guards let them through and ushered them up to the grand manor.

Sheikh Lirahl met them in the front courtyard, where hundreds of oversized, colorful blooms exploded over the walkways. The sheikh approached them, hands outstretched. He was an older man with a white beard and lines on his face from years of stress. He had a scar on his arm that showed his history as a military man. Sybal noted how he stood tall, with squared shoulders—more signs of his discipline. She knew then that he was a serious man and would not have asked for Runers lightly.

"I'm Tzarik and this is Sybal," her mentor said, introducing them. "What can you tell us about your haunt?"

Sheikh Lirahl gave them each a polite bow before eyeing the

massive cage. "What have you brought to my home, Runers?" he asked cautiously.

"Nothing of consequence," Tzarik replied quickly. "Would you be kind enough to allow us to stow it on your land, somewhere safe and quiet, while we investigate?"

The sheikh gave a sidelong glance, clearly curious, but nodded. "I'll have my men put it in the warehouse. It's empty now and no one should disturb...it." He waved some men over and Tzarik warned them not to look inside the cage or make loud noises.

"Thank you," Tzarik said to the sheikh as he led them through his grand manor and up some marble stairs to the top floor.

"No matter," Sheikh Lirahl replied. "Were I not desperate—and dare I admit, afraid—I might have refused."

"Tell us about this haunt," Sybal said, she and Tzarik flanking the sheikh. "The patents were vague, but we thought it sounded like an abu Al'salasel. A chain demon. What have you witnessed?"

Sheikh Lirahl began to sweat. "Torment. Strange fear emanates from the rooms."

"Whose rooms?" Tzarik asked.

"Mine," Sheikh Lirahl replied. "My wife is ill with fear. My children are terrified of the night. They are with their mother's family now. I want to believe it is such a lesser demon, but I fear it's something more."

Sybal watched Tzarik stop outside a large library and look in. "What do you feel?" she asked, waiting for her own sulfates to run. A slight tingle started to stir, nothing more. But Tzarik went stiff. She saw his breathing pick up. He took one step towards the library, then two steps back. She came up alongside him, reaching out and waiting for something. Nothing more came to her.

"What is it?" she asked.

Tzarik swallowed. "I don't want to say, in case I'm wrong. Sheikh Lirahl, have things in your house moved?"

The sheikh nodded. He closed his eyes and calmed himself. "The first night, it was in Hila's room."

He led them farther back into the top floor, opening a door into what looked like a young girl's room. It faced into the city. A canopied bed took up most of the middle. Gauzy curtains overlooked a small, flower-covered balcony. A golden mirror and a few other things a young princess would use made up the room.

"It came in, opened the door," Sheikh Lirahl explained. "She said she saw it here. Watching her. She thought it wanted her. It came back again and again until she was wild with fear. Then it destroyed her mirror." He moved into the room and pointed to the mirror in the corner. "This one is new. But it shattered her mirror and then..." He shuddered. "It dragged her over the floor, cutting her. But then, it moved on. Every night, it attacks. Then I had dreams."

Sybal watched the sheikh tell his story, frightened and interested.

"It showed me things," Sheikh Lirahl went on. "I dreamed I had such terrible powers. I subjugated my people. Destroyed my home. I became a tyrant over Mahal. It reminded me of the wars and the sacrifices I have made in battle. The memories terrified me, but more than the scars of battle, what I could become terrified me. But then..." Sheikh Lirahl steadied himself. "It laughed at me. Said I could never bind it like that. The terror that sits over the house is undeniable. One of my servants hanged himself, and he never saw the thing."

Sybal glanced at Tzarik. He had gone pale and his eyes turned dark.

"Did you speak to it?" Tzarik asked.

Sheikh Lirahl nodded.

"While you were awake?" Tzarik asked more aggressively.

The man nodded. "It's here all the time. It fills me with terror. I am afraid of what it might do if I deny it."

"Deny it what?" Sybal asked.

Sheikh Lirahl stammered and Tzarik's eyes bored into him. "Deny it...me," the man whispered. "I don't know how much longer I can refuse it. I used to be strong, Runers. I am a man forged in battle. But I cannot allow this thing to hurt my family anymore. I don't understand. It spoke of freedom, of peace. But how can it say such things when it torments me so?"

Tzarik grunted, nodding. "Leave the manor. Have all your men, farmers, miners—everyone must leave."

"Why?" Sheikh Lirahl and Sybal asked together.

Tzarik took one last look into the study, his shoulders sagging under the truth. "What you have, sheikh, is an unbound djinn."

Sheikh Lirahl cursed and drew a holy circle over his heart and then his forehead. "How can you be sure?"

"It wants to frighten you into submission," Tzarik explained. "Djinns are demons of destruction, and thrive on the terror they can bring us. There is no magic on the map like that of a djinn. They are hungry for sentient fear. It makes them strong, gives them life. But djinns are slaves to evil gods. They are demons—the highest level of demon. Some of the best destruction they can cause is by possessing a sentient and granting that sentient wishes. Mortals are generally evil, selfish creatures. Djinns know they will use their power for great harm.

"But this one spoke of freedom? It's not bound, but that doesn't mean the soul can move on to the afterlife. It doesn't want to possess you. That would limit its power. It wants you to bind it to an artifact, to make wishes upon it. When a djinn grants a wish, it gets stronger. This one may want to grant you your three wishes or have you only request two. Then it wants you to wish it free. A free djinn may pass to the afterlife. But it may come back as well, free in our realm. The stories say not many djinns wish for binding, but this one must be powerful—has granted perhaps thousands of wishes already. It will make a deal with you, request that you grant it its freedom from the shackles that bind it to its god. Do you understand?"

Sybal thought back over all she'd learned the last few years. "A mortal with the powers of a djinn is a sorcerer."

"Oh, no!" Sheikh Lirahl cried. "I would never become such a monster. Magic such as that is outlawed. All magic outside the temples and such as you is heretical."

"You wouldn't mean to," Tzarik explained. "The djinn's will would meld with yours. You'd be under its command once it possessed you."

"I'd never."

"You wouldn't have a choice. If it convinced you to free it after wishing upon it, it would be stronger. These may be the last few wishes it needs to be strong enough to possess a sentient. That's why it has come to your home."

At this, Sybal's mind went to Sharar. "Could someone find a way to take the djinn's power, but not lose himself to the djinn?"

Understanding her, Tzarik furrowed his brow meaningfully. "Yes. If they had a book that told them how."

Sheikh Lirahl cast his eyes between the two of them, confused. "I don't want it, even then."

"You won't," Tzarik promised, marching down the hall towards the master bedroom.

"Then send it to the next life," the sheikh begged.

"We can't do that," Tzarik replied. "We must bind it. Trap it here. Subdue its powers and hide it. It must not be used," he added when the sheikh looked up, intrigued. "Leave and don't come back until tomorrow morning," Tzarik finished.

"You will have it gone by then?" he asked. Sybal also wondered if they would. She didn't know the first thing about djinns, bound or otherwise.

"Either that or it will have killed us," Tzarik said. "In which case, you won't want to come back."

"How did you know?" Sybal asked as she and Tzarik prepared for the night ahead. They stood in the sheikh's bedroom. The room was huge and circular, boasting many windows. "You knew when you entered the doorway to the library. Like you could see it."

Tzarik sat on a wide bench near one of the many windows. He held the sheikh's family crest in his hands at the end of a long chain and worked on the smooth back of it, chiseling halat onto it with a small set of tools. He had her painting the same rune on the floor in goat urine. She gagged at the smell, waiting for him to answer and explain their binding spell.

"I've encountered one like this before," he said softly. "Just once. Nothing has made my sulfates crawl the same way a djinn does. They are pure evil; their only purpose is to cause suffering. They control everything, from the elements to the very emotions you feel. They have limits, but what they can do is enough to destroy kingdoms."

She dipped the horsetail mop into the vile bucket again and continued to draw halat on the floor. She had to remember where she drew it because the urine blended in with the sandy-colored marble. Of course he'd given her this task, not creating the binding artifact.

"Unbound?" she asked. "How will we bind it?"

"Runers are the only ones who can, really." He shook his hand out, his muscles cramping from chiseling the gold. "It takes runes to bind a demon. We will have to fight it. Be ready for that. That rune you made on the floor will trap it, and we'll have to use our runes to hold it steady. Then..." He flipped the crest over in his hands, wiping away the flakes of gold. "We bind it to this when we have it weak enough. The sheikh was reluctant to give it up, so we're going to remove the temptation."

"Are they all not strong enough to possess?" she asked.

"No," he sighed, brushing away the remaining flakes of gold.

Sybal stopped, crouching to make sure the rune she'd drawn was connected to the circle she drew around it. The setting sun hit the drying liquid, showing her she'd done well. "Then..." She almost dared not ask. "We will have a bound djinn? Like the one in the stories about the lamp?"

"And we will get rid of it," Tzarik cut in, sensing her question. "We will not use it. Making the djinn grant you wishes makes it stronger. A sentient must declare the artifact theirs to become the djinn's master. They can either free the djinn or use it until it breaks free. Or the artifact is lost. Most just devour their three wishes and discard the artifact. You may only be a djinn's master once."

"Will death take away ownership of the artifact?" she asked.

Tzarik nodded silently. She saw on his face that he'd thought about it. If only they could get close enough to Sharar. But she couldn't kill him. She'd seen Tzarik take a life. Murder was not his crime. He could kill Sharar, but the mere thought of the djinn struck fear into him. She understood now what she hadn't that night Tzarik had met Sharar and told him he'd captured Tarkan. She glanced up at him, silhouetted perfectly in the setting sun. No, she wouldn't ask now. He'd told her he'd had experience with a djinn, and she had to trust him for now. Besides, she was about to witness the power of the demon herself.

She stood up, tucking the smelly bucket and horse hair mop away. She removed her runes from around her neck and wrapped them around her left hand. Drawing her opalescent scimitar, she checked the edge. She'd not sharpened it in some time.

"Will our swords cut it?" she asked.

"Orichalcum cuts specters," he reminded her. "Djinns are partially physical, though, as they existed once as physical sentients." He didn't go on.

She hummed in approval, eager to slide her blade through a monster again. "Then perhaps we should—"

The rafters high above them groaned. Both Runers stopped and looked up. A darkness, like a sudden storm, spread out from the center of the domed ceiling. As if the demon sat atop the roof, the entire mansion creaked and Sybal swore she felt it move. Tzarik stood up, pocketing the artifact and unsheathing his own sword. A familiar smell filled Sybal's nostrils.

"Cold ash and sulfur," she mused. "Smells like the Deep."

Tzarik circled the room, looking up. The darkness dissipated and began to creep down the wall towards the fireplace. "Al'Myrahn djinns are ice and ash. Ones from Caerwren or Rhostrana would be made of fire and smoke."

Sybal understood. The hell the mihals spoke of, Nah'jaha, was one of mostly ice. It made sense the demons from there would look like that. "This is an Al'Myrahn djinn, then," she confirmed. "Good. I'd like to strike down a hellion for my people."

"They are rare, so this would be your opportunity," Tzarik said. "It's not like the stories where finding one is all lotuses and lokum. They can do things to you before you take possession of the artifact. Outright kill you, even. The one I fought—with Azar—should have destroyed us. But..." He didn't go on.

A cloud of black smoke filled the fireplace. A blast of cold radiated from it, causing ice to crawl over the stone and up the wall. Sybal saw how this would terrify a normal person. But as a Runer, she relished the hunt.

"The fear has left," a deep, rumbling voice purred from the black, ashen cloud. Sybal swore she saw the faint outline of a man within. The voice laughed. "Runers come to bind me. Do you know what you face?" It shouted the question as it exploded from its hiding place.

A strike of lightning shot out from the cloud, hitting Sybal square in the chest. She screamed and fell backwards, the lightning coursing through her. Her vision went white and blue as the strike ran over her body. She couldn't stop the shaking the shock forced out of her. Her mind reeled, worrying for Tzarik as she heard him grunting. Finally, she got up, shoving her body to her feet.

Something akin to a tornado of smoke ripped through the room. The furniture shot across the space, smashing into the bed and splintering. Ice covered the walls. She spotted Tzarik diving for cover and drawing halat quickly as the demon whipped towards him. Sybal drew halat and thrust the shield towards the monster. It hit the apparition, stopping it. The creature showed itself to her then. It looked like a man. Its skin glowed almost blue, with frost flaking off in the torrents around it. Veins of fire burned underneath, coming off in ashen flakes. Its hair, long and stringy, whipped up and around its face. Its eyes were pure white and glaring. She met them.

"Look at you," the djinn rumbled. "All cut open and dying."

Sybal glanced down at her middle and gasped, dropping her scimitar. The armor around her middle had burst open. White blood poured from her, soaking the floor and carrying her entrails with it. She screamed, pressing her hands into her gut.

"Sybal, don't look at its eyes," Tzarik called from somewhere. "It's a mirage."

She stumbled back and looked again. Her hands pressed into her perfectly intact leather armor. Frustrated with her gullibility, she snatched her scimitar and drew buhkar to vanish. Then she drew jiun slowly, letting the fury rune fill her already pulsating veins. Outside, the sky grew dark instantly. Clouds roiled in, sparking madly and dumping a sudden deluge onto the manor.

The djinn moved quickly, but the more the fury rune drove her, the slower its movements became.

Yes, Sybal, Freja's voice said. *You are fast. Strong. I have made you this way. Let the fury make your god-given strength grow ten times within you!*

Something else joined the fury of jiun in her, then. Whatever it was drew the attention of the djinn. It snapped around to look at her while simultaneously blasting the roof of the manor away to let in the storm. Outside, she heard the people crying out in terror.

"How is this Runer a cousin of mine?" the djinn asked, flickering from view. "What divine touch do you harbor?"

Tzarik burst into sight, slashing at the djinn, driving it toward the halat rune Sybal had painted on the floor. "Don't let it break the rune!" he called to her.

She looked up. The storm raged on, but only outside. Only wind, lightning, and now a rain of fire came into the destroyed room. She grunted, holding her arm up and drawing halat again to shield herself from the fiery embers. The ground rocked, sending a single crack through the rune. They needed to force the djinn onto it.

With a mighty burst of air, the djinn shoved Sybal hard, knocking Tzarik away as well. She careened backwards, slamming into the new mirror the sheikh had put there. It shattered and rained glass down around her. Grunting, she looked up and saw the djinn moving towards her.

"The mirror!" Tzarik called.

Without asking, Sybal grabbed a large piece of the mirror and held it up. Her fingers bled white as she clutched the sharp edges. Carefully, she looked up, trying not to look into its eyes. The djinn had froze, petrified by its own reflection.

"Now!" Sybal shouted to Tzarik. She dropped the mirror and ran to hack at the djinn to drive it back.

With the monster still partially dazed by its own spell, the two of them battled the djinn into a corner, drawing halat to try to squeeze it out. Annoyed, the djinn raised its arms to the sky, calling down a curtain of lightning. It hit them both and struck the ground, sending them flying. Sybal got up first, driven by jiun. The djinn conjured a cloud of ice in both hands. A snowstorm whirled out in a howling wind. Something glinted in the clouds. Jiun and the fury from the voice helped her draw a shield in time to stop the sharp spears of ice the djinn hurled at her. A gasping grunt told her Tzarik had not been so fast.

She whipped around to see him pushing himself up, wiping blood from his side and shoulder. The ice shards plunged into the wall behind him, having grazed him on the way.

"What are you?" the djinn asked, coming into view like before. It moved towards her. Sybal eyed the slowly vanishing rune on the floor and backed away just enough to lure the djinn to follow her. As the djinn's hovering step landed inside the circle, it erupted into a white glow.

Tzarik charged, halat half drawn, coming around the other side of the djinn. Sybal drew halat to meet him, trapping the djinn. The demon bellowed and hammered against the invisible barrier. The force rocked Sybal to her core and a crack shot down the shield. Tzarik pulled the artifact out and prepared to press it into the djinn's side. But the monster saw.

Roaring, the djinn summoned a pillar of fire over Tzarik. When he moved to dodge, the djinn destroyed his barrier and grasped the Runer's arm. Sybal held her shield, seeing that it had kept the djinn over the rune on the floor.

The djinn laughed maniacally. A loud crack was swiftly followed by Tzarik screaming in pain. Sybal looked up to see the djinn had snapped his arm, forcing him to drop the artifact.

"Bind me, will you?" the djinn growled. "Not by you, Runer slavers. Where is the sheikh?" In a flash, he gripped Tzarik's neck and prepared to squeeze. "I will twist your spine like a rag."

Trusting the fury of jiun and the mysterious power from the voice, Sybal dropped her barrier and dived for the artifact. The djinn turned when it felt the shield fall. Sybal had been able to take up the artifact and dive at the djinn in the second it took the monster to turn. She slammed the medallion halat-side down onto its shoulder. The white rune light blinded her as the djinn vanished, bound to the crest.

Tzarik fell to the ground with a thud, cries of pain melting into groans. Sybal ducked to his side and held him. She drew artiah over the wounds from the shards of ice and then picked up his arm. She apologized as she squeezed the bones into place, pulling another shriek of agony from him. She drew artiah slowly over his arm, mending the bone as best she could. After the first pass, she did it again until his hand stopped shaking.

"You'll need to be careful for a bit," she whispered, gently stroking his arm.

With the djinn gone, the fire stopped falling from the sky and the clouds receded. Sybal found herself gasping for air, adrenaline and the last attack of jiun making her quake. She looked out over the utterly destroyed wall to the city and saw the people scrambling to put out fires. Tzarik was right. There was no magic on the map like a djinn's. She held Tzarik close to her, more for her own comfort than his, and thought about the power the djinn had shown in just a few minutes. She ran her hand over her stomach, recalling the horror of the mirage.

"How do we get rid of it?" she asked.

"We'll throw it into the sea as we cross to Alika," Tzarik replied. "That should keep it hidden for a few hundred years." He eyed her, calming himself.

She saw the look in his furrowed brow. He was thinking the same thing she was: they wouldn't have beaten the djinn without her immortality. Was that what he'd wanted to say before, about Azar? She guessed not many Runers walked away from an unbound djinn.

"Is fighting a sorcerer any different than fighting a djinn?" she asked.

Tzarik didn't meet her eyes as they stood up. "Yes. A djinn is a creature, a monster. A sorcerer is a man, immune to bindings and runes." He stopped there, but she sensed he wanted to go on.

She understood; she'd be dead if not for the touch that strengthened and preserved her. If they'd faced the djinn without the curse, neither of them would have lived to walk away.

THE SHEIKH DIDN'T MENTION the destruction when the Runers came to get their pay, mutely handing over a heavy bag of gold to them. Sybal took a handful for her own purse after Tzarik, then put the rest into their saddlebags. Tzarik began to make his way back to where they had hidden Signar when Sybal stopped him.

"We haven't slept indoors in weeks," she said. She tilted her head to a public house a few streets down from the sheikh's manor. "Hot food, a bed, a bath." She groaned the last word. Just imagining it made her yearn for it even more. She hoped the idea of nudity and hot water had an effect on Tzarik. She looked down at him demurely, gently tangling her fingers in his hair. "Time alone. Inside, on a mattress."

His heart rate picked up, so she let her hand trace the vivid vein on his neck. "We cannot leave Signar," he argued futilely. She heard the want in his voice.

"He's asleep," she whispered, moving closer to him. She pressed her index finger under his chin, making him look up at her. "We'll leave before first light."

He didn't respond, a mix of comments, excuses, and worry swirling in his blue eyes. She took his hand and pulled him into the city to a public house down the street, tossing a few coins to the stable master to set their horses up for the night. Wasting no time, she shoved past a large man at the counter.

"One room," she told the innkeeper, a young man who looked

taken aback at her eagerness. "Have dinner brought up for two. And a bath."

"Two tubs?" the innkeeper asked.

Sybal smiled. "One."

She paid for a bottle of mead, took it and the room key, and led Tzarik up the stairs to the rooms above the common area. A lady bard sang a sweet, sad song, her gentle voice penetrating the wooden floor to reach their room. The small room had a window that overlooked the street, letting in a cool desert night breeze.

Sybal drank from the bottle, then handed it to Tzarik. He hesitated just a minute, then tipped it to his lips. As he did, she removed her armor and boots, tossing them into a corner. When Tzarik came up for air, she gripped him, unlacing his armor and devouring him in a long overdue kiss. He melted into her, pulling his arm out of the haphazardly unlaced armor and stumbling as he kicked his boots off.

The side of the bed hit his knees, pulling him down and her on top of him. She let herself crush him, hands running through his hair as she moved to kiss his jaw and neck. Giving in to the loss of any remaining thought, Sybal pulled his tunic over his head, let him reciprocate the gesture, and dived into the black warmth that was their lovemaking. The other comforts forgotten for now.

※

TZARIK WOKE for the second time several hours before the sun rose. The first time had been to wake up Sybal when the two of them had fallen asleep in the copper tub. The innkeeper had interrupted their first round to tell them the bath was ready. They'd moved into the bathroom and continued there in the hot, clean water. Then they'd fallen asleep.

With the night over and the desire quelled, his mind went back to Signar. He could see the sheikh's manor from the window and knew no one would touch the cage, but he didn't worry about someone outside getting in. Signar was a large, strong boy. In his wolf form, he could easily destroy the cage and escape. Tzarik wasn't sure how the wildling would react to waking up alone.

Sybal woke with much prodding. He had fully dressed, saddled the horses, and packed away the food supplies he'd bought before she tore herself from the soft mattress. He paid for two extra waterskins, filled them at the well, and met Sybal on the road out of Mahal. They walked mostly in silence to the sheikh's manor, down his acres of property, and to the storehouse. The guard let them in without any fuss.

Tzarik quickly approached the cage, unlacing the leather ties as quickly as he could. Signar lay inside on his back, long arms and legs splayed out to the sides. Tzarik had never seen him lie like that. He put the key into the lock, which normally roused the boy. He didn't move.

"Signar?" Tzarik called. When Signar didn't move again, panic rushed through Tzarik's limbs. He threw the lock off and flung the door open.

"What are you doing?" Sybal called, running around to the back to see him rush to Signar's side. She waited at the entrance, wary of the wildling.

Tzarik fell to his knees, lifting Signar's head onto his lap. The boy's face had paled so much that the blood dried to his lips stood out like black scabs. "Water!" Tzarik barked at Sybal. He gently smacked Signar's face.

Sybal grabbed a skin and tossed it to him. He caught it deftly, pulled the cork out with his teeth, and tipped some of the fresh well water past Signar's dry lips. At first, the water filled Signar's mouth, spilling over his sunken cheeks. Tzarik's heart raced, and he found himself begging the invisible gods to make Signar wake up.

The boy coughed, spitting the water back out, breathing

raggedly. Then he grabbed the skin from Tzarik's hand and drank ravenously. Tzarik had to pull it away so he didn't make himself sick.

"Not too much now," he said to the Vaeson. "You'll vomit it back up, and that will do you far more harm."

"He doesn't understand," Sybal sighed sadly.

He looked at her. He heard her words, but the softness in her eyes said she was taken in by this caring side of him. Taking the boy's arm, he stood up, instructing him to follow his lead to get his blood flowing again. When Signar stood, he towered over Tzarik. Signar even stood taller than Sybal.

"He'll grow even more," Sybal smiled, seeing Tzarik taking in the giant that leaned on him. "He's only sixteen. He'll sprout like a palm. I did."

Tzarik almost couldn't imagine the monstrous Caerwren man Signar would turn into. But that's why he'd taken the boy. To give him a chance to turn into the Reks he had every right to be. Signar stumbled a little, so Tzarik took his arm to steady him. Sybal made a quick step forward in case he fell. Signar saw her move towards him and immediately fell, afraid, placing Tzarik between himself and Sybal.

Sybal's kind face melted away. "I don't understand why he does that."

Tzarik didn't reply. Signar was not a wild animal, but even wild dogs knew when they were being given tainted food. And who had given it to them. Signar knew Sybal had been the one drugging him. He'd picked up on her dislike of him. Tzarik was just grateful the boy chose to cower rather than attack this time. But that worried him, too. Signar was a wolf, a Vaeson, a Reks of Caerwren. He needed his rage, his strength. Somehow, Tzarik had to teach him to control his wild power, not banish it. He wondered if he could manage such a thing. Binding the djinn seemed like a simpler task than raising the wild wolf.

Chapter 5

Masahk and Runer

The time came for Sharar to mingle discreetly at the docks, looking for his Runer, Amir. It had been some weeks since he'd last seen the Runer. He enjoyed taking Amir to the Dynast Palace because of the rage it brought out of the Vizier, Nasor. The jackal Masahk hated Runers, and Sharar enjoyed the torment Nasor often rained on Amir. The social aspects intrigued him as much as any other.

He eagerly awaited the news Sahir had deemed so important that he dared not send it in written form. He had an audience with the Dynast Pharaoh in a few days' time, and preferred to have his affairs in order before the next step.

The sun hung lower over the ocean, having just risen. He casually paced out onto the labyrinth of docks and piers that made up what the Alikans called the ocean square. Part market, part lawless tussle, part docks, the ocean square moved with quick sailors and merchants transporting goods to and from the jumbled horde of ships berthed there. He scanned the ships, knowing Amir would come off an Al'Myrahn passenger vessel.

A fishing ship bobbed just to Sharar's left, pulling in nets from fishing in the shallows. The ragged mainmast hung at a neglected angle and the men aboard it stank. He could smell them over the fish they hauled aboard and dumped onto their deck. Most of them were missing teeth and shouted in incomplete sentences, showing their total lack of education. Sharar was about to turn away from them when they exclaimed loudly, calling each other over excitedly. The fishermen pointed wildly up into the net that rose out of the water, cranked by a wheel powered by three men. Something inside the net flailed frantically. Something larger than the rainbow-colored fish inside. He stopped to watch.

The captain ran and released the hook, spilling hundreds of flopping fish onto the deck, where their scales caught the Alikan sunlight. Then he saw what had captured their attention and given them so much pleasure. A full-blooded, ocean-dwelling Masahk tumbled to the deck after all the fish, landing with a wet thud. The sailors and fishermen surrounded it quickly. Sharar made his way down the pier, having always been interested in the god-shaped immortals of Alika. Most Masahk had hidden powers they rarely used. Some could bend fire to their will, others could turn invisible, some could read minds, or move things with their minds—the list was just as long and varied as the sentients. He'd rarely seen a full-blooded Masahk off Alika, and many on the continent were half-Masahk.

He saw as he approached that this one was a male. He had blue and white skin, with the tops of his arms, the space near his collarbone, and around his jaw covered in tiny, opalescent scales. He had large, ovate eyes that gave him an innocent face. Something long and tendril-like grew from his head in the place of human hair. He had webbed hands and feet, and wore white and gold wrappings around his waist, as well as gold cuffs around his wrists and ankles. Sharar realized he must be a priest to one of the Alikan gods.

The men on the boat jeered and taunted the Masahk as he tried to stand. One of the men knocked him down with a long harpoon, making fun of his smooth, featureless chest. The Masahk raised his long-fingered webbed hand, begging them to let him go. Sharar approached the gangplank that led onto the ship.

"I hear these fish people are smooth all over," one of them snickered. "How do you plow your fish-wife, my little fillet?"

Another guffawed. "He's a priest. He has no fish-wife. He got no need."

"This is a mistake," the Masahk begged, inching away as far as he could before he ran into the men on the other side of the group that encircled him. "I mean you no harm. I'm sorry I got tangled in the net. I can pay for a new one."

"Shall we see if the rumors are true?" the fisherman cajoled, playfully elbowing his captain.

The captain leered down at the priestly Masahk. He grabbed the harpoon from the fisherman. "Let's take a look at our fine catch." With a grunt, taking the harpoon in two hands, he stabbed the Masahk through his webbed foot, pinning him to the deck.

The Masahk cried out, holding his leg as cold, red blood seeped from the wound. Sharar started, taking two quick steps across the gang plank. He stopped when a few of the fishermen turned to look at him.

"Bare him to his god, boys," the captain laughed.

At his order, three men lurched at the Masahk, ripping his white temple wrappings from him. The Masahk hung his head in shame, covering his face. Sharar didn't understand, since, as the men had said, the water-type Masahk bore no showing human parts. But then the simpletons laughed at him, pointing and making cruel jokes.

"Pray to Ashmalia now, priest," the captain said, grabbing a handful of the priest's strange locks and pulling his head back to face him. "Only women pledge their worship to Ashmalia."

"May she heal your wicked hearts," the Masahk hissed, his large eyes watering in pain.

Seeing the man holding the harpoon start to turn it, drawing more blood and hearing the anguished cry from the gentle Masahk, Sharar ran onto the ship. He grabbed the discarded wrapping and shoved the man aside.

"Let him go, you ignorant brutes," he commanded. "He's not an animal." He gripped the harpoon, trying to pull it from the man's grasp. The man shoved him hard in the chest, pushing Sharar back.

"You one of those weeping naturalists?" the captain asked. "The kind who cries over bees and trees when they are burned for forges?"

Sharar rearranged his robes indignantly. "I am no such thing. But this is cruel. Let him go, or I'll—"

The captain laughed. He signaled his men and two sprang up behind Sharar, grappling his arms. The scholar shoved into one, trying to pull his arm free, but the men held him fast. Another came up before him and punched him hard in the stomach until he stopped fighting. The man hit his wound, making it ignite in new pain. He coughed, moaning, and his knees gave out. The men held him up, making him watch as they turned their attention back to the Masahk.

A gurgling hiss made Sharar look up despite his pain. The Masahk got to his one good foot and flexed his arms. Long, mother-of-pearl claws protracted from all ten of his fingers. He pulled hard, tearing the webbing of his foot that the men had pinned the harpoon with. More blood smattered out as he moved. The Masahk clawed at the captain, making him fall back, then he pounced on the one who had beaten Sharar. The Masahk opened his mouth as he hissed, showing a mouth full of sharp fangs.

The ones who held Sharar dropped him, backing away and

exclaiming in a variety of curses. The captain held his middle where the Masahk had clawed him. A webbed spine Sharar had not seen before flared down the Masashk's back as he threatened the other seamen. One of them backed away to a rack of more harpoons. Seeing this, the Masahk strode to Sharar, put his arm around his shoulders, and hauled him off the ship.

"You fish-whore!" the captain cried, half weeping as his wound bled.

The Masahk ignored them, dragging Sharar away into a smaller street off the docks. Completely bemused, Sharar tried to gather his breath while his wound throbbed under his hand.

"You didn't need my help at all," he grunted. "Why'd you let them mock you like that if you could have fended them off?"

"They had done me no real harm yet," the Masahk replied. He took them to the outdoor seating of a public house and gently lowered Sharar into a chair. "Thank you all the same. You seem unwell, though."

Confused by the priest's tender nature, he squinted up at his scaly blue face. "I have a long-standing wound. They quite angered it with their beating." He couldn't stop himself from curling over a little from the pain.

The Masahk called a server over and ordered cool mint teas for them both. Then he knelt down in front of Sharar. "If I may?" he asked, poising his hands over Sharar's middle.

Sharar frowned. "What can you do?"

The Masahk smiled kindly. "As they said, though they meant it as an insult, I am a priest of Ashmalia. The goddess of healing. That is my Masahk gift." He gently removed Sharar's hand from where he pressed it into his ribs. "If I may?"

Curious as to what the Masahk's power was, he nodded and forced himself to sit up. "What's your name, priest?"

"I am called Het," he replied softly. His long, webbed fingers unfastened Sharar's sashes around his middle and opened up his ornate tunic only enough to look at his wound. Het's large eyes furrowed as he inspected it. "This is a strange scar," he whispered. His cold fingers made Sharar gasp and cringe away. "Something festers inside, refusing to let it heal. Like a curse." He looked up. "How did you get it?"

Sharar grunted, half laughing at the memory. "I was foolish. I trusted a man on Xia who had control of his entire country without them knowing. He had information I wanted. I played his game, waiting for the right time to extract that information. But he was more brute than scholar."

"Xia?" Het asked, frowning and running his gentle fingers over the wound again. "A sigiled blade, perhaps?"

Sharar looked down at his new companion. "You know about the sigiled blades?"

Het shook his head, pressing his palm over the wound. "No. The Wushito are a very secret sect. I know they exist, and I know their warriors use them."

"They take souls," Sharar supplied, not caring if he let the ancient civilization's secrets out to this Masahk. "I assume it's only a matter of time before this one consumes me, killing me."

Het looked up. "You run from death, scholar?"

"They can kill monsters with them, like the blade of a Runer," Sharar went on, ignoring the question. "They can take the soul of a sentient, locking it within the blade. They kill demons with those blades, collecting their souls. If he stabbed me with one, perhaps the darkness within that blade has festered in the wound."

Het nodded, making a small humming sound. "So it would seem. I suppose you are lucky he did not stab you long enough to take your soul? I would call this a malignant wound. I do not know if I can heal it entirely, but I may be able to help. If you'll allow me."

The Masahk asked for consent too much, Sharar thought. "If you think you can," he said.

Het adjusted on his knees, wrapping his hands around Sharar's middle. He turned his eyes to the sky. "Healing is my Masahk gift. But I will also ask Ashmalia to grant you a blessing." Softly, he whispered a prayer Sharar could not hear.

A horrid feeling, like a million tiny strikes of lightning, crawled over the scar. Sharar gasped, cringing away from the Masahk's touch, but his grasp held fast. A moment later, the pain lessened to a dull heat. Het removed his hands, smiling. Looking down, Sharar saw the wound no longer burned black. A pale scar crawled over his ribs where it had been.

"Incredible," he whispered.

Het stood up, taking his robes from where Sharar had dropped them on the table. "Not entirely," he said humbly. "But it will help. I cannot stand to see another being in pain. And you aided me at a danger to yourself."

Speechless, Sharar nodded thanks.

"I am a priest installed in the Dynast temple in Mysir for now," Het said, wrapping his garments on again. "I travel, though. If you are ever in Mysir, find me, my friend."

"I will," the scholar promised. "I am fascinated by your ability. And your nature. How you controlled yourself when those men hurt you is quite fascinating."

Het smiled and gave Sharar a small bow. "I am pleased to have intrigued you, scholar."

Sharar watched the Masahk leave as the server brought out the pot of tea and two cups. He poured himself some and drank, inspecting his painless scar. It would be a matter of time before he knew if the priest's magic had healed him or not. But for now, he'd forgotten what it was like to not be in constant pain.

He re-laced his tunic and tied the sashes around his hips before finishing the tea and heading back to the docks to look for the Runer.

THE SUN SANK SO low it touched the ocean, turning it bright red before the last ship from Al'Myrah pulled in to dock. Sharar glared, tired and hot from waiting all day, as the passengers disembarked. A few burly men with horses and swords came off, but none of them wore the black of a Runer. A few rich sheikhs, a beautiful rani visiting from Bahratt, and a few Xian rice merchants all filed off.

Just as Sharar had made up his mind that Amir would not arrive, the captain of the ship, a tall, sunburnt Caerwren man with chestnut hair and beard, emerged from below deck. The captain led a man in shackles, accompanied by a great red stallion. The man wore the telltale armor of a Runer, had long, messy black hair half pulled up atop his head, and the icy blue eyes. A massive crossbow with orichalcum-tipped bolts was slung across his back. His arms were chained behind him. Sharar recognized Amir at last.

The captain moved behind the Runer with a set of keys and roughly unlocked the shackles. As he did, the Runer looked out over the docks and spotted Sharar. He gave a slight nod and flicked his head, signaling Sharar to leave. Knowing he'd follow, Sharar left the docks and found his horse. He mounted and looked back to see Amir, free now, mount his black stallion and start a slow trot toward him. Sharar clicked his tongue at his horse and started back to his home.

The Runer followed him, often dropping out of sight. But Sharar knew Runers. Just because he couldn't see the man didn't mean he didn't see Sharar. Once they left the merchant district, he made his horse trot, getting to his estate more quickly. He passed through his gate and waited inside for the Runer to arrive. He went to his study where the djinn often waited. He kept the artifact that bound the djinn locked below in his dungeons, hanging from the stone walls where he could keep an eye on it. He hardly ever traveled with it. Tonight, the djinn did not appear when he entered, but Sharar hardly cared.

He moved to a wall-sized map behind his desk and studied it while he waited for his servant to come and tell him the Runer had arrived. His eyes ran over Alika, following a red line he'd drawn from Gypsu to Mysir to the Cradle. He ran his finger over Mysir. For a second, he wondered if he was wasting time here on Alika. There was only one thing that kept him here, and he was steadily losing hope. He needed to find Tarkan, know what the necromancer was doing... and he needed to get back to hunting the Mahit'Onomicon. But thoughts of his son had been distracting him.

"Sira?" a servant girl said softly, opening the study door. "Amir has come." Her voice tilted up, showing her curiosity.

"Send him in," Sharar said, turning to face the doors.

The girl bowed, opening the door for the hunter to enter. Upon closer inspection, the Runer looked gruff and travel-worn. The stubble on his sharp face said he hadn't shaved in days. Dark circles around his eyes told a story of sleepless nights.

"Amir, how are you?" Sharar asked, motioning for him to enter. The girl closed the door behind him.

The Runer walked with long-legged strides up to the desk. He stood taller than Sharar, and had muscles so sharp his armor conformed to them. He was tall for an Al'Myrahn. Amir took up a crystal decanter of an amber drink and drank straight from it.

"This is your Alikan estate?" Amir replied in a gruff, travel-worn voice that reminded Sharar of Tzarik. He wiped the back of his hand over his lips and looked around the ornate room.

Sharar smiled. "If it's not, that makes taking the liquor quite awkward."

Amir scoffed through his nose, half smirking in exhaustion. "I was going to ask. Contrary to what that damned captain of that vessel thought, thievery was not my crime."

Sharar handed Amir a glass. "I've never been able to get a Runer to tell me their crime. They guard that secret so closely."

"I've known you a long time, Sharar, but not *that* long." Amir nodded, downing the entire glass of the amber drink before wincing. "It's the only power over civilians we have. If they don't know our crime, they don't know what crime we cannot commit and will let us into their cities."

Sharar poured himself a glass as well. "The captain bound your hands. Doesn't he know that if you stole something, the runes would take you?" Sharar didn't tell Amir, but he'd sussed out his crime some time ago. The Runer couldn't lie, and he used that to his advantage when the occasion demanded it.

The Runer poured himself another helping and took it, pacing around the study. His large, blue eyes took in the artifacts, the maps, the beautiful weaponry, and the other trophies on the walls. "I assume he wouldn't want the monster I'd turn into if I broke my oath upon his ship."

Curious, Sharar watched Amir admire his things. "Do Runers commit suicide so easily?"

Amir faced the scholar. The firelight hit his face just right to let Sharar see a web of scars on his neck and one cross the bridge of his nose. "Yes, sira. We do. We go from city to city, homeless, hungry, thirsty, and in pain. Only to find a haunt and be feared and ridiculed for our status as necessary criminals. Or worse, they attack us, hoping murder was our crime so we don't fight back."

Sharar sensed a personal tale in that detail, but let the Runer go on.

"So we die, with them dolling out the execution they think we deserve."

Sharar appreciated the Runer's thoughtful comment. Not many Runers were as discerning as Amir. "It's a terrible, symbiotic relationship. They hate you for not being punished as they see fit. But they need you to live for their peaceful lotus and lokum lives."

He took a slow sip, watching Amir. So he wasn't the kind of Runer he'd hunted for; he'd often wondered about Amir's crime. The man was not as cynical as other Runers. He almost had a soft nature at times, so Sharar wondered if he was the kind of Runer he needed. No matter. He had information and was often useful.

"What news does Sheikh Sahir have for me?" he asked.

Amir rested his empty hand on the hilt of his orichalcum scimitar. "The Runer you are so keen on. The Butcher of Ala'Nar."

Sharar stood up from where he leaned on his desk.

"Sahir had him pass through Moshav more than a month ago. Maybe longer," Amir said. "The sheikh told him to go to Alika."

A thrill shot through Sharar. Tzarik was coming to Alika. He might already be on the continent if he hurried. "Why?" he asked. "Where has he been? I've been searching high and low for that damned man."

"He had a beast with him," Amir went on. "Sahir wasn't sure what it was. A monster of some kind, like a wolf."

This gave Sharar a small chuckle. "The monster hunter has turned into a monster tamer. Fascinating. I wonder what creature has captured my Runer's attention so well to warrant companionship." He rubbed his clean-shaven chin. That also mattered little. It made Tzarik more fascinating, to be sure. More than ever, Sharar wanted Tzarik bound and shackled under his knife's precision. He was close, and Tzarik had practically walked into his clutches. The Runer wouldn't know Sharar had an estate on Alika. He had everything he needed to force Tzarik's secrets out of his blood.

Amir moved to a display of ancient Xian and Oceanyan artifacts. "Sahir said his apprentice looked quite unwell."

Sharar choked on the drink, coughing and sputtering. "The lady Runer?"

Amir looked up, eyes sparkling. "A lady Runer?"

"She's dead," Sharar snapped. "I saw her with my own eyes. I put her in a coffin." He stopped, the words cut off by understanding. "You saw Tarkan that day in Singad." His mind reeled. "No," he breathed, his hand pressed into his chest as his breath ran out of his control. "He can't have. He cannot bring the dead to life, not like that."

Amir turned to face the raving scholar.

The scholar's hand shook so much, he dropped the glass. It shattered on the floor. "Did he find her?" he cried, gripping his desk. "Did he take her?"

The Runer stood back, only slightly concerned at the madness mounting in Sharar.

"How?" Sharar shouted, whirling to face the map behind him. "She was alive. Are you sure?"

Amir grunted in confusion.

Sharar's eyes flashed from Singad to Moshav to Alika. "Tzarik is coming here. Sybal is with him. Tarkan was in Singad and took her corpse."

He went silent, studying the map.

"My gods," Sharar whispered. "He's here. And he's ascended to Necro'Khan." His blood boiled. Surely, the path to Necro'Khan was written out in the Mahit'Onomicon. Tarkan must have the book. Sharar rounded on Amir. "Tell me everything Sahir heard from the Runers. Tell me if Tarkan is now my great and powerful enemy."

"And if he's not?" Amir asked, pouring more drink again.

Sharar straightened up, trying to calm his nerves. "Then it's here, isn't it? The Mahit'Onomicon is on Alika, and Tarkan is looking for it."

Chapter 6

Dead-Walking

Tarkan walked up the long, winding stairs of the observatory in the temple of the Apostles of Makan Alu'Ekmet. The turret jutted high above the rest of the city and offered a far view of Alika around it. From the tower, he spied the dancing firelights in windows and street lamps of the main city, Gypsu. One golden estate—almost a palace—rose above most of the others. Tarkan knew Sharar's Alikan home just as well as he knew his Hatal estate and the small manor he owned in Ala'-Nar. He wondered if the scholar was in his Alikan manor now. Sahir had told him that Sharar had made it into the Dynast Pharaoh's circle of scholars, but that didn't mean he had the Mahit'Onomicon yet.

Ashkan appeared through the door in the floor, coming up the steps. His soft footfalls told Tarkan he had no fear of his former tribesman. He joined Tarkan in looking out over Gypsu. "You've waited days, Tarkan. You have not consumed. What are you waiting for?"

The pain in Tarkan's throat stopped him from speaking. He tried to answer, but the burns took his voice. He dropped his head in annoyance and shame. No corpse lay in the tower for him to transfer his scars to. He could try to force them onto Ashkan, but he wasn't ready to push the Apostle away yet. And he wasn't sure if forcing his wounds on another, especially a living sentient, would succeed as it had with the corpses.

"I could go to the scholar's estate on your behalf," Ashkan offered.

Tarkan let out a strangled, rasping laugh at this.

"You do not trust me," Ashkan surmised. "That is to be expected. Brother, now that you are Necro'Khan, I have no reason to fight you. To betray you. I never did, even in the early days."

The Necro'Khan raised a pale brow at Ashkan. He wasn't so sure. The Bone-Scriven had been cowards from the start, hiding their scriptures. Yes, the agony was far worse, but the safety outweighed the pain. A Bone-Scriven's eyes wouldn't even turn green until they were an Apostle. The Scriven were safe from all suspicion. He took a deep breath and turned, descending the stairs. He wanted to speak.

Finding a mostly decomposed corpse, he touched it, transferring his wound to the dead. When it left him, his throat opened, and he swallowed ample amounts of air.

"I want to see Sharar for myself," Tarkan said, leisurely walking out of the temple and into Makan Alu'Ekmet's square again. "But I must find a way to do so without risking myself."

Ashkan eyed Tarkan's pale neck. "I have not seen anyone create new spells since Ishmael. It is not written that we are allowed such ambition. We are to follow our texts, not write them."

"The scriptures are but the start," Tarkan replied. "The spells I will create will be far greater than any Necro'Khan's before me. They will bestow such power and might that none will have the strength to take me from my throne."

"You cast without your voice," the other noted. "That is a testament to your strength already."

"It was not always so," Tarkan confessed. "When the wolf took my voice, I thought that would be the end for me. What good is a necromancer who cannot call on his magic? But I forced the blood magic to bend to my will without it, though it takes such strength."

"Tell me what you want to do, Tarkan," Ashkan said measuredly. "I will aid you in any way I can."

Tarkan stopped and looked at a solitary temple outside Gypsu. It waited perhaps three miles away. A candle burned in a portcullis on the side facing them. A kehann, a temple warrior, must be on watch. Tarkan's eyes scanned the moon-lit horizon to find a few farms nearby as well.

"When I pulled the raven Reks from the Deep," he said softly, "I held his spirit in my hand. I dropped it into the Runer like a stone. I could hardly control it, but I want to do that with my own soul."

Ashkan stopped his stride and faced Tarkan. "What you are suggesting sounds more and more like heresy, brother. Nephron will be displeased."

"Nephron knows the man he chose as Khan of his people." Tarkan stopped. "No matter. The gods will be of no consequence to me. Soon, they will fear me. Ashkan, Alika is known for its ancient cult that worshiped death here and joined the necromancers. There are curses and secrets beneath these sands that I will pull to the surface. I will create spells to cast inside the Deep itself. I will use the dead to every advantage. And I will be strong enough to cut down my enemies with a blade. I will forge a sword of blood and metal, imbued with the heart of a Necro'Khan, and the hilt will be scriven bone." He turned to watch Ashkan's face as he divulged his plan. "With this blade, I will command the dead, imbibing them with a flood of blood. They will not be merely risen —they will be undead: sentient risen, gifted unlife by me, sustained by the blade of blood."

As he'd hoped, Ashkan's glowing green eyes showed utter admiration and anticipation.

Tarkan went on. "The blade will pull blood from every living body it pierces, snuffing their life-force, leaving them an empty husk. I will have infinite power, never again needing to consume. Immortal and unstoppable, I will slaughter any on Alika who stand up to me. I will shatter the Pharaoh's dynasty and take his place on the throne."

Ashkan didn't speak when Tarkan stopped, taking in what he'd heard. At length, he said, "There will never be any who can challenge you."

"There is one." Tarkan turned to the east. "Sharar will be a sorcerer, I have no doubt. He has a better chance of finding the Mahit'Onomicon before me. I just need to be ready to take it from him before he devours his djinn."

"How?" Ashkan asked.

"I will show you. Tonight, go to the temple on the outskirts of Gypsu. Kill the kehann who sits on watch there. Bring his body back to me."

"If you plan to cast, you must consume," Ashkan counseled.

Tarkan turned and marched toward the outlying farms. He raised his hand, calling up his risen viper and griffin. "I will. Bring me the body, and as unscathed as you can."

"What do you plan on doing?"

Tarkan couldn't stop the small smile that pulled at his lips, even as his voice began to slip away. "Possess it, using it as a safe vessel of my own."

Ashkan didn't understand, but Tarkan appreciated his unquestioning bow of obedience. They split up, heading for the first step in creating a new necrotic spell.

TARKAN ROSE a dozen corpses from the tombs of Makan Alu'Ekmet to join him and his risen monsters. He rode the griffin as close as he dared get, then sent them and his risen into the larger farmstead. Wordlessly, he commanded his risen to attack the family, wounding them enough to be brought back alive. They needed to be living when he ate their flesh; he'd not risk possession now.

The screams from the home didn't turn his stomach. He watched the bloodshed, remembering how he'd devastated Ala'Nar all those years ago. He didn't care how much death he and his dragon, Rakthar, inflicted on the people, so long as the Runers understood it was their fault. They'd forced his hand.

But they'd stayed by him on Caerwren...

No, he berated himself. *You cannot think of them now. They were a means to an end.* Besides, they wouldn't hunt him. Not now. Tzarik and Sybal owed him a great debt. And Tzarik at least would pay dearly. The lady Runer was god-touched. She had anywhere from months to a few years before whatever god laid claim to her soul took her, forcing her into demonic servitude. Her fall would destroy Tzarik. He'd return to the wild brute of a hunter he'd been when Tarkan first met him.

A man ran out from the barn and spotted Tarkan in the distance. He shouted, pointing, and took up a weapon to defend his property and family from the risen. He'd been seen, but it didn't matter. Let the lowly people of Alika know a necromancer walked among them. If Sharar was here, Tarkan wanted him to know that he was close. And stronger than the last time.

His small horde of risen marched out of the home, carrying or dragging bodies of moaning captives. He remounted the griffin and commanded the others to take them to Makan Alu'Ekmet and the temple. One of the wounded died along the way, but he didn't take the body. No, the kehann Ashkan would bring him would be much stronger. A body better suited to combat.

Once he reached the temple, he waited for his sacrifices and Ashkan to return. He prepared a place in the catacombs of the temple. Grunting and straining, he removed the stone lid of a coffin and took out the corpse inside, tossing its dusty bones to the floor. Like his father before him, he would need a safe place to hide his own body. He didn't know if the spell would work or what might happen once he put his soul into the kehann's body. Would it eventually expel him, forcing him back to his own? Would he have to cast the spell again? He paused then, wondering. He couldn't cast from the kehann's body. The experimental spell was turning risky and dangerous, but he dared not risk facing Sharar in his own body. Not yet.

Ashkan came back, leading Tarkan's horse with the body of the kehann on the back. "I may have been seen raising some dead," he confessed. "But no alarm was raised."

"Well done," Tarkan praised him. "Lay him here." He indicated a spot close to the stone coffin. "When my soul leaves my body, it will fall. Gather it and put it within this coffin. When we leave to face Sharar, we will close it up, protecting me."

Ashkan thought through the instructions. "How will you return to your body?"

He wasn't sure of his prediction, but Ashkan didn't need to know that. "The spell will be sustained by the blood and flesh I consume. When my body grows too weak to hold my spirit in this one, I will be forced back." He glared at Ashkan with a preemptive warning. "Come back to me. Open the coffin."

"Of course," Ashkan promised. He looked away and Tarkan saw understanding on his face.

"Do not think of betraying me," he warned.

"Never," the Apostle promised. "If I could not be Necro'Khan, serving one will be my pleasure. I have no malice for you in my heart, Tarkan."

Not convinced, Tarkan turned his attention to his risen and

prisoners. "Take the other three below," he ordered them. "This one stays. Ashkan, take your ruby blade and remove his flesh."

The man cried out weakly in his beaten state, but couldn't stop the risen from grappling him and Ashkan from flaying him alive. He gathered blood and flesh and left the man to die slowly so Tarkan could consume.

Tarkan stood over his unwilling vessel and examined him. The kehann was tall for an Al'Myrahn, broad shouldered and muscled. He had a handsome face, but Tarkan didn't care for his looks. He needed the warrior's strength. He spent a few minutes laying the man out to avoid any pain when he possessed him. If this spell worked, if the blood could be bent to his new spell, this would be just the start. He would prove to himself that he could bear the mantel of Necro'Khan, and could be stronger even than Ishmael.

Ashkan came down into the catacombs, bearing a pitcher of blood and a silver tray of living flesh. Tarkan drank nearly all the blood and devoured several mouthfuls of the prisoner's tough flesh. "Take the rest for yourself," he instructed Ashkan. "You will also need your strength."

The other necromancer took it without a word and finished it off. Tarkan turned to face the kehann and the stone coffin. He began to hiss his own spell, using the old Porshain language tattooed on his body. At first, the black wind did not respond. Pouring more of his power into his spoken words, the magic devouring the flesh and blood within him, something at last stirred. Tarkan normally felt a mutual communion between himself and the blood. But now he gripped it, controlling it. Bending it to his will.

The whispering of the blood filled his ears as rivulets of red started to pull from his body into the air around him. A strange and unexpected pain jerked at his insides, like something tried to pull his soul from within. He decided that was a good thing and leaned into it.

Tarkan felt his spirit rip from his flesh as his body fell into Ashkan's arms. He remained standing, a veiny, glowing spirit made of blood. Ashkan's wide, green eyes told him all he needed to know about his new ghostly appearance.

He whispered thanks to Ashkan for catching his body, but no words came out. Just the hissing cries of the blood he'd consumed. In fact, he heard them inside his metaphysical skull. They continued whispering and hissing, cutting out all other sounds. Not sure what would happen if he stayed in this supernatural state too long, he knelt by the kehann's body and lay over it, sinking in. As he did, his consciousness slipped away for just a moment as his spirit came to rest.

A sudden gasp brought the kehann to life as Tarkan drank air into the undead lungs. He gasped, his head spinning. When he sat up, the world tilted dangerously and he fell back again. Ashkan caught him, bracing him, and stood up.

The Apostle swore in three tongues before saying, "I will never doubt your abilities. How do you feel?"

Tarkan leaned heavily against Ashkan as he became familiar with his new body. Since the kehann had died only moments before, no stiffness or weakness pulled his limbs down. He picked up one great foot and took a step. Ashkan supported him, stepping with him. The second step already came more easily. Tarkan pushed off his Apostle and walked several yards away into a clearing of the catacombs. He swung his arms, lifted his legs one at a time, then unsheathed the kehann's scimitar. Easily, the man's muscles flexing, he swung it in arches at his sides. It felt magnificent to be so strong.

Behind him, Ashkan gently lifted his vacant body. "The blood still comes," he said, inclining his head toward Tarkan's body.

He was right; tiny droplets of blood lifted out of his soulless vessel, dissipating when they floated a foot or two above the surface of his skin. The spell held and would drop when he was too weak to hold it any longer. Tarkan helped Ashkan put his necrotic body into the coffin and close the great stone lid.

"We will head to Gypsu tonight to see if the scholar is here," Tarkan said. "When I fall, run. Come back and free me."

"I understand, Tarkan," Ashkan promised, locking his green eyes with Tarkan's now brown ones. "I believe you are right. Our gods will fear you."

Chapter 7

The Voice

Tzarik locked eyes with the wolf. The golden mane of the Vaeson shook as his snout wrinkled in a dangerous snarl and his green eyes flashed. The pile of freshly cooked meat made the wolf's nose twitch in anticipation. They had stopped for the night, close to the shore of Hatal now. They had maybe one more night before they would board an Alikan ship and finally reach the shores of Gypsu and the country of the pharaohs.

Above, the moon glowed in a waxing crescent, just visible over the peaks at the edge of Hatal. Tzarik could almost hear the ocean to the east of them, and it made his heart race in anticipation. Around them, the desert night sang with the few bugs that survived in the hot sand. They'd stopped in a small grove of trees where a shallow spring trickled past. They'd picked the spot at the deepest point in the stream to fill their waterskins once again. Sybal sat near the fire, oiling her blade and mending her armor, leather rune cord, and a few other articles of clothing with the money they'd acquired from the sheikh. Tzarik needed to maintain his tools as well, but Signar required as much attention as possible before they boarded another ship.

The boy had come a long way, Tzarik thought. His fits of fear and rage had dwindled down to upsets that set him off. There were times the Runer swore the boy was calculating him, summing him up with his eyes. Hoping he'd been right—that all Signar needed was to not be chained and beaten—he wanted to give him more freedom.

"I know you want this," Tzarik said, holding the dented metal plate of meat up. "But you have to shift back. I won't give it to you otherwise."

Signar's snarl lessened and a large string of lupine drool dripped from his jaws. He licked his lips and leapt at the food. Tzarik stepped back, having anticipated the lunge, and drew halat. The Vaeson crashed into it with a crunch, followed by a high-pitched whine. Signar shook his wolven head, forcing a sneeze down his long snout. He looked up, tilting his head. This time, he looked confused rather than hurt or angry.

"Be calm, Signar," Tzarik commanded gently. He held out his other hand where the runes wrapped around his fingers.

Signar's piercing green orbs flicked to the offending runes and back to Tzarik's eyes. Licking his lips, Signar sat, towering over Tzarik. He waited. When Tzarik only moved forward a step, the wolf leaned onto his front paws, coming to a lying position so he was at eye level with Tzarik. Testing the boy's gesture, Tzarik moved closer, proffering the meat. His sulfates rushed as he got close to the mystical beast. His hand shook as his nerves feared the wolf might snap at him. Cautiously, the wolf moved his head to try to take a piece of meat. Tzarik pulled it away.

"Not until you shift back," he bargained.

"He doesn't understand," Sybal called over the fire and darkness to the cage.

Tzarik didn't believe that. "Signar," he commanded again in the same gentle tone, "shift back. I know you can. Control your wolf." Curious how Signar would react, Tzarik took a bite of the warm meat and chewed while looking the wolf in the eyes.

Signar whined and backed up, marching a tight circle. About the fourth time he made the pass, he finally shifted, shrinking down to the boy again. He growled in his human form and gripped his long, tangled blond hair as he fought to control his frustration.

"Well done," Tzarik praised him.

He set the plate down and backed away, seeing the distress the Vaeson was in. He took in the boy's garments, realizing he had little more to wear than the draping animal hide around his hips. He hadn't bought clothes for Signar because he didn't know where on Al'Myrah to find a tailor who made clothes for such a tall person. And because he had a theory about the Vaeson and the animal skins they wore. He suspected the huge monsters had to wear the natural hides. Some kind of magic in the animals and the Vaeson spoke to one another. When they shifted, the skins shifted with them, not being torn asunder by their massive bodies. It made sense to him, since everyone he'd met on Caerwren wore such skins. They were close to the animals, close to their gods.

When he exited the cage, Signar dove at the roasted meat, devouring it. Tzarik sat with his back to the bars, close to the boy inside, and took a portion for himself. He chewed for a little while, watching Sybal's lithe fingers dance over her work. She moved through the leatherwork just like her hands had through his hair a few nights ago. Yes, he'd been enraged when they'd come back and found Signar passed out from thirst and hunger. It had been the wrong thing to do. But they'd not been able to touch one another like that in some time.

"You don't think he understands your Al'Myrahn, do you?" Sybal asked, not looking up from her work.

Tzarik paused. He'd not considered it. "I don't know that he understands the Caerwren tongue, either." He turned to look at Signar, who had finished his portion already. The boy met his eyes and crawled over to sit just on the other side of the bars. "Do you want to speak Caerwren?" he asked Signar in his native tongue. Then he added in Al'Myrahn, "Or can you understand me when I speak Al'Myrahn?"

To Tzarik's shock, Signar pressed his lips together to try to hide a mischievous smile. His emerald eyes sparkled in stifled laughter. A thrill and an unfamiliar wave of pride shot up in Tzarik. Signar had understood. And something about it had made him smile. The grin made him look like the boy he was.

"You understand both," Tzarik mused out loud, realizing Signar was trying to hide that fact and found it amusing. "But you don't want me to know you do." He smiled and exhaled softly through his nose. He faced Sybal. "His personality is coming out a little. We've made progress."

Sybal granted him a smirk in reply. "I see he understood. I agree: he didn't want you to know that he did." She shook her head. "He has a Skelmir inside him."

"Skelmir?" Tzarik asked.

"Skelmir," a voice behind him said through a grin.

Shocked, both Runers turned and stood up to look at the boy in the cage.

"That was him?" Sybal asked, genuine shock on her face in the firelight.

The voice had been boyish and deep. It couldn't be any other. Tzarik looked through the bars at the boy, studying him. Signar looked suddenly concerned at their reaction and shrank down.

"Well done," Tzarik said to him. He tossed him another bite from his own plate and an orange as a treat. He forced himself to sit back down, taking his eyes off the boy, and faced the fire and Sybal again. "What is that? A Skelmir?"

Sybal eyed the boy. "It's a Northican god-tale. Skelmir was a trickster who would shape-shift to cause mischief for clan leaders. Some stories have him doing harmless things like souring the milk or turning a grogoch against its house. That's a household creature, very small," she explained when Tzarik looked up inquisitively. "They are said to crave cream and so they set up homes in shepherds' houses. They are good luck and often bless the family if they are kind to it. But Skelmir would trick them into causing mischief for the family."

Tzarik looked on Signar with affection. "Skelmir. He knows the word. Someone must have said it to him. I wonder who called him that. Surely not Sjörna."

Sybal stopped her work and frowned into the fire. "Do you think Dain did? When Signar was captured by Northica after the battle? Dain wasn't as cruel to him as the others. Maybe he even showed Signar kindness."

She looked over Tzarik's shoulder at the boy and a softness finally started to show in her eyes as she watched him. Tzarik had hoped for weeks now that Sybal would warm up to him. He knew she treated him badly to keep any affection at bay. Sybal didn't want to get attached to things. Not anymore. Everyone she'd loved had been taken from her. Tzarik understood. That had been his life before her. He'd not wanted to have even the slightest of friendships because people always left him. Or were taken from him.

He looked up at her. As she watched Signar, she turned soft and beautiful in the firelight. The thick chunk of white hair on her head turned orange in the campfire. She'd be taken, too, someday. Maybe even soon.

"We'll speak Al'Myrahn," Tzarik said, going back to the previous conversation. "He's heard enough Caerwren in his life to remember it when the time comes."

"Soon," Sybal reminded him. She stood up, moving to her horse to pack her things up. "We're not keeping him. He will go back to his people, as you promised Skarde."

Of course. But he didn't want to think about that. He stood up, wiped off the plate, and moved to settle in for the night. He stopped when he caught Signar watching his every move. Approaching the bars, he reached between them to touch Signar's long hair. The boy leaned up against the bars to get closer and yawned. Before, he'd worried the wolf would snap his arm off in one powerful bite. Not now.

"We should give him some of the herbs," Sybal called to him, digging in his saddlebag now. "We need our sleep before our final trek." When she pulled out the sachet of herbs, Signar's nose twitched and he sat up.

He saw the herbs in her hands, then faced Tzarik. He begged with his eyes. He understood what the herb did to him, but didn't have the words to plead, to promise to behave. Tzarik's heart twisted upon seeing Signar ask him, in his own way, to spare him the herbs tonight. He remembered how they'd made him ill. Overcome by all he'd seen the boy do so far, Tzarik said, "Not tonight. In fact, we'll let him sleep outside the cage."

"Are you mad?" Sybal called, marching up beside him with the sachet. "What if he runs away while we're asleep? Or has a fit out of fear and attacks us?"

Signar shifted to a crouch on his feet and held onto the bars, shaking his head furiously. He looked Sybal right in the eye, waiting for her to change her mind.

"We'll try it for tonight," Tzarik countered. "I'll watch him."

"You'll be exhausted tomorrow," she argued. "You cannot stay up all night."

"I don't think I'll have to." He went to the doors and opened them, standing aside and gesturing Signar out.

Excitedly, the boy stood up and trotted out. Signar started when he took in the stars above and turned slowly as he examined the entire field of twinkling lights. Seeing him stand outside the cage, Tzarik saw Signar entirely differently. Outside the bars, he looked like a boy. No, not a boy; a tall, powerful young man. The way the moonlight splashed over his pale skin and hit the tarnishing ornaments in his tangled hair, Tzarik could almost see him as the Reks he should have been.

"Signar," he ordered. "Sleep." He got out another blanket from the saddlebags and laid it beside his. The boy obeyed and lay down, facing the fire. Entranced by the dancing flames, his eyes eventually fell heavy.

SYBAL, the voice said kindly, softly. It sounded just like Freja had on holy day mornings when Sybal had overslept and her mother had come to wake her. *Rise, my warrior. Someone comes. They are ones you should feel no qualms about cutting down. I would enjoy their blasphemous souls.*

Sybal took a deep breath and sat up. The fire burned low beside her. On the other side of the fire, Signar slept soundly. The boy had moved closer to Tzarik sometime during the last couple of hours. Tzarik had drifted off as well, his arms wrapped around his sheathed scimitar.

Curious, Sybal got up into a crouch and scanned the darkness around them.

The west, the voice warned her. *Warriors.*

Now she stood up, seeing them. She picked up her belt with her own sword hanging from it and faced the white-cloaked visitors who appeared. Her sulfates jolted through her veins when she spotted the white robes with blue trim that she knew all too well now. The eastern reed hats gave them away, too.

"Tzarik," she hissed, forcing her eyes to not leave the approaching Reavers.

Her mentor rolled over, awake instantly. She knew his sulfates must have run cold, too. Sensing their fear, Signar woke and crouched, his nose twitching.

"Be calm, Signar," Tzarik whispered, holding his hand out to stay the boy.

Sybal caught his eyes flick to the cage and back. She watched regret fill his face as he placed himself in front of the frightened boy. She prayed Tzarik's faith was not unfounded and that Signar would remain calm, not shift, and not run.

"Peace, Runers," the lead Reaver called out in accented Al'Myrahn. He held his hands at chest height, showing he did not hold a weapon. "We are not here to hunt you. But I was hoping we could join you, share your fire and your spring."

There were three of them. One had the ornaments of a master of Wushito and the other two did not. Sybal surmised they were master and two apprentices. The apprentices looked young, perhaps seventeen, and untested. The master looked to be her age and was tall for a Xian. He had torn the sleeves away from his robe either intentionally or during a fight, exposing his thick, muscled limbs.

"Well met," the master said, stopping just outside the ring of weak firelight. "I had my boys gather wood when I saw your dim fire. We walked along the stream for a mile, but couldn't find a place to fill our waterskins. This seems to be the best place."

Sybal checked Tzarik's expression. He looked on edge, the vein in his neck throbbing. One hand stretched out behind him towards a cowering Signar. His hand shook.

"If you want a fight, Wushito master—" Sybal began.

"Ah," the master cut in with a generous smile. "You know our creed. We are not here to fight, Runer-kim. My apprentices have not even begun their training. We are here on a journey of observation. They are tired and hungry."

She examined the two boys. Their lips were chapped and one had a very bad sunburn on his high cheekbones. Neither had weapons. That she could see. The Wushito, especially the Reavers, were known for their stealthy ways. They were the only ones who trained to kill Runers, who could keep up with the magic of the runes in combat.

"Please," the master reiterated, more gentle than before. "They are just boys."

"You are training these boys to kill us," Sybal said, "and you want to share our water?"

The master smiled and nodded. "Yes."

"Fill your skins and be gone," Tzarik quipped. "Do not double back in the shadows."

The two apprentices shared concerned looks as the master signaled them to take the skins and move closer to the hostile Runers to gather the water. Sybal watched them, scanning their cloaks, belts, and tall boots—anywhere they could hide a weapon. The Reavers had hidden blades, strange bombs that would blind them, and she didn't know what else. She remembered the white silk robe Wu-Zhiang had worn when the serpent Masahk had killed her.

Cut them down! the voice of Freja screamed in her head. Sybal almost recoiled from the sudden, loud tone.

Even the likes of Reavers will turn the runes against me, Sybal snapped back. *Not a single sentient. Why do you berate me so?*

There was a moment of silence before the voice turned sweet again. *All you must do is take one more life and you will be with me. Don't you want to see me again, daughter?*

It wouldn't matter, Sybal argued. The boys filled two skins and brought out two more. She glanced at Tzarik where he stood in front of Signar. He had his hand firmly planted on the boy's shoulder. But Signar looked at her, watching her. Not in a way of fear as he had been, but like he waited for her signal.

I have taken an arrow through my heart, Sybal told the voice. *The*

Vorlamir told me I could not cross death's threshold again. I... She stopped as she finally formed the thought in her mind. She'd not said it even to herself. *I will never die again. I will have to watch Tzarik grow old. I will be more alone than he ever was.* The thought brought tears to her eyes, and she took a shaky breath. She'd tried to not think about it. *What will happen if I take a life? Will the runes take me, turning me into a demonic servant?*

"Well done, boys," the master said, touching each apprentice on the arm as he passed to lash their filled waterskins to the horses. "And thank you, Runers." He bowed in the way of his people and rose slowly, eyes downcast. "I...know who you are," he said slowly before finally looking up. "Unless there is more than one Al'Myrahn lady Runer."

Sybal didn't know. She shared a quick glance with Tzarik. "And have you been sent to hunt us?"

"Not at all," the Wushito master replied. "We are on our way to New Gypsu on Bahratt. I wanted to cross your continent, teach the boys of your people and your ways. I understand we—the Wushito—owe our lives to you." He bowed again, deeper this time. "Wushito is an old creed. I cannot say why we use the sigils and you the runes. After I heard what two Runers did on Xia, I pondered these questions for some time."

"And Hiro?" Tzarik cut in. "What of your Di-Huan?"

"They are well," the Wushito master replied, a tinge of relief coloring his sharp cheeks. "Hiro is a good steward, and our young Di-Huan has already spoken his first words and taken his first steps."

Sybal shoved her motherly instincts down and forced the image from her mind to quip, "And what have you learned in your pondering, murderer?"

"I have no answers yet," the Wushito master said sadly. "But one day, I will. If Xai'long sees fit to let me live long enough." He smiled pleasantly. "But other Reavers still hunt Runers. But I need not tell you that some of them perhaps deserve such a death."

When neither of the Runers replied, the master bowed again. "Thank you once again," he said, and left the firelight.

Sybal, the voice cooed. *You let him leave. No matter his personal beliefs, the Reavers still hunt Runers. You should have cut him down and sent his soul to me.*

What do you mean? Sybal wondered, watching the trio leave. *How can I send a soul to you, mother?*

By my command, any soul you take shall come to me. Strengthen me.

Why? Sybal asked.

The voice laughed lightly. *Nothing stops my claim on your soul, Sybal. Not the sulfates. No ritual will cleanse you. Not even immortality will stop my touch. Denying me is futile. Your fate is inevitable.*

At this, Sybal started. *I knew you weren't my mother.* She glared into the fire. *Who are you? Which god thinks it can take my soul?*

The laugh turned from Freja's gentle tinkle to a deep, evil chuckle. *Look to the north, Runer,* it rumbled. *I will make you mine.*

ᚱ

"Sybal?" Tzarik called her name for the fifth time. She stayed still, eyes glassed over, fixed on the fire. Something like frost slowly spread over her cheek. Her lips turned blue from a cold he could not see. "Sybal," he shouted, shaking her by her shoulders.

She gasped, pressing her hands into her chest and wincing. She fell against him and he caught her, holding her tightly. Behind him, Signar watched, still as a stone.

"I'm so sorry," she gasped, wiping at her face. The frost had receded. "I'm tired and I think the fire entranced me."

"Are you sure?" he asked, knowing full well that wasn't what had hypnotized her.

Sybal nodded. She sat down and thanked Tzarik, then lay down and took a deep breath. "Were you afraid of them?" she asked, referencing the Reavers.

At first, Tzarik wanted to reply that he was. But he found he hadn't been afraid like he used to be. "I believed him when he said he wasn't hunting us," he started. "I was afraid of what you'd do. What Signar would do. I didn't want to harm them or give them a reason to harm either of you." He turned to Signar, who had calmed significantly, lying on his side with his arms folded under his head. He watched them. Tzarik knew the boy understood them now, so he'd have to watch what he said.

"But it reminded me of something," he said slowly. He reached over to Signar and covered him with the blanket. Desert days might be warm on Al'Myrah, but the nights could chill one to illness in their sleep if they weren't careful.

"What did they make you think of?" she asked, yawning.

"The sigiled blades," he murmured, thinking. "They were on Mamun's saddle." He was surprised to find emotion well up in his throat at the mention of his old, loyal steed. "I took one from Wu-Zhiang, Yasuke, and ShanBao. I had them wrapped. They wouldn't look like much on the outside, since their blades are straight, and their round hilts are so small. But I know they were imbued with magic. I can't say what they might do in the wrong hands."

Sybal frowned and hummed in agreement. "Sjörna might have thrown them out. They could be lost."

"That's what I hope," he replied. He tossed one last log into the fire for the night and leaned onto his bedroll. He glanced at Signar, who already breathed softly, buried up to his eyes in the blanket. Had Signar seen them? Perhaps he knew what his mother had done with them.

He imagined the night before the battle on the bridge. Sjörna would have slaughtered Mamun and the other horses. Taken their things and disposed of them. Then lashed Signar to her chariot. Had he fought her? Had she beaten him? He shuddered to think. He allowed himself one last glance at the sleeping Vaeson to remind himself that he had made the right choice, then closed his eyes and drifted off to a nightmare-filled sleep.

Chapter 8

Enoch

"The house in Hatal is nearly empty," the djinn reported to Sharar. "I have had most of your things sent here. They should arrive in a few days." The demon waited for his master to reply, but Sharar stood still and silent, facing a window that overlooked a beautiful waterfall. "Sira?" it asked again.

"Where is Amir?" he asked, ignoring the information the djinn had given him.

"Hunting," came the simple reply.

Sharar liked the simplicity of his enslaved demon. And his usefulness. But he couldn't think about his torture devices and scientific instruments that sailed over the Black Sea. He didn't even care about his meeting with the Dynast Pharaoh later. No, something else occupied his mind. He breathed to keep his nerves steady.

"What is it?" the djinn asked at length. "Something ails you greatly."

"Stay out of my mind, demon," Sharar snapped, turning away from the window. "Focus on my instruments coming from Al'Myrah. I need them ready for guests soon." He imagined finally have Tzarik under his roof, trapped, where he couldn't escape. "I will have answers," he growled. "And Amir should be able to find Tarkan. I know he's here. He wouldn't have gone to Porsh to hide, the coward." He still couldn't believe that Tarkan had raised the lady Runer from the dead. What a truly magnificent necromancer he was becoming.

"Sira?" his servant girl piped from the door to his study. "Umm, she's come back."

Sharar turned, frowning. Who had come back? Surely not the harlot from before. No, he'd scared her off for good. Which, of course, meant he wanted her back more than ever. "Who has come?" he asked.

The girl gulped, eyes wide. "Jasmin."

The glass Sharar had been holding shattered on his desk. He felt the blood physically drain from his face. "In the house?"

"I couldn't stop her," the girl apologized. "I'm sorry, sira, I know you said not to let her in."

He didn't need to ask; he knew. But the words shot out of his mouth. "Where is she?"

The girl gulped again, trying to hide behind her hands. "She went below. To Enoch's room."

A wicked, dark glower twisted Sharar's face. "That bitch," he spat.

§

SHARAR TOOK the golden steps of his manor two at a time, whirling past a few other servants. He practically ran down the gilded halls towards a room deep in the dungeon in the back of the house.

Before he got there, he spied Amir dismounting in the back square. The Runer looked tired and weather-beaten, with a fresh scar on his left cheek. He carried his massive crossbow in one hand and led his horse in the other. He shouted for Amir to follow. The servant girl ran behind him, crying and apologizing.

In his dungeon, he reached a door made of thick wood and reinforced with wide, bolted metal slabs. About five locks hung off it, already opened.

"She still had a set of keys," the servant girl sniffled, ducking her head down in case he rained blows on her.

Amir, unsure of the danger, pushed in front of Sharar, drew his scimitar, and yanked the door open.

"I don't fear that whore," Sharar growled, shoving past Amir into the dark prison beyond.

The room had a tall, arched stone ceiling supported by granite beams. The floor and walls, where they were not rows of cells, were all cobbled stone. A few rooms branched off from the larger antechamber, but what waited in the center was what Sharar had protected. He stopped, spying the offending woman with her back to him. She looked up at a large, vitreous orb. The glass sphere was so massive, it reached nearly twelve feet up from the ground. It was held in place by massive, black-stone arches. The inside glowed with bright aquamarine liquid. Suspended in the center, a boy, nearly seventeen years old, floated in the magical liquid. Sharar had often thought he was a handsome young man. He had honey-colored eyes, the smoothest skin—like his mother—and his own sharp, elegant features. But now, black veins and mild distortions marred the left half of his beautiful face. The black veins crawled under his skin down the entire side of his body.

"I thought you'd forgotten about our son," the woman whispered, facing the boy in the orb. Her voice came through a thick sorrow. "You've not been to Alika in so long." She reached up a hand and touched the vitreous orb. She wore a blue veil over her black hair, bound in golden clasps. Her hand was just as elegant and beautiful as he remembered.

"And what have you done for Enoch, Jasmin?" Sharar asked, catching his breath. Amir followed close, his blue eyes latched onto the woman. "Besides lying in another man's bed?"

Jasmin hung her head, her hand still pressed against the glass. "You may hate me, Abigor. But why have you not ended his suffering? Surely he still feels it, still dreams." She gave a small scoff. "I forgot: you enjoy bringing suffering. But to your own son?"

This old discussion again. Sharar bit his tongue and made his way around the orb to look Jasmin in the face. Above him, Enoch, his son, hung in perfect preservation. "Because he is innocent," he replied. "Why have you come to Gypsu, Jasmin? I have nothing for you."

She looked up, squaring her shoulders to him. "Is that so? I know you, Abigor. I have heard the things that hatchling on the Dynast throne thinks you will do for him."

At this, Sharar allowed himself a dim grin. "Sokar'Xenoteph will be a great pharaoh. He will leave his mark on the dynasty, as he hopes. He is wise. He listens to council."

"He listens to you," Jasmin hissed, turning her eyes to her son again. "He's a fool of a Masahk." She smiled dolefully. "Have you done it yet?" she asked. "Are you the Father of Monsters? Have you learned every secret of the map, Abigor?"

"Don't taunt me," he growled. "You wish to know if you speak so brazenly to a sorcerer?"

Jasmin's brow twitched delicately. "I see you have not, then. Or you would strike me where I stand. Turn me into a toad. Smite me with fire and ice. But you cannot, can you?" She smiled and laughed darkly at the look on his face. "You search and search, Abigor, but you never find. You are a scholar and yet you never learn. You will die this way, my love: desperate to have your work known, never finding the answer to why."

As always, her words were spoken with venom. But they had no effect on him. "Your opinion of me ceased to matter some years go, Jasmin. Perhaps you've come to beg mercy of me, now that the Dynast Pharaoh has chosen to search for the Mahit'Onomicon? You know I am close. You know I was always right." He pointed a finger at Enoch. "My ambition started with *our* son. I need to know why."

"And have you remembered him?" Jasmin cut him off sharply.

Something in her tone and movement made Amir take a cautious step forward, but Sharar didn't notice anything threatening. Jasmin's eyes dangerously flicked to Amir.

"You keep them as pets, Abigor." She eased back a little. "This one is no different."

Amir shot Sharar a glance, but his body did not lose its tension.

"I have found one," Sharar said, forgetting Jasmin didn't know about Tzarik. Jasmin's smug smirk faded, pulling his own back to his face. "I told you I was close. Once I have the book, which is perhaps only miles away, I will devour the djinn who will lead me to the one who holds the answers. I will have the Runer and I will save Enoch. You never did have faith in me."

The woman's beautiful bronze chest rose and fell as her breath deepened. She tried not to blink in awe, but her sweet, parted red lips betrayed her. Satisfaction rose in Sharar's chest.

"Perhaps my family was right about you," he added jovially. He moved to a desk behind Enoch and fiddled with a metal pen. "I should have listened to them long before."

Jasmin's eyes flashed. "I am no magi or witch, Abigor," she whispered. It came like a warning. "But the magic you seek is cruel. The runes. They know your intent and will punish you. They know you want their secrets."

He smiled, leaning against the desk. "Yes. But like every

sorcerer before me, I will rain such destruction. I will be remembered for millennia. Everything I do, every discovery I make, will be lifted by the grandeur of my name. If I fall, and it will be centuries after I have risen, I will have gained immortality through my depravity."

That silenced her. She looked away, blinking back emotion. She pressed her palms into her skirt and Sharar noted Amir eye her hands. Like Tzarik's eyes, when Amir looked, using the sulfates to aid him, his pupils turned to thin slits like a cat's.

Jasmin cleared her throat. Her eyes turned up one last time to take in Enoch, where he floated in the blue elixir. "I see I cannot stop you," she whispered. "I suppose I should be grateful you saved my son."

"Enoch is *my* son," Sharar growled.

She'd had enough. Jasmin didn't reply, but gathered her skirts and fled back up the stairs.

"Should I follow her?" Amir asked, taking two steps after her.

Sharar watched her feet vanish out the door. He dropped the pen with a clatter and crossed his arms. "No." He waited for the inquiries. Amir didn't disappoint.

The Runer walked a slow circle around the orb. "I know this poison. Sulfates. They rejected him." He met Sharar's eyes in the dim glow. "Your son was runed?"

The scholar let his mind go back to that day. It had been too long; Jasmin was right. He hadn't thought about Enoch in some time.

"I swore I'd not lose sight of why I spent so long in the seminary," he began. "But I do from time to time. Jasmin was among the first women scholars in Hatal. A very wealthy family. She interested me enough to draw my attention, but I quickly became bored with her. I think she sensed that. I'm not sure what her interest in me was."

He stopped and frowned, rubbing his chin.

"Now that I think about it, her attention to me made little sense. But she would not let me go. One night, we engaged in..." He paused to make a face of disgust. "Primitive, anatomical exploration."

Amir kept the effect of the condescending phrasing off his face, but Sharar saw the Runer understood.

"Of course, the gods saw fit to punish our coupling outside the laws of Al'Myrah."

At this, Amir laughed gently. "Those religious laws mean little to me, scholar. More than half of your ilk engage in such things. But they lie to remain virtuous in the eyes of their caste and the temple."

"Yes," Sharar agreed. "But no matter. So Enoch came into existence." He stopped and pushed off the desk, walking towards his son. The closer he got, the more he saw the horrid blight inside him. Something within him pushed sudden, hot tears into his eyes, which he blinked away quickly. He coughed to clear his throat. "My family thought she'd seduced me. So when she began to show, my father and grandfather flew into a rage. A child outside wedlock was punishable by the temple. A crime."

"Seduced you?" The Runer frowned. "It is rare for such a defense. Did she coerce you?"

Not sure, he stopped pacing and remained where he was, looking up into Enoch's permanently pained, sleeping face. "I could say yes, but I feel like that's a lie. Saying no makes me weak. I have no answer."

Amir grunted almost sympathetically. "She bore the child to term?"

"At my insistence," Sharar went on. "But my father and grandfather would not let me wed her, since they believed lying with her before marriage made her a disgrace. She was a harlot to them. So they forbade our marriage. To keep her quiet lest she change her story and say I forced her, they arranged for her to marry a sheikh from the very edge of Hatal's province. Some village I forget the name of.

"That spring, my boy was born." He remained where he stood below Enoch. "I knew the day he was foretold and so I rode to the man's house. To see my son come into the world." His voice drifted into soft reminiscence and he didn't fight it. "The man tried for years to raise Enoch as his own. Perhaps I made it worse, coming to see him, trying to steal him away." He laughed dryly. "My father hated me for it. I was to pretend I had no son. But I couldn't. Look at him, Amir. He was strong, wise, and had a hunger for knowledge only rivaled by myself. He is beautiful."

Amir scanned the young man. "He looks like a warrior."

Sharar half nodded. "Well, the sheikh thought he'd done Jasmin a favor, marrying her while she bore another man's child. I suppose he did. But he hated Enoch. I don't blame him for not loving another man's son. I doubt I could. So, in a drunken rage with a pair of quadis who were his close friends, he let the secret out. Enoch was not his son. By then, he had pretended for almost seventeen years. Enoch was almost a man, and I'd not seen him enough. I stole him away from time to time, and other times he ran away to be with me. When he was seventeen, he could have left, never again speaking to the man, relieving him of his false paternal role. But the bastard could not wait for Enoch to leave.

"When the quadis learned what the man had done, they blamed him for falling in love with a harlot. The kehann of the temple were called to take him away for breaking the laws of the mihals knowingly and for hiding it from them. The people of the city hated their sheikh. Everything he'd done for them was tainted."

Sharar stopped, that damned emotion rising like a rock in his throat again.

"They came for Enoch," Amir offered.

"By the hells, they did," Sharar sighed. "The sheikh suggested a runing. A dark punishment for evil men, surely." He inclined his head to Amir. "Not all crimes are equal, I know that. But Enoch? He was innocent. He'd done no wrong. I knew from historical runings that the runes understood sin. They could not keep an innocent man alive. That's not how the black oath works."

Amir shifted here, slowly tilting his head as he listened.

"I couldn't stop them," Sharar went on. He took a shuddering breath. " He called for me. But they held me back. The sheikh threw Enoch out into the streets when they saw the runes were rejecting him." He had to stop to control himself. "Enoch had committed no crime. Innocent. So the runes started to destroy him. I had hunted long for a djinn I knew of and rushed to acquire it. That is a whole story on its own. But I brought it back, begging to make my first wish to save my son."

The Runer examined the orb Enoch floated in. "This is not djinn magic. This is water from the Cradle, un-purified. The salts are still in it. Is that what keeps him alive? How did you get so much? No one outside the temple is allowed to use it."

Sharar grunted in admission. "Sokar'Xenoteph. The Dynast Pharaoh. He's near Enoch's age. The magic of the rivers of Alika keeps him alive. Or rather, preserves him. The djinn told me of the few boundaries the demons have: they cannot stop death. They cannot raise the dead. But he used my wish to show me how to save Enoch, to stop his body and the curse using the waters of Alika. I thought I was too late by the time I had learned, but the djinn held Enoch's life as long as he could. We came here and hid him away."

The scholar gently placed his hands against the orb.

"I studied for years after. Looked far and wide to find another like Enoch. Surely there was a Runer alive who was innocent and would tell me so."

Amir grunted a half laugh. "No such man exists. No one else would rune a sentient out of malice like that. Or if they have, they are long dead."

"But can you be sure?" Sharar asked gently.

At this, the Runer halted and frowned. "Perhaps. If the man desired the runing. The runes listen to intent and spirit. But why would an innocent man desire such a risk? Such a life? If he were innocent, and survived to hunt, the people might find out. They would not tolerate an innocent Runer. They'd kill him, most likely burn him on a pyre. He'd be too dangerous to let live with no bridle to hold him back."

"Exactly," Sharar mused. "We would know if such a man walked the map, for he would be infamous. Unless…" He dropped his hands and paced away. "Unless he had grown up in such a way that guarded his spirit from villainy."

"You have someone in mind," Amir prodded.

"I do," Sharar replied. He almost smiled now. "A Runer who I have seen kill. Who has stolen, but hides his crimes so others do not see. Unless he has fornicated with a sentient against their will, there is only one other answer." He waited.

"He has no crime," Amir murmured in awe. "This Runer could hold the answer you seek to saving Enoch. He could show us answers to the runes we have sought for eternity. How does the white flow through his veins, letting him live as a Runer, if he has committed no crime?"

Sharar beamed at Amir. "This is why I like you, Amir. Exactly that."

"Who is it?" Amir asked, standing up straighter.

"Sira," the djinn called from the top of the stairs. He came down in his human form. "Someone approaches from the west. A man in black and a kehann at his side."

Sharar waited for the djinn to go on. It mattered little if a couple of men from the temple came to his door.

"They have a small host of risen with them," the demon finished.

Amir stood up, ready to leap into action. "Necromancers?"

"I do not know the one," the djinn confessed. "But the kehann is not who he seems to be. I can see his spirit within. Tarkan walks in the dead man's body."

An overwhelming feeling of pride and caution engulfed Sharar. "Well done, Tarkan," he praised him. "Dead-walking. He spoke about it perhaps once. He achieved it. Amir, stay by my side. Demon, let them in."

Chapter 9
Facing Fear

Tarkan loved the feeling of the powerful kehann's body as he strode over the sandy ground. The back of Sharar's estate spanned acres. A mill, sheep fields, and a vineyard were just a few things the estate boasted to maintain its power, flow of income, and Sharar's status on Alika. He was sure Sharar was at least on the continent. Whether he was in his home now mattered little. He'd leave his name, tell them to alert Sharar to his presence. That would be enough to get the scholar moving.

To his delight, he spotted the scholar leave out the back garden with a Runer in tow. The workers of the land had long gone to bed, so the fields and rows of grapes were quiet. Tarkan walked with authority up the path to the edge of the garden, glaring at Sharar the whole time. It had been over two years since he'd seen the scholar, and the man hadn't aged a day. His beard and brows were immaculately manicured, as always. His clothes were clean and billowy in the desert night air. The Runer at his side was a tall, strong Al'Myrahn with keen, blue eyes, as all Runers had. His long, dirty hair hung to his shoulders, and a mysterious cockiness kept all fear or apprehension far away. Tarkan wanted to wear his body. A strange desire, but one he'd conjured with his own new magic.

"My old friend," Sharar said agonizingly slowly. He came to a stop a few yards from Tarkan and Ashkan. "Where have you been? It's been some time since I've seen you."

"To places beyond your reach, scholar."

"I see you've brought familiar company to my door."

Tarkan watched the Runer stand beside Sharar, hand casually draped over his scimitar hilt. "Your false words are even more hollow now, scholar," Tarkan said with the strong, un-scared throat of the kehann.

"So I see." Sharar scanned the temple guard's frame unabashedly. "Dead-walking, I believe you called it. I want you to know, Tarkan, I never doubted your potential. I never hated you."

The Necro'Khan didn't believe that. "The torture I suffered says otherwise. If you had known the heights to which I would ascend, you would have yielded to me. Not imprisoned me as you did."

Sharar's swift, golden-brown eyes quickly scanned the area around Tarkan, taking in the few risen flanking him. "You have an Apostle. But...it's not Zeva. Where is the girl?"

Instant fury shot up through Tarkan. "Do not say her name," he warned Sharar. Hearing Zeva's given name come out of the vile man's mouth always sounded like blasphemy to Tarkan. "I have no reason to lie to you. She is gone."

The scholar raised his brows and parted his lips in awe. "So it was she who gave you this mantle? Her loss is your gain."

Tarkan didn't reply, his nerves searing.

"I must admit, Tarkan, I am shocked." Sharar looked too at ease. "I never would have... That is..." The scholar genuinely couldn't find the words. He chuckled breathily and shook his head. "I over-estimated your affection for her, I suppose."

Tarkan snarled and lunged forward, but Ashkan gripped his

arm, stopping him. In the kehann's body, he couldn't command the dead. They were Ashkan's risen. Tarkan could only defend himself as the kehann could: with his sword.

"Would you like to come inside?" Sharar asked with forced ease. He motioned to a salon in the back of the house.

"Never again," Tarkan replied. "I know what waits beyond your walls. I wanted to see you for myself. To know you were on Alika."

Sharar's eyes changed, calculating. "What have you to fear? You are Necro'Khan, are you not?"

"I am," Tarkan confirmed. "And you are not a sorcerer."

At this, the scholar faced him square on again. He licked his lips nervously and shook his head. "This would be a very different conversation if I were, Tarkan. It seems we both have some studying to do. I'd offer you a place by my side once again. We complete one another, as I said before." He offered a sickly, charming smile. Something changed in his face. Any sign of fear dropped away. "I will have you once again. I promise you that."

Tarkan let a dry laugh escape his lips. He noted the Runer's tension building when he didn't show fear. "Sharar, I know what sleeps in the dungeon below your manor. I know why you want to be a sorcerer. Nothing *you* can do will bring Enoch back."

The scholar's smugness melted.

"I know you do not harbor any love for your son," Tarkan went on. "Your desire is merely one of study, observation, as always. You are cold, empty. Enoch is a means to an end."

"Do not say—" Sharar started, but he stopped himself, raising his hand and clenching his fist in powerful self-control.

"His name?" Tarkan finished, leering at Sharar's uncomfortable movements. "Sharar, I wanted to show you what I have become, so you would know the monster you chase now. I need you to witness my power." More than that, he needed Sharar to see he didn't fear him any longer. "I have ways to raise the dead. I have re-written the scriptures, creating my own spells, rites the likes of which the map has never seen."

Sharar looked interested now, though still cautious. "You can raise him now?" His brown eyes took on a familiar, guarded glassiness.

"No," Tarkan replied. "As you see, I have possessed a body. I cannot cast from this flesh."

Keen as ever, the scholar asked guardedly, "Are…you hurt? Some wound or scar has prevented you from coming to me in your body?"

"Astute," Tarkan replied. "I am not fool enough to walk into your home within my own body." Even as he spoke, a jolt shot through him. The connection to his body was growing weak after so much travel and casting. "I have an offer for you, scholar."

Sharar didn't reply, his brow furrowing in suspicion. "You know how I feel about blood pacts, my friend."

Tarkan shook his head. "I want one of your wishes."

"What?" Sharar spat, genuine shock cracking his frown. "You have lost your mind."

The Necro'Khan shook his head. "I can bring a soul back to a body."

He noted the scholar's face turn almost lax with understanding. "He's… His body is…"

"I can make it anew," Tarkan went on. "I have a spell from my father. A body born from a blood ritual from a grave will be more than risen. With a soul intact."

"Tell me," Sharar offered, stepping close to him. "I can offer you healing. I have a friend who can heal you. Perhaps we can…" He didn't go on with his offer.

Taken aback by Sharar's genuine interest, Tarkan eyed him carefully. He glanced at Ashkan, who had the same look on his face.

"What trick are you planning?" Tarkan asked. "I will not walk into your traps so easily now."

Honesty filled the scholar's face. "None. If what you say is true, I genuinely want to heal you. And it won't take a wish. It's simpler than that. Come here in your wounded body and I will show you. I have no reason to lie after what you have offered to give me. And," he smiled warily, "I know you could overrun even my Runer, should you so desire."

Ashkan glanced quickly to the side, taking in his risen.

"Yes," Sharar replied to the glance. "Bring your army. I don't care. Seems a bit unfair and to your advantage, but..." He shrugged. "You didn't come here just to threaten me, old friend. I know you better than that." A warm, snake-like smile returned to Sharar's face.

Had the scholar read his need so easily?

This offer stunned Tarkan. He cast his eyes about, looking for a tell, a lie, a trap. Nothing appeared. Even the Runer at Sharar's side looked confused.

"You may keep your Runer," he offered. If Sharar let him leave now, he'd know the scholar was in earnest. "I will return."

He motioned to Ashkan to follow and turned, walking quickly away. His speed came from a need to leave before Sharar saw his soul leave the kehann's body...and to escape the scholar's knowing, golden-brown eyes. No movement sounded behind him. His risen followed Ashkan's command and shambled after them.

Ashkan asked, "Why did you go to him now?"

"To see him," Tarkan replied. A pain like none before tore at every nerve inside his possessed body. Like something peeled and ripped at his skin and sinews. "To know he has not risen to sorcerer, that he does not have the Mahit'Onomicon now. To know I have time for him to retrieve it for me. He will heal me, and I believe it is because he wants to use me once he has the book. But I won't give him that chance. I will take what he offers."

"He does not have it?" Ashkan asked. "Are you sure?"

"Yes," Tarkan shot back. "He looked for a tell in my face to know if I had it. I would not give it to him. He doesn't know I do not possess it, so he will continue his hunt, just to be sure. But he will want to keep his eyes on me. I know Sharar. He likes games like this. I will play it and have him find the book for me."

The necromancer looked ahead, green eyes serious. "I suggest caution, Tarkan. Bridle your revenge. Calculate."

Tarkan scoffed indignantly. "He will respect the fear in his heart for a time. Until then—"

A sensation, like fire under his flesh, melting off his body, shot through Tarkan. He hissed and his vision turned red. A feeling like falling or flying from a great height turned his mind and stomach and then all went black.

Stone pressed into his back and a sudden exhaustion paired with starvation and unbearable thirst wracked him. Tarkan opened his eyes, and even with his necrotic sight, he saw nothing. Panting, he pressed his hands out to the side only to hit cold, hard stone. He had been dragged back to his own body, the spell giving out. The sensation of hunger, thirst, and fatigue told him so. Grunting, he pushed up on the lid. It didn't budge. A moment of panic made his aching nerves twinge.

"Ashkan?" he called, wondering if he'd blacked out and how much time had passed. Was Ashkan back in Makan Alu'Ekmet? No reply came.

Panting harder, he shouted and pushed again. When he cut his palms on the rough stone, he stopped. Ashkan would come back. Closing his eyes, Tarkan calmed himself. It was better this way. His body would be safe inside such a cage. For a brief moment, he thought about casting the spell again, just to possess a body to open the coffin, but he put the thought aside. He needed to consume. The spell had been strong, and had lasted longer than he'd thought. There was no shame in the fatigue he felt now.

With a final sigh, he dropped his hands and waited for his Apostle.

༄

"The necromancer was foolish to come to you, to show himself to you," Amir said once the pair of them were below the manor again, gazing into Enoch's protective sphere.

Sharar smiled and clasped his hands behind his back. "Hardly, Amir. You forget, I know Tarkan." He smiled at a memory. "You tend to know the things you study inside and out. I've heard him beg for mercy while my hands were inside him, his body cut open upon my table. But before that, we studied together. Hunted the book. It was his research that led me to Xia, to their crypt. But that was a nearly fruitless journey. No, Amir, he will come back. He wants to be whole. He will not be content with dead-walking. He needs his own body. The necromancer's body is more of a tool; the scriptures are the important part. And his immortality." He dropped his hands and considered the blue liquid inside the sphere. "There must be a way to kill him. He killed his father."

Amir didn't respond, letting the scholar think out loud. Sharar liked that about Amir; the Runer knew when to hold his tongue, and almost never offered interjections or thoughts. Sharar considered Ishmael's fate, his frown of concentration deepening. He watched his own eyes in the glassy reflection of the sphere. Tarkan had known how to kill Ishmael. He'd known how to ascend to Necro'Khan. But he'd watched his old colleague's face; Tarkan hadn't given away whether he had the book or not. Sharar had to be sure.

"Ishmael must have hidden the book if Tarkan doesn't have it," Sharar whispered, afraid to disturb his own thoughts if he spoke too loud.

"Then it's in Porsh?" Amir asked.

"No," Sharar corrected. "It's here. Makan Alu'Ekmet appeared when a tribe of Apostles left Porsh, forming sanctuaries outside once Ishmael began to rise to power. Which would mean he was a necromancer before Tarkan was born." He almost stopped breathing, the riddle twisting his mind. "The Makan cities were founded by him nearly a thousand years ago. But he fathered Tarkan."

"How?" Amir asked, crossing his arms and leaning up against the table. "Are they not like Runers? They cannot beget sentient children. If this Ishmael was a necromancer before Tarkan was born...how old was he?"

Sharar raised his brows in shock and awe at the ancient, dead Necro'Khan. Then, he frowned, everything before him blaring out as he thought. "No, that cannot be true. The timeline is wrong. How could Ishmael have been the one who stood beside Acenoth IV? If he hid the Mahit'Onomicon for years, as Tarkan claimed, then Ishmael must have been thousands of years old. He would have been in Alika during the reign of Acenoth, a powerful Dynast Pharaoh. Yet, Porsh fell into malignant destruction only a century ago."

Again, he shook his head.

"I need to see the Halls of History."

"Are the Makan cities so old?" Amir asked, fiddling with a knife on his thigh.

Sharar hummed disapprovingly at Amir's ignorance of history. "Are all Runers so ill educated?" he asked, pacing around Enoch.

"We're base lives." Amir shrugged, unfazed by Sharar's jibe. He even smiled. "You know those remarks don't bother me. We're criminals who got caught, unlike you aristocrats who can buy your way out of a cell. We don't care much for history and schooling."

The scholar allowed him that. "The Battle of the Promise, led by Acenoth IV," he recited as if he stood in front of a room full of eager minds in a seminary, "was fought on Alikan shores one thousand years ago. They wrote about it on the walls of the Dynast palace." He stopped and looked up. "I should show you. It's quite a fascinating history, and was about the time Ishmael was moving. I am overdue at the palace, anyway. We will take the river caravan and be there within two days."

Amir pushed off the table and followed Sharar out. "When will the necromancers return?"

He wasn't sure, but it wouldn't be so bad if they returned and were told that he'd gone out to see the Dynast Pharaoh. "It will take Ashkan a day to return to Makan Alu'Ekmet, where Tarkan no doubt is hiding his body. They will have to consume and recover their strength before journeying back. Perhaps giving us five days. Four for travel, one to interrogate that brat," he said, referring to the young Dynast Pharaoh.

Amir's steps faltered a little. "I'll need to hunt."

Sharar scoffed, putting his hand at the base of Amir's neck and forcing him up the stairs and into the halls of his manor. "A little pain never stopped you before, Runer. I've seen this agony that takes you Runers. I've seen some go weeks without hunting, especially with their runes and blade by their side. You will be fine."

He sensed Amir was going to argue and called for his djinn to accompany them. The monster appeared in his man-like form, wordlessly following. The Runer tensed when the demon appeared.

"It's not just the pain," Amir tried to bargain.

Sharar called for a trunk of his things and a horse to be brought.

"We cannot bargain with the god of the runes," the Runer went on, getting desperate. "All the runes know is that they are unused. Dormant. The punishment is pain, yes, but it can also affect the mind. Drive one mad. If I don't hunt for long enough, the sulfates will take me no differently than if they had rejected me. I'll mutate, die a horrible death."

When Amir didn't go on but followed him out to his own

horse, Sharar said, "It's five days, Amir. They will not take you. Trust me, I have studied the damned things. I know what they can do."

"Studied is not endured," Amir murmured.

Sharar rounded on the Runer. "You will endure far worse if you defy me and do not obey." He calmed himself. "Five days, Amir. I promise. Then you may leave again and hunt to your heart's content."

"And the necromancers?"

The scholar smiled. "I do not fear them."

Chapter 10

Sokar Xenoteph

The palace of the Dynast Pharaoh rose above the green hills and pearl-white dunes of Mysir. In the shape of a pyramid with many spires, it jutted up from the swaying palms and other greenery into the blazing blue sky. The river that ran from Gypsu to Mysir moved quickly, since the rains from the spring filled it. The river caravan had been noisy and filled with bards' songs and chattering nomads, farmers, traders, and warriors alike. Sharar had grown tired of such monotonous noise, since traveling by the rivers of Alika was the fastest way to get around the continent. Despite its desert, Alika had more rivers than any continent, except perhaps Xia. The Three Rivers, as the locals called them, burst from the massive central spring—near the Cradle—where they farmed the magic salt and purified the water.

Sharar disembarked from the colorful boat, paying a man with the black skin of the people of Yenka in the south, and pushed past the crowd of Masahk and humans to behold the grandeur of the palace for the first time in some months. Amir stood close behind him, leading the horses.

"Such majesty for a people who grew from worshiping a god of death," Sharar mused. He took his rolled-up shibboleth from his robes and showed it to a palace guard.

"I should wait outside the walls," Amir offered. "You know how the vizier despises me."

"Nonsense, my boy," Sharar sighed. "Nasor may be a son of a bitch, but he won't harass you anymore. I've had enough of it. Should he try, I won't allow it. You have my word, Amir."

The Runer didn't look so sure, but followed Sharar.

The guard eyed the Runer, lip curled in disgust, but led them and a gaggle of other scholars, dignitaries, and visiting nobility, who had assembled in a glittering parade.

Most on Alika were immortal Masahk of all varieties: brightly plumed avian types sang and cawed around them in beautiful melodies. A dozen different monkey-like Masahk in black, brown, gold, and red fur talked quietly under an awning outside a new structure being built. Even a female Masahk with green skin covered in tiny, beautiful scales with a long, snake-like tail sashayed past them in a dress of white, covered in golden jewelry. She had large, purple eyes and blue claws on her fingers. She smiled at Amir as they passed, winking slyly.

Amir observed the structure being built less than a mile outside the palace. It had been some time since he'd seen the progress the slaves had made, so Sharar took it in as they passed as well. Being built with sandstone, it glittered gold and white in the shape of a colossal falcon head. Atop the head, a line of full feathers arched back majestically.

"Sokar'Xenoteph has commissioned his tomb," Sharar mused. He glanced beyond the gaudy facade to the space behind it to find it leveled, several machines of wood and rope digging deep into the earth. "The tombs of Alika are quite splendid. I believe the sparrow king thinks more highly of himself than I do."

"Sparrow?" Amir asked, taking in the sharp beak of the statue.

Sharar made a thoughtful grunt. "The Hawk King. He's just a boy, his father taken from him too soon. Pharaoh Ramdas II. He took no such title onto himself and died too soon for his tomb to be erected."

"Why do Masahk need tombs? They're immortal."

"They used to worship death," Sharar informed him. "Glorious death. Something they could only taste in battle or by an illness they believed to be brought on by a god. Since it was rare, or so long coming, the tombs were to be beautiful. A monument to something the Masahk longed for at one time."

"And the slaves," Amir noted. "Masahk mostly. Except..." His eyes drifted to a few human slaves shackled together, working with bent backs on the tomb. "They have the lighter hair of Porshains."

The scholar turned to look where Amir's eyes had locked in horror. "Yes. Porsh was raided much in the past by Al'Myrah, when they still allowed the slave trade. By Bahratt, too, but when their magi prophesied the doom that would come from Porsh, they killed all their Porshain slaves and never went back. Alika has no such qualms, breeding their slaves from the stolen cargo when Porsh fell."

The Runer's face showed the slightest bit of revulsion and pity. "Cargo? The humans?"

Sharar didn't reply, but noted the disgust in Amir's voice.

"They are not necromancers, then?" the Runer asked.

"No," Sharar laughed. "They are Porshains from before the Mahit'Onomicon. Alika breeds them here for work."

"And the Masahk?" the Runer asked. "They enslave their own kind?"

Tired of the moral discussion, Sharar waved his hand and

moved more quickly up the long marble ramp that would lead to where the Dynast Pharaoh would be holding an audience. The place where the throne sat was called the outer court. The throne room was on the inside.

"There is a caste system, my savage friend," Sharar said as they passed through square-shaped sunken gardens filled with fragrant, bright foliage. A massive well of blue water sat between four of these large gardens, feeding the palace through channels running along the floor.

"Of course," Amir said dolefully.

Something swished in front of the pair, stopping them. The rest of the herd of dignitaries moved inward, but Sharar stopped. A tall, black-furred, jackal-like Masahk blocked their path. He stood well over six feet tall, his bare canine legs bent with muscle, as were his arms that ended in black claws. His gem-like eyes glared at the scholar and then the Runer. A blue satin cloak hung from his broad shoulders, the rest of him gilded in gold. In his left hand, he carried a blue and gold staff that resembled a shepherd's crook.

"Nasor," Sharar sighed. "Sokar's personal guard dog."

"Every lamb has a predator," Nasor replied. His voice rumbled and shook Sharar's ribs with every syllable. "And every snake its follower, it seems."

Amir glowered at the vizier as his sharp eyes bored into him, but held his tongue.

"Do you not grow tired of abusing the Runers?" Sharar asked. He snapped his fingers at a nearby servant holding a tray of golden goblets filled with sweet wine and motioned them over.

"Lawful criminals," Nasor purred, "do not exist. This Runer is no different from the one who slaughtered my brother in the streets over a game of dice. Protected by the runes and the laws, he walks free even now." His canine lips snarled at Amir.

"Is that why you despise all Runers?" Amir asked.

Nasor's snarl deepened. "Not all, perhaps. Just *you* and the man who holds your leash."

Sharar laughed lightly through his nose.

"I used to be like the other Runers," Amir confessed. "But not anymore."

"Tell me, rat," Nasor ordered, walking a quick circle around Amir and Sharar. He took one of the little golden goblets from the servant and thrust it at Amir. "Make your excuses."

Amir took the proffered drink, but didn't partake. "I met a boy, Ashar, who became my apprentice. Simple as that, vizier. He was good, kind. He changed me some time ago."

"Yet you follow the scholar's coin," the vizier challenged. "You aspire to nothing higher, as I do."

Amir gently smirked. "I don't live in a palace. I need coin to live."

"Then you should bow before me," Nasor growled. "Runer filth."

"Enough of this," Sharar butt in, but stopped when a lizard-like Masahk guard materialized from the air a few yards off, glaring hard at him for moving so suddenly towards Nasor. The Dynast palace's invisible guard were called the Mirage.

"Cowardly bitch," Amir mumbled, seeing the Mirage guard glare at them, her hand on her sword hilt.

Nasor's eyes flashed. He slapped Amir's hand, knocking the little golden goblet onto the stone floor. It spun in place, coming to rest between them. The vizier glared, but his lips curled in a cruel grin. "Pick it up, you filth."

Sharar rolled his eyes, overly tired of the vizier's petty games.

"Scholar," Nasor purred when Amir didn't move, "tell your Runer rat to pick the goblet up from the ground. It's worth more than he is."

Sharar sighed and tilted his head for Amir to acquiesce. "When you're done stalling us, Nasor, I'd like to be taken to the pharaoh. He *is* expecting us."

The vizier waited, eyeing Amir with a sharp, raised brow. The Runer's jaw flexed as he bit back his words. Sharar knew what Amir wanted to say. He'd said it a dozen times. He hated being in the palace, hated the wealthy. Hated Nasor. Sharar couldn't comprehend how Amir preferred sleeping in stables with the animals to the soft trappings he enjoyed when working for him, but Nasor had a way of making him see Amir's point of view. Nasor annoyed Sharar in that he hovered so close to Sokar that they almost never had a moment alone. That made bending the young pharaoh to his will difficult.

At last, his face burning, Amir knelt, hand outstretched for the goblet. When he gripped it, Nasor moved like a viper. The end of his golden and blue crook came down hard and fast on the back of Amir's hand. The Runer grunted, jerking, but the staff held him pinned to the golden floor. He stopped struggling when Nasor leaned heavily on it with a cruel chuckle.

"Enough," Sharar quipped softly. "Nasor, release him."

The vizier smiled and pressed down on the staff, drawing a hiss from the Runer. "I told you, I'd prefer it if you knelt in my presence, you animal."

Amir dropped his other hand, bowing reluctantly out of pain before the vizier. He clenched his free hand into a fist, bridling the rage building inside him.

"Nasor, I am warning you," Sharar growled. He checked the sides to see the Mirage guard watching them. If he attacked Nasor, even so much as shoved him, the guards would be on him in a flash.

"And I warned you," the vizier snapped back, "to not bring this animal into the palace." He twisted the staff, drawing Amir closer to the ground as he cringed in pain.

Having enough, Sharar lurched forward and whipped the staff

from the vizier's hand. As he suspected, the guard shot towards him.

"Don't," Nasor shouted, holding his hands up. "All is well." He faced Sharar, jerking his crook back. Using the hook, he shoved Amir over just as he attempted to stand. "It seems the court is filing out. Shall we?" He smiled and gestured to the throne room.

Sharar held his hand down to Amir, but the Runer smacked it away, standing up, eyes to the ground.

Affronted, Sharar quipped, "Cool down outside, Amir."

Not looking either of them in the eye, the Runer marched back the way they'd come with long, angry strides.

"Control your beasts, scholar," Nasor said with a grin. "Why do you care so much about how I treat such a creature?"

Plastering a pleasant smile on his face, Sharar turned to face Nasor. "I don't like when people abuse my things, you common jackal." The words snapped from his lips like lightning. "You will not treat Amir thusly again when we are in your presence. Is that understood?"

Nasor's smug grin faded into one of amusement. "Your things?" he repeated. "Fascinating."

THE ESCORT LED the pair into the outer court and left them there. A crowd of Alikans of all shapes and colors filled the area as a woman magi from Bahratt spoke to the pharaoh. Sharar took in the grandeur of the outer court, as he always did. The architecture of the Dynast Palace was not to be rivaled by any other smaller palace belonging to the lower pharaohs of Alika. Blue and gold marble covered the floor of the outer court, and mudstone pillars encrusted with rubies and sapphires and gilded with gold lined the main way. The transepts off to the side looked to be supported by pillars of ivory.

As Sharar waited for the woman to finish her discussion with the pharaoh, Amir returned. The vein in his neck and temple had stopped throbbing, but the muscles on the side of his jaw flexed. He didn't speak to Sharar.

At the head of the court, atop many layers of stairs, sat the Dynast Pharaoh on his ruby throne. The Masahk pharaoh held his head high, his youthful face covered by a gleaming, gold mask shaped in the likeness of a hawk. The mask covered his head. Great, sharp wings rose on either side of it. The top had a slit down the middle. The Hawk King's bright green and gold plumage, mingling with soft hair, arched out from this opening like a palm leaf. The black tresses and colorful feathers spilled over his shoulders, which bore a burnished, golden collar. The ornament hung low and broad over his bare, human-like chest. Bracers of matching gold covered the Pharaoh's forearms, a few plumes of feathers softly flowing out of the ends. His hawk-like Masahk legs bent over the ruby throne, covered in white Alikan silk to his avian knees. His taloned feet were bare. Behind him, in place of many yards of fabric where a cape would have hung dramatically from his shoulders, two great, green and golden wings flowed. Few Masahk, especially half-Masahk, had such glorious features. But Sokar'Xenoteph was a full-blooded Alikan Masahk. Still, Masahk wings could not bear the weight of their bodies. Not for a thousand years had avian Masahk flown. Still, they commanded majesty where they hung.

"That's the pharaoh you call 'brat'?" Amir noted sardonically. "I am staggered by his presence. He commands the room without saying a word." He glanced around at the adoring people, some on their knees, even though he did not speak to them. "They love him. Adore him."

The Runer had fallen under the boy-king's spell just as easily as the other peasants. Sharar sighed in frustration as the lady magi continued her oration to the pharaoh. "Don't be such a simple fool," he encouraged Amir. "It's all a facade. Sokar'Xenoteph is a child, desperate to leave his mark on his dynasty. He tries too hard to please his people. To be remembered."

But that was why Sharar liked the boy, why he'd made himself known to the Pharaoh years prior, when he was just a princeling in his father's court.

They waited until the sun touched the horizon. A set of musicians in white blew three strong blasts upon their horns, signaling that court was over and for the people to leave. Sharar stayed behind, waiting. A water-type Masahk appeared from behind the throne, approaching the Dynast Pharaoh.

Sharar started when he recognized the Masahk. He had expected to have to try to hunt the healer down, but he had come to hold court with the Pharaoh. He approached when the last of the people left, leaving just the musicians and two of the Pharaoh's mysterious guard.

The golden hawk mask turned to Sharar when he came into view. The Hawk King stood up, speaking words Sharar could not understand until the golden mask had been pulled away. The young Pharaoh beamed down at Sharar, tossing the heavy gold mask aside to Nasor, who caught it deftly.

"Sokar'Xenoteph, first of his name, long may he reign." Sharar smiled at the Pharaoh.

"Abigor!" the boy king cried. "I was beginning to think you'd forgotten about me and Alika. What a wonderful surprise after a tedious day of listening to politics and religion. Tell me you've found a lizard of some kind that grants wishes, or a butterfly that feeds on corpses. Something fascinating."

Sharar smiled at the boy.

A pair of the Pharaoh's guards laid their hands on their blades when the scholar approached unabashedly, but Sokar'Xenoteph waved them away. He quickly embraced the scholar before leading the way out of the throne room.

"This is the one I told you about, Het," the Pharaoh said to the scaly Masahk.

Het met Sharar's eyes and smiled kindly. He wore the white and blue robes of his temple and looked well. "How does my healing stand?" Het asked.

"Quite well," Sharar replied. "I haven't felt its malignance since."

The Hawk King looked between his priest and Sharar. "You know each other?"

Het nodded. "This is the man who saved me."

Sokar beamed, though he looked tired and exhausted from the day's court. "Of course he did. Abigor is always nearby to lend a hand. He happened to be in the palace when father crossed the river into Ahryu, into true eternity." The boy king sighed and ran his hand through his feathered hair. "I'm sure, as always, you are here for a reason, Abigor, not just to entertain me?"

"Yes, sira," Sharar replied. He reminded himself to have patience with the boy. Immortal or not, the young ruler had bonded with him in his time of great loss. At the time, Sharar had thought it a good plan, but had to practice great patience with the emotional youth. He had to play the Pharaoh's games. "I've come to discuss that history we started to explore. But," he added when the young Pharaoh's face fell, "I could do it with a drink in my hand."

Het smiled knowingly at Sharar, thanking him with his eyes for offering the libation and conversation Sokar so greatly needed.

"That's more like it." The Hawk King smiled and clapped his hands for servants to bring wine. "I want to show you my tomb."

Sokar skipped down the steps, beaming the whole way. Het and Nasor followed at a more mature pace, the jackal keeping his head high as he glared at Amir behind Sharar.

"I don't suppose you have more of that flower?" Sokar asked Sharar in a hushed voice as he led the group outside onto a massive veranda.

Sharar stealthily removed a tiny crystal vial from his robes and handed it off to Sokar. "Don't take it too often," he warned the boy. "I told you, only when you feel faint."

"Abigor," Sokar replied sadly, "I always feel faint when I hold court. I cannot stand before so many people with confidence." The majesty of the Pharaoh melted away, leaving a nervous boy. "Speaking in front of my own countrymen is hard enough, but when the majestic people of other nations come to my ruby throne, my mind spins in that damned golden mask. Why can't I speak before others, Abigor?"

Sharar put a comforting hand on the boy's shoulder. "Everyone has their battles, Your Eminence. You must follow in the footsteps of your ancestors. Think of Acenoth the Great," he said. "A hawk king like you. Brave enough to carry a curse to his grave."

"I hope so," Sokar replied.

Before the pair could go on, Nasor suddenly growled behind them, striking Amir hard across the face.

"Amir, don't!" Sharar cried, reaching his hand out to the Runer. Amir's hand had flown to his scimitar handle. "I think you should wait outside," Sharar said when the invisible guard came into view at the edge of his vision.

"Very well, sira," Amir growled, glaring at Nasor through watering eyes.

"Sokar, I am afraid Nasor has no respect for my colleagues," Sharar said, leading the way into the mud-pits where the slaves toiled on Sokar's tomb.

"The Runer?" Sokar asked. His entourage of servants, carrying shades, fans, and libation, joined them when they entered the hot sun.

"Yes, the Runer," Sharar sighed. "He may be of the lowest caste, but he is in my employ."

"I don't understand," the Pharaoh replied, taking a drink.

The scholar looked up at the facade of Sokar's tomb, smiling.

"Sometimes, my boy, you cannot mind the caste from which a man comes. Look at your tomb. Beautiful craftsmanship. But built by slaves—a people even lower than Runers."

Sokar smiled. "I think I understand now, Abigor." He turned to the vizier. "Do you, Nasor?"

"I do, my king," the Masahk replied softly, but without conviction. "I would like to remind you that the magi awaits in your outer chamber."

Sokar sighed sadly. "I'm sorry, Abigor. I wanted to speak with you and put the politics behind me."

Sharar smiled, but inwardly cursed the vizier. "What does the magi want?" he asked, a little leery of the woman. "Surely not to prophesy with you."

Sokar paled. "I hope not. I... That is..."

"No," Nasor supplied to the panicking youth. "But you must be away, my king." He glared at Sharar. "The scholar will have to wait."

"For how long?" Sokar whined.

"Until we summon him back to the palace," Nasor said. "What is it you want, scholar?"

Sharar consciously pulled himself up taller, though he could never match the height of the pair of Masahk. "To discuss Sokar's ancestors and his mark on his dynasty."

"You have an idea?" the young Pharaoh asked excitedly.

The scholar smiled. "I do, my boy. But I shall discuss it with only you. In the meantime, may I barrow your Ashmalian priest? I have a promise to keep to an old, dear friend of mine."

B.

SHARAR FOUND his way out to where Amir sat, leaning against a garden wall. Their horses stood by him, dozing in the warm evening sun. The Runer flipped a coin back and forth over his fingers, eyes glassy, lost in his own thoughts.

"Amir," Sharar said as evenly as he could. The Runer didn't meet his eyes. "I am sorry for the way Nasor treats you and your brethren. I..." He stopped, mouth open, at a loss for words. No, he wasn't sorry. It just seemed like the social thing to say. He needed Amir to stay by his side. If that meant a little groveling and showing sympathy, then so be it. "Amir," he started again with more strength.

"Shut up, scholar," Amir cut in. He turned his face up to meet Sharar's. "I don't need someone of your caste explaining why I have to endure every beating lying down. You don't have to justify yourself to me." He looked away, pushing himself up and taking the reins of his horse in hand.

Sharar followed him. "I don't want you to think that I—"

"It doesn't matter," the Runer cut in again. He looked at Sharar, his face flat and serious. "I don't care what I have to do for coin. For food and a place to lay my head. Continue to pay me and I will control the urge I have to sever that jackal's head." He offered Sharar a half-hearted smirk. "Besides, I know it's me he hates. Not every Runer, though he'd have us believe that."

"What have you done to anger him?" Sharar grinned.

Amir shrugged. "I'm honored he hates me so."

"You Runers are a reliable lot." Sharar took the reins of his own horse and followed Amir out of the palace walls.

Chapter 11

A Gift of Healing

The darkness around Tarkan vanished in a blast of light. Before he could blink the sunlight out of his burning eyes, the sound of the stone top cracking against the hard floor split his ears. Ashkan's hands shot into the coffin, pulling him out roughly.

"I hurried as fast as I could," he panted, supporting Tarkan. "I also spied a small party preparing to make camp to the south. We can take their blood and flesh." He offered one of the corpses to Tarkan, who sent his wound into the dead body. He coughed, rubbing his neck.

Tarkan didn't express how grateful he was that Ashkan had come back. Part of him had begun to wonder if the Apostle would return. Ashkan could have waited for Tarkan's body to fall into the deep sleep that only a Necro'Khan could achieve. Then, he could have cut off his head and gouged out his heart. But he hadn't.

"That was dangerous," Ashkan went on. He held his palms close and rose the bodies that had collapsed when he'd used his strength to open the stone coffin.

"Yes," Tarkan agreed, sliding down the wall to collapse into a sitting position. "But now we know."

"What?" Ashkan asked.

Tarkan took a few deep breaths. "That he is not sure if I have the Mahit'Onomicon. But I know he does not."

"You are sure?"

The Necro'Khan nodded. "Sharar has been waiting too long to take the powers of his djinn. If he had the book, he'd be a sorcerer by sunrise. Yes, he has patience, but what upstart of a scholar does not? No, he would have risen already. He would not wait."

Ashkan pulled Tarkan up, one arm around his middle, and followed the dead out to keep them within his sight. He whispered a few more verses, commanding them to march to the camp. Tarkan took them over with the last of his strength to allow Ashkan to let go and focus on him.

"He seemed to be well acquainted with the Dynast Pharaoh," Ashkan added once he stopped whispering the verses. Above ground, the sun was setting, casting red light over the dark shapes of Makan Alu'Ekmet and the mess of monsters and bones they'd risen.

Tarkan grunted, nodding. "One of his wishes was to command monsters, animals. Both living and risen. He turned my dragon, Rakthar, against me more than once. He experimented with Tzarik when he first met him, seeing if the risen could be stopped. It was a good wish. Alikans believe that the man who can read the Mahit'Onomicon is what they call the Father of Monsters, a mortal who can tame beasts by will alone."

Screams rose up from the distance where Ashkan focused his eyes. The black wind howled around them, kicking up sand that cut over their faces as Tarkan wordlessly sustained the risen.

"The scholar was fulfilling a prophecy," Ashkan noted.

"Whether there is a mortal among us who *can* tame and control the beasts without the wish of a djinn or not matters little now."

Again, Tarkan agreed. "When I met him, he'd just come back from Alika after Dynast Pharaoh Ramdas II's most unfortunate death." He let the accusation drip from his words.

"You think Sharar killed the Dynast Pharaoh?" Ashkan asked.

Tarkan shook his head. "I know he did. Alikans are the only people who worship a death god. Even we, as necromancers, do not worship Nephron. We are mere servants, following his words. The Mahit'Onomicon is the book that explains life and death, holding every magical secret of the map. If some god did dictate the words to a man on a mountaintop at the start of the world, he would have hidden it where no one—not even a sentient with a djinn—would look for it. Somewhere surrounded by death. Ishmael told me that Alika has long since forgotten its purpose: to protect the Mahit'Onomicon. Sharar has brought that idea back to the Dynast Pharaoh's mind. Ramdas II had no desire to delve deeply into the tombs of Alika. He could not be controlled. So Sharar removed him."

"You were there?" Ashkan asked.

Tarkan didn't nod, only looked vaguely into the middle distance. "He as good as told me."

The risen had slaughtered the entire group of travelers except for two, which they dragged back, kicking and screaming. Tarkan's mouth watered as he thought of consuming the power-giving flesh.

Ashkan hummed, turning his eyes to the horizon. He crossed his arms against the growing night wind. "He will find the book."

"He will." Tarkan nodded. "And I will take it from him."

USING TWO RISEN GRIFFINS, Tarkan and Ashkan made it back to Sharar's estate by evening of the third day of travel. Ashkan parted from him, going to the grounds behind the scholar's house to search out a few dead. Sharar had just gotten in, and his Runer was not with him. Sharar looked exhausted from the travel, but welcomed Tarkan with open arms and a confident smile.

"Where is your necrotic companion?" Sharar asked when Tarkan stood in his foyer alone.

"Close," Tarkan replied in a whisper, the scars in his throat returning. Sharar heard the wound's effect and made a sympathetic face. Tarkan signaled just outside the garden walls where the risen would soon be visible on a dune not far away.

"No risen creatures?" Sharar asked. "Surely a lion, or even a griffin, would be better."

"Would it?" Tarkan asked pointedly, knowing full-well Sharar could control even a risen beast.

The scholar smiled. "When this is all over, you'll have to tell me how that happened," he said, leading Tarkan into the middle of the manor. "Even I never thought to take your voice during our time together. I must note your bravery in returning to me, alone, as you appear to be. But I suppose you're immortal now, aren't you?" He smiled at Tarkan as if they shared a long-standing secret. "I brought a priest of Ashmalia. A Masahk named Het."

"And you are willing to risk your life by healing me?"

Sharar met the cold, blue eyes of his once-captive and his lips made a familiar flex that told Tarkan he was considering it. "Just how much of a Necro'Khan are you, Tarkan?" His voice went flat, more serious than Tarkan had ever heard it.

The Necro'Khan paced further down the halls toward where he knew the entrance to Sharar's dungeon lay. He wanted to see it, to feel its dark presence again. "Greater than Ishmael. But not as powerful as I will be. I hope you are not underestimating me."

"So you have plans?" Sharar fell in step with him, leading him to the lower level now.

The wound flared up in Tarkan's throat, choking him, muting him. He stopped and took two steps toward a side door.

"Ah, of course," Sharar quipped. "Demon, bring the priest."

Appearing from nowhere, the djinn marched down the hall, a water-type Masahk wearing white robes in tow. The priest's steps faltered when he beheld Tarkan. His thin lips quivered as he held back words.

"Fear not, Het," Sharar said, taking the priest's arm and gently leading him to Tarkan. "Tarkan is an old colleague of mine. We studied together for some years. We've left our marks on one another."

Tarkan glowered at Sharar.

"I'm afraid that I cannot. It's not a law of Ashmalia," he interjected when Sharar moved to speak. "It is my own conscience." He bowed, then took Sharar's hand. "I am sorry."

Of course, a priest wouldn't heal a necromancer. Tarkan hadn't expected Sharar to be able to pull through on his offer. Sniffing with disdain, Tarkan turned and prepared to head for the door when Sharar's hand gripped him, pulling him back.

Hissing, Tarkan flexed his left hand, calling his risen.

"Don't," Sharar said quickly. To Het he said, "My friend, please."

"Do you know what this man is?" Het shot back, his wide, ovate eyes begging Sharar to understand.

"I do. Please, Het." Sharar moved closer to whisper, trying to not let Tarkan hear him beg. "If you do this, he can do something for me that I desperately desire. He can undo a great injustice. Please."

The Masahk's wide eyes studied Sharar hard. Tarkan knew his answer before he spoke it. The priest had a big, pure heart, and could not deny the scholar's begging. His breath came in rasping gasps by the time the Masahk shook his head sadly.

Tarkan didn't stop, though, his risen appearing in the garden, frightening the workers outside. He pulled on his arm, yanking it out of Sharar's hands, and glared hard. The scholar really did want him for a purpose, or he would have called his guards and hauled him below when the risen appeared. Het tried to pull away from Sharar when their low moaning reached them inside.

"Do this for me and Tarkan can save him," Sharar begged one last time.

Taken by surprise, Het frowned. "Save him?"

Sharar nodded. Tarkan almost wished the damned priest would give in without a qualm. Sharar was going to give him a chance to test his powers as they were meant to be used. Tarkan needed to know if this spell would work. If the priest stood in his way…

Het swallowed hard and his breathing picked up, showing he was considering it. And was afraid.

Sharar looked him in the eye. "I will show you."

Het nodded. The djinn gave Sharar a glance, but he motioned for it to stay. The three of them silently made their way to a door with many locks. Some opened with a key, others by turning gears. Sharar opened it and went down into the darkness. Tarkan froze at the top step. This wasn't the same dungeon Sharar had locked him in, but the resemblance was striking. The familiar smell hit Tarkan hard, the cold air tingled over his skin, and the gloomy light filtered in through his memories. Steeling himself, he followed the scholar down.

This dungeon was far cleaner, with bookshelves, a desk, and a huge, mysterious machine. A glass sphere hung suspended in the center, filled with the blue, salty water of the Alikan rivers. The water had not been purified, meaning the magical properties still remained. Within the enormous sphere, a boy floated. Tarkan didn't have to ask: the boy was a younger, mirror image of Sharar, except his veins were black on the left side of his body. It looked like a runing gone wrong.

"Oh, Abigor," Het whispered sadly.

"So you see," Sharar sighed, running his hand down the sphere. "He's not alive except by this device I crafted myself, and by the healing properties of the salts. But only his body is alive. He's gone. Do you understand?"

Now Tarkan did, but he wasn't sure if the boy would live outside the sphere. It wasn't like the lady Runer whose own will had kept her body alive. The boy had died and Sharar had preserved him.

"You will bring him back to me," Sharar said darkly to Tarkan. "As you promised." To Het, he said, "Please understand, friend. My son was taken too early. Falsely accused. He is…" He placed his hand against the glass, close to the boy's face. "He is my life's work."

Het took a deep, shuddering breath and eyed Tarkan sideways. "If I do this, you will have this heretic raise your son from the grave?"

Sharar didn't reply, but his answer showed evidently on his face. Het shivered.

"I must beg Ashmalia for forgiveness." He almost choked on a sob. Slowly, he faced Tarkan, raising his hands. "Approach, death fiend," he whispered.

Finally getting what he'd come for, Tarkan took slow steps closer to Het. Below, Ashkan could not see them. He'd not know what was happening, and Tarkan could not call for help. Not yet. Soon, he'd find a way to communicate through the blood, but not even Ishmael had found a way to do that. For now, he was on his own. He eyed the boy in the sphere as he came close to Het. The boy had better have the hold on Sharar that Tarkan hoped he did, or else he'd be in danger.

The Masahk's long, white and blue fingers were cold against

Tarkan's sensitive skin under his jaw. Het pressed his soft finger-tips into Tarkan's skin. His face dropped into sympathy.

"I feel your pain, my friend," he whispered. "I am sorry. This must be torment."

Tarkan couldn't reply. His impatience mounted. He wanted to strangle the Masahk for stalling. Het finally sighed. The blue markings on his body glowed dimly as he used his god-given Masahk magic.

Inside, it felt like something crawled down Tarkan's throat. He gagged, but didn't pull away. Something warm, soothing, passed over the painful scars. In an instant, the pain vanished.

Tarkan gasped. He didn't choke on the inflamed sores. His throat opened so air passed freely down his throat and into his wanting lungs. He staggered back, gripping his throat in shock. He took three deep breaths, feeling the air flow easily. He looked up at Sharar, who hadn't moved, his face stony.

"Well?" the scholar asked.

"It is done," Het said sadly. He hung his head in loathing shame.

Tarkan smiled. He hissed the verses to open the Deep and stepped back from Sharar. The familiar wind whipped around them and the barrier split easily for Tarkan. He called black spirits to him from within.

"What are you doing?" Sharar shouted, shrinking away from the horrifying tear in the Deep. "Tarkan, we made a bargain."

"I'll return." Tarkan gave Sharar a dark smile and gathered the black souls around him. They hissed and screamed as he pulled on their power like blood. "I must prepare. Be ready, Sharar." Now that he had his voice, he could use Ishmael's spells.

The souls writhed around him. Gathering them, he shot up into the green air of the Deep and soared far and away from Sharar and his dungeon. The sensation flipped Tarkan's stomach. It wasn't like flying on Rakthar, but it thrilled him. He took a deep breath of the horrid air. It passed down his healed throat and he screamed in joy.

Chapter 12

Frost

Sybal stood alone with the horses and the cage at the edge of the shoreline. The docks in southern Hatal were far less wild than Singad. Mostly dignitaries, nobles, quadis, and other such ambassadors parted from this side of Al'Myrah. She leaned against her horse, glaring at Signar. The young Vaeson sat inside in his human form, hands clutching the bars, eyes turned towards where Tzarik had disappeared to find them lodging and a ship to at last set sail. With the sun setting, Sybal knew nothing would leave until the next morning. But that was just as well. They had to find a large ship with a cargo hold, and one that they could convince with gold to let them stow a cage with a boy inside. She checked her bag, and she had plenty of the herbal mixture left to put Signar to sleep for hours.

Her horse sighed and shifted its feet. Sybal reached into her pack and pulled out one of the bits of dried meat they had. She tossed it to Signar, but he ignored it.

"It's clean," she mumbled, going for her waterskin. "I didn't taint it this time."

Signar turned to look at her. His green eyes, so much like his mother's, doubted her. She nodded.

"So you do understand me," she said, wiping her mouth. He came to the side she stood on now, hands on the bars, eyes locked on the waterskin. "Hm," she mused with a half smile. "You're proving those Northicans wrong, you know. Tzarik saw it in you before anyone else." She stopped then, shaking her head in disbelief. "You've improved so much. You understand, but maybe you don't have the words yet. Do you want to speak?"

Signar studied her, his face wrinkling in effort.

"Now you just have to control your wild side," she said. "Stop that wolf from bursting out of you." She approached the bars, inches from Signar. He looked at her expectantly. She handed him the water and he drank deeply.

"We'll camp here for the night," Tzarik said, appearing suddenly from behind her.

She spun around, hoping he hadn't overheard her. "With him? This close to the ships and the city?"

Tzarik glanced in at Signar, who perked up the minute he heard Tzarik's voice. "He seems all right for now. Let's make a fire outside the circle of civilization and rest. Our ship leaves at first light."

They pulled slightly away from the busier part of the port. Tzarik found them a spot on the beach surrounded by tall rock spears for privacy, away from curious eyes. Sybal made the fire and unpacked the last of their supplies. Neither of them worried; they could try to hunt the minute they landed on Alika. Signar's stomach growled loudly when she set the meat to the flames.

"I fed you," she hissed softly at him. "You didn't touch it." She pointed to the piece on the floor of the cage.

Tzarik approached the cage doors and opened them, slipping in easily with no thought to his safety. She watched tensely as he picked the piece up and brought it out. He didn't close the doors and Signar followed him out. Sybal tensed, hand on her sword hilt.

"Don't," Tzarik said to her gently. "We have to show we trust him sometime." When he sat by the fire, Signar joined him and reached for the raw meat. Tzarik grunted and pulled it out of his reach. "You'll wait for it to be cooked now," he said, spearing it next to the other pieces.

Sybal couldn't believe her eyes, but she would have sworn she saw the wildling pout. She laughed lightly and took out a clay jug of ale she'd been saving. "The bastard doesn't want his meat cooked," she said, sitting next to Tzarik.

"He's a man and he'll learn to eat like one," Tzarik grunted. "We won't feed him like a wild wolf anymore." He faced Signar. "Understand?"

Shocked for the second time that night, Sybal watched Signar nod. Tzarik finished cooking the food and handed it to Signar. Watching him instruct the young Reks to wait—because the food was hot—and seeing Signar stare fixedly at the food like he expected it to move, set something alight in her chest, made her smile... Made her sigh.

Is this what you want? Freja's voiced asked Sybal. *Is this what you think was stolen from you?*

Yes, she confessed, speaking to the voice. *And he's trying to create it for me.*

And you've fallen for the Vaeson boy, haven't you? it asked. It almost sounded jealous.

At first, she wanted to say no. She hated him. Feared his outbursts. He put them in danger and made their travels a living hell. He'd hurt Tzarik. During the battle in Northica, he'd attacked her. Her eyes flicked to the massive, painful-looking scar that went from Signar's forehead, between his eyes, and down his neck to his collarbone. She'd done that. Then she'd choked the consciousness out of him. When she blinked, she saw it again. He lay beneath her, crying, bloody. And she strangled him. He just hadn't been able to understand. Now he could. Could she apologize?

You are emotional right now, the voice said, almost soothing. *You are open to me. And yet, you defy me. You do not let me direct your blade.*

Sybal shook her head and took a long drink of the ale before taking food for herself. *I will find a way to silence you,* she promised.

The voice gave a dark laugh. *Do not threaten me, lady Runer. I will remind you whose blood flows in your veins.*

ᛉ

TZARIK LEANED against the trunk of a petrified tree that jutted up out of the sandy beach. The whispering waves eased his mind. Across the fire, he watched Signar sleep. The boy had returned himself to the cage, curled in his wolf form. The doors were locked. Must have been Sybal. Glancing at the horizon, he judged from the dip of the moon that the sun would be up in three or so hours. He'd hardly slept, worried about the boy. But Signar had communicated, and that gave the Runer hope. And now he lay still, peacefully asleep.

Sybal wandered back into the firelight from a quick survey and saw him awake. "Why aren't you sleeping?" she asked. "It's my turn to keep watch."

He noted how her brow was furrowed, and she had that glint in her eye like she'd been arguing. At first, he thought she must be doing battle within herself, as she so often did. But when she spoke, a small puff of icy air dissipated in the warmer desert air. She'd been listening to the voice inside her head.

She sat next to him and put her hand on his knee absentmind-edly, watching Signar with him. Her fingernails had a blueish-black tinge to them. Gently taking her hand, he put his fingers between hers and examined them. Even between their thin gloves, he felt her cold skin.

Giving in to his touch, she leaned into him. Tzarik didn't reciprocate her loving movement, concerned about the advancement of the god-touch. She kissed his neck, pulling him out of his darker thoughts. He leaned away, mumbling, "Not now." His eyes went to Signar. The boy was thankfully in a deep sleep from overeating for what must have been the first time in his life. But that didn't mean they could recklessly dive into their physical desires. What if the boy woke?

But Sybal didn't stop. She adjusted to her knees, hands on his face as her lips trailed up his neck to his face. Tzarik gave in then, replying with his own quick kiss before turning away again.

"Don't do that," Sybal whispered, throwing one leg over his. "I haven't had you in too long."

At this, he smiled into their kiss. "I remember a dangerous attempt in a tub not a week ago. I still have a bruise on my side."

She rubbed her head against his, nuzzling fiercely. "Too long for me. I hardly remember it."

A little insulted, Tzarik pushed against her shoulders. She didn't budge. "We can't. Not with him so close." He glanced over her shoulder at the Vaeson. He still breathed gently.

Sybal sat up, unlacing her armor and tossing it aside before throwing her head back. Her long, thick hair splashed out like a wave of golden ice. A desire to touch it overcame him and he tangled his fingers in her hair. She went to work on his leather armor while he touched her neck. Soon, only their tunics and pants separated their skin. Sybal pulled Tzarik up from his sitting position and he twisted, shoving her against the ground to be on top. She smiled darkly and leaned up, biting the soft skin just under his collarbone.

Tzarik knew he shouldn't be giving in, but the natural urges were ones he'd not had a lot of practice fighting against. They'd never roiled up inside him like they did with Sybal. For so long, he'd thought he had no attraction to any sentient. The wild emotions were new and strong. He sat up, running his hands down Sybal's side and taking in her heavy-lidded eyes and the coy smile she gave while biting the corner of her mouth.

That's when he saw it. A small, thin, white trail of ice—like lightning—spidered out from the corner of her blue eye, casting a frost over her skin. It made her paler the more it spread. Her panting breath came in a white cloud. In that moment, the god curse flared up in her, excited by the passions she let loose.

Tzarik immediately withdrew, sliding off her. He'd told her a little about what the curse meant, but not everything he knew. Perhaps now was a good time.

But Sybal followed his retreat. She slammed into him hard, knocking him beneath her now. Tzarik cringed from the impact and felt the campfire close to his hand, which she pinned to the ground just above his shoulder. He glanced back to see the embers close.

"Wait," he tried again. "Sybal, something's happened. Stop."

Her blue eyes turned to white, sparkly, icy orbs. She smiled darkly, lips black and blue. "Tell me what you see," she said in a dangerous tone. Then she dove onto him, biting his neck. Even her teeth touched him like ice. The touch rose to power with her heightened emotions, taking over her sense. She pulled back for just a moment to let him see a fresh, ashen streak take the color from her hair. It spread from her temple, near the ice that came from the corner of her eye. The frost spread over her hairline now.

"Stop," he ordered, squirming under her. With a grunt, he tried to buck her off, using his legs in an attempt to dislodge her.

Laughing at the struggle, Sybal shoved her hand under his tunic. Her cold nails dug into his skin and she dragged her icy claws down his chest. Tzarik gnashed his teeth against the sudden pain. He'd try one last time, then he'd fight her.

"Your blood feels so warm," Sybal cooed, pressing her hand into the scratches.

Behind them, Signar must have awakened. Tzarik heard him whining and yelping in his wolven form behind the bars. He wondered if Signar could smell his blood.

"Sybal, stop," he ordered again, pressing hard against her. She was terrifyingly strong. Suddenly overpowered, he feared he couldn't fight her off, even if he wanted to. The strength came from the curse. The demonic chains that would soon enslave her rose with her passions. "Look at me," he snapped. "Sybal!"

She moved quick as a viper, gripping his throat and choking the breath out of him in an instant. He gagged, his sulfates rushing madly as the threat mounted. She tilted her head as if listening to a voice he could not hear.

The bars behind them clanged madly. He couldn't twist to look at Signar, to tell him to calm down. Sybal held him down with one hand around his throat. Her other hand shot to the belt buckle at his waist and pulled at it.

"Don't," he grunted around her throttling grip.

With that final plea, the snarl of a wolf, quickly followed by the earsplitting crash of metal and wood being torn asunder, made Sybal look up. A wolf howl quickly turned to the war cry of a man. Above Tzarik, where he lay trapped against the sand, a pale body and long yellow hair tackled Sybal off him. Tzarik rolled to his left, away from the campfire and up onto his feet, ready for anything.

Signar grappled with Sybal, both of them growling and snarling at one another. Tzarik stood rooted in fear, watching the two titanic sentients kick up clouds of sand around them as they tussled. Finally, Sybal landed a blow, but Signar didn't back down. He shifted into his golden wolf form and snapped at her. Being larger than her now, Sybal screamed and backed away, looking for her sword. She dived for it, but Tzarik lunged, kicking it out of her grasp. Sybal didn't notice, turning to catch Signar's maw as he dived at her with his fangs flashing.

Tzarik expected them to stop, for Signar to concede, but he didn't. He shifted to his human form, slipping from her grasp, and ducked, tackling her again to the ground.

"Signar, stop," Tzarik commanded, carefully edging closer. "Sybal, don't fight him!"

But the two ignored him, starting their combat over again. They made contact with one another, bloodying each other's noses and making bruises blossom under their skin. Sybal's flesh frosted more and more. Realizing they wouldn't stop until one of them was dead—both mad and wild—Tzarik dashed at them. Determined to put himself between them and break them up, he gripped Sybal's shoulders and flung himself before her. Overcome by the berserk power of the touch, Sybal cracked his skull with her fist and shoved him away.

White light blasted over Tzarik's sight and made his ears ring. The ground hit him hard as he tipped. Her god-given strength would be enough to fracture his bones, surely. He lay in ringing pain, eyes watering, but he struggled to push himself up. He had to stop them.

Before he could get his balance back, something shot in front of him, guarding him. He blinked and found Signar crouched before him, snarling in his human form. Facing them, Sybal stood, gasping. Her hair flew around her in a long, tangled mess, and her eyes sparked with white ice. She clenched her teeth, making her breath come in a hiss. She met Tzarik's eyes, but he didn't dare move from behind Signar's protective stance.

Sybal took an aggressive step forward, but Signar gave a warning sound somewhere between a bark and a snarl. "Don't," the boy snapped.

Something unfamiliar shot through Tzarik then, making almost all the pain disappear. Had the boy spoken again? Excitement and tepid optimism rushed through him. He fought the desire to spin the boy around and ask him to speak.

Sybal stepped forward again.

"No," Signar warned her. Tzarik could almost hear the wolven fangs in his mouth as he spoke.

Tzarik reached up and took Signar's wrist in his hand, hard. "It's all right," he whispered to the boy, pulling himself up. "Signar, don't hurt her." He tried to walk out from behind the protective Vaeson, but Signar moved with him toward the fire, shielding him from Sybal.

All at once, everything melted from Sybal's face. Her shoulders fell and tears filled her eyes. Her skin turned to a beautiful, dark honey color again. She covered her mouth with her hand and turned her face away, crying.

"Thank you," she said to someone Tzarik could not see. "I'm... I don't know what came over me," she wept softly. She covered her face with both her hands and cried.

Tzarik pulled Signar back, hand on the boy's shoulder. "Stay," he ordered him.

"No, don't," the boy begged, but Tzarik pushed past him to Sybal.

Sybal fell to her knees, doubling over on herself. Tzarik knelt before her and lifted her face with his hands as gently as he could. She bravely met his eyes.

She sniffled and swallowed hard. "Maybe it's me who should be in that cage," she offered. "I don't know what's made this monster in me."

Tzarik offered her a small, coy smile. "Fortunately, I know a Runer who has a way with monsters," he said. "But this isn't all your fault. I should have told you the moment you awakened on Caerwren what to expect."

He watched her eyes quickly flit to Signar, then back to her. "I thought I had mastered my impulses," she said.

"You have," he interrupted. "But this thing is preying on your weakness, making you think you're a monster."

Her eyes once again went to Signar. "Like him," she said softly. "He was in such control. I felt it. He turned to his wolf and back again flawlessly. He protected you consciously." She smiled and haltingly raised her hand to his face. He let her touch him. "You did that," she whispered. "You tamed him."

"And I'll tame you if I have to," he said. He added with a grin, "Again."

She laughed sadly and stood up, letting him lead her back to the campfire. Tzarik eyed Signar as they approached, making sure the Vaeson didn't lose control. When he didn't, Tzarik sat her and himself down. He pulled his saddlebag to himself and retrieved a small bag of coffee they'd bought in town. He prepared water to boil. The sun would be up soon. He had to tell her now. Signar sat next to him on his other side, his green eyes latched on to Sybal.

Tzarik took a breath. "I don't know where to start, but I need you to know. I've seen this before. I told you as much once."

Sybal nodded. "Azar," she said, clearly remembering the very few details Tzarik had told her about his past. Her eyes bored into the fire as she calmed herself.

Tzarik nodded. "He was touched when I first met him. He told me he'd been that way his entire life."

She frowned, taking in his story.

"I have never seen another god-touched," he went on. "But we met some who had. Even Azar knew of one. We learned that those who had the touch turned to their demonic forms within weeks or months. This is what I feared for you. I hesitated bringing you back from the Deep, knowing the body I put you in would be a touched one. A cursed one."

She cleared her throat. "I'm glad you brought me back, no matter my state. The Deep was worse than a simple death." She stopped herself there, looking away. He wouldn't press her. She'd tell him more about it when she was ready.

"But I fear something worse awaits those with the god-touch." He poured the boiling water into the beat up and dented brass coffee pot she carried.

"What happened to Azar?" she asked.

"One day he was there. We were on Bahratt, trying one of their dark rituals to strip the curse from him. How much do you know about the magi's rites?"

Sybal shrugged. "Not much. Rahul, my betrothed and the prince of Jarabu, wasn't a terribly religious man. Nor his father. But I know some of the provinces revere the gods more than their rajas."

Tzarik poured her some of the coffee and handed it to her. Signar's nose twitched curiously as he watched him handle the dark liquid. "They believe in the power of virgin blood, torture for prophecy, and ritual power."

Sybal froze.

Deciding to show her, Tzarik pulled the laced opening of his tunic down, showing her a deep, twisted scar over his heart. "I was to be that blood. Nefiri, a magi I've known since then, performed the ritual. While I lay on that black altar, I knew Azar had selected me off the streets for this very purpose."

"How cruel," she gasped.

But Tzarik shook his head. "It wasn't as simple as that. I know he didn't want to harm me. At the very least, I know he regretted it."

Sybal shook her head. "How can you be sure?"

He knew. He took a drink of the coffee and didn't meet her eyes. It would be too hard to explain. "I almost died upon that altar. Perhaps if I had, he would have been saved. Nefiri urged him to take my life for his. But he wouldn't. So he fled, taking me with him. I was more dead than alive when he ran from the temple. I was bleeding to death and...wouldn't have made it long."

Understanding struck Sybal and she gave a soft gasp. "He runed you to save you. It was the only blood he had."

"Yes." His voice came rough, ragged with the memory. "I was the last life he had been told to take."

"What do you mean?"

"Azar had a voice in his head, one that claimed to be his sister, Amaya. But she was long dead and gone. He told me that he slew any and all that the voice commanded him to. He believed that since he did the god's bidding—once he learned it was the god and not Amaya—it might let him live as it had done so far. When he betrayed his god and stopped letting it use his blade, it took his life more quickly. He confessed to his murders and became a Runer, hoping the black oath would protect him. But that oath, our runes and magic, come from the Dohkma—the darkest, eldest god in the north."

Sybal touched the stones around her neck. "I wondered." Her face showed she understood the severity of the black oath now. "The scholars believe the Dohkma is *the* god. The first god who created all others."

"Azar believed that Runers were servants of the Dohkma, sent to cull the monstrous hordes that his creations—the other gods— brought to life. And that is why the sulfates did not save him, since it was a magic belonging to the god who'd touched him. He tried to heal his affliction with a remedy from the one who'd poisoned him in the first place.

"The night he runed me haunts my nightmares still. The morning after, he was gone, leaving behind his scimitar, horse— everything," Tzarik finished.

Sybal suddenly started. "So you're... You're not like me?"

He looked up, confused.

"You're not a criminal." Her eyes rounded and she recoiled

slightly, like she had a plague she was afraid to pass to him. "You were innocent. A child, even." Her eyes narrowed, trying to remember what he'd told her.

"I was fifteen," he supplied flatly. "I was a criminal in that I stole food to survive after I escaped my enslavement. But I was never prosecuted. The runes were not a punishment for me. So, I suppose, you're right."

"You were innocent," she whispered again. She inhaled softly, remembering something. "The Mong Sho on Xia knew it. It wouldn't harm you. I remember watching it attack you. It was like a barrier stayed it. It can only attack the guilty. That's why it went for me and ShanBao." She sighed heavily, her shoulders dropping. "You're not like me," she repeated.

"That doesn't matter," he said quickly. "Why I'm a Runer has no bearing on who I am. You killed Xiao to save your family, to save Ala'Nar. They punished you for it."

"Yes," she agreed. "People don't hate you like they hate me."

"That's bullshit," Tzarik cut over her. "I'm not going to let you wallow in misery and think you have had a harder time of being a Runer. Just as I'm not going to tell you that you know nothing about the world but what your diamond mine education has bought you. That my father's torture, selling me, and living on the streets was more difficult than your life."

She glared at him.

"But none of that matters," he said more kindly. "Everyone has it worse than someone else. If you make your suffering your identity, you will never be anything but what others have done to you, giving them utter control over you. I'm not saying you have to forget what you've been through. Trust me when I say that. But you cannot let it be who you are. I tried that. It led me down dark paths that only end one way. You rob yourself of your chance to make something of your life if you become only what you've suffered."

Signar was perfectly still and silent beside him.

Tears fell from Sybal's unblinking eyes as she watched him. He hadn't intended to make her weep, convicting her. He hated being the reason she hurt. But she'd grown strong in their years together. Become a powerful, talented Runer. A formidable woman. He couldn't stand by and let her be devoured by her sorrow. She'd learned to grapple with her impulses, and he didn't want to see her lose that control.

"All Runers are hated, no matter the blood we lose, the bones we break, or our lives that we risk saving people from their nightmares," he said steadily. "We are all spat on, provoked, hunted, and despised. Even those who aren't Runers are. Everyone has a hateful burden to bear that you cannot see; don't blind yourself from seeing that with your own.

"But," he added when she gave a soft gasp, trying hard to hide her crying. "We are together. You chose me, gods know why. If you hadn't, I'd regret it."

"You were the only Runer in the city," she said with a weak smile.

This stopped Tzarik for a moment. That might not have been true. He might have just been the closest one. Almost like some higher power had placed him there at that moment.

"I'm glad I was," he said out loud. "Rather than comparing sorrows, I want to use our strengths for one another. To try to save you."

Sybal took a deep breath, wiped her tears, and moved to sit closer to him. Signar sat up from where he'd started to lounge and glared at her.

"It's all right," she whispered to Signar, smiling sadly. "I'm not going to hurt him."

The Vaeson watched cautiously as she slid under Tzarik's arm and wrapped her arms around him, lying against his side. She sighed contentedly, her breath shaking, and closed her eyes.

"If I'm not saved, what happens?" she asked. "The Vorlamir said I cannot die again. What does the touch do after I become the god's slave?"

This was the part Tzarik had been dreading. "To be a demonic slave to a god is to become a djinn."

Her arms tightened around his middle as fear took her. He held her closer, leaning his cheek against the top of her head.

"You will lose yourself to the god, unable to deny him," he went on. "Then someone, no doubt a Runer, will bind you, trapping you to this world forever until someone wishes you free. But then, only the void awaits you, should the Dohkma allow it. You cannot go to Janna or even Nah'jaha. Demons do not get an afterlife. And that is what frightens me." He couldn't imagine her in oblivion, alive, feeling, and utterly alone.

She craned her neck to look up at him. "There must be more. Djinn are ancient magical beings. There must be things about them we don't know. We could find out. Perhaps there's a way to…" She stopped. Like him, she wasn't sure what they could do.

"I won't lose you to that fate," Tzarik promised. "There will be an answer in the Mahit'Onomicon. We just have to find it and find a way to read it."

A silence fell then as the sky started to turn purple in the east. Signar lay down against Tzarik's other side and sighed deeply, content. Suddenly, Tzarik felt whole. A feeling like that of coming out of a deep illness overcame him: wellness, strength, purpose. A strange hope filled him. Something about Sybal and Signar leaning against him made Tzarik's chest tighten and his eyes water.

Chapter 13

Magi Ambassador

Tzarik's apprehension rose as they surveyed the docks and the small market square on the shores of the very edge of the Hatal province. Signar had utterly destroyed the cage the night before, breaking out to save him from Sybal. Tzarik had no choice but to trust the boy or poison him to sleep with the herbs. For now, he kept one eye on Signar and one looking for the ship he'd bought information about that could sail them to Alika. As he watched a pirate vessel preparing to leave, the Alikan captain reminded him of something.

"Sira," Tzarik asked the Alikan pirate, who was posting a notice to a board. The notice asked for a few crew replacements. "I am looking for someone. Have you any news about pirates from the west? Alikan men who may have done business there?"

The man, his eyes flashing dangerously in his black face, gave Tzarik a cautious look. "You're a Runer," he said, feeling out the conversation. "What do you want with treasure hunters? We've done nothing wrong, and we won't take your blood as our own, no matter our crimes."

"I'm looking for a friend of mine," he said, passing by the pirate's nervous question. "We were on Caerwren and he was captured by a clan leader, then sold to an Alikan pirate who sailed out from islands west of Northica. He was a younger man, Al'Myrahn. If you haven't seen him, you must have heard of him. The pirate who bought him from Northica would remember him by his incessant speech. He's called Vicdan."

At this, the pirate's dark eyes lit up behind a thick amount of kohl. "The singer," he grunted, giving a knowing half-smile. He finished fastening his notice more securely, then turned back to the docks. Tzarik followed him. "Yes, we ran into Captain Sebak perhaps a week ago. He was preparing to head for Gypsu. Had been hired by some rich man's accountant to sail some of his things across from Al'Myrah. He must be there by now. Still had his bard with him, putting him to work. We can't be too selective when it comes to who we fill our crew with, Runer. The discipline of a ship will make an obedient sailor out of any man."

"Did you speak to the man?" Tzarik asked, just to make sure.

The pirate grunted and rolled his eyes. "No. *He* spoke to *me*. Friend of yours?"

"Something like that. Thank you." Tzarik turned to head back to Sybal and their ship. That had to be Vicdan. The only doubt he had was that this Captain Sebak hadn't tossed the talkative man over the side yet. But Vicdan did have a way of making those around him comfortable, feel listened to and important. So long as he pulled his weight on the pirate's ship, maybe he'd make it a little longer. Long enough for Tzarik to find him on Alika.

"The ship is boarding," Sybal hissed when Tzarik came back. "We have to hurry. But we cannot take Signar aboard as he is." She started to dig in her saddlebag.

Tzarik knew what she was about to suggest before she pulled

out the clay jar of herbs. Signar's nose twitched when he caught the scent. He sadly met Tzarik's eyes.

Tzarik looked at the boy's face, calculating. Of course, the Vaeson's wide eyes begged Tzarik to spare him. Signar hadn't been able to communicate. Tzarik wasn't sure what the mixture had done to him in his sleep. It could have made him feel sick, given him nightmares. The one time, Signar had woken nearly dying of thirst. No, he couldn't give him the herbs when the boy couldn't protest with his own words. His hand went to Signar's long, yellow hair before he could stop himself.

"No," Tzarik said. "I'll go below with him."

"And if he attacks you?" Sybal asked.

Signar locked his eyes with Tzarik's, looking up hopefully, and shook his head.

"He won't," Tzarik promised.

Sybal moaned, desperate. "Tzarik, please don't put yourself at risk."

"I'm not." Tzarik clicked his tongue, gently shoving Signar along towards their ship and leading the horses.

Sybal glared at Signar and growled quietly, "Skelmir," as he passed.

Tzarik led the Vaeson and the horses onto the massive passenger boat before the crew directed him to the dozen or so slings below for the horses.

With the help of the animal handler of the ship, Tzarik got the two horses settled in. He watched Signar while they secured the animals and noted how he sat patiently by, waiting. As if the boy knew trust was at stake, he sat on sacks of feed, hands gripping one another, eyes straight ahead. This gave Tzarik more hope for the wildling's recovery than anything he'd seen before.

THE WEATHER COOPERATED, giving sunny days and windy nights, pushing the laden passenger ship across from Al'Myrah to the blindingly white sandy shores of Alika. Unlike Al'Myrah and its golden sand, occasional red shores, and golden rivers, Alika's sand was white as a cloud and its rivers bluer than the sky. The harbor in Gypsu quickly melted away into the paths leading towards the small cities that made up the province around the larger city. Most travelers parted for the big city while others hurried through the crowds to the river caravans.

By the time Tzarik maneuvered the horses, Sybal, and Signar through to a large kiosk that expanded into an open air lounge, Signar's nose and the tops of his sharp cheek bones were red from the sun. The covered lounge sprawled out, acting as a meeting house for ambassadors, rich travelers, and warriors on the move. A few colorful pipes wafted scented smoke out, several women served drinks to customers lounging out of the sun on colorful cushions, and out behind it, in the open sun, several large fire pits roasted lamb and had pots boiling.

Sybal nodded to it. "If nothing else, we can fill our skins before we move." Her lips were chapped. "We can ask for information, too."

Tzarik grunted in agreement. Signar looked tired from the journey, having not slept at all on the ship. Tzarik wondered if that would help keep him in check, or if that meant he had less control over his wild wolf. It was a risk he'd have to take.

"Signar," he whispered as they approached the open air lounge, "be calm. Do you understand?"

Lids droopy, face red, the Vaeson nodded. His emerald orbs brightened when he smelled the lamb on the spit several yards away. He licked his parched lips and honed in on it.

"We'll eat, don't worry," Sybal grumbled, pulling Signar closer to her as they approached the lounge. "It's like this boy's stomach has no end; just a bottomless pit inside his gut."

Tzarik laughed gently through his nose. Sybal had never been a starving young man. She wouldn't understand.

Checking the faces of the patrons carefully as he approached, Tzarik meandered closer to the front bar of the lounge where a fat man from Bahratt in a turban shouted orders at his staff out back. His face perspired profusely and his voice sounded worn down.

"Eh, Runers," he sighed, spotting Tzarik approach. He squinted at Sybal, lips curling up with the effort. "A lady Runer. And a white man." He looked nervous. "How can I be of service to such as you three?"

"We're here to meet a scholar from Al'Myrah," Tzarik half-lied. "A rich man. He was to get us an audience with the Dynast Pharaoh."

The man laughed suddenly, his corpulent belly shaking under the yards of silk and gold wrapped around his middle. "Audience with the Dynast Pharaoh? Sira, one cannot just walk into the palace and speak to the Hawk King. You'd have a difficult time getting in to see the lower pharaoh of Gypsu. The Dynast Pharaoh? What does a Runer want with the god-incarnate who watches over Alika? An *Al'Myrahn* Runer," he added, glaring now. "Does your sultana not have enough husbands to satisfy her? Has she set her sights on our Hawk King?"

"Guard your words," Sybal snapped, glowering at the man.

"Then what do you want?" the man said, moving quickly around his tables of storage, pulling out a small barrel of mead and handing it to one of his workers.

"As we said," Tzarik replied. "We're looking for a scholar from Al'Myrah. We were told by a reliable source that he'd be in Gypsu."

The man sighed and leaned against the table. "I might know the man. Not many Al'Myrahan scholars pass our shores. Dignitaries, yes. But not men of the seminary. Wish I could remember more."

Gritting his teeth, Tzarik pulled his coin purse out and tossed the man a Bahratt rupee. He made sure to let the bag jingle and let the man see the various kinds of coins inside, tempting him.

"Ah, yes," the man said, biting the coin, then pocketing it. "There is one naturalist from Al'Myrah who has a large estate in Gypsu. Comes and goes often from the docks. Been there for several years now. Always has large shipments. Is fond of the mint liquor."

Sybal shot Tzarik a look, nodding. "Even my family has homes in various cities. That makes sense for him."

"Mm." The man nodded. "There was something else, too. Oh, what was it?" He faked thinking, scratching his black beard. His eyes hooked to the purse.

Tzarik tossed him another rupee. He hated the peasants' games, having played them often. It wasn't a hard game to learn the rules for. They'd tell you anything if you had something shiny to give. He'd played many times and hated it now. He just had to let them think this was his first time, or else they'd not spill their secrets.

"Oh, yes." The man smiled and scratched his cheek with the coin. "That Al'Myrahn scholar has had a standing audience with the Hawk King for most of his life. Which is very odd."

"A standing audience?" Tzarik asked. "What does that mean?"

"He can see the Dynast Pharaoh whenever he wants," Sybal supplied. "Why?"

"Hardly matters," Tzarik said. He wanted to be shocked that Sharar had a permanent audience with one of the most powerful rulers on the map, but it didn't come as a surprise. The rich, charismatic man could probably talk a fire into putting itself out. "How do we get an audience?" he asked the shop keep.

At this, the man's eyes became cautious. "Oh, that's not something I can tell you. And to find out would cost you greatly."

Annoyance at the common rabble boiled up in Tzarik. The people of these large cities liked to play with Runers, make them squirm. Their payback for Runers being convicted criminals who walked free.

"It helps if you know the right people," a smooth, deeply feminine voice said from behind them.

Tzarik knew the voice far too well. His entire body froze on the spot, not letting him blink or breathe. Sybal noticed and gently took his hand before turning around.

"Who are you?" Sybal asked the woman.

Tzarik didn't need her to reply to know. The sound of her voice, the clinking of the golden chain from the diamond stud in her nose to the golden hoop on her ear, the swishing of her red, silken robes and veil, were permanently burned into his brain, etched on the inside of his skull. The scar over his heart panged in agony, taking his breath away in a wave of pain.

"Tzarik knows me," the voice said. "Don't you, *cousin?*"

He steeled himself and turned to meet her dangerous, kohl-lined eyes and mocking, red-lipped smile behind veils of gold and red.

"Nefiri," he grunted, having to force the name out of his constricted throat. "Why are you on Alika?"

The beautiful magi smiled and held her ground, unafraid of him, as she always did. "I'm an ambassador. You know that. I speak for our Maharaja and our magus off Bahratt's shores. Even to your sultana. I was wondering when I would see you again. It's been years." Her dark brown eyes slowly turned to Sybal. "I see why you haven't been to see me in some time." She clicked her tongue, speaking slowly, letting each word hit him hard. "So this is what your loneliness has brought you to? Desecrating the holy temple that is a woman's body with the sulfates." She shook her head slowly. "I'm disappointed in you, Tzarik."

"Who are you?" Sybal shot back, repeating herself. Her face paled as her sulfates rushed to her cheeks in rage. "I chose to be runed. They had to pay Tzarik to take my life."

At this, Nefiri let out a loud, melodious laugh. "Of course they did. You haven't changed at all, have you?" She reached out and touched his arm, holding it tight in her long fingers.

Tzarik's skin scorched under her touch. He'd not forgotten what her hands felt like. Cutting through any other unpleasantness, he quipped, "Are you here on diplomatic business, then?"

But Nefiri wouldn't let him change the subject that easily. Her mysterious eyes snapped to Signar. Fear jolted Tzarik into action and he quickly placed himself between the magi and the Vaeson. "No," he growled darkly, even going so far as to lay his hand on his scimitar.

Nefiri ignored his threat and slowly raised her hand over his shoulder towards the boy. Tzarik thought quickly: should he smack Nefiri's hand away, or would that trigger Signar to danger, making him lash out and lose control? His mind reeled in the milliseconds it took to make a choice, but before he did, Nefiri froze.

She stopped, her hand just beside Tzarik's face. Her eyes lost some of their sparkle and she swallowed hard. Was that the tiniest drop of fear he detected behind her coy eyes? He glanced back at Signar and saw the boy give the first stony, hard, warning glare he'd ever seen.

"To my tent," Nefiri said, clearing her throat. "We can speak there." She turned and called back, "No magi tricks, Tzarik. I can help you."

FARTHER AWAY, a massive caravan of two dozen tents, vardos, elephants, camels, and other pack animals spread out over a quarter of a mile in the middle of the desert. Tzarik recognized the markings of other ambassadors, magi, kehanns from the temples of Al'Myrah, and other such dignitaries on their way across the continent. Nefiri had a large red tent, with half a dozen attendants, servants, and a kehann with her. The tent had draping walls, making four rooms. She led them to one with a table on the ground surrounded by lounging chairs and a large free-standing mirror in a corner. The entire room smelled of amber and myrrh. Tzarik remembered the scent well.

"I am curious about you, sabi," Nefiri said to Sybal. "Sit next to me and let us get acquainted."

Sybal gave Tzarik a quick glance, but didn't get a reply before Nefiri pulled her down to sit. Nefiri moved quickly. Her questions were never to be answered. They were ornaments for her fake civility. She was to be obeyed. She was the closest to the magus, the head magi on Bahratt. She saw visions and knew prophetic futures no one else did.

Tzarik led Signar by the arm, keeping him close.

"Last I saw you, Tzarik," Nefiri said with a gentle smile, "you were looking for the comfort of my company, plotting your final days." She met his eyes as her servant poured them tea from a crystal carafe. Her kehann guardian stood close. "I told you to find a purpose." She motioned to Sybal. "Is she the result of that? Now you are on Alika, wearing jade from Xia, and a medallion of passage from Caerwren." Her eyes flitted to each item as she spoke. "By Krishvu, you have traveled far and wide." She looked honestly intrigued and impressed. At one point, he would have thought her praise valuable.

"Can you get us to see the Dynast Pharaoh or not?" Tzarik asked. The less time he had to spend under Nefiri's tent, the better.

"The Dynast Pharaoh?" Nefiri asked. "Sokar'Xenoteph, first of his name, long may he reign," she added in a traditional Alikan blessing for the Dynast Pharaoh. "Reaching a little high, aren't you, Tzarik?"

Tzarik's face went stony, impassive. "We have it on good

authority that's where our next hunt lies. I won't tell you more, witch."

Sybal shifted, indicating she'd heard Tzarik holding back.

"I can help you," Nefiri said after a moment. "I was in his court not two weeks ago." She drank the tea slowly, but kept her eyes on him. Then she stood up and moved to a table with the map on it. She studied it before humming. "You have gone far. And brought a piece of Caerwren back with you." She smiled at Signar. "What is he? I feel something in his aura. Something wild."

"He's no concern of yours," Tzarik shot back. He hadn't sat yet, not willing to be vulnerable in her presence. "Tell me why you're here and how you intend to get us into the palace."

The magi smiled again, slowly approaching him. "It's easy for me. But the palace is not fond of Runers. Not the Dynast Pharaoh himself, but those around him hate Runers. The vizier, Nasor, had a brother killed by a Runer." She stopped for a moment, forcing her eyes away from Signar. "Why do you need to speak to the Dynast Pharaoh? The boy king. What is on Alika that interests a Runer such as you, Tzarik?"

"Monsters and death," he quipped. "You know my business."

"Do you ever think about me?" she asked suddenly. She was close behind him now. "The only reason I think about you is because I know how much seeing me upsets you." She smiled and reached around from behind, running her long nails down his throat. "I miss how you always came crawling back to me, wounded, bleeding, desperate." She leaned her face close to his neck.

Tzarik, quick as lightning, seized her wrist and shoved her away. Nefiri smiled, eyes wide with shock. She laughed darkly and stepped away. Her eyes went to Sybal, clearly understanding why Tzarik had pushed her away the moment Sybal's eyes flashed death at her.

"Perhaps we could prophesy together tonight," she said, eyes locked on Sybal, but speaking to Tzarik.

"Fjaen," Signar snarled softly, glaring at Nefiri.

Tzarik started at the Caerwren word. It meant demon, or monster. He prayed Nefiri might not know that. But the magi laughed gently.

"Kasamar," she called to her kehann. "Take Tzarik to the stables. Let him pick a third horse and have it saddled. They will leave at sunrise."

The kehann, Kasamar, marched forward, motioning toward him. Tzarik quickly glanced at Signar, then Sybal. She gave him a trusting look, nodding so minutely that the others didn't catch it. She told him with that look that she'd take care of them. Tzarik begrudgingly let the kehann lead him out of the elaborate tent.

SYBAL WATCHED her mentor leave and felt every muscle in Signar's body tense next to her. He gave a small whine like an abandoned dog and looked around, nervous.

"Now," Nefiri said with a smile. She floated onto the cushions, elegantly seating herself across from Sybal. "Tell me your story, sabi. Not even in my dreams have I seen a woman Runer." She shook her head, looking impressed. "Astounding. And no doubt terrifying. What a world you must inhabit."

"It was," Sybal said quickly. She felt if she just told the magi what she wanted to know, she'd trade stories, help them get the information they wanted. "At first. Well, no, not at first. I was too bold and foolish to know the dangerous life I'd chosen. It wasn't until the fall of Ala'Nar that my choices became real to me."

"I heard," the magi said gently. "Terrible, what happened to the city."

"But Tzarik..." Thinking about him eased her discomfort and

almost made her smile. "He's been strong for me. Struggled with me."

"He is wonderful at surviving," Nefiri offered.

This piqued Sybal's curiosity. "You seem to know him well. From long ago." She scanned the magi. She didn't look much older than Tzarik, but then again, the magic of the magi was mysterious to her. Dark. "You knew him before…"

"Before he was a Runer? Yes," Nefiri said with a condescending smile. "When he was just a boy. Probably not much older than…" She nodded to Signar. "Who is this boy he's picked up? Tzarik never seemed like the type to collect a child."

"He's not a child," Sybal replied, hoping to dissuade the magi. "Tell me how you met Tzarik."

At this, Nefiri smiled darkly and giggled through her nose. "I see quite clearly what you are to each other, sabi. He is not your Runer master, and you are not his apprentice."

"He is," she cut in. Her mouth went dry. "He trained me."

"I'm sure he did." Nefiri poured herself more tea. "I see the love in your eyes. In his. How perverse."

This made Sybal's blood boil. Beside her, Signar gently touched her arm, steadying her. He had sensed her mounting hate for the woman. She thanked the boy in her mind, also surprised by his initiation and calm demeanor.

"Have you lain with him?" Nefiri asked simply, taking a sip of tea.

Sybal sputtered. She suddenly wanted to leap up and flee the tent. She hadn't been a proper lady in high caste company for some time, but she felt even among the savage world of Runers that the question was out of line.

Nefiri smiled and nodded. "Did he tell you I was his first?"

What was this woman trying to do to her? Sybal started to lose control of herself, her rage, confusion, and hot temper flaring up. She thought of her Northican blood now that she'd seen her people. She imagined wielding a mighty axe and severing Nefiri's neck. She'd strike so hard, the magi's gilded head would spin, flying yards away.

"He mentioned you," she whispered, forcing the quiver in her voice down.

The magi grinned. "Virgin flesh makes for the most vivid prophecies."

Sybal's heart stopped. She knew how the magi prophesied. "What?" she stammered, lips numb. The world dropped out from under her. Tzarik had told her bits of the story, just enough for her to understand. "The ritual for Azar? Before Tzarik was runed?" Her stomach turned. "Tzarik..." She almost vomited, covering her mouth. "He was fifteen," she hissed, hoping she'd misunderstood, but condemning the woman at the same time.

The darkest smirk overtook Nefiri's face over her tea cup, then. "He was."

Unconsciously, Sybal fumbled for Signar's hand in the maze of cushions under the table, out of Nefiri's line of sight. He slipped his hand into hers and gripped it tightly. The boy's instincts were strong, and at this moment, she was grateful for them. She squeezed his hand hard, and he reciprocated. She couldn't imagine someone as twisted and somehow beautiful as Nefiri with a boy of Signar's age. Then cutting open his chest to get to his heart in a savage ritual. Tears drowned her eyes, blurring her vision. She dared not blink and let them fall, letting Nefiri see her story had the desired effect.

So that was what Tzarik had thought of the first time they'd made love. When she met the magi's eyes again, she saw written on Nefiri's every feature the glee she felt at making Sybal uncomfortable.

Sybal swallowed and cleared her throat. She had to maintain a stony face, not let the magi get under her skin. "You've been in the pharaoh's court?" she asked instead. To her shock, her voice came steady, strong.

The magi's glee faded a little. "Yes. I had been staying at the embassy there just outside the palace. A word from me and you could take my rooms while I am away in Yenka. Then you need only to send a message to the vizier that the embassy wishes to have an audience with the Hawk King. They will take you to him promptly."

The Runer finally met the magi's eyes. All the teasing cruelty had faded from her face. Sybal realized she had passed the test. Nefiri had wanted to enrage her, to see if she'd lash out. But she hadn't. At last, she was able to control herself and play the game. Pride filled her. She rubbed her thumb over the back of Signar's hand where they still gripped one another, letting him know she was all right now. He didn't let go.

"I may have another piece of information for you," Nefiri said, all playfulness gone. She turned rigid, back to her professional temple demeanor. When Sybal didn't ask, she added, "But I want something in exchange for it."

"We have some money," Sybal offered.

The magi shook her head and sat up. Her eyes locked on to Signar. "I don't know what he is, but I feel the magic in him." Her eyes turned to those of a huntress. "Let me prophesy with him tonight and—"

"Damn you!" Sybal cut in, shooting to her feet. She reached down and yanked Signar up, gripping him close and tight. "May every god damn you!"

She whirled around, fleeing for the exit. She expected the magi to run after her, call her servants to stop her, but no such cry came. Sybal hauled Signar out, apologizing to him over and over, tears cascading down her face. Outside, the sun blinded her. She cast around, but had no idea which direction the stable tent would be, so she marched towards the way they'd come in. She let herself weep audibly. For Tzarik. For the boy he'd been and the tortures he'd endured. She understood now. And the magi bitch had had the nerve to ask to use Signar just as horridly.

Sybal doubled over, sobbing into the desert evening. She let her emotions wash over her, cleansing her one last time.

Strong arms gripped her and pulled her into an embrace. They wrapped around her shoulders tightly, holding her steady. The body that held her was tall. Not Tzarik. Realizing Signar was hugging her, her heart broke again, and she reciprocated, wrapping her arms around his middle and burying her face into him. She didn't deserve his mercy. Not after how she'd treated him, how she'd attacked him on the mountain. He would be a kind and merciful Reks. Perhaps too much so. As he held her, she regretted every harsh word she'd said to him, every blow she landed on him, and every scar she'd given him.

A few worried travelers watched them, curious and afraid of the weeping they'd heard. Signar's hand rested against her head while she gathered her breath. Once she controlled herself again, she pulled away. He was so tall that she had to look up at him. It was a strange sensation, looking up at someone.

His emerald eyes looked at her with sympathy. And...gratitude? Had he understood? She hoped not, but there was little chance of that. The boy understood more than she thought.

"Are you all right?" Tzarik called, running up to them. Their horses and the additional one came trotting up behind him.

Sybal nodded. "I'm sorry. We're fine." She took in the gift horse. It was tall, thick with muscle, and had a golden coat with a white mane and tail. Tzarik had picked it just for Signar.

Looking concerned still, Tzarik held up a thick piece of parchment with a red seal. "A letter of introduction for the embassy," he said. "We will stay there and be able to see the pharaoh as soon as we ask."

Shaken, Sybal took the letter and opened it. It was written in a spidery yet elegant hand. The words were very formal and short, asking that the bearers of the letter—which she specified were a Runer, a woman Runer, and a boy from Caerwren—should be allowed to stay in her rooms adjoining the palace until her return, and they should be treated no different from the visiting magi.

"Why?" Sybal asked, breathless from surprise. "What did you promise her?"

Confused, Tzarik shook his head. "Nothing. She gave it to me when I came back. She said you went out ahead."

Not convinced that the magi had undergone a moral transformation in the minute between gloating about what she'd done to Tzarik as a boy and him finding her, she cautiously folded the letter and handed it back to him. "That gets us a little closer. Let's hurry to try to reach the embassy before the week is too old."

She mounted her horse and watched Tzarik coax a very wary Signar onto his. It took several minutes, but eventually, the three of them rode towards the Dynast Palace, closer to Sharar than they'd been in some time.

Chapter 14

Power in the Blood

Tarkan heard Ashkan exclaim when he reemerged from the Deep into their temple hideout. He appeared in a flash of black and green. The smattering of souls he'd used to soar across the land screamed and moaned, vanishing into the ether. Ashkan stood before him, face paler than usual, mouth agape. Tarkan smiled, knowing the power he commanded over dead souls frightened the Apostle. The hissing and cries of the damned dissipated into the halls of the Palace of Apostles in Makan Alu'Ekmet. He waited a moment; the thrill of being volitant left his head spinning a little.

"You returned sooner than expected," Ashkan noted, following Tarkan out.

"Traveling with the souls inside the Deep is quick," he mused. "But we must prepare to leave on foot. Raise the creatures and fill a wagon with bodies. I must cover myself." He went about, pilfering black cotton from the dead in any form. Unlike Ashkan, he had to wrap every part of his Scriven skin to hide it.

"Where are we to travel?" Ashkan asked before he moved.

Tarkan stopped for a minute to think. "East. Towards the shores that face Xia."

Ashkan made a shocked grunting sound. "Do you expect us to travel by boat to the east?"

"No," Tarkan shot back. "But travelers from the east will take the river caravans down to Mysir."

Understanding, the Apostle asked, "What kind of traveler are we looking for?"

"Masahk," Tarkan replied.

"One of your theories, your experiments?" Ashkan asked. He approached Tarkan and aided in cutting the fabric into strips, beginning to wrap his left arm entirely to hide every mark.

Tarkan smiled and hummed. "On Caerwren, I drank the blood of a Runer. I was desperate for any strength."

"A risk," the Apostle reminded him.

"Yes. But I felt the blood in me. It was foul, and burned and cut as I drank it. But it gave me strength. I saw as Runers do, acquired their instincts." He thought back, trying hard not to live in the memories too much. "The Runer blood protected me in the Deep that time, I am sure of it."

Ashkan slowed his work for only a moment as understanding dawned. "Masahk each have a magical gift, given by their god. This is what you seek by consuming their blood. Taking their power into you by their blood."

"Yes," the Necro'Khan replied passionately. "If I am able to keep Masahk blood with me—more than one sentient's blood—I will have more power to match Sharar. We can let out their blood until they are within an inch from death, and their immortality will sustain them long enough to heal. They will not die. I have no fear of possession." He smiled, turning his face up to the sky. "I will have infinite abilities at my disposal."

Finishing the wrappings, Ashkan stepped back. "Never has there been a Necro'Khan such as you, Tarkan."

The groveling didn't become Ashkan, but his family had never had strong wills. There had only ever been three Necro'Khans before him in the history of the map. Like the three sorcerers that had deceived sentient kind along with them. But the Apostle was right. Tarkan had paid his dues to reach for the crown that belonged to him.

"And Sharar?" Ashkan asked.

Tarkan didn't care what the scholar did in the week it would take him to test his experiment. "He had a chance to take me today, and he didn't. He fears what he does not know, the scholarly fool. He does not know what I can do, so he did not try to hold me there. Let him play diplomacy with the pharaoh. When we return, he will understand how much he should fear me."

ⵣ

THE FAMILIAR MODE of travel brought every memory back to Tarkan threefold. His thin boots sinking into the sand with every step reminded him of the century of travel he had behind him. The old wagon, painted black with the ash of burned dead, creaked and rumbled. The second set of footfalls was not familiar, though. Ashkan had a long, wide stride, and his breathing was quiet, hidden behind the desert wind. More than once, Tarkan fell into melancholy memories, tempted to look back. But he knew he'd not see her there.

She was gone.

No; this time, he traveled alone.

Before Zeva, he'd walked the desert sands with Shiva, his last apprentice and Apostle. Ashkan and his wife, Elahel—traitors at the time in House Nashira—had joined them. Tarkan had walked with his three Apostles for sixty years before Zeva. He'd lived a hundred and nine long years without her in his life. But those years were almost forgotten, swallowed up by the nearly fourteen years he'd spent with her. The other years meant nothing when compared to the few he'd had with her. That was the time of his life he'd remember forever.

"Do you remember Zeva?" Tarkan asked Ashkan as they left the sparse jungle patches around the main city. They didn't sleep, walking through the night. They'd consume soon, restoring their strength.

Ashkan had been walking behind Tarkan out of respect, but now he strode abreast with him to answer his question. "Better than I remember Shiva," he replied. "I think in her heart Shiva was jealous of the girl. It might have been what drove her to part from us and act the way she did."

That *had* been why she left. She'd tried to excuse her parting from their small tribe, but Tarkan knew the truth. Shiva had left perhaps six months after Tarkan had taken Zeva from her family. The morning after Shiva left, Zeva, only five years old, had been overcome with nightmares. She'd ran to Tarkan in the night, weeping and screaming. He'd given up hope before that she'd ever not be afraid of him and his tribe. Before, she'd been terrified of the necromancers, weeping piteously every day.

"Elahel thought Zeva'd die of thirst from all her crying," Ashkan remembered. "She was right to be terrified of us."

Of course she was. Zeva had had powerful instincts. Her kind nature and empathy had opened her up to the true feelings and intentions of everyone around her. She'd understood more than she'd ever let on. That was why she'd apologized when Shiva had left. But at last, Zeva had overcome her fear and bonded with Tarkan.

He closed his eyes, remembering that night. They'd been still as statues around a camp fire. They'd been running from a pack of bounty hunters who had recognized Ashkan in the city as the necromancer who had cursed many people over the last ten years. Ashkan had cursed far too much, which was often the reason for their constant fleeing. That night, Tarkan had been standing watch, surrounded by the risen, eyes peeled for the bounty hunters. When Zeva had begun to wail, Shiva had cursed loudly, saying the child would draw every hunter to them. Tarkan hadn't had time to argue back before the girl had shot out of her blankets near the fire and run to him. He'd knelt on a strange new instinct so she could fly into his arms. And she had, wrapping her tiny hands around his neck and burying her head into his shoulder. She'd blubbered about her nightmare, not making any sense. But it hadn't mattered to Tarkan. He'd held her close for the first time, comforting her into silence. She'd wrapped her tiny legs around his middle when he'd picked her up and eventually calmed, but still clung to him, head on his shoulder.

Tarkan moaned as something in his chest ached. A sharp pain stabbed his red diamond heart. The pain came so sudden and strong that he gasped, pressing his hand into his chest, doubling over. He half expected his heart to thud against his hand, since that's where the pain came from. It didn't. The ache prolonged into a sharp cramp. Confused, he breathed, trying to release the tension.

"What's happening?" Ashkan asked, coming to his side.

"My heart," Tarkan said, wincing. It shouldn't be feeling pain. It shouldn't feel anything. It was dead, hardened to diamond. Why had it suddenly pained him, like it was trying to beat against the impenetrable shell?

The ache subsided and he straightened up, pushing Ashkan away.

Two days passed as they traveled from the main settlements and cities of Gypsu, until they reached the base of a small, sandy mountain. There, they passed caravans coming west from the sea. The travelers meandered in small groups south towards the river.

Some continued east to Gypsu. The necromancers paused on a dune and watched the travelers.

"We want to find the ones who break off from the others," Ashkan said, studying the herd. "Something we can take quickly, silently."

Tarkan ran his eyes over all the potential victims. He looked for the obvious signs of Masahk sentients. Even a half-Masahk would do.

"We could take the river down to Mysir," Ashkan added. "The Masahk slave villages there would have more than enough for you."

"Also many witnesses," Tarkan hissed. "Alika is not as ignorant of necromancers as Al'Myrah. They would know us on sight." He half-heartedly gestured to the black wagon. "I'd rather not fight my way out."

His eyes caught a small, mishmash tribe of Masahk and humans break from the larger caravan. They led two great draft horses lashed to a vardo towards a little worn path that weaved over a more open part of the desert. It was late, so Tarkan wondered if the small tribe knew of an oasis on the path to stop at. He nodded towards them, flicking his wrist for Ashkan to follow him. Their undead mounts—two griffins—pulled the wagon at his bidding.

Their wagon lumbered over the uneven ground, but kept a good distance from the group of travelers. Even from far away, Tarkan heard a lady bard singing to them as they marched. Every line or so, the others chimed in with a ruckus call back, singing with her. They had no fear. They must come to this part of Alika a lot.

As he'd guessed, the travelers stopped their vardo just outside a perfectly circular oasis surrounded on one side by rocks and elegant palms. One of the travelers exclaimed that the fig tree was still there and in bloom. Tarkan stopped his wagon atop a dune and kicked at the sand. It was fresh from a day of wind, loose, and would be easy for the risen to move underneath. He'd not been able to hide his risen on Caerwren like he could on Al'Myrah and Alika, thanks to the soft, shifting sands. He signaled Ashkan to begin his spell, since the Apostle needed more time than he did to raise the dead.

Once Ashkan's risen had clambered out of the wagon and were standing, Tarkan waved his hand wordlessly, raising the other half. The risen followed his thoughts, burrowing into the sand and moving towards the camp. The sands were loose, but it would still take them a moment to reach the camp.

"Stay," Tarkan ordered Ashkan. Consuming an entire waterskin of blood, he opened the Deep—the blood he'd just consumed vaporizing inside him—and walked inside to approach the travelers in the spirit world.

On Alika, the Deep burned red. The sands and sky almost blinded him with their fiery shapes and shadows. Everything sentient-made vanished. His own body, being flesh, did not glow in the Deep like his soul would have. He glanced back and recognized Ashkan among the standing risen. Ashkan's bones appeared under his ghostly shape. The Bone-Scriven hid the scriptures under their skin, chiseled onto their very bones. The words appeared fiery green in the Deep. His eyes, green outside the Deep though they were, blazed brighter here.

Turning back to the travelers, he approached them, invisible on this side of the barrier. The Masahk stood out, their spirits glowing golden, with dust-like orbs glittering around them. The others were simple white ghosts. Mortals. He watched the spirits move, not sure what tasks they did around their camp. The bard continued to sing while the others set up. There were four of them: two Masahk and two mortals. One Masahk had fox-like qualities, and the other Tarkan could not quite place. A badger, perhaps?

Satisfied, he turned and walked back to Ashkan, who was concentrating on his spell. Tarkan slipped out of the Deep, appearing next to his Apostle.

"One made fire," Ashkan said, his eyes blood red as he cast. "An elemental gift."

"It doesn't matter for now," Tarkan offered. "I only need to know if it will work. Make the risen attack."

At his command, Ashkan spread his fingers wide, palms up. He slowly raised his hands, blood-red eyes unfocused. Tarkan took in Ashkan's shaking hands as the blood slowly leaked from him in thin, red rivulets, vanishing into the dark wind. He'd been that weak once. Not long ago. But never again.

Tarkan turned his attention back to the travelers, who screamed for only a moment as the risen slew the mortals and wounded the Masahk. Tarkan marched towards them, unafraid. Ashkan had been right, and one Masahk hurled fired at the risen, trying to fend them off. He cried out when the bard fell to a risen sword. With the two mortals down, Tarkan commanded the risen to subdue the Masahk before he entered the firelight.

The Masahk's eyes widened in terror when they saw him, swathed in black, blue eyes glowing.

"Death fiend," the one with animal traits he could not place spat at him. He opened his mouth to keep talking, but Tarkan ordered a risen to cut his throat.

The fox-like Masahk cried in horror at the callous, quick execution. "Why?" he begged, struggling against the risen that held his arms behind him.

Tarkan ignored his blubbering, catching the red-gold blood of the Masahk in his hand. He tipped it between his lips, splashing most of it down his neck. The fox-like Masahk moaned loudly in disgust, tears cutting tracks down his face.

The Necro'Khan waited, eyes closed. The warm, golden blood shot through him. He felt it ignite a fire down his throat, into his gut, and out to his fingers. He opened his eyes and a quick blaze ignited, blinding him before it vanished. He gasped, feeling the fire in his veins. Tarkan held his hand out, reaching into the blood he'd consumed. Heat waves rippled over his palm before a small burst of flame, like a large candle, appeared there. He gasped in shock, holding the flame like he'd held a soul before.

Looking past the flame at the stunned Masahk, he smiled. "There is power in your blood. More than just your immortality. It is yours no longer."

"What are you?" the Masahk gasped, more horrified now than before. "How did you take his gift? The fire belongs to him!"

"It did," Tarkan mused. He made a motion to toss the fire and a small arc of flames burst from his hand. Shaken, he stumbled back, extinguishing it immediately. He laughed at his own surprise. After that, he felt the blood dissipate. He'd not drank much, so this didn't disappoint him. But now he knew.

He stepped away, signaling his risen to finish off the fiery Masahk.

"The other?" Ashkan asked once he made it back to the wagon.

"Take him with us," Tarkan ordered, still reveling in the heat from the blaze he'd created. "We need living flesh to consume for some time, and he won't die as easily as a mortal."

Chapter 15

---◇---

The Halls of History

Sharar wanted to return to the Dynast Palace. Amir returned from a hunt, a fresh scar on the left side of his jaw from his ear to his chin. Sharar let him rest in a room set aside for him on his estate. He prodded the Runer about his hunt, curious about what he'd been paid to dispatch, but Amir never cared to discuss his battles. So Sharar contented himself with rifling through the Runer's saddlebags while he slept. He found the black box all Runers carried and discovered Amir's newly stocked with bottles of fresh sulfates.

"Damn. If only he'd speak," Sharar mumbled as he put the Runer's things back.

There were nine ingredients to the sulfates, and Sharar knew seven of them. Mostly poisonous minerals and tinctures. He'd never been able to deduce how the men with the vile concoction in their veins had lived longer than a few days.

"Something else must keep them alive," he mused over and over to himself. And the ingredients required a hunt, whatever they were. And Amir came back exhausted, wounded, and shaken. However, the ingredients had been gathered; at least Sharar knew they were worth the trials to get them.

He'd asked Amir on separate occasions to tell him the ingredients, but the Runer was stubborn and silent when he wanted to be. But that was what he liked about Amir; he was quiet and meek at times, but had a will of iron and an undying loyalty to his fellow Runers. Sharar had thought about using a wish to get the knowledge of the sulfates, but—especially now—he couldn't waste the djinn's power like that.

Once Amir had regained his strength, Sharar set out with his Runer to Mysir to once again spend time with the young Pharaoh. He knew now where he had to go to get the answers he sought. The Halls of History were, of course, the place to start, but now he had a date to track down.

The Dynast Palace lay quieter than last time. No people clamored for their Pharaoh's attention, no workers streamed in and out of the structures being built. The palace guard led Sharar and Amir in, knowing them, and took them to an open balcony overlooking the gardens.

"Is the Hawk King not in court?" Sharar asked the guard, who turned to leave.

"Not today, sira," the guard replied. "Our Pharaoh desired a day of rest and gave the slaves an edict to remain at home."

"And will we see him today?" the scholar pressed.

"You will when I say you will," the deep voice of the vizier answered for the guard. The jackal-like Masahk entered slowly, his lupin claws clicking on the golden floor.

Sharar sighed deeply, not hiding his dislike for the vizier. "Nasor," he said, giving the slightest bow of his head he could manage.

"Abigor," Nasor replied, "back so soon? What could possibly bring you back to the Dynast palace twice in a single month?"

"I care about our Pharaoh's well-being," Sharar replied with a genial smile. "He's seemed tired of late. Exhausted, even. I'm here to lend my support and council. If only I could speak with him alone."

Nasor gave a gentle grunt, seeing through Sharar's facade. "Gilded words from a foreigner," he said, pacing a circle around Sharar and Amir.

The metal of his gold and blue staff clanged loudly with every other step he took. The shiny blue silk of his cape made deep fluttering sounds as he whipped it around.

"And your Runer," Nasor grumbled. "I don't know why you continue to defy me, Sharar. I said to leave your animals outside the palace walls."

"I've not done anything to you," Amir said with contempt.

"Do not speak directly to me," Nasor hissed back. He marched up to Amir like he might strike him. When the Runer held his ground, the Masahk stopped.

"I grow tired of your barbaric games, vizier," Sharar sighed, running a finger over his manicured beard.

"Have you?" The jackal reached a hand toward Amir, sharp black nails on the end. He gripped the Runer's face, forcing his new scar into the light. Amir grunted but didn't fight.

"Getting into trouble, scholar? Not taking care of *your things*." Nasor clicked his tongue.

"From a hunt," Amir growled, answering for the scar.

Nasor snapped his claws back. He swung his hand, backhanding Amir across his scarred face. Sharar took two quick steps forward, but stopped himself. Amir inhaled sharply from the shock, hand over his wound. He slowly turned back to face them. White blood leaked between his honey-colored fingers. Sharar saw the vein on Amir's neck throbbing, showing his restraint. He appreciated the Runer's strong will. If he had the chance, he'd let

Amir kill the vizier. When the time came. The Runer deserved that much.

"Enough of this show of power, vizier," Sharar barked. "Amir is my colleague and will be treated with respect." He calmed himself and held his head higher. "Your abuse displays a weakness I don't think you understand you are showing. You're a pathetic man."

Nasor glared at Sharar.

"Now," the scholar said, "take me to Sokar."

⁊

NASOR LED them down a set of open air stairs from the balcony into the expansive gardens below. Amir hung far back, eyes downcast. The gardens spanned four great sections around the Dynast Palace, one on each corner, and acted as supplemental supplies of fruits, herbs, honey, and other such crops, as well as elegant meeting places for dignitaries. They also shaded the water supplies that bubbled up from a spring beneath the palace.

Sokar sat under a patch of shady palms around an ivory table. A servant fanned him, and he wore only a simple white garment around his middle, showing his body's light, colorful feathering. He sat across from a magi draped in red and gold who spoke seriously to him. Sharar recognized her from the court before. Sokar looked tired, leaning his elbow onto the chair back, his head tilted onto his palm. When he saw Sharar, his eyes brightened.

"Ah, Abigor, I am so pleased to see you," he said, louder than necessary. He stood up and came to Sharar, taking his hand and pulling him to the table. "This bewitching ambassador from Bahratt has just been telling me that the king of Jarabu has adopted a son and named him heir. She was saying something very fascinating about intercontinental alliances and gold. *My* gold, of course."

Sharar glanced at the magi. Her golden eyes flicked from Sokar to him quickly. "Nothing quite that simple, Your Eminence." She stood up to face Sharar. She was tall for a woman, had broad shoulders, and black hair clasped in gold that hung all the way to her knees; a testament to how long she'd been in her profession. "They call me Nefiri," she said.

Sharar gave her a proper bow, bending at the waist to let her know he respected her. "Abigor Sharar, at your humble service. This is my Runer, Amir."

The magi, Nefiri, smiled at Sharar and gave Amir a second look before quickly averting her eyes. "Young Sokar has spoken about you. Perhaps you can convince him that international relations are important at a time like this."

"At a time like this?" Sharar asked for clarification. "You are widely traveled, it seems. Is something amiss in Bahratt that is Alika's business?"

Nefiri pressed her red lips together hard under her veil, gathering her patience. "Sira, I hear from your accent you are Al'Myrahn. How can you not know that your own sultana has started the search for a certain...threat that has recently appeared on the map?"

"That does sound serious, Your Eminence," he said with a playful smile to Sokar. "And she's right: the solution is your country's gold mines."

The magi cursed, planting her palms hard on the table. "I see I am out-manned now. Sokar." She looked at the Pharaoh like she might when scolding a child. "Maharaja Saksham has adopted a young man as his heir. His son died in their palace not four years ago. Attacked by a death fiend."

Sokar sighed and looked up at Sharar. "Is death not a part of our faith?"

Nefiri nodded and looked away. "The religious war Bahratt and Alika had twenty-two years ago should not rise again, no matter our differences. Maharaja Saksham wrote the treaty that binds

Alika to Bahratt still. You must understand, Your Eminence. Hatal is not far from your shores, where the sultana fear-mongers her own people. Afraid of this necromancer."

Sokar stood up and beckoned Sharar to his side while the magi took the other side. "Magi, I want to leave my mark on my dynasty. My father was taken before he could."

"Does the treaty not count?" Nefiri cut in, aghast.

Sokar went on, ignoring her. "Should another in our line die thusly, one of the lower pharaohs—Shepteth from Zhigo or even damned Nasphiri from Gypsu—will put their offspring on my throne. My dynasty has held the ruby throne for many lifetimes. I know the temple is afraid our dynasty is growing weak. They hold nearly more power than I over my people. Priests of Krah and Ashmalia hover at my doors every day to remind me. I cannot be the link that breaks our mighty chain."

Sharar noticed the magi looking eager now. "I have spoken with the rajas of Bahratt. I know Maharaja Saksham will agree with them and the Tashid temple. We must be ready if Al'Myrah falls to fear. The three of us—Alika, Bahratt, and Al'Myrah—are the hub of the map, Eminence. The center of the civilized world. It is our duty to protect the map."

Sharar stopped walking, frowning at the magi, not believing what he'd heard. "You think Al'Myrah will be the one to succumb to fear? What do you anticipate my country will do if this necromancer grows his power?"

Nefiri smiled condescendingly at Sharar. "I expect the sultana to make a rash decision. She plotted once to kill Kalil, her first husband, idiot boy though he is. Once the truth of his death came out, that would send a message to your people that she is afraid. She has ideals of beating the necromancer to her country, destroying it before he can."

He'd not heard of such a plot, but that didn't mean it wasn't plausible. He often thought the sultana was too hot-headed. She made pacts with religious orders, dealt too much in international trade, and had even once inquired about the Rhostranan slave trade, even though such practices were outlawed on Al'Myrah.

"Let him seek council, magi," Sharar said at length. "Leave him to his vizier, his temple priests, and the kehann. These matters cannot be decided upon when he is alone. Unless," Sharar glanced around in mock observance, "that's why you chose to approach today."

At this, even Nasor arched a dark brow at the magi.

"I do not appreciate your insinuations, sira," she shot back, her golden eyes narrowing dangerously. But she stopped herself before saying something she'd regret. "Sokar, I have given up my quarters to visitors," she said with finality.

Sokar sighed and looked away.

Nefiri ignored his immature reaction. "I will be in Yenka for some time and have given them access to the embassy."

"Why?" Sokar moaned. "I cannot abide more visitors here on diplomatic missions."

"They are not," Nefiri said simply. "You will find them fascinating, Your Eminence." She stopped following the men around the garden and prepared to leave out a side gate. "They are Al'Myrahn —" She suddenly stopped. Sharar caught her eyes flick to him. "Al'Myrahn visitors," she finished with far less gusto.

"That is fascinating," Sokar replied, rolling his eyes. "But if you'll excuse me, I promised Abigor I'd show him the Halls of History."

"Great Pharaoh—" she started again.

"That will do," Nasor butted in with a deep growl. He inserted himself between the magi and the Pharaoh.

"I will think on what you've said," Sokar said, defeated. "I will request your company again soon."

Satisfied, Nefiri bowed, kept her eyes on the ground, and left the gardens. Sharar let the young man lead them into the palace and down several passageways before speaking.

"That does sound serious, Your Eminence," Sharar offered. "Perhaps I am concerned as an Al'Myrahn."

"I suppose," Sokar replied. "Nasor has said as much. The high priests of the temple are more wary, as are the kehann."

"It would be them in battle," Nasor offered. The kehann were the temple's warriors. Theirs would be the blood that dampened another religious war with Bahratt.

"Nasor," Sokar said dully, "go back to your scrolls and dignitaries. Please."

The vizier glared hard at Sharar and Amir before bowing to his Pharaoh and turning, disappearing with a wide swish of his blue cape.

"Enough politics," Sharar sighed. "Show me the year 687 on these walls."

"But Abigor," Sokar teased, "it's only 313."

He smiled, allowing the childish joke. "Pre-Cradle," he added. The Alikan calendar had started over when the Cradle was created 313 years ago. Other map-altering events had taken place on Al'Myrah at the same time, putting Alika, Bahratt, and Al'Myrah on the same calendar. Each continent used to follow their own years. Now, the unity helped bring them together.

"Why that year?" Sokar asked.

The three of them walked through the academic wing of the palace to the open air transept that led to the great library. Every scribe's scroll and every historical event were stored there. Past the rooms filled with scribes and scholars, they entered the darker places where the histories decorated the walls in bright, colorful images.

"I recently spoke with a friend who mentioned his..." Sharar stopped. He couldn't say father, even though it was true. Tarkan had mentioned Ishmael and, according to his research, the last

Necro'Khan had ascended one thousand years ago, when Acenoth IV was on the throne. "A friend mentioned his ancestor," he said instead. "During Acenoth IV's reign."

The Dynast Pharaoh led the Runer and the scholar down deep, dark halls. He took a torch from a sconce in a room full of scribes before going into the black labyrinth. "I don't know why you make me walk this maze with you, Abigor," Sokar said. "I studied enough as a child."

"There is no such thing as studying enough," Sharar said genially as Sokar led them down the left side of the Halls. "Never stop learning, Your Eminence."

The three of them walked on for some time. The images on the walls covered every inch of stone. The deeper they went, the more etchings and paintings there were. The ceiling rose easily twenty-five feet up. Every inch of the wall was covered over in faded history. Soon, the ceiling became covered, and it came lower, the older Alikans not stacking the Halls as high.

"650, 660, 670," Sokar counted off as they passed narrower halls on the side. He stopped and turned one last corner, holding his torch aloft to light a few old oil lamps along the walls. "687," he announced. "One thousand years ago."

Sharar had lost count of the turns, and the pressure in his head told him they were deep underground. "Incredible," he mused. "At this time, Al'Myrah brought the written word to Alika."

"And now we use your language," Sokar replied with a smile. "But we still write our histories in these images." He smiled fondly at his country's unique art style.

"What is this?" Amir asked. He whispered unintentionally, in awe of the sight before them.

The scholar backed away to take in the long wall. "They call it the Battle of the Promise, or the Battle of the Plagues."

Amir didn't react, showing he had never heard of the event.

Sharar expected this. He liked the Runer for his strong will and powerful frame, but he was quite as ignorant as all the others.

"It was a battle led by Pharaoh Acenoth IV," Sharar began.

He walked a few steps away and pointed to an etching with faded paint. A Masahk in gold armor wore a helmet much like Sokar did when he met with his audience, only this one was in the shape of a jackal. However, huge wings spread out behind him. He held a great staff with a scythe on the end. The figure faced an army flocking towards him. "An unkillable army flooded Alika. Acenoth couldn't stand up to them, and even neighboring countries came to Alika's aid. So many died," he added sadly. "Many thought this immortal host was sent to wipe sentient kind from the map. An apocalypse of sorts."

Amir walked farther down the hall, intrigued by the story now. His keen eyes flitted over the carvings and paint. Sharar followed him, the images showing the progression of the battle. "These men are under the Pharaoh," Amir noted. "Facing the others."

"That is where I am interested," Sharar said, joining Amir in looking at the mysterious army depicted under Acenoth IV. "Acenoth went to the salty spring where the Three Rivers begin and prayed for a miracle. Before the Cradle, the people had to purify the water themselves," he added as an aside, as if giving a lecture. "Acenoth took a host of men—his One Thousand and One—with him. He begged his god of death—Nephron, they call him—for victory over the immortal host, and had every faith that the god would hear him and bless his army. But the One Thousand and One were not as steadfast in their faith. They fled."

Sharar stopped and took a lamp from the wall, leading Amir two more paces down. Sokar followed, enraptured by the way Sharar told the story.

"Alika still stands," Amir reasoned. "They must have overcome their enemies. Masahk are immortal. They stood a good chance."

"In battle," Sokar supplied, "we are as mortal as you. A blade may take our lives, a poison, an illness. Not time."

"Acenoth was gifted a tome for his faith," Sharar went on. "One already in existence. It had been spirited away from—what I am guessing—was Xia. In that book lay the secrets of every beast, creature, and immortal on the map."

"Ah," Amir grunted, understanding now. "You think Nephron gave him the Mahit'Onomicon?"

"I do now." Sharar looked up at an image of the ancient Dynast Pharaoh. His wings were spread wide, and a book hovered over his right hand. He faced a monster.

"What is that?" Amir asked, shaken by the thing Acenoth faced.

The monster was a large, blue, slit-pupiled eye. Black tendrils wreathed it. From behind, four white wings splayed out in a tangle of black tentacles. Somehow, the eye looked like it glared.

"Nephron," Sokar offered. "We no longer worship him, as he brings death. Ashmalia brings life."

"Why don't you worship him?" Amir asked.

"Worshiping death is barbaric," Sokar whispered, taking in the evil eye. "We're wiser now. And we enslaved the people who brought such a god to us. Retribution for a lifetime of darkness."

"With his new power, Acenoth destroyed the risen host." Sharar pointed to a depiction of the jackal-masked Pharaoh, smiting hundreds of small warriors. In the very back of the risen host, a black figure stood, faded. Sharar eyed it. Could that be Ishmael?

"This figure," Sharar said, pointing. "Does he appear again?"

"Here," Amir said from several steps away. "He's holding the book."

Sharar joined his Runer in looking at some faded part of the wall. The paint was thin, almost like someone had scrubbed at it for years. A black-clad figure held a tome, hovering over its poorly painted hands. *So Ishmael had the book,* Sharar thought. His eyes took in the symbols and imagery. He spotted a few that meant eternal life.

"Ishmael had the book," Sharar said to his listening audience, translating the symbols and pictures. "According to this history, it endowed him with eternal life." This sent a little thrill through Sharar. "He was advisor to Acenoth." He stopped when he spotted an image of Ishmael handing the Mahit'Onomicon over to Acenoth. "He left Alika," he mused softly. "He gave Acenoth the book. Look." He pointed excitedly. "See how he now has the scriptures on his flesh?"

Amir hummed in thought. "The necrotic scriptures are copied from the Mahit'Onomicon. Ishmael wrote them on his flesh and took them back to Porsh." The Runer frowned gently. "He must not have put the locking script on his heart."

"He wouldn't, not yet," Sharar mused, now following Ishmael's journey. "He would have taken the scriptures home, gathered willing Apostles. He would have known how to make Scriven and Apostles from the scriptures and would not have done it to himself yet. He saw himself as the king of necromancy and wanted an heir. He most likely went back to Porsh, started his following, and gathered necromancers to himself. Then, when he was ready, he took a wife from Alika long after Acenoth died. Tarkan and his brother were the harbingers of Porsh's demise."

Sharar stopped for a breath.

"By then, everyone would have known Ishmael as the father of necromancy. He brought it back to the map." He locked his eyes on the small, black figure behind the army in the first image. "He destroyed Porsh for his position as khan."

"But, Abigor," Sokar asked. "He gave up the Mahit'Onomicon. How did he live so long without it?"

Sharar gave a weak smile. "Perhaps once I have the book, I will know. I cannot pretend to understand necromancy."

"Will you become a Scriven when you find the book?" Sokar asked.

"Never," Sharar assured the youth quickly. "I have greater plans."

"And Acenoth?" Amir asked.

"Since his One Thousand and One fled during the Battle of the Promise, he cursed them," Sharar said. "Their bodies would remain whole, even after death. They should never know peace. They were buried under Acenoth's palace in tombs. Alive. Until they fulfilled their purpose, rising and fighting for the one who sits on the throne, they should not pass the river into Ahryu."

"Why does it matter if their bodies are whole?" Amir asked. "Are they not decayed?"

Sharar ignored the Runer's question. He'd not been this far into the Halls before and was closer than ever to finding what he looked for, now that he knew *what* to look for. He stepped away, his strides picking up pace as he scanned the walls.

"It's a curse," Sokar said in Sharar's stead. "We do our best to preserve our dead. Without that preparation, which only comes from the temple and a high priest, you would be a blight on the map. They did not have it."

Amir glanced around. "And the palace is built on that blight?"

"It will be safe to open the tombs only if..." Sharar's words faded in his throat as he found the image he sought: the burial of Acenoth. The Pharaoh lay on a golden sarcophagus, arms crossed over a thick, reddish-black tome. "It will be safe to open the tombs if there is a man who can read the Mahit'Onomicon," he finished in a whisper.

"Open the tomb?" Sokar gasped. "But the curse..."

"Sokar," Sharar said softly, almost endearingly. "Who am I?"

"And he will be known by three signs," Sokar quoted. "The prophets said one of the signs would be the man's ability to tame the monsters and command them with his will." His eyes turned up to Sharar in utter reverence. "And I've found that man. You're right, Sharar."

Amir gave Sharar a look that was part admiration, part disbelief. Amir knew Sharar had acquired the power by a wish. He'd forced the prophecy to come true. There were no gods at work here.

"This could be my mark," the young Pharaoh mused suddenly, eyes wide, raking over the historical images. "I could set them free. The answer was here all along."

"Isn't opening a tomb full of curses a risk?" Amir asked.

Sharar glared silently at his Runer. It had taken Sharar a decade to track the book down. He'd studied more histories than any scholar in his seminary. He had followed Runers, sultans, and had traveled far and wide looking for a hint as to where the book lay. He thought he'd come close in Xia, but the old Wushito fool had led him on. The only thing ShanBao protected was the crypt, and Sharar had no use for that.

"I tracked down Tarkan thinking he'd know," Sharar said, his voice heavy. "He didn't. Every time I thought I was close, it ended in nothing. Not this time, Amir. I will not let the idea of a blight stop me."

"Will you take it?" Amir asked Sharar.

The Masahk answered first. "It will stir my people," he said. "Opening the tomb of the One Thousand and One would bring great fear. It will be difficult to do it in secret, but do it we shall." He turned to Sharar. "Abigor, I have decided you shall have the Mahit'Onomicon, should it rest with Acenoth. You've been by my side all my life. You were there when father was taken from me. If what this magi fears does come to pass, I shall need you by my side once more."

For once, the urge to hurry rushed through Sharar. He'd been slow, methodical up until now. And here the Mahit'Onomicon was, perhaps only a mile from him. He'd bore through the earth himself if it meant holding the book by the next morning. But he couldn't throw away all the progress he'd made in the last decade and a half. And he wanted to see what use Tarkan might bring to him. For now, the Necro'Khan demanded his respect, but soon, he'd have Tarkan trapped under his boot again.

All in good time, he told himself. *And soon. We know now.*

Sharar faced Sokar solemnly. "I will help you make your mark on your dynasty," he promised. "You will surpass even Acenoth once I have the Mahit'Onomicon in my hands."

Sokar's boyish face turned serious. "I must prepare my court and the temple for the excavation," he said. "You understand this will take time?"

Sharar held his temper, trying to match Amir's iron will. "Of course, my friend. I will wait."

"And we must show the people you are the Father of Monsters," he went on.

Sharar wasn't sure how this could be done, so he waited, seeing Sokar's face light up.

"We will use the coliseum," the boy whispered with a twisted grin.

Chapter 16

The Bone-Scriven

Sharar and Amir wrapped themselves in cotton to keep the hot summer sun off the back of their necks as they stood on the docks in Gypsu once again. Sharar surveyed the cargo ship on the docks as the crewmen hauled crate after chest after crate off the ship. A few of his things had finally arrived, and he was eager to get his scientific equipment set up. After all, Tarkan and his Apostle would be returning any day now.

Amir waited in the shade of an awning where arabas were rented out to travelers, messengers sifted through missives that needed to be delivered, and other such workers waited. He leaned against the thick front post, looking bored.

"If you're going to stand there, at least get us a second wagon," Sharar called back to him. "I underestimated the size of some of these chests." He looked back to the ship and finally saw the last of his crates being unloaded. He was about to turn and signal Amir when a familiar face caught his eyes. "Amir," he hissed, flicking his fingers to signal the Runer to follow him.

Sharar ducked into the crowd and approached the small ship. It had every sign of being a pirate vessel, right down to the gilded crewmen on board. They seemed to have come back from a good haul. But the gold and stolen treasure didn't interest Sharar. No, he'd recognized a bright, honey-soaked smile on a particular young man among the pirates. He'd only seen the man once, maybe twice, but he'd left a lasting impression on Sharar.

Standing up to look, the scholar spotted the man he sought. A thin, strikingly handsome man sauntered down the gangplank, a wheel fiddle thrown over one shoulder. Behind him, the captain swore at his back, making rude hand gestures. Finally, the young man turned and made a mocking bow to the captain.

"You are too kind, captain," the man sang brightly. "I owe you my life, as it were. And I shan't forget it."

"If I see you again, you damned peacock, I'll swing you from the highest yardarm on the next ship we take," the captain replied. "Mark my words. I'll kill you if you come back."

"I'd expect nothing less. Don't disappoint me." The young man smiled again, coming up from his bow. He turned and hurried down the plank.

"Amir," Sharar hissed. "Get him and bring him."

Without asking why, the Runer sprang into action. Sharar dashed after him, leaping over cargo to keep an eye on Amir as he bore down on the hapless jongleur. The start of the chase made a few citizens shout at the Runer, cursing him. This drew the jongleur's eyes back behind him. He at first frowned curiously at the running Runer, then his eyes snapped to Sharar's. The scholar didn't need to hear the singer's sudden curse to know he'd recognized him. The young man's eyes snapped from Sharar to Amir, then back again before he broke into a gallop towards the city.

Sharar's breath came in gasps as he tried to keep up with the Runer. The jongleur scampered between two large market stalls and almost vanished, but Amir caught up to him. His prey slipped on the sand, but quickly recovered and dashed to a ladder leading up onto the roofs.

"Don't let him get away!" Sharar shouted to Amir. But he didn't need to tell the Runer.

Amir reached up and seized the man's ankle, pulling him hard. The jongleur cried out as he fell, hitting the rungs on the way down and finally landing hard against the ground. Sharar ran to the pair. Amir flipped the singer over onto his back and pinned his arms hard. The wheel fiddle had cracked and lay in two pieces beside them.

"Help!" the jongleur shouted desperately. "Get off me, Runer scum." He tried to wiggle free, but Amir held him fast. "Gods, you Runers are strong brutes," he panted.

Sharar's lungs burned when he finally stood over Amir and their captive. He glared down at the young man, trying to recall his name. "Vicdan, isn't it?" he asked, gasping. He was delighted when the slightest bit of fear tinted Vicdan's eyes.

"Honored you remember, scholar," Vicdan replied. He struggled against Amir, but couldn't so much as shove the Runer. "What do you want? You cannot possibly have a use for me. I'm not one to discourage the usefulness of any sentient. I believe every one of our gods' creatures has value, even if they cannot see it themselves. But really, what can I possibly do for—"

Amir pressed hard on Vicdan's wrists with a growl, shutting him up.

A small crowd had gathered, curious at the strange sight.

"We've caught the thief," Sharar called to the people looking on. "He's been steeling from me for months. Please, step aside so we may bring him in."

"Lies!" Vicdan cried desperately. "They're kidnapping me and are going to—"

Amir balled his fist and slammed it into the side of Vicdan's head, cracking his skull hard against the stony road. The young man instantly went limp. Amir stood up, grunting in satisfaction.

"Bring him," Sharar ordered, turning back to his cargo.

Amir lifted the jongleur and carried him to the araba he'd been in the middle of paying for. He tossed the unconscious Vicdan into the back with little care and then helped Sharar get his things loaded onto the wagons. The scholar paid both drivers and then slipped into the araba with Amir and their captive.

Once they were on their way, Amir asked, "Who is he?"

Sharar looked at Vicdan's limp frame. A large bruise blossomed under the bronze skin on his face already. He looked pathetic. "He knows Tzarik," he answered simply. "I doubt he knows where they are now, but he'll know something."

Amir looked doubtfully at Vicdan.

SHARAR SHACKLED Vicdan in his dungeon so that he hung from his wrists, his toes just able to reach the cold, stone floor. A thrill shot through him as he looked at his captive. Amir stood back, arms crossed, leaning against the dungeon wall. Sharar took everything but Vicdan's tunic and pants, letting the cold seep into his skin to wake him.

"Does the pain of others bring you pleasure?" Amir asked darkly after a moment.

Sharar heard the judgment in his voice. "It is the best way to understand a living thing," he replied simply. "Eternal agony is a powerful motivator, isn't it, demon?" He addressed this question to his djinn, who loomed off in a corner.

"Do you wish to know my thoughts?" the djinn asked softly.

"Always," Sharar prompted, ready to slap Vicdan into wakefulness.

The djinn's blue eyes trailed up from Vicdan's bare feet to his limp fingers over his head. "Something is amiss about him. There is a power just beneath the surface of his skin."

Intrigued, Sharar said, "We shall soon see what lies under the flesh."

"I caution you," the djinn replied before vanishing into the shadows.

This held Sharar for a moment. He scanned the jongleur up and then down. He had no markings on him. Bore no scar to show where he'd taken a dark oath. He stepped closer and did see a few thin white scars on his forearms. Having been familiar with the marrings on sentient bodies, Sharar saw these scars were less than a year old. He found a definite bite wound on Vicdan's neck as well.

"A few scars," he mumbled, frowning. "Nothing out of the ordinary."

"I'm...insulted," Vicdan moaned, coming to. "Not out of the ordinary? How dare you. I am extraordinary."

Sharar smiled at the bold young man. "My djinn seems to think you harbor a dark secret. I look forward to digging it out of you."

Vicdan struggled against the restraints, straining to get a good foothold on the ground. He moaned in pain and stopped. "My head is splitting," he groaned. "I don't think you've done any real damage, though." He glared over Sharar's shoulder at Amir. His dark eyes flicked back to Sharar. "Go on then, scholar. Tell me what you want. I'm an open book."

"How generous." Sharar leaned back against the wooden table where a myriad of his instruments were laid out, waiting to be whetted with Vicdan's blood. "How fairs our mutual friends?"

"The Runers?" Vicdan asked. He looked offended. "Left me for dead. I hope they rot."

"So you've seen them?"

"Yes. Unlike you, scholar, I go outside every now and then."

This didn't amuse Sharar. A dislike of the young man began to grow. He pushed himself up and approached Vicdan. "Where did they leave you? Al'Myrah?"

"If only," Vicdan sighed. "I couldn't wait to get back to warmer shores."

Sharar raised his brows, intrigued. "Rhostrana?"

Vicdan blanched, realizing his gaffe. "I don't know what good it will do, knowing where they were. As far as I know, they're still on Caerwren. Far out of your reach." He tried to smile smugly, but the pain on the left side of his face made him drop the grin quickly.

"So Tarkan was on Caerwren," Sharar mused out loud. He crossed one arm around his middle, resting his other elbow on it, tapping his chin. "Vasaras. So Tarkan did bring back the lady Runer." He scoffed in admiration. "Amazing. I chose my necro-mancer wisely. Though Tarkan didn't mention it. I suppose he wouldn't."

"They say talking to yourself is a sign of insanity," Vicdan moaned through a smile. He twisted his wrists and lost his footing, sliding to a hang that drew a shudder of pain from him as the metal cut into his wrists. "You made a bad choice of captive, though. They won't come for me, if that's what you're hoping."

He wasn't. He just wanted to know what they had been doing since their run-in on Xia. He clicked his tongue. "Are they on Alika now? Sahir told me they were coming, remember, Amir?"

The Runer nodded.

"They would have come into Gypsu if they came from Moshav," Sharar went on, thinking out loud. "They're close. *So* close!"

Vicdan's face paled and he swallowed. "What can you want with them? You have a Runer already." He nodded to Amir.

Sharar smiled and laughed lightly. "But none like Tzarik, my boy. And now, definitely none like our lady Sybal. I like rare finds, you see." He approached Vicdan again, coming so close he could hear his breathing pick up. "Like you. What is it about you that drew the attention of my djinn?"

The younger man opened his lips, hunting for the right words. He smiled. "I can't say. Maybe he thinks I'm handsome."

"Amir," Sharar called, stepping back. The Runer marched forward.

Vicdan began to panic. "Any savagery is unnecessary, scholar. We are both men of learning, are we not? What do you want me to tell you?"

The Runer approached, taking his runes from around his neck. He held artiah in his palm.

"Oh, no," Vicdan whispered, turning serious. "Not that. Don't, please."

"Don't worry. I won't kill you yet," Sharar promised.

"That's not what I am afraid of." Vicdan gave a weak, nervous grin that was really more of a grimace.

Sharar signaled Amir to go on. The Runer slowly drew the rune before Vicdan, the white runic light glowing brighter the more he drew. Something appeared under Vicdan's skin. Sharar stumbled forward, not sure he'd seen what he thought he did. He came right up behind Amir. The Runer stopped, mouth open and stepping back, still holding the light aloft.

"What the hell?" the Runer asked.

Artiah revealed hidden magic, hidden forms of monsters. The light from the rune splashed over Sharar's captive, illuminating his eyes. Vicdan's eyes had been a soft, dark brown before. But under the rune light, they blazed green. Sharar took a step back, seeing something else appear on Vicdan's face. Green, softly glowing scriptures emerged under his skin. Sharar recognized them. He'd seen them a thousand times on Tarkan's skin.

Breathless, Sharar ripped the jongleur's tunic open. His ribs also glowed with bright green scrawl. Speechless, he took Vicdan's face in his hands and turned his head to see the scriptures around the sockets of his eyes, on his skull, and down his jawbone. Necrotic scriptures covered the man's entire skeleton in glowing green.

"Incredible," Sharar breathed. "Bone-Scriven."

Vicdan grunted, struggling to release himself from Sharar's grasp. "Despite your gentle, callous-less touch, scholar—indicating the soft life in which you must find yourself—I am repulsed by your hands upon my face."

Overcome with a maelstrom of emotions—joy, rage, excitement, anticipation—Sharar ripped his hand away and slapped Vicdan so hard across his face that his own palm stung. He reveled in the cry of shock it drew from his captive. He turned to Amir, grinning wildly, and rubbed his stinging palm.

"A Bone-Scriven necromancer, Amir," he gasped. "The ones Tarkan called traitors. The gods do smile upon me!" He faced Vicdan again, leering. "Check yourself, my boy. You won't be making such jovial comments for long."

The jongleur forced a shaking smile through the tears filling his eyes. As artiah faded, they returned to brown. "I just might. Ask anyone. I'm quite a stubborn ass."

Chapter 17

Sorcerer's Blood

Tarkan stood in the shadows of the courthouse of Gypsu, watching between the great pillars of the temple of Ashmalia. She was the goddess of the moon, healing, and life. Her likeness, a great fowl-like Masahk with long, flowing tail feathers and a crown of plumes on her head, swooped over the entryway to the temple. Her wings spread over where several of her priests knelt in prayer and thanks. The setting sun turned the white marble goddess orange. Ashkan made his way toward Tarkan, through the last of the city's people on their way home from their daily toils. He'd gone to buy himself food, since he was not sustained by the black magic like Tarkan was.

The Necro'Khan missed feeling the mortal hunger, and the relief that came from consuming fresh fruits or an evenly cooked lamb. Now he only consumed living flesh to feed the magic. When Ashkan joined him in the shade of the courthouse, he let his eyes run over the priests inside Ashmalia's temple again.

"What are you looking for?" Ashkan asked around a mouthful of grapes.

"Blood work will thrive under a blood moon," Tarkan replied easily.

"The blood moon was during the summer solstice." Ashkan followed Tarkan's eyes into the temple. "There is a full moon in two weeks."

Tarkan nodded. "If the gods will not heed my needs, I will make them conform to them. I will force the next full moon to be a blood moon to empower my spell for Sharar. By spilling the blood of Ashmalia's priest on her altar—a heretical act—she will turn the moon red in mourning for his blood."

"This is a rite like no other," Ashkan mused.

"By my design," Tarkan agreed. "No spell I cast, no ritual I scribe, will be like any other upon the face of the map." He pushed up from the courthouse wall where he'd been leaning and stealthily weaved his way out of the city back to their wagon. "You will return to Sharar and prepare the grave."

"Grave?" Ashkan asked, close behind.

"For a grave-born to rise, there must be a grave," Tarkan reasoned. "Even a shallow grave will do. Draw the circle of blood and ash and prepare the site for my return."

"Tarkan," Ashkan asked, stopping and taking the Necro'Khan's wrist in his hand to halt him. "Why are you doing this for him? Why try to raise the boy? You cannot bring him back as Sharar imagines."

Tarkan yanked his wrist out of Ashkan's grip. "On the contrary, my Apostle. I will bring the boy back *just* as the scholar imagines."

Ashkan waited, mouth open slightly in shock. "How?"

"I am Necro'Khan. The dead will obey me. I will not simply raise Sharar's boy. He will be more than a risen. He will be an undead, a sentient soul inside a body sustained by the power of blood. Not only will this allow me to grow my power, but I must bide my time while Sharar hunts for the Mahit'Onomicon. I need him to find it." He continued his march to the wagon.

Ashkan kept up with him, matching his stride. "Are you not afraid of him? Of the power he will wield once he's a sorcerer?"

"I anticipate it."

The Apostle stopped, once again taking Tarkan's arm. He spun the Necro'Khan to face him. Tarkan saw in his green eyes that Ashkan finally understood. He grinned darkly.

"You want his blood," Ashkan breathed. "The blood of a sorcerer."

"A Necro'Khan sorcerer." A thrill shot through Tarkan's dead heart. "The most powerful being on the map in all of history. And you will witness this. Once we raise Enoch, you will take me to Elahel."

Ashkan frowned, taking a step back. "For her bones?"

"They are the core I need for my blade of blood." He needed one other key component, but he wasn't going to tell Ashkan he needed Ishmael's heart. Ashkan needn't know the heart of a Necro'Khan would be the key to the blade's power. "You will tell me where you have them hidden."

The Apostle kept his face expressionless. "Of course, Necro'Khan."

Once again, Tarkan pulled away. "Go to Sharar. Prepare the grave and bury the boy in the earth. The damned scholar will have all you need, no doubt." He approached the wagon and their risen mounts. Digging into his bags, he pulled out his black box and took the orichalcum dagger out. He slipped it into his boot and pulled the cowl of his cloak far over his face. "I will return to him once the moon is full and red."

"Yes, sira." Ashkan bowed and took the reins in his hand to lead the mounts and wagon away.

Tarkan watched him go, still as a statue, until Ashkan vanished over the dunes. No, he didn't trust the necromancer as much as his actions showed. But he needed him, for now. Tarkan had not missed the sudden, frozen mask over Ashkan's face when he'd mentioned Elahel. There was a time jealousy had eaten at Tarkan for Ashkan and his wife. Elahel had born a child before becoming an Apostle. Scriven could still conceive. Somewhere, Ashkan had a son. He'd made them give up the babe when it was only hours old. Then, he'd forced Ashkan to make an Apostle out of Elahel, taking away any chance of their happiness. Bearing a child as a Scriven had been such a risk, but the love Ashkan and Elahel had for one another had outweighed the risk.

The city quieted quickly after the sun set, so Tarkan easily slinked back toward the temple. He waited until most of the priests went deeper into the temple to sing their evening prayers to the interior mass.

Yes, he needed the Scriven bones of a necromancer for his blade—the blade that he would smite the continents with. Never had he wielded more than a knife. He wanted to feel the weight of a sword in his hand, to smite down his enemies with the sharp metal. Like no Necro'Khan before him, he'd fight his own battles, sword in hand. If Ashkan would not give up Elahel, his Apostle's bones would do just fine.

A priest came out of the temple to light the single candle in a white lantern above the archway, signaling that others waited inside. It was meant to be a light to those in need. Tarkan moved in the shadows, not blood walking to preserve his strength. He recognized the priest as Het, the one who had been with Sharar. Tarkan grinned. This somehow made the idea of letting his blood even more appealing.

Tarkan followed Het just inside the grand foyer of the temple. When the Masahk passed under the likeness of Ashmalia, he struck. Rushing from the shadows, he came up behind the Masahk, gripped his chin, and plunged the knife into his chest.

Het gasped and tried to cry out, but Tarkan stifled his cry with his cold hand. Grunting in effort, he cast Het to the stone floor of the temple. His golden-red blood spattered out. Het moaned and rolled over, trying to stand up. Tarkan stood in front of him, pressing his boot into Het's chest, shoving him back to the ground.

"You," Het gasped. "What have I done to deserve your ire?"

Tarkan pressed the knife to his throat. "If not yours, it would be another." With all his strength, he pushed down, slashing the Masahk's throat.

His immortal blood splashed over the steps, dripping down. Tarkan rubbed his hand over the wound, then smeared the priest's blood onto the altar. Het went pale and still. Tarkan stepped up to the altar and spat on it before turning away, leaving the dying Masahk choking on his own blood.

℥

"Where is Tarkan?" Sharar asked when Ashkan shoved past him into the manor. "Necromancer!" he shouted when Ashkan didn't stop. Sharar called for Amir and ran after Ashkan.

"He is preparing your rite," Ashkan replied, marching through the manor and out the back into the utter darkness. "Where is your cemetery?"

Sharar stammered, not sure why the necromancer asked. "Behind the garden, around to the west. But there's only the family who lived here before buried there."

"Doesn't matter," Ashkan quipped. "We need a grave. Do you have blood and sentient ash?"

"Of course I do." He followed the determined necromancer, curious about what made him plow ahead with such determination. "Where is Tarkan?"

Ashkan finally stopped, surveying the cemetery before them. A few graves were marked and one mausoleum stood a few yards away behind the black wrought-iron fence. Amir rushed up behind them. He panted behind Sharar, having looked for them inside first.

"He is forcing a blood moon," Ashkan grunted. He raised his left hand and soon a wagon appeared, pulled by risen horses. The necromancer went to it and pulled a shovel out from the back. "The blood and ash, scholar," he commanded.

Sharar didn't move, signaling Amir to stand close to him, just in case. He knew very well what lingered inside the black, locked wagon. The moon above shown white and partially full. "What does that mean? How is he summoning a blood moon? Tell me and I will take you to gather the things you need," he added forcefully when Ashkan turned to face him.

The necromancer waited a beat before answering. "He's summoning it with a heretical act: spilling the blood of an Ashmalian priest on her own altar. She will mourn the death and turn the moon red. He is at the temple now."

A strange feeling sparked in Sharar's chest. Something like fear, but for not himself. "A priest of Ashmalia?" He glanced at Amir and saw the Runer come to the same conclusion.

"I can be there and back in an hour," Amir grunted. He turned and ran to the stable to fetch his horse.

The scholar waited, hoping he was wrong. He met Ashkan's green eyes. "Follow me below. I have what you need."

With heavy steps, Sharar led the necromancer below into his dark underground. Yes, he had stores of sentient blood and a few small chests of ash. He had a vast collection of what his father would have called oddities. His collection was larger now than ever. He took a lantern from the top of the stairs and led Ashkan down.

The dark passageway led past his dungeon, the room where Enoch waited, and some more of his hidden storage rooms. When they passed the dungeon door, locked and fastened, Ashkan stopped. Sharar walked on a few more paces before he realized the necromancer had halted. He faced the dungeon door.

"What's behind this door?" Ashkan asked.

Sharar frowned. "My prison cells. Nothing that concerns you." Then he saw it; the corners of Ashkan's eyes stirred and a green glow emanated softly from under his skin.

"You have a necromancer behind this door," Ashkan whispered, not asking. He faced Sharar, stony. "Open the door, scholar."

There was no use in fumbling for a reply. The necromancer knew. If he denied Ashkan an answer now, he might inform Tarkan simply out of spite. Sighing in resignation, Sharar pulled a ring of keys from his sash and opened the door. He stepped aside and Ashkan entered.

The necromancer walked slowly, inspecting the cells carefully before stopping before an open one where Vicdan hung from his wrists. Thankfully, the jongleur had passed out, his head hanging back, limp and silent. Sharar tensed, wondering how the necromancer would react. He laid his hand on the scimitar by his side. At least below the ground, the risen would have to shamble down to them. He'd have seconds to incapacitate Ashkan if he struck out.

"Bone-Scriven," Ashkan whispered. He reached up and touched the part of Vicdan's arm that was exposed from his torn tunic. "Not an Apostle." He glanced sideways at Sharar. "You are wise to have a necromancer in your possession. You do not trust Tarkan."

Sharar scoffed dryly. "Trust a man who I killed a thousand times over? Of course not." He eyed Ashkan. "But he is only Scriven?"

Ashkan nodded. "Once he is an Apostle, the only sign will be in his eyes, like his brethren and the Runers. As you see upon me."

Sharar caught Ashkan freeze a moment, his brow furrowing.

What is he contemplating? Sharar wondered. He studied Ashkan's face harder, but only saw thought on the surface.

Vicdan moaned and tried to lift his head. "Gods, everything is stiff and hurts," he grumbled. He opened his eyes and glared at Sharar before he caught sight of Ashkan. With another moan of effort, he raised his head between his arms and blinked. "Ah," he sighed, realizing who and what Ashkan was.

"Who are you?" Ashkan asked, genuinely curious.

The jongleur smiled wearily, even though he was pale and perspiring. "Vicdan Nashira. Same as you, I take it."

"How are you a Nashira?" Ashkan asked. He scanned the captive up and down. "Where have you been? Your tribe?"

"Ala'Nar," Vicdan replied. He coughed, his lips chapped and dry.

Ashkan looked around and found a single basin and carafe. He poured water from it and offered it to Vicdan, who drank sloppily. Sharar waited, fascinated.

Vicdan swallowed and moaned again, twisting his bleeding wrists. "I was born there," he went on. "My family was owned by an Alikan sheikh. Not very glamorous, I'm afraid."

"A Porshain slave family?" Ashkan asked.

Sharar noted the sympathy that entered the necromancer's face and tone.

"As so many of our brothers were," Ashkan added. "Were you Scriven?"

The jongleur half nodded. "Father was. They overthrew the sheikh, took his home, his land, his wealth. Then I came along." He closed his eyes, tired. "I never knew the slave life. I have my father to thank for that. But he was of house Nashira. Scriven during the fall of Porsh. An ancient, vile man, honestly. I suppose when he fled, the Alikans captured them all." He clicked his tongue sadly. "I miss our gilded halls. But I brought that on myself. I didn't know I was Scriven, like so many Bone-Scriven. I suppose we forget the memories of the months of pain and agony. When I was to be made an Apostle, I ran away. Denounced the scriptures. Father was so pleased," he added with heavy sarcasm.

"You cannot leave them behind," Ashkan offered. "They are part of you. Forever."

Vicdan looked away, forlorn. "So I found out. Between ages thirteen and twenty, I spent most of my time running away, only to be caught and brought back. Met a kindly jongleur from Rhostrana who took me in. Treated me like a pet." He smiled weakly at some memory. "He was always ready to take me back in when I ran away from home. But, of course, some years later, he...was gone."

Sharar shook his head. "Why would you deny yourself such a power?"

Vicdan gave him a dirty glower. "Not everyone is as macabre and ambitious as you, scholar. Some of us find all the pleasure we need in a well-sung song, in the arms of a pretty barmaid, or in the honey glaze of a prime lamb over a fire." He narrowed his eyes at the scholar. "When was the last time you had a good shag, scholar? It might do you good."

Sharar let the juvenile insult roll off him. "Necromancer, we have work to do." He turned to leave, but Ashkan didn't move.

"Scholar," Ashkan murmured, eyes locked onto Vicdan. "You would have more to bargain with if you had an Apostle."

"No, please." Vicdan began to babble, to beg to not have the locking script on his heart broken, but Ashkan ignored him.

"I could do it," the necromancer went on. "Tarkan would not know. He will not be as strong as the Necro'Khan, but once you are a sorcerer..."

The ulterior motive was palpable behind the necromancer's words. "Go on," Sharar prompted, curious if he could get Ashkan to divulge his secret motivation. "How would having this imbecile made into an Apostle help me?"

Vicdan sniffled, eyes red, waiting for his fate to be discussed.

Ashkan waited a moment. He reached his hand up to Vicdan's face, gently taking his dirty hair between his fingers, rubbing the fibers together. "Scholar," he said carefully, "you will want all the strength you can get. Tarkan has discovered how to take power from the blood he consumes." He faced Sharar now, giving him a serious glare. "He consumed the blood of a fiery Masahk and was able to bend the flame to his will. I saw it with my own eyes."

Understanding hit Sharar like an avalanche of sandstone. The damned Necro'Khan had almost hidden his plan. Sharar had come very near to underestimating Tarkan. "He is waiting for me to ascend to sorcerer," Sharar finally admitted out loud. "He thinks he can overcome me, take my blood?"

Vicdan stopped his moaning and listened now.

Sharar's mind reeled, and he fought to regain control of himself. The hand holding the lantern shook slightly. The damned Necro'Khan had nearly tricked him. But could Tarkan overpower Sharar once he was sorcerer? Sharar wasn't sure he wanted to give Tarkan that chance. "When is he returning?"

"At the full moon," Ashkan answered.

First, Sharar thought of the djinn. No, he only had one wish left. He had to strike Tarkan down himself. He'd done it before. "Once I have the Mahit'Onomicon, he will not be able to stand up to me," he whispered. "He doesn't see that. Blinded by his new strength."

"Are you certain?" Ashkan asked.

"I will be a sorcerer," Sharar spat back. "Yes, I am certain. Though..." He grinned. "It may be a magnificent battle." Could there be a passage in the book that would help him take the necrotic powers from an Apostle like Vicdan, and bestow them on himself? It was the only power a djinn did not possess.

"Tarkan is coming back?" Vicdan asked. "Will you kill him, then?"

Sharar shook his head, still lost in thought. "No. I need him to..." He stopped. Was it worth it? To let Tarkan bring Enoch back and flee again?

The choice stared down at Sharar in his dungeon. His son, or his enemy's blood? The question of whether Tarkan could raise an undead being also needed consideration.

Enoch or Tarkan?

"But I must ask, necromancer," he said, pulling away from the maddening conflict, "why have you told me this? Are you not his Apostle?"

Ashkan faced Vicdan again. He touched the jongleur's high cheekbone where the scriptures lay hidden. Vicdan cringed away, making the chains rattle. "Tarkan has far-reaching plans. He needs the bones of a Bone-Scriven Apostle. The only ones he knows he can find are the bones of my wife, Elahel. I'll not allow him to have her."

"Gods, no," Vicdan cried, pulling again on the chains around his wrist.

"Even if this Scriven is a reluctant Apostle," Ashkan offered, "you can bargain him to Tarkan if ever you needed. Or you can use him once you are a sorcerer. He's as good as any necromancer."

The choices seemed like a bargain to Sharar. Despite Ashkan knowing he had the Scriven now, he did not sense the necromancer would betray that knowledge to Tarkan.

"You won't tell Tarkan I have such a Scriven?" Sharar asked to be sure.

Ashkan didn't face him and didn't reply.

It didn't matter what this Apostle wanted or tried to hide. Tarkan was the goal, the target.

"Sira," Amir called from above. His boots clamored down the stairs. He panted, sweating from his effort. "I found Het."

That strange feeling came into Sharar's chest again. "And he's gone?"

Amir nodded. "Dead, his blood painted over the altar of Ashmalia."

Something stung Sharar's eyes. He blinked and raised his head.

"The stronger Tarkan is, the stronger I will be when I take him down and steal everything that has made him Necro'Khan. The Mahit'Onomicon will tell me how. Apostle, can he bring Enoch back?" That still mattered.

Ashkan nodded. "I have no doubt."

The next full moon was in less than a fortnight. That would give Sharar time. He faced Amir. "I have a game of politics to play. Nothing a show of power will not solidify. But this gives me time. Amir, we must go to the Pharaoh."

The Runer sighed despondently.

Sharar approached Vicdan. He touched the Scriven's side, running his hands down the ribs that bore the hidden scriptures. Vicdan squirmed uncomfortably, glaring at Sharar. "Necromancer, my demon will see to your needs. Amir, we leave for the Dynast Palace at first light. My meeting with my old friend is long overdue."

"Friend?" Vicdan gasped. His eyes went wide suddenly. "You don't know where they are. They could be anywhere."

Sharar couldn't stop the smile. "They could be. I must rein them in."

He signaled Amir to follow him. The Runer sighed, head down, and followed him out.

Chapter 18

Monster

Tzarik watched Sybal's chest gently rising and falling while she slept, curled by the fire. Next to him, Signar snored softly, mouth open. Sleeping on the ground didn't bother the boy. He'd probably never slept in a bed. Sybal always looked forward to when they got to sleep indoors. She had been raised that way, unlike him and Signar. She'd been looking forward to entering the embassy, despite the dark glower she wore when discussing the magi. Tzarik pulled half his hair up, tying it into a knot, and prepared to move.

What had Nefiri said to Sybal when he left? Had the magi made him leave on purpose, to speak to his apprentice alone? His hand went to the ugly scar over his heart. Had Nefiri told Sybal about the ritual? About what she'd done to him? He clenched his eyes tightly, pressing his fingers into them to sponge out the images.

A long-fingered hand touched his leg, tapping him. He looked down to find Signar's green eyes open and on him. They were

Sjörna's eyes, but his face was more Kjarton's. Signar sat up, biting his lip as he tried to speak.

"What is it?" Tzarik asked softly, not wanting to wake Sybal yet. He'd delayed long enough, leading them around and around Mysir's border, never going in. He wanted to make sure Nefiri was gone before they arrived. And part of him hoped he could find an opening that did not require them to be so formal; bringing letters, staying so near the palace. He didn't like being trapped inside walls like that. It had been a few days. Sybal would want to enter the city when she woke. Even he grew tired of his hesitation.

"I... I am..." Signar frowned, fighting to find the words. He got frustrated and pounded the ground with his fist. Tzarik grabbed his wrist, placing his other hand on his shoulder to calm the wild Vaeson before he lost control.

"It's all right," Tzarik offered. "You don't have to speak. We'll go into the city today. Get food, some place to wash, a soft bed."

Signar tilted his head like a dog trying to understand.

Tzarik laughed lightly. "You'll see. Once you do, you'll no doubt rue this day. You'll want to sleep indoors for the rest of your life." He stood up, pulling Signar with him. "You deserve better than you were given. Maybe this will make up for some of that." He turned to wake Sybal and call the horses.

"Tzarik," Signar said.

The Runer's heart leapt into his throat. He spun back to face Signar.

In halting Caerwren, the boy said, "I... am sorry."

Tzarik frowned. "For what?" Realizing Signar might not be able to verbalize more than that, he stopped himself. "Never mind, don't answer that." He gently slapped Signar's shoulder. "You have nothing to be sorry for, Signar. Nothing."

He reached down, heaving up his saddle, and whistled for his horse.

"Sybal," he called, kicking her shin. "Wake up. We have to reach the embassy with plenty of daylight left."

Sybal groaned, rubbing her leg and glaring up at him. "At last. I thought you'd never take us in. What stalled you for so long?"

"I wanted to be sure she was gone before we entered," he confessed, tightening the girth on his horse. The animal put its ears back, eyeing him sideways. He glared back at it. He cursed Hiro in his mind for making him name Mamun. The loyal mount's gruesome death would have been far easier to bear if he'd not had a name. "Don't look at me like that. You're not getting a name," he growled to it.

The horse snorted, stamping its feet. Tzarik ignored it at first, but then the thing tossed its head, whinnying loudly. He stumbled back. The horse reared up then, screaming as its hoofs clawed at the sky.

"Careful!" Sybal cried, holding her own mount to calm it.

Tzarik reached up for the reins, but the massive horse was far too tall, tossing its head and the leather reins out of his reach. The thing bucked and reared again, snorting violently and pinning its ears back. It locked its brown eyes onto Tzarik.

Just as the thing readied to charge, someone gripped the back of Tzarik's cloak and whirled him out of the way. Signar put himself between Tzarik and the wild horse. The boy, over a foot taller than Tzarik, raised his hands up to the creature, calling to it. The horse reared up, ready to bring its sharp hoofs down onto Signar. Tzarik shouted for him to move, but he didn't.

"Aye!" Signar growled at the horse, standing his ground. He reached up and grasped the reins, yanking it down. "Calm," he commanded in Al'Myrahn. His other hand went to the back of the horse's head, forcing it to stay still. "Be still."

The creature whinnied and tried once to pull away, but it was clear Signar was far stronger. It locked its knees, eyes wide at the powerful sentient that held it.

Signar approached it slowly, moving his hand from its head to its neck, patting it and whispering. "Alvakar," he said over and over, soothing it. "Aye," he sighed gently with a final pat. "Alvakar."

Shocked, his body still tingling from the near harm he'd come to, Tzarik marveled at the boy. Sybal stayed back, calming her horse and keeping it in check.

"Are you all right?" she called to Tzarik.

"Yes," he panted back. "What the hell spooked it?"

"I think it knows you despise it." Sybal smiled now that the danger had passed. "That was incredible. Signar," she called so he knew she spoke about him, "well done."

The boy smiled, petting the horse's nose before handing the reins back to Tzarik. "Alvakar," he said again, pointing to the horse. "His name."

"A horse from western legend," Sybal supplied, swinging up onto her horse. "Made in the hellfires of Tierheim and who broke free. Became the one who guards the sun, according to those on Caerwren."

Tzarik sniffed in disdain. He would, of course, acquire a hell horse. Perhaps the heat of Alika and Al'Myrah had angered the beast. It was, after all, a horse of Caerwren. Massive, strong, sure-footed—but also a hellion. Everything from Caerwren had a temper he could not abide. He smiled at Sybal.

Then he watched Signar mount his horse easily and join Sybal, facing the city of Mysir's borders. Something swelled inside him, forcing a smile of admiration onto his lips. He realized as he mounted Alvakar—and he would call the beast that—that he was proud of Signar. The boy had made leaps in his progress to master himself, so much that he'd been able to calm the horse.

It was a small test, but Signar had proven he was no longer the wildling they'd freed from Northica.

THE CITY that the province of Mysir was named for reminded Tzarik of Hatal in its busyness, its rushing throngs, many streets, and mix of sentients. The river from the north cut through the very center of the province. It took them a few hours to get past the outer rings of the royal city into the middle, where the Dynast Palace stood. It jutted up from the city like a pyramid of gold, reaching for the sapphire sky. The other rivers and larger streams of the city flowed around them, being used for transport and travel. Large structures with mill wheels pulled and pushed ferries and rafts up and down the rivers. The Three Rivers flowed from the massive spring where The Cradle purified it, giving fresh water to the entire continent. Only once in his life had Tzarik used salts from Alika in a magic tincture. The salts often enhanced other magical properties, but were hard to come by. The religious orders of Alika protected The Cradle and the salts they pulled from its waters.

Signar's eyes darted from street corner to shop to public house, unable to keep up with all the stimulation. Every sound made him jump. Street performers with bright, waving veils put him on edge. The sooner they left the sights, sounds, and smells of the city behind the embassy walls, the better. Tzarik trusted the boy, but this would be a real test. He slowed his horse to let Sybal take the lead so that he rode next to Signar.

Sybal led them toward the Dynast Palace, where guards stopped them and made them wait outside a small keep while they sent a runner to the embassy to check with the servants there. Tzarik showed them Nefiri's letter, but they still halted.

"Not just anyone—let alone Runers—get to dance into the embassy," the guard told them roughly. "It's too close to the Dynast Pharaoh. The common pharaoh in Zhigo or Yenka might let you wander into their palace grounds, but not the Dynast Palace." He looked the strange trio up and down.

Tzarik didn't engage the man. He leaned forward onto the horn of his saddle and waited. Beyond the keep, slaves worked to build the top of a grand tomb in the likeness of a hawk. The slaves were a mix of Masahk and a human people with honey skin and dark brown hair.

"Porshains," Tzarik mused, realizing who the people before him were. Al'Myrahns had black hair and dark brown eyes. While Porshains were very similar, they tended to have more golden or light brown eyes, along with dark brown hair.

Sybal joined him, coming up beside him on her horse. "I forgot Alika still deals in slaves like Rhostrana."

Tzarik gave a sharp hiss through his teeth. "Convenient, since Rhostrana only enslaves Masahk. How can they barter their own people?" He ran his eyes over the workers. These Porshains were not like the necrotic houses that had destroyed their country. These were the ones those houses had made suffer.

"They came to Alika to flee the fall of Porsh," Tzarik mused. "Perhaps if Al'Myrah had been more welcoming to them, they'd not be here, trapped in generational slavery."

Sybal's face went impassive. "I find it hard to pity them."

"They didn't destroy Porsh," he reiterated. He glanced sideways at her. She'd become so cold, so callous, since Caerwren. He missed when she was impulsive, emotional. Yes, he'd found it irritating at the time, but at least she'd felt then. Was it the touch of the god that made her this way? Or was he not giving her enough credit? Was this really her?

A taskmaster shouted at a fallen slave, screaming for him to get up and back to work. The shackle and metal ring around the slave's ankle—for securing them during the night—clinked as he struggled to stand. The taskmaster shouted again, cracking a whip.

A sharp gasp behind Tzarik made him turn. Signar had closed

his eyes, cringing away as if the whip had cracked over his head. When the cracking blow fell, Signar flinched and turned his face away.

Realizing the sounds and images brought back memories, Tzarik jerked his horse around to the guard. "Let us inside. I showed you the signed letter."

"No, sira," the guard said, not moving from where he sat, using a knife on a block of cheese. "Not until the runner returns."

Aggravated, Tzarik spun back around to watch Signar. The last thing they needed was the boy shifting into his massive wolf form, attacking the guards, and possibly slaying dozens or hundreds of the helpless slaves. But his worry partially melted away when he saw Signar now sat still. His eyes had gone dead, but at least he didn't look volatile anymore.

His nerves fraying, Tzarik waited.

The sun had crawled down the horizon by the time the runner returned, confirmed the magi had mentioned that Al'Myrahns and a western boy would be coming, and they were let into the palace's grounds. A dozen guards flanked them, escorting them across the gardens, over the open fields where priests gazed at the coming stars, and through a few outer wings to the embassy.

The small manor consisted of two floors and its own land. A balcony on the second floor surrounded the entire structure. Open windows, billowing with veils, covered most of the walls. A luscious garden shaded the cobbled area around it. Out behind the manor, a pool of fresh, blue spring water bubbled up, surrounded by short palms and colorful flowers. Tables and chairs dotted every room. A few servants moved through the halls when they arrived, lighting the oil lamps in preparation for them.

A servant girl in pink silk hurried up to them. She smiled, a ring of gold in her nose. "I prepared the bathing pool for you, if you so desire."

"I desire," Sybal said quickly, sliding off her horse and leaving it behind to the stableman. "And so do both of you. Your stench has turned my stomach long enough."

Tzarik smiled, following her inside. The girl led them deeper into the house, into a room made of wooden walls with no roof. Gray stone surrounded a hot spring. Sybal audibly moaned and immediately dropped her belt and went to work on her armor when she saw it. A few plates of fragrant soaps, oils, chunks of amber and myrrh, and six different hairbrushes waited around the side.

Sybal turned to face Tzarik. "Wait with Signar outside. I'll call you when it's your turn."

A little disappointed, he waited in the doorway, watching her undress.

"I feel your lustful eyes on me," she said without turning, but he heard her smiling. "Go on."

Sighing, Tzarik turned and rejoined Signar in a room with a large table. Already the servants had piled it high with roast meat glazed with honey, fresh fruit, and bowls of savory vegetables. Half grateful Sybal was not there, he attacked the food with abandon, Signar joining him. They ate some of every dish, not caring to sit around the table. Tzarik poured himself some dark purple wine and drained the goblet. He offered some to Signar.

The boy sniffed at the golden glass, his face wrinkling.

"Try it," Tzarik urged him, picking through a pile of grapes. "I can't take you back to Altevine if you won't drink. That might be heresy among your people."

Tentatively, Signar raised the glass to his lips. Tzarik watched him, finding the pained look of apprehension on the boy's face amusing. Signar tipped the goblet, taking a large drink. He blanched, a shiver vibrating down his whole body. He shook his head and put the goblet down.

"Well," Tzarik sighed, taking the wine for himself, "perhaps it's an acquired taste. This is as easy as alcohol comes, though. Alikan wine is sweet." He shrugged, remembering the powerful, clear drink he'd had on Caerwren. "You're going to have to find a way to enjoy it. No one on that savage continent is going to follow a Reks who doesn't drink."

"Reks?" Signar asked.

As before, the sound of the boy's voice shot a jolt through Tzarik's nerves. He looked up from the food. "Yes. You will be... No. You *are* Reks of Altevine. I promised Skarde I'd bring you back."

Saying it made him realize it was true. Someday, he'd have to give Signar up. Take him back to that savage land. Perhaps never see him again. The weight of the truth pressed down hard on him.

"Tzarik?" Signar said gently from where he sat on the floor with a plate of food.

The Runer looked up, unable to stop the sad smile that pulled at his face. He'd never get used to hearing Signar say his name. "What is it?" he asked as gently as he could.

The Vaeson went through his now-familiar tells of trying to find the right words to say. The way his eyes danced back and forth through focus, how he chewed on his bottom lip, and the frustration and anger that welled up, knotting his sharp muscles. Tzarik saw the wild rage slowly build in the boy.

"You don't have to say it correctly," he offered. "Speak however you can. It doesn't matter if it's Caerwren or Al'Myrahn."

"I..." Signar started again. His hands fiddled with a stem of a fruit he held. "I am..." He stopped and finally made eye contact.

Something in his eyes was familiar to Tzarik: fear of showing weakness. Curious, he pushed himself up and took a few steps in the boy's direction. Signar turned his face down then, his cheeks turning red.

"You can tell me anything," Tzarik offered. "Nothing you can say will make me think you are weak, Signar." He scoffed in good humor and touched his shoulder, remembering the bite. The boy was anything but weak. "People will teach you that certain things you say make you appear weak, but that's not so between you and me."

"To say things… makes me weak?" Signar asked, still not looking up. He spoke in a strange mix of Al'Myrahn and Caerwren, replacing words he didn't know in each language with the other.

"No," Tzarik corrected. He sighed and sat down next to the Vaeson. "The map is full of people who are full of bullshit," he started. "They will tell you not to say something because it's not what's right for who you are. You come from a place where your people are more afraid of weakness than the gods that torment you. I suppose I understand. To protect myself, I barred certain emotions from myself. Kept myself alone so I never had to experience loss. Perhaps this is weakness to admit, but…I don't know how to teach you these things. When I took you from Northica, I thought I could save a scared boy."

"Regret?" Signar asked.

"No," Tzarik answered quickly. "I was not ready to take on the task of teaching you, but I don't regret taking you."

"But," Signar started, fighting for his words, "you…save me. I know this."

Just seven words in a row from Signar sent a thrill through Tzarik. Pride once again swelled in his chest. "Yes," he confirmed. "But I didn't know if I did the right thing. Taking you from your people. I acted out of fear of my own past. I put your entire country at risk, taking you off its shores. I don't know how to teach you to be a good Reks. A good leader to your clan."

Signar met his eyes. "You save me. I am Reks now." His face suddenly fell. "Alone?"

This was what Tzarik dreaded. "Yes. Alone. But I won't abandon you. I promise." He sniffed quickly, running his hand under his eyes, and said, "What was it you wanted to say before?"

The boy went back to fiddling with the apple in his hand. "Hard to say," he mumbled.

"Not to me," Tzarik reminded him. When Signar didn't go on, Tzarik nudged him with his elbow.

Sighing in defeat, Signar murmured, "Thank you. For... saving me."

Tzarik looked ahead, taken aback by Signar's thanks. "Showing gratefulness, thanks, is not weakness, Signar," he said, going back to the start of the conversation. "You may be glad, grateful."

"But," the boy cut in. He tapped his chest and shook his head. "My heart hurts." The confession drove a sudden, loud cry from him. Embarrassed, he dropped his face into his hands and pulled his knees into his chest, turning away.

Tzarik finally realized what the boy had been trying to communicate. He wanted to thank Tzarik for saving him, but the emotion, the feeling of being saved and freed, overcame him, making him want to weep in thanks. Signar had not wanted to weep. If only the boy knew how much Tzarik understood. He'd had the same maelstrom of emotions when Azar had saved him. Freed him. For the first time in his life, he'd felt safe. He had no walls, no roof. Just standing by Azar's side was more than enough. He'd never thought he'd feel that way, and the strange sensation had brought him to his knees.

Cautiously, Tzarik moved, raising his arms to take Signar into an embrace. At first, the Vaeson resisted, his shame holding him rigid. So Tzarik waited, not wanting to force him. After a chest-rattling sob, Signar fell into him and wrapped his arms tightly around him.

"She... hurt me," Signar said after getting control of his voice. "I don't...to remember it. I Don't...."

"Want," Tzarik supplied the missing word. "You don't want to remember it."

Under Tzarik's fingers, on the boy's bare back, thin, welt-like scars pressed into his touch. He realized what Signar spoke of. "It's not weakness to hold on to the memories of those who have hurt you," he counseled. "You are strong enough to not let them consume you. But it's harder when that pain comes from those who are supposed to protect us."

Signar took a deep breath. "I'm… afraid. Always," he confessed. "Afraid to hurt someone."

Tzarik gently pried the boy's arms off now and held him out at arm's length, looking him hard in the eyes. "You are a Vaeson, Signar. Harm is in your nature."

The boy swallowed a sob. "I cannot do good."

"You can," the Runer went on. He suddenly knew what to say, now that he'd let Signar break down for just a moment. "You are a man, but you are also a monster. A man *should* be a monster. There is nothing wrong with your aggression; don't discard it. A man with no aggression is worse than one capable of it who cannot control it. You are a wild wolf, and that is a gift. But you must choose when to be tame by controlling your wild heart. You must not forget or discard that aggression. Master it, and it will make you strong—strong enough to take down other monsters. When there are monsters in your path, you have to say, 'I will do good nonetheless' and face them as your tamed, wild wolf. For now, you're right. You're not fine the way you are. You must always strive to grow your aggression. And you must master it. Take your power under your control and you will be strong."

He held Signar's gaze, not letting the boy shrink away.

"Do you understand?" he asked.

After a moment, Signar nodded. "I will try."

"And I will help you," he promised, clasping his shoulders hard.

The door opened. Sybal stood in an Alikan robe of bright red and green, braiding her long, wet hair. She sighed loudly, smiling.

"Your turn," she said to them. "We are going to get that gold nest on your head clean, Signar. I will have it shining like an

Al'Myrahn sunrise soon enough." She stopped, hands freezing in her hair, and shot a glance between the two of them. "Are you two all right?" she asked.

"Yes," Signar said stoutly.

She smiled. "Come on, then."

She led them back into the room with the hot spring and waited while they entered the steaming water. Tzarik almost groaned as the warm liquid engulfed him. He sank, closing his eyes and letting his head fall backwards. His wounds ached, and the muscles in every part of his body were tight and sore. He let himself float against the side while Sybal attacked Signar's long, yellow hair with every brush, waiting with the soaps.

"Here." She handed him a circle of soap and a cloth.

Signar sniffed at the soap and made a face similar to what he'd done when tasting the wine. Tzarik watched him through one partially open eye.

"Scrub yourself, you filthy goblin," he ordered when Signar moved to stealthily put the soap back while Sybal was distracted with his hair.

Glaring at Tzarik, Signar did as instructed.

"Are you intending to bring him to see the Pharaoh?" Sybal asked. "Because I don't think he should be left here alone." She began to plat small braids back into Signar's hair now that she had him clean.

"Yes," Tzarik answered, rinsing suds out of his own hair. "He will come with us."

"He needs clothes, then," Sybal sighed, eyeing Signar's grimy garments in the corner.

"Animal skin," Signar said. "The cotton gets...." He made a motion like tearing cloth with his hands.

"Destroyed?" Tzarik supplied.

Signar nodded.

Tzarik grunted, nodding as well. He'd theorized as much. "I doubt we can find such animal skin in the city," he sighed.

Sybal hummed in thought, inspecting her work on Signar's hair. "He has been controlling his wolf well. Perhaps it is a risk we can take." She looked down at Tzarik.

He nodded. "I think we can."

Sybal dumped some of the fragrant oil into her hand and ran her fingers through Signar's hair. "We will go into the city, then. Find you something to wear before we see the Pharaoh."

Tzarik eyed them across the steaming spring. "Be careful."

"I will," Signar promised.

Chapter 19
Eye to Eye

Sybal couldn't stop the smile that spread over her lips as she watched Signar take in the market square the next morning. The day before, he'd seemed overwhelmed, jumping at every sound. Now, he moved through the people and drew the eye of every local. Standing head and shoulders taller than most—save the Masahk—with his bright yellow hair and pale skin, he was hard to miss. This was the only thing that worried her. Several eyes followed her and Signar through the streets. Of course, his near nakedness drew their attention as well.

She led him to a tailor first, wanting to get him clothed more than anything. She stood under the stall's awning outside the door of the sandstone part of the shop. The quick-witted tailor kept trying to sell her more and more expensive fabrics, but they had little money to spare.

"I'm a Runer, old man," she said at last, picking out some black cotton. "Do you think I have money for Xian silk and Alikan gold trim?"

The man stammered some excuses, but Sybal didn't hear them. Something to her left made her sulfates tingle. Eyes were on her.

She turned and met the eyes of a fellow Runer across the market. He stood over a warlock's stall, examining herbs and crystals. At first, she thought it might be Tzarik, but he was too tall. He had the same long, dirty hair and scruffy face, but stood a head taller than most. His blue eyes sparkled when she met them with her own. Something like a pale blush rose in his cheeks as he cautiously grinned at her across the square.

Smiling back just as guardedly, she nodded to him. Of course the Runer was struck mute at seeing a woman Runer. She was the first, and had grown used to the reaction.

The Runer had a handsome smile that drew her eyes back to him. His eyes suddenly dulled and the smile faded, but he remained locked on to her. Then his face turned down and he looked away. Had he recognized her?

She turned back to find Signar, but felt the man's eyes still on her as she did. She thought he might dash across the market to speak to her.

As she scanned the area, she turned to see a girl swathed in form-fitting red garments and a deep hood watching her. The girl looked to be partially of Bahratt and Alikan blood, with dark skin and piercing golden eyes. She looked past Sybal to Signar. Sybal sized her up quickly. The girl was short, perhaps seventeen. She was lean, though, muscled, and had the golden ring of a magi in her nose, but everything about her told Sybal that she lived on the street. She was dirty and rough.

The girl moved around the stall, pretending to look at the wares, inching closer to Signar. When she drew close, Sybal heard the light, metallic tinkling that came only from lock-picking tools. The girl was a rogue, a thief. Realizing this, Sybal let her move through her motions. She'd be disappointed if she tried to pick-pocket something from her or Signar.

But the girl swiveled around to face Signar. The Vaeson jumped, having not seen her approach. The girl smiled at him.

"You're foreign," she said. She reached a hand out towards him. "May I?"

"What do you want?" Signar asked, quickly overcoming his initial fright.

The girl kept her sweet smile on his face. "Can I touch your hair?"

Confused and at a loss for words, Signar nodded. The girl reached up and ran her long, thin fingers through his newly washed hair. She made a soft cooing sound and giggled.

"So soft," she mused, repeating the action. "Pretty. Why are you so pale?"

Signar shifted and Sybal realized he was reacting to the touch. He no doubt had feelings tingling through him that he'd never experienced before. Her heart softened a little for the girl; yes, she was a thief. But right now, she was genuinely interested in Signar. She found him fascinating.

"All on Caerwren are like this," he replied haltingly. "Some paint themselves blue."

"Where's that?" the girl asked. Her hand went to his bare arm, feeling his pale skin.

"Far," Sybal interjected. She reached over, taking Signar's hand and pulling him towards the tailor now.

"You his mother?" the girl asked, having just noticed Sybal and looking a little perturbed at being interrupted.

She didn't reply, pulling him away. Signar craned around to look at the girl as Sybal hauled him away.

"Come see me again, yellow head," the rogue called with a grin.

As the tailor made the clothes—mostly black—for Signar, Sybal leaned her elbows on her knees and shook her head. Had Tzarik thought about this kind of thing—girls, feelings, and all that came with it—when he'd argued to take the boy? Probably not. No, she wouldn't discuss those things with Signar. That would be Tzarik's job. He'd taken the boy. He had to deal with all that came with the young man.

⚡

SHARAR LOOKED out a window of his quarters to see Amir striding through the grounds with bags of fresh supplies. The Runer had an uncommon bleakness in his countenance. When Amir entered the quarters and strode past Sharar, he asked, "What has you in such a miserable mood?"

The Runer went to the small table near a bookshelf and helped himself to some purple wine there, tossing the bags of potion makings down. Sharar sensed he was about to try to dodge the question and cut it off.

"Don't, Amir. You cannot lie, remember? You are terrible at avoiding truth, and even worse at hiding your true feelings."

"I am, perhaps, a terrible Runer," Amir said after taking a drink. "It would be simpler if I had been tried for murder. But bearing a false witness? That sentence has made my life hell."

"It's one of the reasons I like you," Sharar said, still eyeing Amir curiously. "What the hell has you so despondent? Tell me." Sharar knew Amir could not lie. He didn't know the entire story, but lying under a courtly oath had landed him with the runes.

"I saw something fascinating in the market while buying supplies," Amir offered, clearly pained by what he was about to divulge. "A Runer."

"Truly fascinating," Sharar quipped dolefully. "What made him so compelling?"

"A lady Runer," Amir corrected. He swallowed hard, looking away.

Sharar froze, his hand halfway through turning a page of a

great tome laid out on the table before him. "An Al'Myrahn, woman Runer?" he asked haltingly.

Amir lowered his head, hiding his face. "She was tall, but had our skin. Her hair was…"

Sharar waited, brows raised as Amir relived the memory.

"Beautiful," Amir murmured. "I think she had some western blood in her."

Lightning flashed through Sharar. He dropped the page and straightened up. "You are sure?"

The Runer cocked a brow. "Yes."

"Where were they?" Sharar barked. His blood ran hot and he couldn't seem to breathe properly. "Was there a man? A Runer with her?"

Amir shook his head. "So this is the pair you've been hunting?"

"Yes," Sharar whispered. He rubbed his fingers against his thumb in anticipation. "They're here. They must have followed Tarkan." He looked up. "Well done, Amir." At last, he'd gotten the break he so desperately needed. "We have work to do now. Tell me what else you saw."

Z.

THE RUNERS WAITED for the runner to the palace to return with a few guards, who then escorted them through the golden halls to the main palace. Tzarik led the way, Sybal and Signar behind him. The two tall Masahk guards stopped them outside the throne room, where Tzarik heard speaking inside.

"Well," Sybal sighed, smoothing her hair and holding herself higher, "we've made it to the Dynast Pharaoh. I hope we're not too late."

"We'd know if Sharar was a sorcerer by now," Tzarik assured her. "Do you think he'd wait to show his power? By how he talks, he's chased this for years."

"Is he here because the Mahit'Onomicon is here?" Sybal asked. She leaned forward, half trying to listen to the conversation taking place inside.

Tzarik shifted his feet, glancing up and down the hall. He felt eyes on him, but saw no one. Slowly, he picked up a swath of black fabric wrapped around his shoulders and moved it to cover the bottom half of his face. He motioned to Sybal to do the same, concealing their immediate identity. If Sharar was close, he wanted it to be harder for him to spot them at a distance. All three of them hid their faces with wrappings, giving Tzarik a small sense of security.

"Sahir told us that the Pharaoh believes Sharar is the Father of Monsters," Tzarik said. "The one sentient able to read the text. It must be some sign they were told that would mark the man who could read it."

"But he made a wish," Sybal reasoned. "He's not some prophecy fulfilled. He has that power because of the djinn."

This was why Tzarik hated the gods, their prophets, the magi, priests. Once something as nonsensical as a prophecy was announced, any fool could make themselves the one to fulfill it. "I thought the map had grown too wise to follow prophecies," he mumbled, adjusting his belt on his hips. "I'm the fool for thinking sentient kind would leave such things behind."

Sybal didn't reply. Of course, she was religious and might believe in such things. In the past years, Tzarik had come more and more to understand the existence of the gods. But he hadn't liked any of them. Maybe one day he'd find one to trust, to put his faith in. For now, he despised them all.

"Enough!" someone shouted inside.

The Runers started, tensing for the body that marched towards them from within. Every other step was accompanied by the loud clang of metal against marble floor.

"Speak to me when you are of sound mind, you ignorant boy!"

A tall jackal Masahk burst out from the throne room. Robed in white, gold, and a thick blue cape, he swung around the hall towards them, chunnering angrily. The clang came from a great gold and sapphire crook he held. He stopped when he saw them.

"Runers," the Masahk growled. "In the Dynast Palace." He was about to shout at them, but stopped when he spotted the tall white western boy behind them. "Who are you?" he snapped instead.

Tzarik held up Nefiri's letter, sealed with the red wax of the embassy. "We are here to see Sokar'Xenoteph, first of his name, long may he reign." He quoted the traditional Alikan greeting when one spoke of the Dynast Pharaoh. Normally, he'd not stoop to the level of the upper caste, but he sensed the jackal was already in a livid mood.

"From the embassy?" the Masahk asked, lowering his voice. He cautiously stepped towards them. "Are you associated with Bahratt? No," he corrected, taking them in. He whispered excitedly, "Al'Myrah?"

Cautious, Tzarik nodded. "We're from Al'Myrah. But we're not associated with the embassy. We simply are acquainted with Nefiri, the magi who was here."

"She saw fit to give you—Runers—a letter of passage?" he asked. His amber eyes shifted quickly back and forth down the hall. He leaned in. "I don't know what you want with our boy king," he began, "but I've had enough of you Al'Myrahns coming to our shores and bending his ear to your will."

"Al'Myrahns?" Tzarik asked. "Like a scholar?"

Nasor gave a low growl. "I don't care who knows how much I detest the scholar. He has warped the mind of my..." He cleared his throat. "Of the Hawk King."

Sybal stepped forward, gently touching Tzarik's arm to signal to him that she was going to do some prodding. "We know the scholar. You can trust us. It's because of him we're here. Can you tell us more?"

"Trust Runers?" The Masahk shook his head, one of his sharp canine ears tilting behind him to catch a sound they didn't hear.

"Do you have a choice?" Tzarik asked. "We have traveled far to stop this scholar. Does that not make us allies?"

The Masahk drew a deep breath, looking at them as if he'd like nothing more than to beat them with his crook. "Treachery is everywhere," he mused. "You could be in league with the scholar."

"We can prove we are not," Sybal whispered, seeing more movement from the way the Masahk had come. "Come to the embassy. Speak with us. On your grounds."

The Masahk straightened up and said stoically, "I am Nasor, the vizier to the Dynast Pharaoh."

Tzarik gave him a slight bow. "Tzarik and Lady Sybal from Ala'Nar." He halted for just a second before motioning to Signar. "And Signar, our ward."

Nasor gave the tall Altevine boy a bow from his middle. "Honored to meet one of the men of the west," he said, hand over his heart. "If you are lying, I will have you killed," he warned them. "I will have you flogged and then dragged behind a chariot until death takes you. Do you understand?"

"Vividly," Tzarik replied.

Nasor nodded, a cruel glint in his eyes. "I will present you to his eminence."

When they followed the vizier into the throne room, Tzarik heard what his sulfates had tried to warn him about. The soft padding of bare feet followed them at a distance. If he'd not been on alert already, he'd have missed it. He noticed Sybal's eyes flit to where the sound came from, too. Signar's steps slowed, and he sniffed the air like a wolf on the trail. He looked in the same direction. Seeing this, Tzarik decided he was glad to have a wolf with them. His animal senses would be priceless in certain situations.

The throne room was a long marble hall. The sides were lined with pure, clear water and large clay pots with palms and ferns spilling out of them. Gold and blue pillars lined the long walk towards the ruby throne. The seat of the Dynast Pharaoh took even Tzarik's breath away for a moment. He knew the white sands of Alika flowed with gems, but hadn't known exactly how much. The back of the ruby throne fanned out like the tails of a peacock. Being ruby, light from behind cut through it, making it look liquid. Two fan-bearers stood on either side of the Pharaoh, as well as a few other Masahk and human guards in royal armor.

The Pharaoh himself sat with great command on the throne. Being Masahk, Tzarik saw he'd be tall when he stood. His long avian legs splayed out before him, ending in golden talons. His two great, shimmering green wings flowed over the arms of the throne where he rested his wrists, encased in gold gauntlets. He wore the traditional golden mask of the pharaohs. This one was shaped like a hawk, glaring down at them. Some Masahk had more animal-like faces, and others did not. He guessed the Dynast Pharaoh did not, or he would have foregone the mask when taking an audience. It had the desired effect; Tzarik felt like he should show reverence to the sentient on the throne.

"Your Eminence," Nasor called in his rich timber up to the Hawk King. "I beg to put before you two Runers of Al'Myrah and a man of the west. They come bearing a letter signed by the magi ambassador, Nefiri."

At the mention of the magi, the Pharaoh sighed and turned his head away. "I told you to keep all politics on hold, Nasor," the Pharaoh replied. His voice was stony, steady, but young. As he spoke, the wave of hair and feathers that fanned out from his mask shook, glittering. "Why will you not heed my words and wait to see the display in the coliseum?"

"Sira, er, Your Eminence," Tzarik stammered, stepping forward. "We've come a long way. All the way from Altevine."

At this, the Hawk King faced him again, showing interest. "You must have been there during Vasaras."

Tzarik nodded.

"I am interested in that," the Pharaoh went on. He leaned back into the throne, raising his head high. "They understand the value of death on Caerwren. Do they not, golden hair?"

Signar didn't shrink under the Pharaoh's question. "A...good death, perhaps," the boy replied slowly.

Tzarik felt pride again for Signar. The boy hadn't had time to give words to the thoughts and beliefs he had about the ways of his people. Especially the madness his mother had brought to the continent. He had assumed that Signar wouldn't be as bloodthirsty as she had been. But then again, even Skarde on Northica indulged in the Eldritch Hunt. The bloodshed. Would the boy follow in his traditions? His reply to the Pharaoh's question gave Tzarik hope.

"I value the dead, like my ancestors," the Pharaoh went on. "Also a well-lived life. I plan to live that life."

"Your tomb told us as much," Tzarik countered.

Sokar'Xenoteph laughed. "If you are here, bearing a letter from the ambassador, I will give you a message for her." He leaned forward, elbows on his knees. "Tell her I will finish what Acenoth IV started. I will raid his tomb and take from him what he stole from Alika. That should remind her who she spoke down to for so long."

Tzarik had no idea who Acenoth IV was, but understood what the young Pharaoh implied. "The Mahit'Onomicon is buried in a tomb?"

Sokar nodded. His lips quirked up in a smirk under the hawk-like mask. "Under a cursed tomb. A malignant tomb. No pharaoh since Acenoth has had the power to retrieve the book, let alone use it. I will be that pharaoh, a curse-breaker."

Sybal shifted. "I've read more stories than should exist about what happens when one opens a cursed tomb. Is this really what you intend to do, Your Eminence?"

Tzarik heard Sybal's unspoken question: did Sokar mean to

simply hand the book over to Sharar? Nasor had been right; Sharar's hold on the boy king was strong.

The great golden hawk's head nodded, and he sat back, easing his hands to the arms of the ruby throne again. "I don't need your ambassadors, your magi, to leave my mark on my dynasty. I am not afraid of Acenoth and his curse. I have the man for the job. The one to read the book, to raise my legacy."

"The Father of Monsters," Tzarik supplied. "One who can control the beasts of the map."

"A tamer of the untamable, a master of the monsters. The very one." Sokar's voice dripped with hubris. "And he is my life-long friend."

"What?" Tzarik couldn't stop the exclamation.

"The scholar was with me when father crossed the river into Ahryu," Sokar said. He shrugged. "Or Du'ith. Perhaps he landed in our hell because his heart was not worthy of Ahryu. But I was not always so disappointed in my father. I wept for his death. The scholar says loss of immortal life is worthy of mourning. But he stayed with me through the shameful burial of my father in grand-father's tomb. I shall suffer no such embarrassment."

The Pharaoh's voice echoed down the throne room into silence.

Sybal glanced down at Tzarik. He read the distress on her face, too. They were too late. Seventeen years too late, it sounded like. Had Sharar known where the Mahit'Onomicon lay this whole time?

A guess, Tzarik reasoned. *He went to Xia to investigate leads there and came up empty-handed. He must have returned to Alika, thinking he was right the first time. But he waited. He needed Sokar on the ruby throne before he dug into the cursed tomb.* The only hope they had was that this tomb didn't actually hold the book. Tzarik didn't need to know where the book was. He just needed to know Sharar didn't have it. He should have killed the scholar four years ago when he had the chance.

Or Tarkan. But they'd not seen any sign the Necro'Khan had appeared on Alika like Sahir had claimed. Not yet. If Sharar was on Alika, Tarkan might be as well, hunting the scholar down.

"We simply offer a warning," Sybal said when Tzarik didn't reply. "And might suggest listening to those close to you." She inclined her head to Nasor. "And perhaps acquiring more personal guard. I count two."

Sokar smiled. "I am guarded." He raised his long fingers and snapped them.

Movement at the corner of Tzarik's eye made his hand fly to his scimitar and turn. Sybal turned the other way, putting herself between Signar and the strange, rippling movement. Where once nothing had been, a pack of scaly Masahk appeared. They had lizard-like features, their large, iridescent green scales making them blend into the air around them.

Tzarik understood, as he'd seen monsters and smaller lizards do a similar trick. Each Masahk had their own gift. These guards vanished.

"The Mirage," Sokar said proudly. "The Dynast Pharaoh's personal guard. They use quieter means of execution. Some trained on Xia before returning to the Dynast Palace. I assure you, I am well protected."

Sybal gave Tzarik a wary glare, dropping her hand from her sword. "So I see."

"Runers," Sokar said, standing up to his full height. With his long wings hanging behind him, his Masahk height, and the way the feathers in his hair jutted out the top of the mask, he looked like a giant. "Come to the coliseum two days hence. You will see why I have nothing to fear."

"The coliseum?" Sybal echoed. "Pharaoh Ramdas I outlawed that bloody display."

Sokar smiled. "And I brought it back. I need my people to see the Father of Monsters display his power, to show he is the man the priests saw in their visions. A man who can tame the monsters. It is the only way to quell the fear they will have when I excavate Acenoth's tomb."

"The people are wary of the malignation?" Tzarik asked.

"Of course," the boy king replied. He sighed. "I am tired of conversation. If you wish to persuade me, I insist you come to the coliseum and witness first."

Tzarik swallowed his reply and his warning. "I'm afraid of what I will see."

Chapter 20

Hunt and Capture

The next morning, Sybal raided the embassy's closet, rifling through the gaudy, gilded garments. Tzarik had mentioned a hunt to her, but they'd not moved since Sokar had invited them to the coliseum to put Sharar on display. However, she wanted to hunt, to move. Waiting only left more time for the voice to whisper in her ear. So she spent hours brushing and braiding her hair and trying on clothes she'd not felt the likes of in years. The embassy had no short supply of gilded clothes.

She put on a blue dress that hung off one shoulder and had a crisscrossing golden middle. Her bronze skin clashed brightly with the blue, making it stand out. She looked at herself in the mirror, hardly recognizing herself, despite the rich dress. She turned, looking at her bare back. The dress dipped low enough to show her entire back. The scars from the flogging she'd received before her death stood out. As did the bite mark from the snake god that had chased her. She wrapped her arm around herself and touched the scars. At least now she looked like a proper Runer. Like Tzarik.

The revelation about his innocence still spun in her. *I thought the runes might not take a sentient who didn't deserve it. At least, one they think didn't deserved it,* she thought. She turned and started to pile her long hair up onto her head. She'd not cut it since before her trial. The white streaks in it caught her eye. Gently, she touched them. The voice had been silent for a time.

She scoffed. "Have you lost interest in me?"

"Never," the gruff, smiling voice of Tzarik said from behind her. He stood, leaning against the doorway to the room, wreathed in sunlight from outside. The room opened up onto the grand garden. Her eyes went to the exposed skin of his hard chest, which his wide open tunic exposed. Heat rose in her. He held his belt, sword, and crossbow in his hand.

She gave him a wan smile and held her arms out. "Like the day you met me," she said. "Though, they feel like foolish clothes now." She touched the pearls and gold lacing, her face reddening.

"Then shall I take you out of it?" Tzarik offered, sauntering into the room, tossing his weapons onto the bed and taking her hands in his.

Sybal laughed into his hair, sinking into his embrace. They'd made love only a few times, but every time she thought about it, her toes curled and her ears burned. She prayed that the sensation never went away. She let him turn her to face the mirror as he slid kisses down her arm.

"You wore black in the court," he murmured against her skin. "I remember."

She stopped, about to turn and return his kisses. The memory came back. She'd put on black to hide in the shadows on her way to assassinate Xiaoh. "Yes, you're right." Turning, she lifted her head to invite his kisses onto her neck and moved her hands down to his hips.

Signar appeared in the doorway then, walking quickly. When he saw them together, he stopped and turned, his face scorching red.

"Signar, come back," Sybal called. She pried Tzarik's hands off her and shoved him away. "What is it?"

The Vaeson's eyes turned nervous in his bright red face. He held up a patents. "Tzarik...wanted a hunt."

Sybal crossed her arms over her mostly exposed chest and the silly blue dress while Tzarik took the patents from Signar. She couldn't help but look at him lovingly as his eyes whipped over the page, right to left.

"What is it?" she asked.

"Perhaps a pishaca," he mumbled. "Ectoplasm trails, black smoke, eating of sentients. Nothing we couldn't handle."

"Can I go with you?" Signar asked, his eyes already saying he knew the answer.

Tzarik shook his head. "Stay inside. Stay hidden. It's not far. We should be back before sunrise."

Sybal checked out the window to see the setting sun turning a brighter orange. "Now?"

"Yes," her mentor replied, rolling up the patents and gathering up the weapons he'd discarded so quickly just a moment ago.

She wondered how he could discard the mood they'd been in so quickly. He'd always been more unfeeling than normal sentients.

"Sybal," he ordered shortly, "get changed. Meet me outside. Signar, stay."

Sadly, the Vaeson nodded.

TZARIK KNELT near the well-traveled path that led into the sacred rock formation. A few patches of trees and jungle oases scattered around the dune-made valley. The sun had long since gone down, making the pishaca hard to track.

"Draw atan," Tzarik ordered softly. "We may be able to find the ectoplasmic trail."

Slowly, Sybal did as he'd instructed and held her hand at chest height. The soft white light let him see a shiny black smear over one of the tall, sacred obelisks. He pointed to it soundlessly. She understood and moved beyond it, him following. On the other side, they lost the trail. Tzarik knelt again, wondering if the thing would even come back when the vein in the right side of his neck tingled.

He stopped, holding his hand up to stay Sybal. They both froze. Someone, a sentient, moved to their right, coming out of the jungle oasis. Sybal pressed up against the side of the obelisk to hide and he quickly followed. Four sets of horses' hooves pushing through the sand reached their ears.

Tzarik craned his neck around in the dark to look. His Runer eyes took in the dim light from the nearly full moon above. The white sands of Alika brightened the light considerably. Two men riding Alikan warhorses and two horses lashed to a wagon came into his line of sight. He could only make out the men's silhouettes because they wore all black. They didn't speak Al'Myrahn, but Tzarik couldn't hear well enough to determine what language it was.

"Runers," he whispered to Sybal.

She opened her mouth to reply when a loud crackling snap cut off her voice. In a flurry of black smoke, something appeared from the air directly in front of her. A long whiplike tail flailed as the creature attacked Sybal. She couldn't help but scream as the thing latched on to her with sharp claws. Its mouth popped open with a hiss, exposing rows of sharp fangs.

Tzarik shoved himself up and fired a bolt from his crossbow. The thing vanished just as it had appeared, dodging the bolt.

Sybal panted, unsheathing her scimitar and putting her back to his.

"Pishaca," he remarked easily. "Flesh eating, smoke monster."

"It's spirit?" Sybal asked, eyes flashing around the rows of sacred stones.

"Both spirit and corporeal," Tzarik answered. "Orichalcum is our best option."

"You there!" one of the other Runers shouted in Al'Myrahn, rushing up to them. The man stood tall and carried a straight, cross-shaped blade. He looked to be just over twenty years old and had the wild, untamed eyes of a new Runer. "Stop. This is our hunt." The man's accent was strange, but Tzarik recognized it as Rhostranan. He'd not spoken Rhostranan or heard it in years, so he was grateful the man spoke in the language of the east.

"Vitaly," the second Runer called, stopping his friend. "Don't attack them. They are our brothers." The second Runer was a tall man of Bahratt descent. He shoved the hot-headed Rhostranan behind him and faced Tzarik. "Apologies. I am Ashar. This is my apprentice Vitaly. We were sent to capture the pishaca."

"Capture?" Sybal asked.

The crackling sounded again, and in a puff of black ectoplasm, the creature appeared. It gave a demonic screech and leapt at the Runer called Vitaly. The Runer didn't raise his sword fast enough and the man-sized creature tackled him to the ground. The pishaca lurched, biting the young man's shoulder and ripping its head back and forth to draw blood and rend his flesh.

Tzarik shot a second bolt at the thing, making it vanish and reappear several yards off. Vitaly grunted in pain, eyes wild with fear.

"Help me!" the Runer called Ashar cried, unsheathing his own gently curved Bahratt blade.

Tzarik joined Ashar's side and charged the pishaca. Sybal broke from them, taking the left flank.

"Ashar!" Vitaly cried from where he'd been left lying on the ground.

Tzarik ignored the young man's pleas, knowing if they could subdue the pishaca, they could save him from the cursed poison slowly entering his veins. Tzarik caught Ashar hesitate; he feared for his apprentice. Hesitation would cost the Runer his life. But he understood the urge Ashar had to protect his apprentice.

"Go to him," Tzarik ordered. "We can kill the pishaca."

"Don't," Ashar asked, half stalling to head back to Vitaly. "We need it alive."

"Alive?" Tzarik growled. Behind him, he heard Sybal enter combat with the monster. His eyes snapped back to the other Runers' horses and the wagon. A black box with orichalcum chains rested on it. He didn't care why the Runers wanted it alive. "This is our hunt," he shot at Ashar, ready to take out the other pair of Runers to earn the coin.

"We've been paid," Ashar pled. "You can turn in the patents for the hunt money. But we need the creature."

With no time to do battle within himself, Tzarik nodded. "Fine. If we can, we will capture it."

Ashar nodded thanks and ran back to Vitaly. "We'll join you," he promised, vanishing into the standing stones.

Tzarik dashed into the maze of stones to find Sybal. She drew halat, shoving the pishaca off her. The monster reared its clawed hand back, preparing to strike. As it did, Tzarik exhaled hard, firing a third bolt from his small crossbow. The bolt struck through the monster's hand and pinned it to an obelisk. The thing screeched, pulling on the orichalcum-tipped shaft.

With it trapped, Sybal arched her scimitar behind, about to slash. But the pishaca pulled itself free and vanished after landing a hard kick into Sybal's chest. She grunted and fell against the desert sands. Tzarik ran to her, pulling her up and keeping his eyes sharp.

"Wait," Ashar called, rejoining them. Vitaly stood with him, the wound on his neck still black, but healed over with a quickly drawn artiah. "Use these to weaken it." He pulled something small, black, and round from Vitaly's belt and handed it to Tzarik.

"What is this?" Tzarik asked as Ashar handed one to Sybal, too.

"From Rhostanan Runers," Vitaly said proudly but weakly. "Made with black powder and a catalyst that makes it explode upon impact. Inside is orichalcum dust. The blast may harm you a little if you are too close. Stay clear of the dust. But it will help slow the monster."

Sybal smiled, weighing the little bomb in her hand. "Inspired," she mused. "I must journey to Rhostrana some day and meet your Runers."

Vitaly grinned, but his face was pale.

"Drive it to the crate," Ashar instructed. "Once the dust from the black powder bomb does its work, it will be weak enough to force inside."

The four Runers fanned out, rushing to the sides of the holy stone field. Tzarik kept his eye on the other three. He never had trusted other Runers much. Ashar and Vitaly didn't seem like other Runers, though. It was clear Ashar had great affection for his apprentice. Most Runers didn't care whether their apprentices lived or died. Except for him.

He looked up at Sybal and saw her snap into action. The pishaca came for her again, but she blocked it with halat, swung her sword, driving it back, and tossed her bomb toward it. The pishaca screeched. The bomb went off when it hit an obelisk behind the monster. A flash of light and a crack like deep thunder accompanied the sudden glittering puff of orichalcum dust in the cloud of smoke.

Ashar and Vitaly rushed forward, battling the thing. Tzarik joined them, understanding now that the orichalcum dust prevented the monster from blinking away in a cloud of smoke. The pishaca screeched as Vitaly landed a quick stab with his

straight blade, driving it back to the crate. Ashar slammed his
bomb against another stone, making a second explosion force the
pishaca back. Tzarik joined them until the thing turned and ran
headlong into the black crate. Tzarik took his crossbow up
quickly, pinning it once again with a bolt, giving Vitaly and Sybal
—the two taller Runers—the second they needed to slam the crate
closed. Tzarik and Ashar jumped on it then, lashing the chains
around it, locking it.

The black and the orichalcum trapped the monster. It writhed
and shrieked, banging against the sides, but the thick, ensorcelled
wood held. Tzarik and Sybal sighed, meeting each other's eyes.

"We need some of those," she panted, smiling.

"Come to Rhostrana some…day…and…" Vitaly stopped talking, going weak. He collapsed, his hand clamping over the wound
on his neck.

"Vitaly!" Ashar cried.

"Sulfates," Tzarik barked to Sybal, who had already run to
Ashar's horse.

"I don't have much," Ashar said, kneeling by his apprentice.
He inhaled sharply to hide his emotion, pulling Vitaly's armor
and tunic aside to see the damage the pishaca had done. "Please,
help me," he begged Tzarik. "He's my first; I don't want to lose
him."

"Calm yourself," Tzarik said as steadily as he could. Ashar was a
new master and still had raw emotions, letting them scramble his
brain. "It's a simple poison. This kind of wound happens all the
time." He pulled his dagger from a small sheath on his left thigh
and cut Vitaly's wound open. To his relief, Ashar didn't try to
stop him.

Sybal knelt next to him, opening Ashar's black box and taking
out the sulfates and needle. She went to work preparing it while
Tzarik gently cut open the young man's wound. Using his fingers,
he pushed roughly into the skin around the wound, forcing it to

bleed out. Black-tinged sulfates spurted out, making Ashar exclaim in worry.

Together, Tzarik and Sybal quickly let out the poison from Vitaly, set up the sulfates to replenish the ones he'd lost, and wrapped the wound after a few passes with the healing rune. In a matter of minutes, the young man was lucid again.

Calmer now, Ashar said, "Thank you, Runers." He sniffed and swallowed. "I don't know what I would have done if you were not here."

Tzarik eyed the Bahratt Runer. "How old are you?"

"Twenty-one," Ashar replied. "Vitaly is eighteen."

"You're his mentor," Tzarik said sternly. "You know what to do and would have done exactly what we did. He's lucky you care so much. But you must keep your head cool."

Ashar laughed dryly. "That's what my master used to say. He was a stoic type. You remind me of him. He often told me I was led by my heart too often and not my head." He gently touched Vitaly's shoulder. "But I do not see the point in not caring for them."

"Your master must have been a very caring man."

"Not at first," Ashar admitted with a smile.

Tzarik quickly glanced up at Sybal. "Caring means they can hurt you," he sighed, standing up. "But I'm learning it's worth it." He held his hand out to Sybal, who took it, pulling herself up. "What do you want with a captured pishaca?"

Ashar stood up, letting Vitaly rest. "We were hired by a scholar to capture creatures for a display in the coliseum tomorrow. This was the last one he wanted."

"A scholar?" Sybal shot. "Tzarik, the coliseum."

He understood. "Sharar wants to show his power to Sokar's people. This is how he's doing it."

Ashar frowned. "You know the scholar? You know what the Pharaoh wants with these monsters?"

Tzarik nodded. "Thank you for telling us." He glanced at Vitaly. "He'll be ready to move in an hour. Let him rest once you are safe."

Ashar thanked them again as they departed. Sybal marched with purpose to their horses.

"Do we try to stop him? What do we do?" she asked.

"I'm not sure yet," Tzarik answered, genuinely unsure. "I thought the Dynast Pharaoh would be our best option, but he's under Sharar's spell."

"We could find Sharar, put a sword between his ribs," Sybal suggested savagely.

"Not when he's in the palace," Tzarik countered. "He may have bodyguards. We need to find him alone, and..."

"Kill him?" Sybal whispered. She swung herself up onto her horse, watching him.

He climbed up and turned to head back into the village to get their reward. "We might not be safe at the embassy," he mused. "Especially if he finds out we're there. But it's not just Sharar we have to worry about," he reminded her. "We need to find Tarkan before he does something to endanger the entire map."

Sybal frowned in thought as they rode back. "He may only want to kill Sharar. Out of revenge."

Tzarik arched a brow sideways at Sybal. "You know him. Do you think that's all he wants? He used us to gain this power and now he's been set loose onto the map. He won't be satisfied sitting by."

His apprentice took a deep breath. "We don't know where he is. We know where Sharar might be. Let's focus on him before he finds us."

"STOP," Tzarik ordered Sybal. He squinted ahead at the embassy. "The door is open." His heart hammered, then leapt into his throat.

"Signar!" he called, abandoning all silence. He threw himself from his horse and charged into the front gates. "Signar!"

He knew before he entered the inner rooms that he would not find the boy inside. Few signs of a struggle showed within. A rug had been bunched up in a corner like someone had shoved it there. A single vase lay shattered on the floor. Tzarik ran through the rooms, shouting for the boy even though he knew the Vaeson was gone.

Anger filled him, mingling with a font of guilt. His eyes stung and he couldn't stop a quick gasp that welled up.

"Signar?" Sybal called, checking a few more rooms. "Tzarik?" she asked, fear squeezing her throat. "What happened?"

The Runer looked around, blinking to clear his eyes. "He knew. He knew we were here," he growled through gnashed teeth.

Sybal gasped, pressing her hand into her chest as sobs welled up in her.

Tzarik ran outside and remounted his horse. Sybal, crying, galloped after him. Together, they charged down the path to the palace. Tzarik wasn't sure what they were going to do. Was Sharar still in the palace? Would he come for them? Why had he taken Signar?

"Sharar took him?" Sybal gasped as Tzarik slowed to think. "Why?"

"The coliseum," a deep, steady voice said. "I tried to warn you, Runers."

The Runers turned to see Nasor slowly gliding up from the palace stables in a chariot. A servant hung on to the back. The vizier's blue cape fluttered in the desert wind. He glared down at them, his gold and sapphire crook planted firmly on the floor of the chariot.

"What do you know about this?" Tzarik demanded.

Nasor raised his head. "I do not trust Runers."

"Do you trust Sharar?" Tzarik snapped.

Nasor held his gaze, brow furrowed for some seconds before he sighed and half glanced back over his shoulder. "I told you. Sokar's ear is bent to that man from Al'Myrah. He is easily led by ideas of glory and ascension."

"Answer my question," Tzarik cut in. "Did he take Signar?"

The vizier closed his mouth, but his amber eyes glinted as he nodded almost imperceptibly. "I am sorry for you, Runers. I do not have many I can trust, but..." He glanced away in deep thought. "I could release the boy for you by morning."

"You can?" Tzarik asked. "Have you seen him?"

"He's in the garrison under the coliseum," Nasor replied slowly.

Tzarik almost ran then. Imagining Signar chained in a cage again made him wild with worry. The boy could turn into the wolf at any moment, giving himself and his entire country away.

"Take us to him," Tzarik demanded. "Now!"

"Wait," Sybal said, pulling on his arm. "We could endanger him. We cannot storm the palace's garrison."

"I cannot leave him caged," Tzarik cut back. He felt his emotions getting the better of him, turning him wild. He stopped, breathing steadily. Of course, she was right. "Vizier," he asked as softly as he could, "can you get him out?"

The Masahk nodded. "But not tonight. We must wait for the morning. Come to the coliseum. Be ready to run."

TZARIK MADE them ride a good distance away from the embassy and find a public house to stay in, not wanting to lay his head in the embassy since Sharar knew they were there. They sat in the room. The sun would be rising in a few hours. Pressing his hands into his face, Tzarik took a deep breath to calm himself. He heard Sybal's leg tapping with an anxious rhythm. His hands dropped and he glared over at her. She pinned him with her gaze.

"Sharar will make him fight in the coliseum," he mused gently.

"Because he's a Vaeson?" Sybal asked.

Tzarik shook his head. "Skarde was sure not many—if any—knew about the shifters of Caerwren. Sharar just wants to get to us."

Sybal swallowed a sob. "He'll hurt Signar. Because of us."

"He's strong. He can hold his own in the coliseum." Tzarik dropped his head. "But that's what worries me as well. Half the city will be there to watch whatever show Sharar has planned. If Signar shifts..."

"He will," Sybal confirmed. "He's come so far, controls himself so well. But in a real life or death situation, he will lose the discipline he's gained. His wildling will take over. Tzarik, what do we do?"

This was exactly what Skarde had warned him about. He'd put aside the Northican Reks' worry, determined to save Signar from his torture.

Tzarik gripped his knees in determination. "Saving Signar is worth the risk," he said, resolved in his choice. "When we get him back, we'll move. I'll..." He almost choked on the emotion rising in his throat. "I'll take him back."

Sybal gasped, snapping her head up, eyes full of tears.

"He's strong and smarter than they gave him credit for," Tzarik reasoned. "He's tamed enough to be Reks of Altevine."

"Tzarik, no. He's not ready," Sybal began, but he stopped her.

"He has to be. I've done all I can, I'm sure." That was a lie, of course. But with what little help he'd given the Vaeson, Signar might be able to return to Altevine and take his throne, even though it broke Tzarik's heart to even think about losing Signar to Caerwren.

"We need to sleep," he sighed. He stood up and poured two goblets full of wine, handing one to her. "We will rise with the sun and go to the coliseum at first light."

Chapter 21

The Coliseum

Sharar slowly strode down the underground halls of the coliseum's garrison. Arms clasped behind his back, he inspected the monsters Sokar had collected for him. Sokar walked on his left, smiling proudly. Amir, on his right, eyed the creatures as well. The garrison was half-lit by sunlight cutting in through the grates above and pouring in from the entrance to the coliseum ahead of them. Guards, kehann, and even a priest stood watch in the garrison. Men and Masahk prisoners waited in the sandy cells.

"Runers ahead," Amir mused, nodding slightly.

"Yes," Sokar beamed. "We have acquired some monsters only a Runer can guard. A crocatta and something called a pishaca as well."

Amir's brows went up, part in judgment, part in amazement. "Those are corporeal haunts. Mostly supernatural, but also physical. You expect a sentient in your bloody arena to defeat it? Only orichalcum can cut through something like that. Not to mention it's fast. And eats sentient flesh."

Sharar fought valiantly to hide the knowing smile from his Runer. "Indeed, all true. But the monsters are not here to test the prisoners of the coliseum. They are here for me." They passed a cage with something akin to a horse-sized tiger in it, long fangs jutting out from its upper maw and a forest of spines running down its hunched back. "Ah, a mahsnir," he mused. "And a western wyvern. How did you find one?" He faced the cage where a half-mangled green wyvern shuddered, all four of its limbs on the ground. The wings hung limp and bleeding at its side.

"A group of hunters from Rhostrana," Sokar replied. "Not Runers. They hunt large monsters like dire wolves, dragons, wyverns, and other such creatures that don't always require a Runer."

"How marvelous," Sharar agreed.

Up ahead, a gaggle of black-clad men stood near a large, black crate bound with glittering, pearlescent chains. Sharar recognized the Runers and the kind of entrapment they guarded. This had to be the pishaca. He scanned them for one Runer he had hunted down and requested specifically. Before he spotted him, Amir called out, "Ashar?"

Sharar smiled.

A younger Runer leaned out from the group. Judging from his darker skin, Sharar guessed he was some sort of Bahratt and Al'Myrah mix of blood. He was shockingly attractive for a Runer, his smile brightening his eyes.

"Amir!" Ashar called back in a boyish manner. He pulled apart from the others and jogged to Amir, arms wide. They embraced, roughly slapping one other's shoulders and backs, audibly laughing in the joy of being reunited.

"You know one another?" Sharar asked, feigning ignorance.

The younger Runer gave Sharar a quick bow of his head before turning back to Amir. "My former master. I was his apprentice for a year, and we hunted together for another two, apart from the Trial. It's been a few seasons since I've seen his hideous face."

Sharar noted how they'd not let go of one another, still clasped in the affection that only comes from men who'd bled together and shed others' blood together. He didn't try to hide his dark smile now. He'd been curious about his stoic Runer's attachments and had thought a former apprentice might show him. He had been right, but there was one more experiment to do.

"No doubt an epic tale of how you met lies between you two," Sharar mused.

Amir's face went impassive for a moment before taking solace in Ashar's gaze again. "I was a different man then. Ashar changed me."

Ashar kept his beaming smile.

"I never thought you'd make it this far without me," Amir added, a gentle jibe in his tone.

"And I thought I'd kill you in your sleep long before the Trial was over," Ashar replied just as quickly. "Come to see my handy work as always, master? To steal my techniques and coin?"

"Never," Amir beamed. He inspected the black crate. "I see you still forge your own metal." He lifted the orichalcum chain around the box, inspecting it. "You never did trust a smith to make you a strong blade."

"Nor the chains that bind the nightmares we hunt," Ashar agreed. "Why force another to forge it when it was my trade before? It won't harm me now."

"The blacksmith with a heart forged from gold. Are you still doing the trade?" Amir asked.

Ashar nodded. "When I can. I live on Al'Myrah now, have a smithy there, and work when the hunt allows. I have my own smith apprentice, Ari. He's a good boy from Bahratt. He's taken a wife, though. And I have an apprentice of the runes," he added as a joyful afterthought. "A boy from Rhostrana. He's learning quickly. Perhaps when this is over, I'll introduce you. He was wounded while fighting the pishaca, but he's strong, Amir. You will get along with him well."

Amir hadn't taken his eyes off his former apprentice, still shining approval and admiration on him. "All the best ones are strong, then they leave us."

"Neither of them will," Ashar promised, turning back to the crate. "I don't make Ari forge orichalcum. My forge won't see this glittering metal until I return. And Vitaly is... Well, I think he's still too scared to hunt alone."

Sharar had to stop himself from making a sound of disgust. He hated nothing more than Runers with moral centers. He preferred the ones like Amir, who could set aside their emotions, their personal beliefs of good and bad, and simply get a job done, who could take humiliation and a beating. Amir had that shining center he despised, but the Runer could stifle it and do the work Sharar asked of him. If things in the coliseum didn't go as planned, though, Amir's fortitude would once again be tested. Sharar ran his eyes over Ashar once more before turning to Sokar.

"This is a perfect menagerie you've assembled, Your Eminence," he said to the Pharaoh.

"I am glad," Sokar sighed, turning slightly serious. "I was afraid to find the one creature you could not control. Assuming there is such a thing. I don't doubt you, Abigor. I only want my people to see. I need them behind me."

Sharar offered the young Masahk a warm smile. "I don't see your caution as doubt, my boy. It is a good thing, to be certain. But you are not wrong. There are limitations to my god-given gift. I once tried to control a mori, something of a blood fiend from the west. I could not. They still have their souls intact, unlike similar sanguine creatures. There was a monster on Xia I could not control, either. Perhaps something too close to a god. But, my boy, that will change once I have the Mahit'Onomicon, once you have stolen your glory from the tombs of Acenoth and done what no pharaoh since has." He gave Sokar a proud smile. "I do this for you, my boy."

The Pharaoh fell into his praise, his pointed, feathery ears perking up as he shared the grin. His pride faded, though, as the familiar clink of Nasor's golden crook came around the garrison's corner. The jackal Masahk marched down to them, his blue cape hanging long down his back, the ends snapping.

"Your Eminence," Nasor grumbled, "you should not be in the garrison alone."

"I am not, as you see," Sokar replied, motioning to Sharar and Amir. "And I won't be removed."

Nasor glared at Sharar. "Of course, my king. You are safe among monsters because you have found the Father of Monsters." His tone dripped with loathing. "Can you control a djinn, sira?"

The vein in Sharar's temple pulsed, but he kept his face perfectly placid. "No. Not yet. But I will. I promise you that."

The jackal's canine face lost much of its assured glaze. "The people have assembled and the gladiators are fighting," he said instead to Sokar. "You must go to your box so the people see you. Our guests await you."

"So you did send for the dignitaries?" Sharar asked, following Nasor out as he pulled Sokar along. He moved up alongside the boy to avoid his long, feathery trail.

"Of course," Nasor replied. "Sheikhs, scholars, priests—I would not want to disappoint you, sira."

Sharar noted the jibe. He stopped suddenly, seeing a prisoner he'd hoped to not miss. In the last cell, a tall, pale young man stood. Sharar faced his captive, finally taking him in. The western boy stood well over six feet tall, broad shouldered, his yellow hair long and tangled down his back. The Runers had dressed him in black, no doubt for protection. Sharar approached the cell, keeping his eyes on the boy's face.

"I was wondering when I'd meet you," he said simply. "Oh, forgive me," he said, this time in Caerwren. "You barbarians in the west don't know our dialect."

"Not so," the boy replied in Al'Myrahn. Sharar noted his Altevine accent. "They taught me to understand."

Interested, Sharar came as close to the bars as he dared. He quickly checked behind the boy to see he was shackled, arms behind his back. He was. "What do they call you, boy?"

"Signar," came the curt reply, "of Altevine."

"Signar of Altevine," Sharar said, trying the foreign name on his tongue, "why did my old friends take an interest in you? I know Tzarik and Lady Sybal. They wouldn't take just anyone under their pathetic wings. No, you have a secret you are not telling me. What is it?"

Signar's bright green eyes glowered at Sharar, his jaw tightening.

Sharar smiled, giving a quick laugh. "You know, you look at me the same way he does. I see Tzarik in you. The same defiant eyes, stubborn chin. He's had quite an influence on you."

The boy's left brow gave the smallest twitch, showing his amusement at the words he took as praise.

"Yes," Sharar said, nodding again. "You are Tzarik's boy, no doubt. I could not have asked for better prey. But let me ask one last time before you're torn apart on the bloody sands of the coliseum." He squared up to the boy. "Why did Tzarik, of all people, take you under his charge? He's a Runer, a killer. He has no capacity for affection. So, why?"

Signar's eyes flashed playfully. "Why? Because when we're in town, I can reach the liquor on the top shelf."

Sharar couldn't stop the burst of laughter that shot from his gut. He let the glee roll off him naturally, running his hand over his manicured beard. "Yes, you are perfect for him." He cleared his throat and took a deep breath, clasping his hands behind his back. "Give the people of Alika a good show, my wild boy. They've never seen red blood on white flesh."

※

THE SUN SCORCHED the roaring crowd that packed the stone, step-like seats around the arena. Dust and sand clogged the air, kicked up from the four combatants below. Sharar glanced down to see two sets of Masahk chained together, fighting two other similarly chained Masahk. They moved like wild animals, roaring and snapping at each other. Blood caked some of the sand under their feet. It had been a bloody battle.

Nasor led Sokar to greet the nobles and dignitaries who'd come to partake in the bloody show. Sharar waited patiently for the pleasantries and cultural greetings to pass. They were here for him; he knew that, and didn't need to insert himself. A sheikh from Yenka, his black skin shining with sweat, gave Sharar a guarded glance from under the yards of colorful fabric swathed around him. They moved under a gold-tasseled awning where servants poured wine and brought out food.

The vizier whispered conversation to some of the nobles until the man from Yenka faced Sharar. "So you are the scholar, the man who claims he can control the gods' creatures and their damned alike."

Sharar looked at the man over a golden goblet. Below, one pair of Masahk slaves slaughtered the other, finally winning. "I studied at a seminary in Hatal, sira, as well as the academy in Rom. A claim is a theory, conjecture. Not proven. Today, I will prove my power to you and to all of Alika. I would guard my words more carefully in the face of suspected strength."

The man's face turned stony as he backed away to join a woman draped in gold.

Sokar watched the servants clear the arena. "Shall we, Abigor?"

"More than ready, my boy," he replied.

Nasor stood by, his face tentative. His body went ridged as his knuckles gripped the crook hard.

The Pharaoh gave the signal to his guards lower down the seats and began to introduce Sharar, explaining who he was, and the mark he hoped to leave on his dynasty with the scholar's help. Sharar stood brazenly at Sokar's side, but his eyes scanned the crowd before them. Many on Alika wore white or blue. Runers would be easy to spot. Tzarik and Sybal had to be close, if not already on their way to him.

"Amir," Sharar whispered, leaning slightly towards his Runer. "Eyes open. Watch for them."

The Runer nodded.

"My friend," Sokar said loudly, getting Sharar's attention. "Will you show my people that you are the Father of Monsters?"

Having not listened to the boy king announce him, he gave no verbal reply and simply nodded. He stepped up to the edge of the royal box and looked out into the bloody arena. "Bring the beasts," he called.

Below, two gates clanged open on the opposite end of the coliseum. The mahsnir ran out into the sun and sand, screaming a tiger-like roar to the crowd around it. A hush had fallen, making the animal's yell almost deafening. Sharar focused on the monstrous cat, feeling for its mind with the gift the djinn had given him. He touched the wild creature's consciousness easily, forcing it to stand still.

"I have it under my command," he informed the nobles behind him. "Bring out the wyvern."

Prodded by guards, the wounded wyvern shambled out, snapping with its long, sharp maw at the men. When it spotted the mahsnir, it shrieked and flapped its broken wings helplessly. The mahsnir seemed to not notice the wyvern. Sharar felt the cat pull against him, wanting to turn and claw at the struggling wyvern, but he held it still.

"Even now," he told the nobles who watched in awe, "I can feel her pull. She wants to attack, to rend the wyvern. I sense her lust for violence." Opening his mind even more, he grappled with the wyvern as well. More intelligent than the mahsnir, it took a moment longer. But soon, he had the animals bound, walking a calm circle around the arena together like old friends.

"Great Du-ith," the man from Yenka whispered. His mouth hung open, eyes wide. The people around the arena began to laugh at the display before them.

"But I can do more than that," Sharar smiled. Boasting had never been his favorite thing to do, but proving doubters wrong gave him a little bit of a thrill. After this, no one would stop the boy king from digging into Acenoth's damned tomb. He signaled the Runers to bring out the black crate.

"You are certain you can control this monster?" Amir asked, his eyes fixed on Ashar as he accompanied the box.

"Faith, Amir," Sharar whispered.

Below, the Runers unlocked the crate and jumped back as the monster burst free. In a whirl of black mist and foul wind, the pishaca exploded from its cage. The thing had the vague shape of a man, but moved in blinks, disappearing and reappearing in black smoke. A long, bifurcated tail lashed out from behind it when it ran on all fours every other blink or so. It snarled and snapped at the helpless wyvern and mahsnir, leaping at them like a hellion uncaged.

"A pishaca!" one of the Bahratt nobles cried.

Sharar let go of the mahsnir's and wyvern's minds. He waited until the creature had mangled the mahsnir and the wyvern and turned on the Runers standing by. He'd been inside a creature's mind once when it had died. Never again.

A few guards remained in the arena to see the supernatural monster up close, but now they screamed and scattered. The pishaca vanished into a puff of black smoke, appearing before them. It raised its clawed hand and tore the guard's belly open, spilling his insides onto the sand.

One Runer, Ashar, ran to the aid of the other guard, drawing the shield rune.

"Sharar?" Amir's voice was strained. "Take its mind. Make it stop."

Instead, Sharar wanted to watch Amir squirm for a moment. The Runer's icy eyes whipped back and forth between his former apprentice and the pishaca. He took in the familiar pulsing vein in Amir's neck, the rapid rise and fall of his chest. Fear did marvelous things to the bravest of men.

"Sharar!" Amir begged as Ashar was put on the run.

Turning his face back, the scholar took over the mind of the pishaca. It had just killed one Runer and had turned on Ashar now. The creature froze, gasping and panting where he held it. An audible cry of surprise went up as the manic monster turned still. Ashar scrambled back away from it, watching it carefully. The other Runers had run, leaving him to defend the foolish guards.

"My dear sabis and siras," Sharar said easily, turning to face them. "As you can see, even without the book buried in Acenoth's tomb, this is my power. Sokar'Xenoteph, first of his name, has allowed you to see it so you may choose wisely to stand with him." He flashed the boy a quick smile to make him feel included. "No matter the political unrest from other nations, Alika will never need to fear."

Even the man from Yenka nodded mutely.

"For the last display," Sharar went on, "I will pit my creatures against a man."

Ashar turned to leave when the last gate opened to reveal the pale figure of Signar of Altevine.

"Stay, Runer," Sharar called. "Only you can deal the killing blow."

Ashar nodded and moved to the side.

The guards stabbed at Signar with long spears to get him to exit the garrison. He winced in the bright sun but stood tall. Sharar scanned the crowd. Surely the Runers would be on this side, knowing where the royal box was and that he'd be in it.

Where are you damned fools? he growled inwardly. He glanced around for guards he could command to take them, should he need. There were very few, but enough, he thought.

Instructing Amir to once again watch for Tzarik and Sybal, he forced the pishaca to attack the western boy. The monster leapt, blinking into blackness, only to appear behind Signar. The boy ducked and ran, his long legs carrying him far. He pulled an axe from the sand, left from the previous battle, and faced the pishaca.

How brave, Sharar thought. Signar had no hope of actually killing the supernatural monster, but he faced it anyway. The boy had Tzarik's damned courage and Sybal's impulsiveness.

He let the pishaca take back some control, letting its instinct guide it in its attacks against the boy. He found that his own mind hindered the creature, so he relented more. Soon, his mind only pushed the monster to attack faster, harder, to not shrink when Signar landed a mighty blow with the axe into its shoulder. The people gasped in awe when Sharar forced it to keep fighting.

Watching Signar, he saw the boy struggle—not struggle to fight or keep up, but his movements waned and faltered. He seemed distracted. Curious, Sharar forced the pishaca to blink four times in a row, flashing around Signar. Once he got the monster behind him, it leapt, teeth wide, and latched onto his side. Sharp claws wiggled into his flesh, piercing his side so the pishaca latched on fully. Signar screamed, throwing his head back.

Two things happened at once. A sudden burst of movement below finally brought two black-clad forms into view, one tall, the other shorter by a head or more. Sharar recognized Tzarik's gait easily, and Sybal's long braid flashed ashen in the sun. This almost gave him pause, but a wolven howl from the arena drew his eyes back. Where once the boy had been, now a monstrous golden wolf writhed in the sand. The shock took Sharar so thoroughly that he let go of the pishaca's mind.

The monster went savage on the wolf, but the wolf tore at it as well. Locked in feral combat, the creatures kicked up sand, black and red blood spraying out every time one landed a savage bite. Sharar reached out to the wolf, searching for its mind, the Runers forgotten.

Amir flashed in front of him. The runic barrier appeared and vanished in a blinding flash. A large, black arrow shattered on it. Sharar shot a quick glance down and saw Sybal pull another arrow from a quiver on her back and aim up at him.

Sokar screamed for guards to take the Runers.

"I'll deal with the Runers," Nasor growled, quickly snaking through the crowd and vanishing.

A tumult began to rise from the audience just below them. Sharar forced himself to focus on the creatures. Never had he seen something as magnificent as the wolf. Yes, he'd seen and studied werecreatures, but this was not the same. Those monsters looked ugly, humanoid, almost. This was a pure, real wolf. Its coat alone— gold and shimmering—brought him awe.

Focusing on the wolf, the pishaca went unbridled. The monster snapped into smoke, appearing beside Ashar. The Runer shouted in shock and flipped out his scimitar to fend off the beast.

Sharar felt it. Reaching carefully, he touched the wolf's mind.

The creature had a much stronger will than any of the other creatures he'd ever bridled. He almost heard coherent thoughts. But for the most part, it was a wild animal's mind. The wolf felt terror, shame, rage. Shouts went up around him, but he ignored them. After a moment more, he grappled the wolf's mind, subduing it. The creature whined, thrashing against his control as he forced it to lie down.

No, the boy's voice cried in his mind. *Let me go!*

Something bucked against Sharar's will, throwing him off. The thrust came so hard and forceful that he thought he physically felt something hit the inside of his skull. Blood trickled out from his left ear. He stumbled back and watched as the wolf melted away back into the shape of the boy. Beside him, Amir shouted something. He scanned the arena to find Ashar lying still in the sand.

Mostly naked now, the pale boy leapt up and ran to the fallen Runer. Signar took up his scimitar and turned on the pishaca that had once again locked its hunting gaze on him. The boy winced from the toxic tang emitting from the sword, but held his ground. The pishaca blinked into puffs of smoke as it ran towards him, snarling. Signar angled his body, putting himself between the fallen Runer and the wild monster, bent his legs, and prepared a swing.

The pishaca leapt, diving like a jaguar. Signar feinted to the side just enough and swung the orichalcum scimitar. He brought it up in a graceful arc, cleaving the monster clean in two from the sheer power of his arm. The pieces of the pishaca spiraled away from one another, slapping wetly against the arena floor. The black blood soaked Signar as he dropped the scimitar. The boy stumbled, hand over his stomach. Then he lurched forward, vomiting from the toxicity of the blade.

"Sharar," Sokar shouted perhaps five times before the scholar tore his eyes away from the boy below. Confused, he faced Sokar.

"Those Runers," Sokar said, sounding like he was repeating himself, "they tried to kill you."

Sharar panted, realizing he had been holding his breath while he'd fought Signar's wolven mind. "Where are they? Where did they go?" He scanned the area. "Where is Nasor?" he growled.

"Sira," a servant called, shaken by the roaring of the blood-thirsty crowd. "A message came for you. I was instructed to deliver it no matter what."

"I don't care," Sharar barked, shoving past the servant. He scanned the hallway that led out to the stairs, looking for the tall Masahk. He'd vanished already.

"But, sira!" the servant begged, chasing after him. "It came on a carrion falcon. And it's…" He gulped. "I can see it's written in blood."

Sharar stopped. He couldn't catch the damned Runers now. He'd lost his chance, distracted by the wolf. He glanced back below. No, the wolf boy was gone, ushered out by the coliseum guards. Ashar was gone as well. Annoyance made him grind his teeth. He had to trust that Nasor would catch the Runers. Rather, trust his hate of Runers.

The servant quickly held out the letter. Sharar recognized Tarkan's tight, sharp scrawl. Of course the necromancer would send him a letter by falcon just as he had Tzarik within his grasp. He snatched up the letter and read it. A copper tang emitted from the letter, confirming the servant's suspicion. Tarkan had written the letter in blood.

It detailed how he was ready for the rite…and that it had to be done the next night on the full moon. That it would be a blood moon. He'd have to hurry.

"I have to leave now," he growled, frustrated. "Amir!" He looked around. The Runer had run off. No doubt worried about his former apprentice. To the servant, he growled, "Find Amir and tell him he must follow me to my estate in Gypsu. Now. And tell his eminence to find those Runers and hold them in captivity once they are caught. Do not, under any circumstances, let them leave the prison."

Anger boiling his blood, he left, trusting the damned boy king to follow his orders and find Tzarik and Sybal. He'd not lose them again.

Chapter 22

One Wish

Sybal threw the kehann against the wall, winding him. The temple guard had chased them down the tunnels of the coliseum, forcing them deeper into unknown darkness. She followed Tzarik, trusting his instincts. But his shorter frame shot through the low-hanging doorways and avoided natural pillars like stalactites jutting down from the ceiling. She hit them, slowing her escape. The kehann caught up to them, shouting for them to stop.

She clashed with him as he leapt to his feet, shoving him hard against the wall with her forearm. The man gasped, clawing at her arms.

"I've...come...from Nasor," the kehann gasped.

Tzarik stopped his retreat and cantered back to Sybal.

"What does that mean?" Sybal growled, dropping her scimitar and pulling out a small knife to hold under the man's ribs.

"He wants to help you," the kehann grunted. "To escape. He has your boy. The scholar is distracted, but we cannot say for how long."

Sybal glanced sideways at Tzarik. Even in the dim torchlight under the ground, she could see he wanted to hear the man out. She hissed a warning, then released the kehann. He fell to his knees, gasping for air and coughing. Tzarik gripped her arm, holding her back to allow the man a moment.

The kehann cleared his throat and stood up, unafraid. "The scholar left. He ran for his horse and is heading to Gypsu. He received a letter from a carrion hawk, written in blood."

The Runers exchanged glances.

"So now Nasor has the pale boy," the kehann went on. "He said to come to his wing of the palace and retrieve him and he will speak with you."

"Can we trust the vizier that much?" Sybal asked Tzarik. Her voice echoed into the caves, mingling with the sound of dripping water farther down.

Tzarik adjusted his cloak and grunted. "I think we can. His loyalties lie with the dynasty and Alika. Sharar is here to open a cursed tomb. Nasor will want to stop him. Especially now that they've seen the power Sharar has."

"Then we proceed with caution," Sybal agreed. To the kehann she said, "Lead the way, sira."

The kehann nodded and led them back the way they'd run. He branched off and ascended a long set of stairs that brought them up and out a door that snaked back through the underground prison adjacent to the coliseum. Most of the people had cleared out and few eyes watched them move into the palace. The walk was long and made Sybal uneasy, but she kept her mouth closed and eyes open.

The halls of the palace were mostly empty. Only the internal waterways, birds, and the rustling of the leaves just outside the pillared walls whispered.

"Where is the Pharaoh?" Tzarik asked.

"Within," the kehann replied. "Our Hawk King is…shy of his people. The crowds exhaust him."

"Can we see him?" Sybal asked.

"No," the kehann replied curtly. "I cannot take you to him. But perhaps the vizier will."

Sybal scanned the way they took through the wide-open interior. She looked for the Mirage, the invisible Masahk guards who watched over the Pharaoh. A few servants moved quickly from room to room, and some remaining nobles lounged in the gardens outside.

The kehann stopped outside two great brass doors. He eyed them before pushing one open and slipping inside. The Runers waited a moment before he reappeared, pulling them within.

The vizier's chambers sprawled out in a single, wide-open room. It spilled onto a balcony that overlooked the temple and the keep where the kehann of the temple housed themselves. On the other side, a massive hanging garden filled with colorful flowers and fruit grew. Near the back was a long lounge with a golden floor. Across it, the pale body of Signar lay. His eyes were closed and his arms hung limp. An Alikan witch knelt next to him, her hands working over the bite of the pishaca.

"Signar," Sybal gasped, rushing to his side.

The witch looked up, relief filling her face. "Oh, thank Amuteph," she gasped, wiping sweat from her brow. "You can help him."

Tzarik joined Sybal, his hand quickly going to the boy's sallow face. "He's poisoned from the bite," he informed Sybal. He moved Signar's hands from where they were pressed into the ravaged flesh.

Sybal pulled out artiah. "Will this help?"

"First, the poison must be let," Tzarik instructed, giving the witch a leery glance. "You should have known that."

"I... I..." the woman stammered. "I didn't know if I could cut into him. He was..." Her large brown eyes shot back and forth from Signar's wound to his face.

She'd seen the wolf, Sybal realized. "Thank you, then," she whispered to the woman. "For waiting."

Tzarik pulled his small blade from his thigh and gently cut deeper into Signar's wound. The boy moaned and squirmed only a little in his delirious state. The blackened blood flowed out. Sybal watched Tzarik squeeze the wound until the blood ran red.

Sybal drew artiah slowly and the flesh scarred over. The black veins under Signar's white skin cleared.

The witch audibly sighed and sat back on her heels. "Thank you. I was not sure what to do. There is only so much healing herbs and crystals can bring."

Sybal held Signar's hand. "Thank you for your effort," she said honestly. "You probably stayed the poison with your remedies."

The witch looked up as Nasor entered, his massive frame filling the entryway from the balcony. She bowed to the vizier and backed out, taking her leave.

Gratitude towards the vizier filled Sybal. His initial meeting washed from her mind. She wanted to weep and thank him for saving Signar, but she held her ground. She turned back to the young Vaeson and noticed his breathing become less ragged. His eyes danced under their lids. She gripped his hand with both of hers. Giving in to her emotions a little, she bent her head and kissed the back of his hand. When she closed her eyes, thanking Layth'asad for keeping Signar safe, Tzarik's hand gently rested on her back. She thanked Tzarik for not condemning her. For not reminding her how much she'd hated the boy only weeks ago.

So, this is what you protect? the voice whispered. It came soft, curious. *I do not understand.*

"You do not have to run," Nasor said softly, appearing behind them, not wanting to disturb the reunion. "Sharar has left for

Gypsu. No doubt more of his heinous experiments need his attention. You have four days at the very least to recover and leave."

"We're not leaving," Tzarik replied, his hand still on Sybal's shoulder. "We know what Sharar is after. We know more about him than you and can help you stop him. And he knows we're on Alika. He will come after us either now or after he has the Mahit'Onomicon."

Nasor nodded, his jackal ears twitching in alert. "He has an obsession with you in particular. I've heard him speak of you. Why?"

Sybal raised her head, looking at her mentor, waiting for his answer.

"I can't say why," Tzarik answered honestly. He reached down and stroked Signar's sweaty locks off his face.

"Your western boy…" Nasor stopped, trying to find the right words. "He is unique."

"I'm afraid we cannot discuss that," Sybal replied, ending the inquisition there. "It is not our magic to divulge."

"So be it," the vizier replied with a gentle nod. He took a deep breath, crossing the room to a desk. "I must confess, I despise Runers. In the past, I have treated your brethren badly."

Sybal shook her head. "That's not uncommon. We're used to it."

"But, as you said, I despise Sharar more." The Masahk unrolled a map and traced the lines that outlined Caerwren. He hummed a moment in thought. "Stay if you must. I cannot make you flee. But if you choose to put yourself between Sharar and the tombs, I hope you do so with commitment."

"Won't you try to council Sokar?" Sybal asked. "Won't he listen to you?"

The Masahk turned his face away, looking up into the sky. "He will not. It's not a matter of Sokar's pride any longer. Acenoth is his ancestor. It is a matter of the dynasty, Sokar's mark on history."

"He could be written into history as the Pharaoh who stopped a sorcerer," Sybal suggested.

Nasor shook his head, his ears drooping slightly. "There is no sorcerer yet."

Sybal opened her mouth to reply, but Tzarik stopped her with a look.

"Go back to the embassy," Nasor suggested. "Sharar might think you have fled, and I will encourage this thought as best I can. The ambassador from Bahratt should be returning soon as it is."

"We won't be here long," Tzarik said. He motioned for Sybal to help Signar stand. She did, gathering the boy in her arms. "Let us talk in private, to plan."

"Of course." Nasor gave them a stiff bow again. He halted, as if something pained him. "You cannot know what it means for me to ask this of you. If you choose to stay, Runers," his tone turned serious, "I pray you will trust me. Help me save my king from the twisted brambles the scholar has planted in his mind."

"LEAVE NOW?" Sybal asked, her heart falling. They stood in one of the bedrooms of the embassy that they'd taken for themselves.

Tzarik rummaged through the wardrobe, finding more clothes for Signar. Almost nothing was long enough for the tall boy. Sybal collapsed onto the bed, back bent in defeat.

"We have very little time," Tzarik replied. "It will take Signar and me weeks to travel to Caerwren and back. More than a month of travel, if we're lucky."

"But you don't have to leave now," Sybal begged. "And let me come with you. I cannot stay here, hiding every day, waiting for Sharar to come back."

"No," Tzarik replied. "I need you to watch Sharar and keep an eye out for Tarkan. With Sharar gone from Mysir, I need you to try to speak with Sokar. You know far more about interacting with a royal court than I do."

"What if they find the book before you're back?"

"Pray that doesn't happen."

She reached her hand out as he passed, pulling him onto the soft bed. He let her, looking her in the eye. She searched his face, desperate to see if he, too, had any doubts about leaving Alika so suddenly. But as usual, his stoic visage gave nothing away besides his resolute decision. Unable to think of words to argue with, she kissed him, putting her arms around his neck and pressing him down underneath her.

He opened his mouth to argue back, but she covered his lips with her hand, shaking her head. "Why do you have to leave for Caerwren now?" She straddled his hips, sitting atop him, looking down into his blue eyes.

"Sharar will become a sorcerer," he started, "unless we can stop him. But I don't think we can. I must get Signar to safety."

She shook her head, confused. "Then why leave? Signar has months before they want him returned."

"The blades," Tzarik replied. He took her arms in his hands and tried to gently push her off, but she slipped her hands out, pressing her palms into his shoulders to fortify her hold on him. "The sigiled blades I took from ShanBao, Wu-Zhiang, and Yasuke are on Caerwren somewhere. Most likely in Altevine. I don't know what their magic is, but I saw those same sigils on the Vorlamir's blade in the Deep. They must be powerful magic, soul-binding. They used those sigils on the scrolls and their blades to send sentients and supernatural creatures alike into their crypt. Once Sharar is a sorcerer, a simple blade—perhaps not even orichalcum—might not take his life. Those blades may be the answer we need to end him."

Sybal sank into his words, remembering the mysterious weapons the Wushito used. "We could get another blade. Xia would be a shorter journey. And Hiro could arrange for a Wushito blade to be given to you. You don't even know where the blades are on Caerwren. They could be lost or destroyed."

"I doubt they were destroyed," Tzarik sighed, squirming under her once again to try to get up.

She didn't let him. She wanted to touch him, to feel his scarred skin under her fingers. Especially if he was just going to leave again. She leaned down, pressing her chest onto his and laying her head down under his chin. He gave in, running his fingers through her long hair.

"They are sigils from the Deep, perhaps the god's language, even," he went on. "The Vorlamir, whatever he is, has the power of life and death, and they are his sigils. They are the only thing I can be sure will end Sharar. And I know they will be in Altevine. Sjörna killed Mamun. She wouldn't have wasted the saddle, the swords. She might not have known what the sigils were, but she'd have known they were magic. She'd have kept them somewhere like a trophy. Like she kept that Reks' axe above her throne. Yes, I know they are in Altevine. And..." His voice grew thick. "It will be safer for Signar to be on Caerwren among his people than with us."

"You'll leave him?" Sybal gasped, sitting up.

Tzarik's brow furrowed in mild confusion. "Yes. It is his place."

"I will not stay," the gentle voice of Signar said.

They both turned to see him standing in the doorway, wrapped in a white cotton sheet. The bandages on his torso bled through. Sybal rolled off Tzarik now that he watched them. She stood up.

"You have to," Tzarik argued back, joining Sybal in standing. "You are Reks of Altevine. Your people need you."

"And they will have me," Signar agreed. He entered the room and came to the foot of the bed. Returning to something of his old, wildling self, he sat on the floor, leaning against the brass bed frame. He looked up sadly at them. "But I can't stay. Not yet. That man..." He looked away, reliving the events in the coliseum. "He was in my head. I heard him speak to me. I know he heard my thoughts."

Shock shot through Sybal. "Sharar?"

Signar nodded. His long fingers clenched into a fist of determination around something in his hand. "He spoke to me. He commanded me." He clenched his fists, trying to find the right words. "My wolf...obeyed. I couldn't fight back. Only his thoughts... in my head."

Sybal knelt next to Signar, taking his hand. "He can only control beasts. But you are a man."

"The wildling is an animal," Signar said darkly. "I will go to Altevine, show them I have control over myself, and test it for myself. I want to face their... trials and banish the wildling once and for all. Then," he looked up at them, his green eyes serious, "I will face the sorcerer with you, and he will not control me." He spoke as he often did, weaving Al'Myrahn words in with the Caerwren, mixing the languages he knew. He spoke haltingly, but more sure than ever before.

Sybal knew they couldn't put Signar, and in turn Altevine, in that kind of danger. But she didn't argue with the boy. Instead, she said, "It will take too long to travel to Caerwren and back."

"No, it won't," the boy interrupted. He stood and held up his hand. He held the pendent from the sheikh's house, the one that housed the trapped djinn.

"Damn," Tzarik cursed quickly.

"We never rid ourselves of the djinn," Sybal moaned. "How did we forget?"

Tzarik gave Signar a quick glance before looking at her meaningfully. She remembered now; they no doubt had been preoccupied with the loose, wild wolf when they'd crossed on the boat, since Signar had broken the cage before. Neither of them had been ready for him to be free while crossing.

Tzarik snatched at the golden chain, but Signar easily held it out of his reach. This made Tzarik's face burn with what she guessed was embarrassment and rage.

"You will not bind to that djinn," he growled. "The stories of stupid men who use the wishes for wealth, fortune, and fame are false. Binding to a djinn is more dangerous than the stories tell."

"I've thought of that," Signar argued. "I will make a, uh…deal with him."

"No," Tzarik barked again. "Do you not understand the cost of magical oaths?"

Signar didn't reply at first. "The bargain is for one wish," he said after a moment. "Then, we release it. Free it."

"What?" Sybal gasped. "So it can destroy again? Bring fiery hail from the sky? Possess an innocent sentient?"

"It won't," Signar cut in.

"How do you know?" Tzarik asked. He glared at the boy now. "You don't understand these demons, Signar."

Something akin to hurt quickly flashed over the boy's face. "I do, Tzarik. I watched my mother for fifteen years. She was wicked. Mad, even. But she never broke a, er, an oath. 'Betraying my word does me more harm than them,' she used to say. Like her—like me—this djinn will take our deal to be free. It made so much destruction because you were trying to bind it. Now we will free it."

"Demons are liars," Tzarik tried again. "It may promise to go peacefully once it's free, but it won't. It will bargain simply to gain the freedom to torment sentient kind. Why do you want to use the djinn?"

"To get to Caerwren quickly and return," Signar said simply. "One wish: for it to open a… portal to Caerwren like the sorcerers in the stories, let us through, and then take us back once we have the blades. Once it's bound to me, it must trust me as well to only use one wish. It will keep its word once I release it. I am sure. And if it doesn't," he added when Sybal stepped forward quickly, "we use those blades to send it to the crypt like the demon hunters you spoke of just now."

Sybal tried to read Tzarik's face. His feet apart and locked knees showed more worry than anger. "Then let it bind to us," she reasoned. She held her hand out to Signar.

Hesitantly, Signar handed over the pendent.

"The djinn is bound to the artifact?" she asked Tzarik. "So if we command it to return, it must?"

Tzarik nodded. "We shouldn't, though. A djinn is not something to bandy about lightly."

"I won't," Signar promised.

Taking a deep breath, Sybal said, "Djinn, the one within this pendent, come out. We have a deal to make with you."

She grunted, shrinking away from the now-floating pendent as a flash of white and black smoke crackled out of it. The demon materialized, reeking of sulfur and ash. Its red eyes glowed like coals in a black face. It looked shapeless, yet also humanoid as it floated before them. It laughed darkly, taking in each of them in turn.

"What have you summoned me for, deathless one?" he rumbled to Sybal. It laughed darkly in delight. "You cannot bind to me."

"No?" Sybal asked. "Why not?"

The djinn's red eyes rounded in fascination. "One god already holds the shackles to your soul. I cannot take an oath from one already bound."

"Then bind to me," Tzarik said through shallow breaths.

The djinn spun to face him, a hot wind whirling off it as it turned. "Are you prepared for a binding, Runer?" it laughed. "You who fear the demonic servants of gods you deny?" It stopped, eyeing Tzarik. "No. Not you. I cannot take an oath from one already bound."

Sybal flashed a look at Tzarik. "The runes stop a djinn binding?"

"Never," the djinn cackled. Its teeth glowed white and sharp against its shadowy face. "I can smell another demon on this one. I'll not take what belongs to another djinn."

"I don't have a djinn," Tzarik argued back. "I've only ever fought one other djinn in my life, and I bound it, sending it away."

The monster leered harder now. "Poor, foolish mortal doesn't know the binding on his soul." It rumbled a laugh. "Understood or not, I will not bind to one already bound."

"Take me, then," Signar said, stepping forward. "But I only want one wish."

Intrigued, the smoky demon drifted closer to the boy. "Only one? Then what, mortal?"

Signar squared up to the djinn. "Freedom. But under the condition you do not harm anyone with your unbound power."

At this, the monster growled slowly, arms flexing. "It is my nature, my one desire." He inhaled, closing his eyes, then spread his fingers wide. "The only act that makes me feel alive and free."

"If you cannot agree to this," Signar cut in, "then I will not bind to you. You will remain imprisoned in the artifact."

The creature opened its eyes, glaring, but considering. "You do not understand the nature of the djinn," it said softly.

"I will one day soon," Sybal added. "Perhaps I'll find you when that day comes."

"Ah," the djinn breathed, realization dawning as it took in Sybal's ashen hair. "The northern god has staked a claim to your soul. Soon, a sister you shall be." He hovered slower to Sybal. "Alive as well, when you turn. Most are dead, rising from death as a djinn. Not you." A vile pleasure soaked the monster's voice. "I take great pleasure in suffering. Call upon me when you join the demons, lady Runer." It cocked a smoky brow, grinning. "Make that part of the bargain."

"Fine," Sybal snapped. "But be warned, demon." She glowered at him, never having felt so sure of herself before. So dangerous.

"When I am a djinn—and if you have done anything to harm this boy today, or hide suffering in your bargain—I will find you. And I will reap such agonies on you with the power of my god that you will wish upon yourself to end it."

The djinn hummed in delight, its sharp smile returning. It drifted for a moment in silence. At last it said, "I agree. Boy." He faced Signar. "Speak your wish. I am—" it bowed where it floated in the air, "—your humble servant."

"What about the binding ritual?" Sybal asked. "What does he have to do? I've read stories of djinns who request their master's harm themselves so the first wish is healing. A master of a djinn must perform some task."

The smoky demon hovered back, away from the trio. "Sometimes a riddle is asked. Sometimes a task, as you say. I once witnessed a djinn command a woman to hatch twelve perfect eggs under a toad. She was soon devoured by the monster that comes from such a rite. The beasts hatched from the eggs and killed her entire village." The djinn smiled and chuckled deeply to himself. "Perhaps he was a fool. What if the woman would have wished for his freedom?"

"No tricks," Sybal barked. "I have made you a promise already. You are powerless unless you have a master right now, and we are bargaining your freedom."

The djinn lilted side to side as it thought. "The company you promise is far greater, my sister."

Beside her, Tzarik shifted stiffly. Sybal didn't want to think about it. About the years that would pass without Tzarik by her side. Her eternity without him.

"One wish does not strengthen me much," the demon finished.

"But the freedom," Signar reminded him. "Free to use your power for yourself, bound to no sentient."

The djinn hovered, perfectly still for a moment. "Very well," he growled. "No ritual of binding need play out today. Speak your desire."

Confused, Sybal watched the djinn for any sign of a trick. Unsure what she looked for, she called out to the voice. *You heard my bargain with this demon,* she said to it. *I will be yours, make no mistake. I go willingly when the time comes. But remember my promise today.*

The voice replied, still in Freja's soft tone, *Oaths are worth more than sacrifice. I have heard you this day, my daughter.*

"A portal," Signar said. "Take us to Altevine in Caerwren, safely. And then, when the time comes, return us here."

The djinn quivered, the smoke around its shadowy figure vibrating. "A portal? That is all? To travel in the blink of an eye to the continent of the barbarians?"

Sybal noted it sounded disappointed. She supposed, with how desperately they begged, the djinn expected more. Somehow, this made her smile.

"Yes," Signar replied. "Safely there, and safely back when we say."

"And my freedom?" the monster asked.

"The moment we're back on Al'Myrah," Signar reiterated.

"Only the one wish? No more once you are upon the icy rock?"

Signar nodded. "I'd dare not."

"This confuses me," the djinn confessed. "But I shall do it." The djinn reached out, gripping Signar's shoulder.

Signar screamed and jerked away, clutching the same spot. Something like the smell of burning flesh punctuated the air. In a flash, the djinn vanished and the pendent clattered to the floor. Tzarik shoved past Sybal, kneeling by Signar. The boy slowly pulled his hand away. There on his skin, perfectly burned onto him, was the handprint of the djinn.

"Is that his mark?" Sybal asked. She reached to her belt to pull off a tiny glass bottle of ointment for burns. While she administered it, Tzarik quickly moved around the room, gathering up two fur cloaks and boots for Signar. "You're going now?" she gasped.

"We have very little time to spare," Tzarik said. "They said Sharar has left, but we cannot know for how long. In the time we are gone, go to the palace. Try to stall Sokar. But please—" he stopped to look her meaningfully in the eye, "—be careful."

"You be careful," she shot back. She embraced Signar tightly.

The boy took up the pendent once he'd swathed himself in the fur cloak. "Now?" he asked.

Tzarik double-checked his belt and provisions. "We'll go. Leave the horses. We'll find horses there. I'm not sure how they might react to a portal."

"Tzarik," Sybal began again, but her voice was cut off, pulled from the air by a sudden loud crack.

Before them, a blue and black portal burst open, whirling like the eye of a storm. Wind ripped from it, pulling them towards it.

She lunged away from it slowly, escaping the pull.

"Sybal," Tzarik called. "Do not act rashly. Be calm. Stay safe." He held tight to Signar. Then he glared into the portal, trepidation written in every line of his face.

"Be careful," she called over the roaring wind. "Tzarik, come back to me." She looked at Signar as he wrapped the heavier cloak around himself. "Signar, keep him safe."

The boy nodded.

The duo took one step toward the portal. In a flash of blue lightning and a burst of hot cinders, it vanished, swallowing Tzarik and Signar with it.

Chapter 23

Grave-Born

Tarkan stood outside, eyes soaking up the rising blood moon. The red orb slowly crawled over the horizon, making its way into the starry blanket above him. Clouds began to fill the sky, a threat of late summer rain noticeable on the gentle breeze. The more clouds filled the sky, the bloodier it turned, reflecting the red light from the mourning moon. He stood over the grave Ashkan—and no doubt the Runer Amir—had dug some days ago.

Ashkan approached, coming out of the scholar's home, holding a bag that clinked with the bottles of items they needed for the rite. Sharar would join them soon with his dead boy.

"You have done well," Tarkan said to Ashkan. "I will remember it when I have the book in my hands."

Ashkan moved around the open grave, sprinkling the ash. "How certain are you this will work?" he asked softly.

"I have faith," Tarkan replied. "My father spoke of many spells our tribes did not partake in. Taught me how to perform some of them. I never had the strength before. There is more in the Mahit'Onomicon than a list of beasts and how to raise to sorcerer." He turned back to the manor. "Is Sharar here?"

"Below," Ashkan replied. He broke a sealed bottle of blood, dumping it into the grave. Then he repeated the motion, making a pool of red mud within the grave.

"Ashkan," Tarkan whispered, his mind wandering far, "when you are finished here, go out and find Apostles. Bring them to Mysir. Spread my message and tell them their Necro'Khan calls them."

Wordless, Ashkan bowed his head, then went back to preparing the ritual. "They will flock to you, Tarkan." Some kind of caution salted his words.

"I am ready for their veneration," he assured his Apostle.

Tarkan watched for a moment before turning back to the house. He walked silently down the dimly lit halls to the dungeon below. It was nearly pitch black except for a torch Sharar held. The light came into view when Tarkan entered the round room where Enoch waited. Sharar stood behind the contraption, slowly emptying the salty water from the glass orb. Amir stood by, watching, stony-faced and silent. Tarkan noted hard lines etched over Sharar's face as well.

"Things are not well in Mysir?" the Necro'Khan asked, keeping his tone neutral.

Amir's eyes flitted to Sharar, waiting for his answer.

"Keep your focus here, Necro'Khan," Sharar hissed. His eyes locked on to Enoch's slowly descending body. "If you fail this experimental rite, your immortality will be tested."

Tarkan could read the scholar like the scrolls he poured over. He had the look of a hunter who had spotted its prey, given chase, and lost. What had he found? The Mahit'Onomicon? No. If he had, he would have it now.

His eyes snapped to Amir. Had Sharar ran into the Runers?

Were Tzarik and Sybal on Alika? Why would they come here? Unless they knew... Tarkan chided himself inwardly. They had tracked him. He'd been focused on his plans and growing his power, so much that he'd not thought the Runers might be tracking him down. And they wouldn't be hunting him because they were concerned for his health. Surely they should be more concerned with Sharar finding the Mahit'Onomicon. They had, after all, helped Tarkan ascend to Necro'Khan. Why would they try to stop him now?

He damned them in his mind. If they wanted to find him, he'd make them pay for what they'd done to Zeva. For turning her against him, using her. He'd kill Sybal and then take Tzarik captive. Sharar was obsessed with the Runer. Yes, he wouldn't kill Sharar's prey. He came back to the present when he felt Amir's eyes on him.

"Once the water is drained," he commanded Sharar, tired of the circles his mind ran, "bring his body to the grave. We are ready."

He took the back exit that came up outside the cemetery, cutting across to rejoin Ashkan. The Apostle had staked severed goats around the grave, preparing the Blood Path for Tarkan. Tarkan stood over the grave and recited the verses to open the Deep. Having consumed voraciously, he felt no weakness as the blood was pulled from his pores and into the black wind. Before him, the blood combined with the dirt and sand to make a thick mud. The blood from the goats flowed freely, with much more to give.

"You will help me cover the body," Tarkan commanded Ashkan. "Then I will pull the blood from the sacrifices."

"Understood," Ashkan replied, backing away from the crackling opening to the Deep.

Once he had the rift in his sights, Tarkan backed away, too, waiting for Sharar and Enoch. He looked upon the gruesome rite before him, satisfied. Once he had performed the rite and the boy was raised, he would know beyond a shadow of a doubt that he had the strength needed to finish what he'd started. He could leave, find the Scriven bones of Elahel, and forge the blade with which he would smite the map. This was his last test. And the wound it would do Sharar only added to his elation.

"Where is she, Ashkan?" Tarkan asked, his long white hair whipping around his sunken face. "Where is Elahel?"

"Why?" Ashkan asked, but his tone changed. "She is safe, resting in peace, as all necromancers should. Even I cannot bear to raise her."

"Her bones," Tarkan replied, eyes fixed on the tear in the barrier. Beyond it, the Deep burned orange with flaming sand. "I need her bones."

"No," Ashkan replied, horrified. "Let her sleep in death. Use another's bones."

"Will you offer me yours?" Tarkan asked, grinning darkly.

"I am not eager for death," Ashkan confessed. "But what if there was another?"

At this, Tarkan scoffed and almost laughed. "House Nashira is full of traitors. Are you turning on your own? You would offer me one of your brethren? Is it not customary for the followers of Nashira to burn the dead? To stop the bones from being stolen?"

He saw Ashkan visibly deflate. Even if Ashkan wanted to find another dead Bone-Scriven, it would be impossible. Yes, House Nashira burned their dead, turning their bones to ash in the hottest fires. The bodies in Makan Alu'Ekmet were simply Scriven. Only the urns in the catacombs housed Nashiran bones.

Tarkan jolted inside as he thought. Ashkan had been in Makan Alu'Ekmet for some time. Guarding what? An epiphany hit Tarkan. She was there. In the catacombs. His body relaxed into elation. Elahel was in Makan Alu'Ekmet.

"Tarkan," Ashkan said slowly. "What if Sharar had another necromancer in his possession? Would that worry you?"

This gave him pause. He watched a pillar of fire strike the sand inside the Deep, the heat wave bursting out from the waiting rift. "I don't know what Sharar wants with our tribesmen," he confessed. "I only know that one of the few things a djinn—and therefore a sorcerer—cannot do is bring back the dead. I am the strongest necromancer. Another would do him no good."

"Unless," Ashkan went on, his tone cautious, "he thought that within the pages of the Mahit'Onomicon lay the secret to ascension...even with another Necro'Khan on the map."

"It cannot be," Tarkan assured him. "Sharar is a fool if he believes that. No, he only wants to collect. He will never unlock the power of the Mahit'Onomicon because he will not have the chance."

"And you?" Ashkan asked. "Once you have it, what then?"

Tarkan couldn't stop the grin that spread across his lips. "The tomb of Acenoth will be open. The halls of his tomb must be flooded with blood to raise his One Thousand and One soldiers. If I can raise this one boy, then I will repeat the spell on a grander scale. I will cast and raise his army. Not simply risen, but undead. Souls within immortal bodies. One thousand and One grave-born at my command."

Ashkan shifted. "Yes. But then what?"

Tarkan kept the grin on his face. "That is for me alone to know, Ashkan. If you choose to follow me, you will see. If not, you will be trampled underneath."

Behind them, Amir approached, carrying the dead Enoch in his arms. Sharar came behind him, torch in hand. The scholar's steps faltered when he beheld the red, crackling rift, and the gruesome ritual set out before him.

"Place the boy in the grave," Tarkan ordered the Runer.

Amir grimaced, but obeyed without a word. He slipped, splashing the red mud onto himself. But then he laid Enoch down. Tarkan ordered Ashkan to bury the boy even as he sank into the bloody mud. As he did, the Necro'Khan flexed his fingers, pulling the blood from the sacrificial goats and mixing it with the dirt. It created more bloody mud until the boy was covered.

"How...?" Sharar began, but he stopped himself.

Tarkan stepped up to the grave, the wind ripping his voice from his throat. "Enoch," he called softly into the Deep. "The Necro'Khan calls you. Come back from Janna. Follow my voice."

He felt more than saw the soul of the boy pulled from the afterlife. A dozen voices cried out in protest as he once again plundered the world of the gods, taking a soul that rightfully belonged to them. Tarkan looked into the Deep, reaching into the rift to grasp Enoch's soul.

In the distance, amidst the wavering heat and flashing fire of the Deep, a huge shape appeared. Tarkan focused on it, knowing how the deities might be enraged at his presence there. The creature walked slowly over the burning sands, one golden paw at a time. The closer it got, the more he recognized the outline of Layth'asad, the lion of Al'Myrah. He stopped, wondering if the god saw him. The lion was larger than even a draft horse, his white, beaming eyes roving over the Deep. He didn't see him. The mane, made of fire, did not smoke. A flame whipped at the end of his tale. When the god lifted his paw, a flaming print remained behind for only a moment in the sand.

Why is he here? Tarkan wondered. Had the opening summoned the god? He waited, not wanting to draw the god's attention to him. Then, a golden wisp shot past him, over his shoulder. Realizing it was the boy's soul, he stepped back, out of the rift.

Layth'asad turned his burning eyes on Tarkan. Slowly, the god's lion face turned to a snarl. But he didn't charge. Carefully, Tarkan closed the rift. It took his eyes a moment to adjust to the sudden darkness. A familiar weakness wrung the life from his body. He stumbled backwards into Ashkan, who caught and steadied him. An exhaustion took Tarkan. Before them, the mud bubbled slightly.

"What now?" Sharar shot at the necromancers.

"Wait," Tarkan panted, pulling himself up. "He will rise from the grave, born of the earth and the blood."

Amir stood back, hand tight on the hilt of his scimitar. "What if it's like a drekavahk?" he asked. "What if Enoch returns as a monster?"

Sharar shot Tarkan a look. His face pled with hope that the outcome would not be so dire. It was strange to see the scholar so worried.

"He won't," Tarkan assured them. "Of that, you can be sure." But how long would the body last? How long could the soul stay in the undead body without being sustained by blood magic? In this case, he wasn't sure. In the case of the One Thousand and One, he knew they'd stay, sustained by his blade and the oath they had to fulfill. And he'd have Acenoth himself among the ranks. "Stay if you must, but he will not rise until the blood moon sets."

He straightened his robes, flexing his now bone-thin fingers, and turned to leave.

"Where are you going?" Ashkan asked, chasing after him. "What are you doing now?"

"To find Elahel," he answered, unafraid of any wrath Ashkan might show. He was sure now that he could do what needed to be done. He'd cast his father's five spells. Now was the time to climb to greater power than even Ishmael. And better still, he knew where to find the dead necromancer's bones. Ashkan would not have burned her. He loved her too much to desecrate her. No, the fool would have held on to her, kept her hidden.

"Tarkan, no," Ashkan pleaded, reaching out to stop him. "Have I not done all you asked? Why must you torture me like this?"

"Her death will have meaning now, Ashkan," Tarkan replied. He whispered the spell to bring up the souls. He'd use them to escape Ashkan's begging; the necromancer would not be able to follow.

"You don't know where she lies," Ashkan tried again.

Tarkan smirked. "I do. There is no other reason for you to have been in Makan Alu'Ekmet all these years. It is the perfect hiding place. She is there. I will find her, and I will forge her bones into a blade so imbued with our necrotic magic that all will be in awe of the spells I will wield."

"Tarkan!" Ashkan shouted, lunging at the Necro'Khan to try to stop him. "Leave her be, please!"

The souls shot out of the earth like a geyser of oil, enveloping him. Ashkan shouted, trying to fight them away to get to him. But the darkness took over Tarkan's senses as the souls carried him into the Deep like a strike of lightning. The last thing he heard was Ashkan's pleading call.

SHARAR DIDN'T REALIZE the moon had set and the first purpling rays of the sun touched the horizon. He had stood still, eyes fixed on the muddy grave, since Tarkan left. Amir sat behind him, arms crossed and head down, dozing. The cool night hadn't yet given way to the warm morning. Birds woke in the trees in his garden on the other side of the wall. The streams seemed to grow louder the brighter the sun got. He watched the bloody mud, waiting. Surely by sunrise the spell would have worked. If it hadn't, he'd have to decide what he wanted to do first: hunt down Tarkan and put an end to the damned necromancer at last, or pursue the Mahit'Onomicon.

Behind him, Amir gasped, waking up with a jolt. The Runer's quick breaths told him all he needed to know: something was happening. Like all Runers, Amir's sulfates would alert him to monsters, danger, or the presence of supernatural events. Amir leapt to his feet, scimitar in hand, and joined Sharar at the foot of the grave.

"Is it Enoch?" Sharar asked softly. Finally, his hand holding the lantern began to shake, making their shadows quiver.

"Something is coming," Amir grunted, rubbing the sleep from his blue eyes. He gently pulled Sharar away from the grave, his icy orbs fixed on it like a falcon about to dive. "Stand behind me." He placed himself between Sharar and the grave.

Just then, the muddy earth moved, almost like it pulsed. Something leapt inside Sharar as anticipation filled him. He gripped the lantern hard, looking over Amir's shoulder. The earth bubbled in one central area. Then, a grunt sounded below the earth.

"Enoch!" Sharar cried, but Amir held him back. The Runer slowly backed away from the grave.

"Wait," Amir commanded, holding his sword out. "Whatever is coming is making my sulfates rush madly."

Then, a pale, thin hand burst out from the earth. It was so sudden both men jumped. The hand flailed back and forth as if trying to find something to grab on to. It splashed into the mud and pushed until the second hand broke the surface.

"Wait," Amir said again when Sharar tried to lunge forward. "We don't know what kind of spirit or creature this rite may have created." He shook his head. "There is no such thing as making an undead. Not like the mori or other bloodsuckers."

Sharar's breath came shallow. "Are you saying Tarkan failed or lied?"

"I don't know."

At last, a loud cry of effort came up from the grave, muffled but strong. It sounded too human, too sentient, to be a monster. And Sharar knew the voice. Knew it almost as well as his own. Enoch had a high, boyish voice. That was the kind of voice that struggled to break free. And he knew the hands: long, lithe fingers that had played the lute and been strong on a bowstring.

As the first rays of the sun hit the earth, a head covered in dark brown hair struck up through the mud. The body that came out was dirty, but Sharar recognized the bronze skin and wild brown eyes. Unable to stop himself, he shoved Amir out of the way and dashed to the grave. He slid onto his knees and reached out to Enoch. The boy spotted his father and gripped his proffered arms. Familiarity exploded into the boy's eyes.

"Help me," Enoch wheezed, his lungs weak.

"I have you," Sharar promised.

With all his strength, he pulled Enoch from the grave until his whole body slipped out. Not caring that he was utterly covered in mud and blood, Sharar pulled Enoch to his chest in a tight, desperate embrace. Enoch gasped and coughed, too weak to recip-rocate. Sharar didn't care. He gathered his son in his arms and hugged him again.

Amir appeared beside him, offering Sharar his hands to help. He took the Runer's proffered hand and grunted, pulling himself and Enoch up. The boy moaned and his legs gave out immedi-ately. Amir moved to catch him, but Sharar beat him to it. He held Enoch tight, supporting him entirely, and headed for the house.

"F-father?" Enoch gasped, looking around. "What...? Where...?"

"Don't talk," Sharar whispered. The three of them stumbled over the threshold and to the bedroom that had been prepared for Enoch. A hot bath and food waited inside.

"Where am I?" the boy asked anyway. "What happened?"

Realizing he wouldn't wait to ask questions, Sharar sighed. "What do you remember?"

They entered the room and, with Amir's help, lowered Enoch's cold, mud-caked body into the bronze tub. A servant woman brought in another huge pitcher of hot water and a tray of bath cloths and soaps. She shook madly as she put them down, lips biting back any comments. Her eyes were wide and focused on the ground before her. She quickly retreated.

Enoch hissed from the heat of the water. He turned his head

up, looking around the room and taking it in. "This isn't our home," he said, his voice quaking.

"This is my estate on Alika," Sharar offered. He went to work on Enoch's hair, picking out the mud and wiping away the blood. "Do you remember it?"

His son made a small noise, indicating that he did a little. "I feel so cold," he said. "So..."

The way his face twisted in confusion drove a stake through Sharar's heart.

"Did Sheikh Mahis—" Enoch choked. "Did he..." He shook his head. "I remember the room covered in blood. My blood. There was a Runer."

"Yes," Sharar said sternly, not willing to lie to his resurrected son. "Mahis had you runed. I saved you as long as I could. I took you away."

"How?" Enoch asked. He shook despite the hot water.

Sharar dipped the washcloth into the water, running it down Enoch's back. "I did what I had to. But you're here now."

His boy didn't reply. His sad, brown eyes flit from the bloody water to Sharar, to Amir, then back to Sharar. "I don't understand, Father."

Relief filled Sharar at the steady, constant conversation. He finished cleaning the blood and mud from Enoch and helped him dress before letting him sit and eat. Once he dressed and ate, some of his strength came back. Moving slowly, Sharar guided Enoch through the manor and around the grounds, letting him get his legs back. As the morning wore on, no sign of the runes or death showed on Enoch's body. Like he had been born anew.

In the privacy of his own mind, Sharar praised Tarkan. He'd always known the Porshain had the potential to be Necro'Khan. And the drive. He'd admired Tarkan's resilience and will. Yes, he'd doubted that Tarkan could raise an undead—a living soul inside a dead or dying body—but now he had no doubts.

Since Enoch was too weak to do much else, Sharar walked inside the garden with him, talking about before. They discussed the past until soon, Sharar felt Enoch would once again ask about how he had been awakened. What had happened.

Sharar let Enoch take the lead, seeing where the boy would walk to. He led his father to the stables.

"Mahis bought me a horse once," Enoch mused, leaning heavily against the stable doors and taking in the magnificent stalls before him.

"Was he never kind to you?"

"Sometimes he was."

"How much do you remember?" Sharar asked.

"Everything," Enoch said with a sigh. "Like I awoke from a long sleep."

Sharar smiled down at his son. "Do you remember when you ran away for the first time?"

Enoch smiled and gave a weak laugh. "I was four. Mother and Mahis had an argument and I decided then I cared for neither of them. I wanted my father. The man who loved me, who risked his life to come and find me. I put some sort of herbal mixture in Mahis's wine, making him ill. He had to keep excusing himself from the audience he had with the quadis." Enoch laughed now. He looked up at Sharar. "When I climbed out my window, my nurse shouting after me, I saw you waiting. I remember running to you."

Unable to stop himself, Sharar placed his hand at the back of Enoch's head and pulled him in for an embrace. He kissed the top of his head and held him. "That's the day I taught you to shoot a bow. I remember how impressed I was the next time I saw you."

"I practiced," Enoch beamed gently. "I wanted to impress you."

"You never failed," Sharar confessed. "Your sword skill, your artistry with the lute… I loved everything about you."

Enoch pulled away, smiling, and looked back at the horses. A moment of silence passed before he spoke again.

"Will you not tell me what happened? How long has it been?"

Sharar swallowed hard and focused on the white Al'Myrahn mare inside the stables instead. It hurt to not look at Enoch right now, but he didn't want to meet the boy's eyes as he confessed. "It's been nearly five years since…" He stopped.

Enoch frowned and faced Sharar. "Father… Did I die?"

Now he had to meet his son's wide, sad eyes. "In a way, you did. I kept you preserved, knowing one day I'd bring you back."

"How?"

Pushing past the question, Sharar opened the stable half-door and went inside. He led Enoch in, taking his hand. Together, they made their way to the white mare's stall. Sharar reached up and stroked the animal's long, pristine neck. Enoch joined him, still frowning in concern.

"Enoch," Sharar began, "I've studied magic most of my life, despite it being outlawed in Al'Myrah outside the Masahk and the temples."

"And Runers," Enoch murmured.

"I've studied the Runers," Sharar added quickly. "Or at least, I am trying. To save you."

Enoch looked up, eyes curious.

"I was able to save you because of a djinn I found," Sharar said, eager to let his son know exactly what he was doing to bring him back.

"A demon!" Enoch cried.

Sharar reached out, grabbing Enoch's wrist as he pulled away. "He's not like other djinn, my son. You recall the studies I started here?"

Enoch nodded.

"Well, I'm close," he whispered. "I've waited and planned, putting everything into motion with precision. And, with the news of my necromancer coming here, I knew I was right. When I told the Dynast Pharaoh I was the one they called the Father of

Monsters, he told me about Acenoth IV and the Battle of the Promise."

He waited a moment. Seeing his son shrink away from him cut his heart deeply, like he didn't think possible. So he stopped. But, being his son, Enoch understood.

"So you intend to…become a sorcerer?" Enoch asked haltingly. "Because of me?"

"Yes," Sharar whispered before considering his answer. When Enoch stepped back, gasping, he corrected himself. "Not entirely, though. You know I have this burning need for knowledge. I cannot stop learning. I must know why things happen the way they do."

"No, you don't," Enoch shot back. He turned and stumbled over the uneven stable ground, then pushed outside the stable and made his way out into the grounds.

"Enoch!" Sharar shouted. He ran after him, catching up easily. Enoch gasped for air, his legs and lungs weak. Sharar gathered him in his arms and whispered, "What I am doing is not wrong. My motives are purely scientific. For understanding. To know why the world is the way it is. Stop, Enoch."

Gasping, the boy stopped and collapsed into his father's arms. He took deep, shuddering breaths. Giving in, Enoch said, "Talk to me about other things."

Grunting, Sharar helped Enoch up and held him tightly as they turned toward the orchard. "Of course, my son."

Content to simply have his boy back, Sharar turned to other topics of conversation. Thinking he had the rest of his life to convince Enoch of his motives, he began to explain the Al'Myrahn trees he'd had imported and left talk of djinns and Runers for later.

ⴲ

"FATHER," Enoch sighed, his face going pale. Dark circles appeared under his beautiful brown eyes as the sun set. "We've discussed politics, the seminary, the academies in Rom, and even the sultana's harem. I remember how you speak when you are avoiding a conversation. I feel…" He swallowed. "Go back to talking about your studies. About becoming a sorcerer."

"Why?" Sharar asked. "I don't want to upset you again."

Enoch's face turned dark. He stopped walking and froze. "When I died, I heard it in my blood. Voices. The runes, perhaps. I was told I had been taken, that I'd died. I remember a light. Perhaps even the form of Layth'asad himself."

This made Sharar's heart falter once again. He faced his son. "Why are you saying this?"

"Because," the boy replied softly. "I feel… I feel it again."

"What?" Sharar gasped, gripping Enoch's arms. "No. How?"

Over Enoch's shoulder, he saw the sun dip below the horizon. Had the entire day passed already? Time ran cruelly fast.

"So he hasn't found a way." Despair filled Sharar. "He knew. He did this to me out of malice."

Enoch went limp for a moment in his hands, almost collapsing before standing up again. "I feel so cold. It hurts again."

Sentimental panic almost forced a string of babbling worry from Sharar's lips, but he bit it back. "Enoch," he begged instead. "Can you hold on?"

Enoch stumbled and fell into Sharar's arms. He shook.

Then he reached a cold, clammy hand up to Sharar's face. "Father, listen to me." He spoke with urgency. "You don't have to do any of the things you said on my behalf. You're not that man. Don't—" He choked before going on. "Don't hurt anyone. You can stop now. It's not too late."

"It is," Sharar whispered, but Enoch's words stabbed him deep. "I have to finish what I started."

"You don't," Enoch insisted, his face growing paler and paler. He winced with a pain Sharar could not alleviate.

"I can't stop, Enoch. I did this for you. You know of my burning desire of knowledge. I can't control it. Years of my life have gone into studying all I need to find the book, to consume a djinn. Why ask me to throw it all away?"

Tears filled Enoch's eyes as the shuddering overtook him. "So I might see you again," he whispered. "In Janna. We can be together in the afterlife. Please, Father."

Emotion consumed Sharar even as he tried to rise above it. "Enoch, I... I can't. I won't."

Face twisted in sadness, Enoch nodded in defeat. The boy went limp, crumpling into Sharar's arms. "Help me, Father," he whispered. His eyes turned milky white.

"Not again," Sharar growled through gnashed teeth. "Tarkan, why?"

Enoch went rigid, mouth open to gasp for air that would never come. His face twisted into familiar pain, then he went still.

Chapter 24

---◆---

Apostle of the Bones

Sharar didn't hear the necromancer and the Runer approach him from behind. His legs had long since lost the sensation of the cooling sand beneath him. His bent back ached, but he'd not registered it until Amir touched his shoulder. The weight of Enoch in his arms had numbed as well. He lifted his head, his neck cramping in stiff pain. Ashkan stood several yards back, brows furrowed in an expression impossible to read. Concern? Pity? Revulsion?

Amir knelt down before Sharar and soundlessly pried his arms off Enoch's now stiff corpse. The black veins from the rejected runing stood out against the moonlight under his son's perfect skin. Amir grunted, pulling the body back until it was out of Sharar's line of sight. Sharar didn't look up, feeling the necromancer's eyes on him.

"I should have known," Sharar croaked into the night air. "That he couldn't last. Wouldn't stay."

"He felt no pain," Ashkan said stoically. "His soul only left, returning to Janna. You should be grateful for that."

Why was the necromancer trying to comfort him? Assuming that's what his words meant. Sharar wanted to stand, straighten his back to his full height, but even thinking about moving made his bloodless legs tingle. He'd just fall, and before the necromancer, that would be worse.

"Grateful?" he whispered in disgust. "Grateful I watched him die a second time? That with his dying breath, he begged me to stop everything I have worked for for the last twenty years?" He collapsed onto his knees.

Amir returned, reaching down to him. "Get up, Sharar," he commanded. "The Necro'Khan left last night. When will he be back?" He directed his question at Ashkan. "Why are you still here?"

Sharar took Amir's proffered hand and leaned heavily on the Runer as he forced his body to move. He'd been sitting for hours, it seemed. The moon was high in the sky now, white and round, clean, pure.

Ashkan took a cautious step toward the duo, his hands together in front of him. "Tarkan left, transporting himself through an ancient and vile means. Enslaving the souls of the dead."

"I don't care," Amir interrupted gruffly. "What is he planning to do?"

"You want to know why he left?" Ashkan asked, dropping his hands. "Did he know Enoch would revert to his death?"

"Yes," Sharar answered quickly. He motioned to the house, directing Amir to take him inside. Every step shot tingling pain through his legs as the feeling started to come back.

Ashkan joined them. "I think he did. The blood could not last. It never does for us."

Sharar noted his tone. He'd dealt with men with ulterior

motives his entire life; he knew what that tone signified. "And what does that mean to you?" he asked.

The necromancer didn't respond right away, eyes focused on the lantern outside the back door. "Tarkan has started down a path he planned long ago. I should have known, coming from a man as ambitious as Ishmael, that he'd not stop until he reached the peak of whatever mountain he thinks he's climbing."

"Speak plainly," Amir snapped. He kicked the door open and set Sharar down on a lounge, calling for water.

Sharar watched Ashkan's pale, un-Scriven face in the dim fire-light. He looked like a haunt, swathed in black. "This was an experiment?" he asked. Something inside him raged at that. Tarkan had used his son as an experiment. Sharar had often done terrible things for the sake of discovery. He knew that. But it hadn't happened to him. "Perhaps I have had too much of an influence on him over the years," he said dryly.

A servant brought a pitcher of water and Amir poured and handed him a cup. Sharar took a long drink, almost coughing as it soaked his dry throat.

"What is he doing now, necromancer?" Sharar asked Ashkan. He was ready to command Amir to beat the answer out of him. But he was not ready for the necromancer's accommodating reply.

"He is traveling to Makan Alu'Ekmet."

The scholar and the Runer shared a quick, startled glance.

"Why did you— That is, are you speaking the truth?" Sharar stammered.

"I see the shock this brings you," Ashkan replied. "But I am not lying. I have no hope of stopping Tarkan, since he travels through the Deep the way he does. So I must find other avenues of hurting him."

A smile Sharar could not stop twitched in the corners of his mouth. "Why? What has he done to you?"

Ashkan replied, "I was his Apostle before Zeva. But before that, I was a Scriven for House Nashira."

"Ah," Sharar mused slowly. "His enemy."

Ashkan tilted his head slightly. "Not entirely. Tarkan rebelled against his father then. The enemy of his enemy became his tribe. My wife, Elahel was with me when he joined us. Of course, then I did not know he sought the power to break the chains that tied him to Ishmael. And then, to you. Tarkan is driven by his need for total freedom. To never again be bound."

This brought some clarity to the Necro'Khan's suddenly trusting behavior. Sharar had thought he'd never see Tarkan again. That the then-necromancer would bury himself in a crypt some-where and never reemerge. But he'd overestimated Tarkan's fear. He did not shrink away into the darkness. He rose, ascending to heights of power Sharar had never thought he could achieve.

"And now you're back to being enemies?" Amir asked.

Ashkan paced away from them, studying a tapestry on the wall. It hung a dozen feet long and almost two dozen feet wide. Sharar watched him, knowing he'd speak again soon. The necromancer ran his eyes over the entire tapestry before turning to face them again.

"This is a Xian work of art?" Ashkan asked.

Ignoring the necromancer's dancing game, Sharar obliged him. "Yes. Depicts the rise of Shen Mi-long, the mythical third Di-Huan of Xia and his battle with the red dragon. There is symbolism in the flowering trees, but I never was one for allegory and such things. He was a great man. A real leader."

Then he saw what had drawn Ashkan's eyes. The necromancer studied the blade in Shen Mi-long's hand.

"The sigiled blades of Wushito," the scholar supplied. Even saying the name drew a phantom pain to his side. His hand went to where the wound had festered for two years. It was still gone, healed. "The sigils were given to the man who wrote the Xai'de Jing."

"Xia's name for the Mahit'Onomicon," Ashkan added, more for his own clarification.

"Yes." Sharar sat up. Amir stood, helping him to his feet. "Through my research, I have come to two conclusions: that the orichalcum the Runers use, created by the Dohkma—the god in the Silent Tower in the north—is an abomination of the sigils. Or that the sigils are a way mortal kind found to emulate what the orichalcum does without being bound to a god. I assume the sigils come from the Mahit'Onomicon as I have found not a single Wushito who knows what they say. Just what they do. There is one symbol on every blade, and that same symbol is engraved on a golden door over a crypt on Xia."

"Which do you think is true?" Ashkan asked. "Which came first, orichalcum or the sigils?"

Sharar half shrugged. "I have spent my life studying the runes and the Runers. Tarkan and I began our study of Xia together some years ago. I believe the crypt to be the end of that magic, though. I watched the Wushito use their sigils to bind haunts. The blades slew beast and sentient alike. But they didn't use them for combat. No, they reserved the sigiled blades for slaying the supernatural or taking a soul. After some time, I deduced that the sigils bound the souls within the blades."

He halted his speech a moment, remembering the faint wailing he could sometimes hear from ShanBao's blade. "I think some gathered souls within their blades. Monsters and demons, too. Perhaps they thought it made their strike more potent. But other Wushito then caged these souls inside what they called the crypt. It was locked atop the Hallow City behind wards, sigils, and other protections."

He stopped suddenly. Ashkan turned to face him, frowning

slightly. Even Amir turned his face to the scholar, a thoughtful look filling his blue eyes.

"No," Sharar almost laughed. "It can't be an..." He looked up at Ashkan. "You would know better than I. Could an opening to the Deep be hidden inside the crypt?"

So many unspoken thoughts, theories, and answers flashed over Ashkan's face that Sharar wished he could read the fiend's mind.

"I'm sorry," Ashkan said, his honesty still shining through. "I don't know. Perhaps. The Wushito is such an old creed, rivaled only by the Runers. And Xia guards its secrets so fiercely that even the brightest scholar might not know."

For now, Sharar decided that had to be the answer. Thank Layth'asad Tarkan had never gotten to Xia. They'd fallen out before Sharar had sailed to the east. But the Necro'Khan knew. They'd discussed it many times before Tarkan had turned on him. He made up his mind then to go back. He'd have to return to Xia and finish what he'd started someday.

"Ashkan," Sharar asked, using the necromancer's name. "What was it you wanted to say before? I sensed you were going to proposition me. I am curious to know what one like you might bargain with me for."

The moon peeked down into the wide-open windows, splashing their shadows across the floor. Ashkan's face turned serious.

"As I said, I cannot stop Tarkan from taking Elahel. He wants her bones."

Amir made a pained face, imagining something Sharar could not guess at.

"Why?" the scholar asked.

"Bone-Scriven," the necromancer offered easily. He pointed to the sigiled blade in the tapestry. "He told me he is forging a blade, but I didn't understand. Perhaps made of orichalcum. He plans on using her bones, bearing our scriptures, within the blade."

For one of the rare times in his life, Sharar listened to something about magic he did not understand. "What would that do?"

"I fear..." Ashkan moved closer to Sharar now. The warning glared brightly in his eyes. "I fear he will use it like an artifact. A way to channel the blood magic. To make it more powerful, and sustain it longer than any amount of consuming will. He is creating new spells because the magic bends to his will. Because he is Necro'Khan. *This* is why Porsh fell. Because one necromancer thought he deserved more power than what our holy texts gave him. Being master of the blood makes one its author. Creator. With something like that, Tarkan will be able to perhaps command hordes of not just risen, but undead."

"But it didn't last," Sharar cut in, remembering his once again lifeless son in his arms.

"But with an artifact, they will." Ashkan said it like a promise.

"And he's gone to forge this necrotic blade?" Amir asked.

"He is well on his way," Ashkan replied. "And he moves too quickly for me to stop him."

At last, Sharar understood. He breathed out in triumph, smiling at the necromancer. "The jongleur."

"Yes," came the hissed reply. "I can make him an Apostle."

"And then?" Amir asked, his dull mind not seeing the end. Sharar admired the Runer for so many of his bullheaded qualities, but could not stand how slow he was most times.

"Then," Sharar supplied, "I will have the Mahit'Onomicon. I will be a sorcerer. I will force that bastard below our feet to do as I command. Make him mine. I will have a chance to take Tarkan down if I can bridle even a fraction of his power. If I have one of his own kind at my side."

The Runer nodded now, rubbing his chin, which needed a shave. "You need to hurry, then."

"I do," Sharar agreed. "Necromancer?"

"I can do it right now," he offered. "It is not a ritual. All it takes is a stab of my ruby blade to his heart."

Sharar smiled.

SHARAR LED the march to his dungeon, oil lamp in hand. The other two followed right behind him, now accompanied by the silent human form of his djinn. The scholar spared no ceremony, unlocking the garrison door and flinging it open hard. When it hit the stone wall behind it, Vicdan looked up from where he lay on the wet, cold floor. He blinked and slowly pushed himself away from them.

"To what do I owe the pleasure of your company?" he asked, clearly straining to keep his voice jovial. "Are we going to go for a walk as friends? Please say we are. I am in desperate need of some sun."

He tried to move his legs but hissed. The manacles around his ankles were Sharar's personal favorite. Metal spikes of varying sizes lined the inside, making the wearer more placated and still than if they were normal shackles.

"Even if we were, you'd have to wait until morning," Sharar said. He motioned for Amir and the djinn to pick Vicdan up off the floor.

"What can you possibly want to do to me?" Vicdan moaned in good spirits as Amir pulled hard on a chain wheel, lifting Vicdan's arms over his head. "I have it on good authority that you are fascinated by some, shall we say, irregular activities. And for once, I thought we might have something in common, but perhaps not."

Sharar smiled, easily pacing around the now hanging younger man. "Your light words, in instances such as these, are what fascinate me."

"Oh, scholar," Vicdan said sarcastically, "at least get to know me before flattering me."

Ashkan ripped open Vicdan's shirt and went to a table alongside the wall where he'd placed his black box.

"Can you at least tell me your name first, before you start to disrobe me?" Vicdan sputtered, looking down at his torn shirt. "You lot move quickly. Haven't had a plowing in a while, is that it? I typically don't go for your sort, but I'll make an exception because you're so rich." He offered Sharar a smile, drunk on exhaustion.

"Incredible," Sharar mused, shaking his head. "In the face of harm and possible torture, you choose glee."

"I've come up with far more riddles and jokes since the last time you beat me," Vicdan offered. "They're much better than the last ones. Shall I give you a recitation?"

Sharar leaned in close to his prisoner's face, making Vicdan grimace and try to take a step back. The jongleur was rank from his torture and the damp of the dungeon. Still, he held his place. "You will be my slave. You will have no choice in the matter once I have the book. I will be on my way to fetch it after we're done here. I should have it already, but Tarkan delayed me."

Vicdan's eyes quickly flitted to Ashkan and back. "I see. Scholar, I am a terrible choice for your own personal necromancer. Go find another. They're crawling over Al'Myrah. They probably have one on Rhostrana, for all I know." He stopped and laughed lightly, making Sharar glare at him. "I'm the best you've got?" He shook his head. "I am disappointed in you, scholar. Sorry for you, too."

Growling, Sharar brought the back of his hand across Vicdan's face hard. It didn't sting badly enough, so he repeated the gesture until his knuckles bled. Satisfied when Vicdan choked, he stepped back.

"Get this over with, necromancer," he hissed.

Vicdan spat a large blob of blood and mucus onto the ground as Ashkan approached. "I don't want to live for eternity amongst the dead," he sighed. "I'm going to make a terrible immortal. And a worse necromancer." He met Ashkan's green eyes. "We're brothers in the tribe, you know? Why are you doing this for him?"

Ashkan purred dangerously, "I could flay your flesh from your bones and give them to Tarkan, but I won't. I'm giving you a chance."

"Oh, you are too kind," Vicdan said.

At last, when Ashkan lifted the ruby dagger, a quick moment of panic shot through Vicdan's brown eyes. That's all Sharar ever wanted: to see the courage and defiance melt away from his subject's face, replaced by fear. He took a deep breath, savoring the fleeting moment.

The jongleur flailed his legs only once before stopping, the spikes drawing more of his blood. "It's no use, scholar," he began, eyeing Ashkan, who was making his way to him. "I don't have a hope of standing up to Tarkan."

"It's not you I have to trust," Sharar said simply. "It's myself. I trust that when I am a sorcerer, I will have all the power I need to make you a worthy adversary."

Vicdan gasped for air as the panic finally set in. "I think you overestimate yourself. You think you're so smart and have found the way to ultimate power—"

"Enough!" Sharar cut in.

At the same time, Ashkan plunged the ruby dagger up to the hilt into Vicdan's chest. The necromancer whispered a few words that quickly flitted away on a brief, gentle wind. Vicdan gave a few strangled gasps, fighting for breath, before he went still.

Sharar watched, a tinge of worry filtering into his heightened and burning emotions. "Do the scriptures reject Apostles like the runes?"

"If they do," Ashkan sighed, "it would have happened when he was made Scriven." With a grunt, he jerked the ruby blade from Vicdan's chest.

The jongleur's head tipped forward between his arms and his rasping, rattling breath filled the air.

"Stop fighting them," Ashkan whispered. "You will lose that battle. Give in, let them take you."

Fascinated, Sharar stepped closer. He couldn't see or feel whatever had told Ashkan that Vicdan was fortifying himself against the words engraved on his bones. Vicdan gasped, unable to get air into his lungs, grunted, and moaned through gritted teeth. It sounded like a battle.

"Let them awaken, brother," Ashkan whispered, more gently this time. He placed his palm softly against Vicdan's cheek, whispering something else Sharar could not hear.

Finally, Vicdan gasped and his head dropped back. He took in several breaths of air. Before Sharar's eyes, the wound on Vicdan's chest healed over, leaving him without a blemish again. Amir stepped forward without Sharar having to instruct him. He gripped a handful of Vicdan's hair and forced his head up. The singer blinked, his vibrant green eyes flashing in the darkness.

"Damn it," Vicdan muttered, as if nothing worse than losing a game of dice had just happened.

Something akin to relief flooded Sharar. He breathed easily and stepped out of the cell. "Demon, see to it he consumes. Force him, if you have to. I want him strong to cast the five spells."

The djinn bowed mutely.

"Amir, quickly," Sharar barked. "We will wait no longer. It's time for Sokar to make his mark on his dynasty, open the tomb of Acenoth, and give me the power I've spent a lifetime searching for."

Chapter 25

---◇---

Corpse-Eater

White light blasted into Tzarik's eyes, like flashes of the brightest lightning in pure darkness. Every strike blinded him, making his eyes water, and sent a thudding into his skull. The wind turned from hot torrents to cold gusts, taking his breath away and filling his lungs with cutting frost. A terrible moment passed when he hung, suspended in the air, Signar shouting in the distance. Then he rushed again, falling onto the rough, rocky, cold ground of Caerwren. When his back hit the ground, his brain continued to spin, making his stomach swirl until vomit choked him. He coughed, spewing it up into the air like a geyser before turning over to empty his mouth.

The first thing Tzarik noticed was the brittle grass under his fingers, which stuck out from the cut-offs of his black leather gloves. He gripped it, willing the world to hold still and stop spinning. When he opened his eyes, the horizon blurred, making him nauseated again, so he clenched them closed. Heavy footfalls approached him, a hand gently lying on his shoulder.

"How are you standing?" Tzarik asked Signar, recognizing the long legs that crouched next to him.

"I suppose I have the stomach for it," the boy replied.

Tzarik grunted in annoyed admiration, pushing himself up. Heights made him that way, too: nauseated, unnecessarily afraid, palms clammy, his body shaking. He waited a moment longer, then halfway pushed up, not sure if his stomach would revolt again.

Signar gripped him under his arms and hauled him up, steadying him. "Will you survive doing it again?" he asked with a light smirk.

"Careful, boy," Tzarik warned him, unable to hide his own weak grin. "Just because you tower over me doesn't mean I cannot take you down if need be."

"I believe you," Signar replied.

Finally, being able to see, Tzarik took in the place the djinn had thrown them to. The pendant still hung around Signar's neck. Tzarik glared at it, daring the demon to go back on his deal and remain attached to Signar. He didn't trust the ashen slaves of the gods.

Tall, straight trees surrounded them. Dark green leaves sprouted from the tops, the gray trunks shimmering in a late morning frost. But the animals did not sing and cry, as if it were late morning. Tzarik perked his ears up and scanned the thin forest. Between the trees, a tall figure moved quickly, determined. He couldn't be sure, but he thought a strange orange aura of fire wavered around the figure as it dashed in bursts through the trees. Caerwren had many strange monsters and creatures to be wary of.

"The sun is low," he mused, not wanting to run into the fiery figure while they were isolated. It vanished.

"It is the very end of summer," Signar replied, almost whispering. He began to walk through the trees, turning so the sun hovered behind them. "The sun will not set until autumn, what we call Mayvon. It's probably midnight. That's why it's so quiet."

"Is the year so old?" Tzarik asked, following the boy carefully. "It seems only weeks ago we were fleeing these shores."

Signar nodded, his keen green eyes flitting from shadow to dell, tracking things Tzarik could not see. "I can hardly believe the thoughts I used to have then," he confessed. "I understood so much, but didn't have the words to say them."

A small light of pride lit inside Tzarik at hearing this, though he didn't believe he could take credit for it. Signar was a clever and smart boy. The people of Caerwren had forced him to be wild, convinced his mind could not comprehend even simple things. Signar had believed it as well, leaning in to his wild nature. He hoped now the boy saw differently.

"Do you know where we are?" Tzarik asked after a few more minutes of walking with the sun behind them. Despite the sun hovering above the horizon, the shadows lay dark.

"East, towards Altevine. We are close." The Vaeson sniffed the air. "See?" He pointed through the trees.

Tzarik narrowed his eyes, looking for signs of life. A few pillars of smoke rose in the east, but due to the hills and valleys of Caerwren, he couldn't see much more. He trusted Signar. A thick, gray mist hung over the ground, hiding the round, gray rocks and moss. Small forest creatures dashed around and under it before scurrying up the trunks of the trees.

A sudden, familiar smell of decay hit Tzarik hard as a wind rushed up from the north. He stopped, his sulfates whispering in his ear. He reached a hand out to stop Signar and they both froze. A branch snapped to his right. Above them, the forest creatures quieted. Signar unconsciously crouched low, like he used to do when hiding behind Tzarik. This time, though, his eyes glared, looking for the danger.

"I smell death," he whispered.

"Something is coming for whatever died," Tzarik agreed. "My sulfates are cold as ice."

Then he heard it: a moaning almost like the thick branches of a tree when a heavy breeze pushes through them. Then, the rhythmic clicking and clacking of wordless communication, followed by a low hissing like a smooth spring. Without more wind, a patch of flora to Tzarik's right rustled and vanished.

"A ligda," he informed Signar. "A corpse-eater. They prey on weak or dead creatures. They are creatures made to blend into the dark green foliage you have here on Caerwren. Some parts of Rhostrana, too. Maybe Xia. They are drawn to corpses. You won't see them until it's too late. Their skin is green, and they have scales almost like the bark of these trees over most of their bodies."

"Yellow eyes?" Signar whispered, his body going perfectly still.

Tzarik snapped his head up to where Signar focused. He saw it. Crouched in the shadows of thick bushes under trees so old their branches bowed down towards the earth was the thin, long-limbed figure of the ligda. Its long hair, made of whip-like leaves and earthen tendrils, made it hard to see. A pair of small, three-pronged antlers arched over the back of its head. The thing's huge yellow eyes didn't waver from them when Tzarik spotted it.

Ligda liked to kill living victims and then place them around their territory to come back to later. They only had a taste for dead flesh. They were drawn to battlefields or ransacked villages filled with the dead. Curious, Tzarik glanced around. What had drawn the ligda to this spot?

As they watched the monster crouch in the bushes, something hissed a hunter's roar behind them. Tzarik hardly had time to spin, hand flying to his scimitar, when a second ligda tackled him hard. They had long, powerful back legs to leap like man-sized frogs. Their front limbs—more like human arms, with long black claws on the end—were elongated to allow them to run on all fours.

The force of the monster's leap ripped Tzarik far from Signar. The second ligda screeched, baring its gray teeth. It raised a clawed hand and swiped at Tzarik, trying to rip his throat open. He grunted, blocking the attack with the black leather gauntlet on his forearm. His other hand scrambled to find his dagger on his thigh. The scimitar was too long to try to pull out from this position. As he pushed against the ligda's chest, it snapped its jaws, trying to bite him.

Sparing a quick glance over, he saw the first had bounded at Signar. The damned monsters had planned the trap. Knowing they would focus on the first one, another had sneaked up behind them. Signar rolled away from his attacker, looking around wildly for something to defend himself with.

"Signar, fight it!" Tzarik commanded. "Use your wolf."

He knew the boy thought shifting into his wolven form meant he had failed, but it wasn't true. Signar was a Vaeson, and was allowed to use the god-shape given to him. He just had to control it when he transformed.

With a growl of effort, Tzarik flipped the ligda to his left. The second it took the thing to crash and roll back onto its feet, he was able to pull out his scimitar. The ligda howled at him, almost like it cursed him. They began a slow circle, eyeing each other. Behind him, Signar transformed. The huge golden wolf appeared, sundering the clothes on his body. The great monster growled and snapped at the ligda.

With his eyes only on Signar for a half second, the ligda pounced. Tzarik fended it off once, landing a good slash with his scimitar to its right arm. The ligda screeched and flailed. It flew up the trunk of a tree, skittering over the branches. With the predator several yards above him, Tzarik shot a quick glance at Signar as he chased and snapped at the ligda that attacked him. The monster seemed far less interested in the monstrous golden wolf than the boy from before.

"Don't let it bite you!" Tzarik shouted. "They'll have eldritch mucus and will poison you."

No sooner had he said this than the ligda finally latched onto

Signar's back with its fore-claws. The thing pulled itself up and buried its teeth deep into Signar's shoulder. The wolf yelped and reeled his head back, snapping at the creature.

Above Tzarik, his ligda dropped, mouth wide, limbs splayed out like a spider. Tzarik thrust halat above him, drawing it as fast as he could. The barrier flashed into existence for only a second, but long enough for the ligda to land hard against. Tzarik knelt, pulled his dagger from his thigh, and jabbed it upwards into the soft flesh under the ligda's jaw. He saw the white metal shove up through its wide open mouth and into its skull. The monster flailed, trying in a last desperate attempt to claw at the Runer.

Tzarik jerked his dagger free and turned to fend off the last one. Signar dropped to the ground, unable to force the monster off him. The wolf rolled onto his back, growling fiercely. His weight was enough to make the ligda screech and panic as its ribs were crushed. It finally let go and Signar snapped up. He whipped around, striking like a viper at the ligda. He crushed the monster's skull in his jaws and whipped it back and forth, like his more primal brothers having caught a rabbit.

The ligda went limp almost instantly, its limbs snapping and cracking until Signar finally dropped it. Tzarik stood, legs bent, ready to mist if Signar should lose himself to his wolven madness. He scanned the wolf for signs of continued aggression and held one hand out towards him, the other gripping his runes.

Signar snarled, black blood covering his otherwise golden face. His hackles still rose from his neck to his tail. He shook his head, sniffing at the dead monster.

"Signar," Tzarik tried, wary of getting too close. He'd been tackled by Signar before, ripped back and forth, just as the ligda had. He had no intention of feeling those teeth in him again.

The wolf panted and shook his great body. "I'm fine," he growled, pacing around the area in his Vaeson form. He put his nose to the ground and sniffed.

A bit of relief filled Tzarik as he saw the hackles along Signar's spine lower. "I need to look at that bite," he said, coming closer. "Might need to pull the poison and cauterize the wound if the runes won't heal it. Sometimes, those kinds of eldritch wounds don't stop bleeding."

The wolf sighed and lay down so Tzarik could attend to his bite. Assured now that Signar was in complete control, Tzarik drained the poison and drew artiah over his massive shoulders. To his relief, the wound weaved itself together. Tzarik gently pushed aside Signar's mane of golden fur to inspect the scar.

"If we're not careful," he said, patting the great wolf, "you'll have more scars than I do before your eighteenth name day."

Signar gave a strange, wolfish smile and stood up. He shook like a dog, his tail wagging slightly.

Suddenly, Signar stopped. His sharp ears pointed to the sky, turning on instinct.

"What do you hear?" Tzarik asked.

The wolf went perfectly still. "It's him," Signar whispered. "He's...calling me?"

Tzarik glared into the shadows of the trees. "Who?"

Slowly, Signar took three steps towards the east. "He knows I've come back. Raudnir knows I've returned to Caerwren. I hear him howling."

This confirmed a fear Tzarik had. Greater forces than just his promise to Skarde would come for Signar on this gods-damned continent. Forces he could not fight against. If he were able, he'd slay every god. He often wondered if he'd actually killed Bolemesh, the spider goddess, so that he'd know it was possible. For all he knew, she had spawned again, clawing her way up from the gruesome earth in the Deep. It was her realm, after all. Now another god was coming after someone he cared for. If given the chance, he'd bloody that god, too.

Throwing his head back in a dramatic arch, Signar shot an

earth-shattering, bone-tingling howl into the cold air. It rang so loud that Tzarik dropped his dagger to cover his ears. He howled long, until Tzarik's entire body shook from the note. He closed his eyes, afraid his shaking vision would make him ill again.

Signar stopped and swiftly shifted back to his human form. Naked, he gathered the remnants of his cloak and tied it around his middle.

"The animal skins are not destroyed when we shift," he explained. They began their slow march towards Altevine again. "Since we are their brothers, the magic keeps it whole."

This brought up another magical aspect of the Vaeson Tzarik had wondered about. "And the Vaeson blades? They come to your command."

"Given by our gods." He looked ahead. "I was five when I saw a Reks pull their axe from a stone in Gidenmore. Mother said he was the last of his kind. Perhaps that's why Gidenmore sided with Rom and Hovandel against us."

"They are not Reks like you?" Tzarik asked.

Signar shrugged. "In a way, they are. But in many others, they are not."

The boy stopped in his tracks. The smell of death and decay that had hit Tzarik before came back tenfold, turning his stomach. He clamped his hand over his nose and focused ahead. Something —two dozen somethings—hung from the thick branches of the trees ahead. Tzarik took Signar's hand and pulled the boy behind him.

In the trees hung over two dozen bodies. The corpses hung by their necks, arms unbound and loose at their sides. Their hands had been cut off at the wrists, frozen blood still red. As they cautiously drew closer, Tzarik saw their mouths were stitched closed.

"Stay," he instructed Signar. "They could be cursed objects."

He moved closer, looking up at the lowest hanging body. Small sprigs of rosemary and other woody herbs protruded from between the stitched lips. He scanned the others and saw the same. The bodies had been stuffed with herbs of banishment. Whoever had put them up had wanted to keep something inside the line of hanging dead. The way the hanging bodies angled around the copse and out of sight told him they most likely hung in a perimeter around Altevine. Confirming his suspicion, he found every hanging body wore a wolf totem. His heart dropped.

"They're all from the clans of Altevine," he whispered, confused and worried. "Someone took your people, killed them, and is using them to ward against your clanlands."

"Why?" Signar whimpered. "What have my people done to deserve this?"

Had Skarde done this? No. He'd sworn to protect Altevine. Perhaps he'd even sent Dain to act as steward in Signar's absence. Had they done so and another clan attacked, removing Northica's hold on Altevine? And if so, what were they trying to keep inside Altevine?

Signar gave a soft sob behind Tzarik, trying to hold his head high and blink away the emotion.

"We'll find out what has happened," Tzarik promised, leading the way under the gruesome wards.

Just then, voices reached them. Men grunting orders, the sound of metal clanging, and the gentle crackling of a fire. Tzarik moved cautiously through the mist and the rays of the midnight sun until he spotted the forms. Three men moved amongst the trees, cutting down the Altevine clansmen. They had a pyre nearby where they laid the bodies. A fourth form stood near the pyre, singing a guttural chant, arms raised. Tzarik recognized the white leather and black paint of the Volra.

"Don't bother with ceremony," a young man shouted to the other two with him. "Just get them down. They will have new bodies in Rahrgalah." His words came in the accent of Zealmor, with a few twists of Altevine.

Tzarik crept closer. The forms of the three men were black against the white mist and trees, massive swords on their backs. The low-cut scabbards allowed for them to be drawn easily and showed the pearlescent sheen: Runers.

"If we take them down," one of the other Runers said, his accent entirely from Altevine, "they'll just kill more and put them up. And I cannot blame them."

"Get them down," the younger Runer ordered gruffly. "We're not helpless yet."

As the younger Runer turned to pick up a body from the forest floor, Tzarik thought he recognized the boy. He had long, strawberry-blond hair that looked like it hadn't been washed in days. A rough patch wrapped around his head, covering one eye.

"Tage?" Tzarik whispered, wondering if this was the apprentice of Korvoth, a Runer he'd had the pleasure of hunting the mori with the last time he was on Caerwren. Korvoth had been a great Runer, strong, with an almost bard-like personality. "Tage?" he called, stepping closer.

The Runer stopped and looked up. He squinted into the mist with his one good eye. "Tzarik?" he called back. "What are you doing back here?" His eye flicked from Tzarik to Signar and his mouth dropped open in a gasp. "Signar Wolf-tor?" he whispered in awe. His eye flit to the hand-shaped brand on Signar's shoulder only for a second before they went back to his face. He took a few cautious steps back, eyes wide.

"No need to fear," Signar said. "I am no longer the wildling I once was."

"You speak," Tage stammered, still in awe. Behind him, the other Runers furrowed their brows in shock. "Is the wildling tamed?" Tage gasped, then fell to his knees and bowed his head to Signar.

Tzarik, taken aback, stumbled.

"We've been waiting for you, Reks," Tage said, his voice still strangled with awe and what Tzarik read as relief. "Have you come to take Altevine back?"

Signar came abreast with Tzarik and looked down at the kneeling Runer. Behind Tage, the others stopped, and the Volra pressed his hands into his chest, eyes wide. The old shaman abandoned his chants near the pyre and ran to join Tage in kneeling, mumbling about how the wildling was no more. Tzarik glanced back at Signar and expected to see him looking uncomfortable, unsure about what to do. But he didn't. Signar's face smoothed over with stoicism.

"What has happened? Tell me," the Vaeson said steadily.

Tage raised his head and stood up. Tzarik saw now he had to be only a year or so older than Signar. On rare occasions, a Runer was taken on as a young apprentice. Tzarik looked around for Korvoth.

"Dain was seated in Altevine," Tage said quickly. "He had a few around him for council, including myself and Korvoth when he found out Korvoth knew you. There are some other Runers as well, since Dain valued us."

"Does he no longer?" Signar asked.

At this, Tage nodded mutely. "There was an uprising. The Vilderkin who prowled the borders of the canton came in, unsatisfied with Northica's presence in our thronehall."

Tzarik grunted at this, shaking his head. The wild barbarians of Caerwren were unreasonable, driven by primal fear and hate.

"But Dain didn't care about them," Tage went on. "Even when they broke our borders."

"Why not?" Signar asked. Tzarik saw agitation rising in the youth's shoulders.

"The…" Tage swallowed hard, eyes serious. "A malignation has sprung up within the canton. From the bog."

Understanding hit Tzarik, cold and hard, in his gut. "Of course," he sighed. "We should have known. The place where Tarkan ripped open the Deep, where we brought Sybal back, and Kjarton." He stopped and his eyes went to the east where Altevine lay behind the thick mist. Would *she* know where the rip in the barrier was? Could she come back through?

The red wolf would just be one of a dozen haunts trying to escape the Deep. Other creatures and spirits would already be roaming Caerwren.

"So Aras, the Vaeson Vilderkin who took the thronehall," Tage went on, "does not stop the other clans from killing our people and making them into these." He gestured to the remaining corpses. "To keep the malignation within Altevine."

"Is the malignation strong?" Signar asked.

The young Runer tilted his head, thumbs in his belt as he thought. "Some days are worse than others. But the sun seems to keep them weak. Thank Raudnir for Beltire. But soon it will set and we will have nights again."

"And Aras?" Signar asked. "A Vilderkin? What god does he follow?"

"He is a thunder hawk, like Dain. But you know the Vilderkin do not worship their god. He wanted to purge everyone loyal to Dain." Tage sighed. "He..." The boy choked and looked away, his eye suddenly shining with tears. "He took Korvoth. Had him..." He couldn't go on, his throat closing. "I wasn't ready for him to leave me," he gasped.

Instant empathy for the young Runer filled Tzarik. Sorrow for the loss of the great, brave Runer he'd known also filled him. Knowing the barbarians of Caerwren, Korvoth had most likely not had a good death. Or a swift one. Tzarik looked away from Tage, clearing his throat. No, Korvoth didn't deserve whatever had happened to him. Neither did Tage.

Signar took Tage's shoulder in his huge palm and squeezed hard. "You are brave to stay after that."

"Altevine is my home," Tage said through a thick voice, encouraged by his Reks's words. "Korvoth stood up to Aras. He tried to save Dain. Aras has no order. Only drunken revels. His men burn farms and hurt the people, then wonder why the city has no food. He has many, many slaves."

"He tried to save Dain?" Tzarik cut in quickly. Ice filled his gut.

"He lives still," Tage said, seeing the effect his words had. "All the other Northicans Skarde-Reks planted in Altevine were killed off in the dead of night months ago, when Aras took Dain captive as a thrall. He wants to sacrifice him to Isodel, his own goddess. Thinks it will stall her taking his god-shape, as all Vilderkin lose their shape, eventually. That day cannot come soon enough." Tage spat angrily. "But Aras enjoys humiliating Dain as a thrall in the thronehall too much to kill him yet."

Signar looked to Tzarik, pleading with his eyes. "Dain was kind to me," he whispered. "Spoke to me like a human. Called me Skelmir. Tzarik, please—"

"No need to ask, boy," Tzarik said, his own blood rushing. "Tage, take us there now."

Chapter 26

---◆---

Sheikha Sybal El'Freja

Sybal stood on the second-floor balcony, looking in the direction of the inner walls of the Dynast Palace. Tzarik and Signar had only been gone twelve hours, and already her mind spun and her nerves bunched under her skin in worry. The sun shone hot on the top of her head, and a gentle breeze pushed her whitening hair into her eyes. She slowly pulled her hair back, regretting letting it down out of its braid.

She couldn't sit and hide, let alone in the embassy where anyone could find her. And Sharar? Surely he'd return soon. She scanned the streets constantly, worried he'd appear again. She wasn't safe loitering inside.

Your inaction disturbs you, the voice of Freja said gently.

Sybal jumped at the sudden reappearance of the voice. It had been some time since it had tried to sway her, guide her sword. "You know me, Mother," she said darkly, knowing full well the voice did not belong to Freja. "You know I cannot abide sitting by and waiting."

And yet you will not raise your sword on my behalf.

Growling, Sybal pushed herself up off the alabaster railing and marched back into the interior of the embassy. She made her way to the master bedroom where she and Tzarik had slept. The wardrobe still hung open from when Tzarik had gathered warm cloaks for him and Signar. The blue dress she'd worn before the Vaeson had been taken from her hung clean and spotless over a chair. A servant must have come in, taken the dress from the floor, and hung it up again.

She reached out to the blue silk and ran her hand over it.

You were a lady once? the voice asked. *Why do you not use that to your advantage?*

Sybal frowned. "What do you mean? What can that do for me?"

The voice hummed in light thought. *How does your family's land stand? What has become of it?*

Sybal hadn't thought about it. Her family was dead. Ala'Nar hated her. Surely they would have ransacked the estate. Or the miners would have taken it for themselves. She'd not gone back since. A sudden curiosity took hold of her.

"We had powerful friends in Ala'Nar," she reasoned. "Other families like our own. Father had a quadi in charge of his legacy. I wonder if he stepped in when we all…disappeared."

Deciding, Sybal dressed in the gold and blue silk, discarded her Runer boots for gold slippers, and moved to the embassy's study to write a letter. The great library was lined with scrolls and books and opened up into the back gardens. A servant there trimmed the fruit trees, ignoring her as she rushed around the room looking for ink and paper.

The only parchment she could find bore the symbol of the embassy in Mysir. This would tell anyone the letter fell into the hands of where she was, but she didn't expect anyone to be on the lookout for letters. She quickly scrawled a short missive, remembering the quadi's name to be Sira Sabari. She inquired about the estate, her claim to it, the condition and the workers, and signed her name. The man would know her signature as it littered every log, journal, and order from her home. She had been the one to run the mine when her father had started to step down. Abdul hadn't had the strong hand she'd had.

Sybal went out to the servant in the garden and asked where to post the letter.

The servant pointed to the palace. "The royal messengers. But if you want it to go quickly," he offered, "the vizier has courier falcons that go to nearly every major city."

She thanked him and took a deep breath before marching into the palace. There could be no possible way for Sharar to be back yet if he had left after the incident at the coliseum. She would be safe inside if she could find Nasor. The palace buzzed with servants, guards, merchants, and every other caste of people on Alika. She wasn't sure where Nasor would be this time of day, and had to walk the halls for some time before a servant pointed her to the throne room.

Curious, she made her way there. The wide isle leading to the ruby throne was packed with Alikans as they came to discuss and listen to the Dynast Court. She pushed her way in to see not Sokar on the ruby throne, but Nasor. The jackal Masahk engaged in a heated argument with a priest, his clawed hand gripping his blue and gold crook. She moved closer.

"Damn the gods, Chaseth!" Nasor barked, slamming his fist into the arm of the ruby throne before shooting up to standing. He towered over most in the room.

The people closest gasped, and the priest looked mortally affronted.

"Is that your true sentiment, Nasor?" the priest called Chaseth asked quietly. "In this court? At this time?"

"The Father of Monsters be damned," Nasor said in a more

apologetic tone. "He's a liar, Chaseth. Our king has been blinded by his silver tongue."

The priest looked around, touching a large golden symbol on a chain around his neck. "Not here, Nasor. The people will hear. They were there. They saw him at the coliseum. They understand what this could mean for Alika. Do you not have any pride in your country or your king?" The priest stopped himself and calmed a little. "Think of Sokar."

"I am!" Nasor growled. His long, black ears pressed down like an angry dog into his hair. He snarled quietly and turned away. This landed his eyes on Sybal. He blinked, not recognizing her at first. "Excuse me."

"But the people," Chaseth called.

Nasor pushed through to Sybal, quickly touching her shoulder and beckoning her to follow him. She did, sensing the priest's growing anger. The vizier led her out of the throne room, over a small bridge that crossed an indoor stream to his quarters in the palace. Much like the library in the embassy, scrolls and books covered the walls. Astrological instruments made of glittering gold dotted the areas, with open walls to look out into the stars. Nasor went to a great desk and poured a drink from a gold carafe into crystal glasses. He handed one to Sybal, then pointed at the parchment in her hand.

"Sending a letter?"

"Oh, yes, if you could," she said, remembering it. She held it out to him.

Nasor took it and moved to a small balcony on the left. A massive golden cage housed half a dozen large falcons there. The great birds perched on branches of trees growing inside the aviary. Nasor opened a small door on the side and the birds fought to be the one chosen. Deciding on one with dark feathering, he slid the letter into the small pouch on the bird's leg. Then he raised his arm high and the bird shot into the air.

"You're not going to ask what I wrote?" Sybal asked, joining Nasor in a slow march around his personal garden.

The Masahk waited a few strides, eyes fixed on the horizon, before he replied. "You're not going to thank me for saving you?"

Sybal's lips fell open, lost for words.

"Exactly," Nasor sighed. "Runer, I trust you more than the snakes within the Dynast Palace. And...I hate Runers."

Sybal glanced up at the towering sentient. "You are right to distrust Sharar. We don't know what he will do once he ascends to sorcerer, but we know he is cruel. He has tortured, killed, destroyed—all in the name of knowledge." She looked ahead. "Do you know he has a djinn? You know he wants to become a sorcerer?"

"I suspected." Nasor inhaled deeply, then let the breath out slowly as his eyes roved over the palace's grounds. He stopped, facing a grand white fountain splashing with the blue water of Alika. He set his crook down. His hands empty, they hung at his sides. Much of his grandeur and authority melted away. His ears drooped slightly. "I am at a loss. Sokar was taken with the scholar when he was a child. Perhaps the loss of his father encouraged his attachment."

Sybal blanched. She couldn't imagine Sharar being even falsely affectionate with anyone. "But Sokar won't listen to you?"

Across the wide stream in the garden, the young Pharaoh appeared. He wore no gold or adornments. He moved slowly between the fountains and ornamental statues, seemingly distracted.

"He wasn't in court," Sybal noted.

Nasor shook his head. "Our young king does not like the crowds. He cannot control his fear of letting his people down and often foregoes court. The weight of his golden crown exhausts him. He is descended from Acenoth IV, and the burden of the dynasty is too much for him. He's a gentle boy. But he was not made to rule. No, he won't listen to me. I was his father's vizier, not his. He says I try to make him into his father, but I hope I do not. Sokar has so many good qualities of his own. But he's too soft.

"We have a story." Nasor paused, taking on the tone of a bard. "Once, there was a snake that lived near a gorge in the land. The snake didn't think of the gorge as an obstacle and didn't care for it. It meant nothing to him. He lived in peace on his side, having all he needed. Until one day, a hawk flew over the snake's nest to the other side. Enraptured by the hawk's ability to fly, the snake waited for it to pass by again. When it did, the hawk carried a large, fat desert mouse in its talons. The snake wanted such fare. So he called to the hawk the next time he flew over and asked the hawk to carry him over the gorge. The hawk refused, knowing the nature of snakes. 'But I am in earnest,' the snake replied. 'I only want to hunt. I will not harm you.'

"So the hawk took the snake over the gorge to hunt. On the other side, the grass was long and the snake could not see far. He had to work twice as hard as on the sandy side he'd come from. The hunting made him weary. So the snake wanted to go home, but by now, he was hungry. Too hungry. 'Take me back, hawk,' the snake said. Having trusted the snake once, the hawk joyfully took the snake in his talons to bring him home.

"But the snake, overcome by his nature and his hunger, struck the hawk. The fall was long, and the snake ate the hawk as he fell."

Sybal frowned, tilting her head.

"You understand." Nasor nodded. "The snake was so overcome by his nature, his hunger, that he did not stop to think that he would fall to his death if he ate the hawk. All he knew was the hunger." The Masahk shook his head sadly. "Some blame the hawk. But...my hawk is too young to understand."

"You care very much for him," Sybal mused. "I didn't expect that."

Nasor closed his eyes. "His father and I were as close as brothers. He was a good, strong pharaoh. Sokar was robbed of him. And in his place, a snake appeared."

Curious, Sybal asked, "You've known Sharar for some time, then?"

The vizier clenched his clawed hand. "For fifteen years. He came to us as a student, fresh from the philosophical academies in Rom. Ambitious, hungry. Sokar was but a hatchling." He looked across at the young Pharaoh fondly. "When the young hawk was but a decade old, his father was taken from us. Young Sharar stepped in like the older brother Sokar never had. I believe he was an opportunist."

A sudden thought struck Sybal. "Do you think Sharar killed Sokar's father?"

The Masahk didn't reply, but the way his brows furrowed and the deep sigh that filled his chest answered the dark question.

She looked back at the prince. He'd stood and stretched his wings before letting them fall back down his back. "I met a hawk-like Masahk on Caerwren," she said. "Do Masahk not fly?"

Nasor smiled at last, if only weakly. "The gods saw fit to not bless those with wings with the ability to fly. There are stories on Alika, the birthplace of the Masahk, that say at one time they could. Thus, the first pharaohs were of the hawk. Who else would be a god incarnate, worthy of leading the god-shaped people, than one who could also touch the sun? You will find many of our pharaohs—especially the Dynast Pharaohs—in the Halls of History are hawks. Or falcons. Acenoth was the last to fly over his kingdom. Sokar has quite a legacy to live up to." The vizier's face fell again and his shoulders slumped.

The more she looked at the young prince, the more her heart went out to him.

One day, the voice whispered, *I will harden your heart. It is this*

love of others that maddens and intrigues me. That stays your blade. It
went silent before adding, *I don't understand it.*

Closing her mind to the damned voice, Sybal said, "Can I speak
with Sokar? He doesn't know it was me Sharar wanted captured at
the coliseum."

Looking as if he'd like nothing better, Nasor said, "Of course. I
will introduce you."

༄

SOKAR HAD DISAPPEARED from the garden, moving around the front
of the palace walls. Nasor led Sybal through the outer areas.

"He does not leave the palace much," the vizier explained. "This
unnatural fear of the public eye has been a burden for me to bear.
The more time he spends behind our golden walls, the more I
worry for him. Sokar is trapped between his fear and his need to
put his mark on history, on his dynasty."

Sybal followed the Masahk closely. "Is that why he looks for
ways to endanger his people?" Her tone cut harshly.

"Lady Sybal," Nasor asked kindly, "please do not think Sokar is
cruel."

Her eyes shot to the slaves they passed as he said this. Human
Porshains and Masahk alike toiled in the hot sun, covered in mud
from making bricks, backs bent under the pull of miles of rope as
they erected the grand facade of Sokar'Xenoteph's tomb. "He has
much to change if I am to believe that," she replied. "He could do
many other things to leave his mark."

"Sokar would tear himself in two if he tried to dissolve the
slave trade," Nasor said sternly. "He cannot be all these at once.
You ask much of him."

"He is chasing power," Sybal shot back.

Nasor did not reply to this. They came around a bend of thick alabaster pillars into a grand arbor. A marble floor rose up before them where architects, builders, stonemasons, a few priests, and Sokar stood around a table in the shade.

"I do not want to disappoint him when he returns," Sokar was saying. "Keep looking. We must have something to show him."

When the workers saw the vizier, they bowed deeply and quieted down. This caught Sokar's attention, and he turned to see who had interrupted. His youthful face fell into dismay when he spotted Nasor.

"Why are you here?" the Pharaoh asked. The maps before them showed he'd been in the middle of something.

"Your Eminence," Nasor said, ignoring the boy's disappointed tone. "May I present Lady Syb—"

"Sheikha Sybal El'Freja," Sybal cut in. She would know for sure once the quadi replied if she indeed was Sheikha, but for now, the title was needed. She bowed deeply to the young Pharaoh. "I am a lady of Al'Myrah. My family owns land in Ala'Nar."

Sokar bored his hawk-like eyes into her. He then held his head high, tossing his feathery hair over one shoulder. "Why are you here?" He shot a sharp look at Nasor. "As you can see, I am very busy." He gestured to the maps. One of them was heavily annotated, with a large black circle in one area not too far from the palace. "I am on the cusp of finding the entrance to Acenoth's tomb. We've been searching for some time." He smiled tensely. "I think I've found it."

Good. He hadn't recognized her. Tzarik had been right in suggesting they wear the masks the first time they entered the palace. They'd been hiding from Sharar, but not the choice proved useful again.

"I'm here to warn you," Sybal said, her eyes flitting to the map and back quickly. Were they too late? No weakness or doubt remained in her mind. She had to speak plainly, but gently, as a sheikha. Sokar seemed to have a delicate sense of emotion, and she didn't want to drive him away.

The boy king waved his hand, shooing away the architects and builders. He pressed his palms into the table and leaned heavily on his arms. "About the tomb? So Nasor has told me."

Sybal tried to read the young Masahk. His golden-green eyes flicked over the plans before him and the smooth skin around his eyes tightened. His hands gripped the table hard.

"The man who told you to open that tomb is preying on you," she tried gently. "He wants to open Acenoth's tomb for his own ends."

"For the Mahit'Onomicon," Sokar interjected. "I know this, sheikha. I am not afraid of the man who can read a book written by the gods for sentient kind. Had we known Acenoth held the tome, we would have opened his tomb long ago, I assure you. But Abigor spent his life hunting down the book. I've known him all my life. To be the one who can help him achieve his goals... I am honored. And the glory this will bring to my name?" The boy sighed in admiration and shook his head. "To be the first pharaoh to hold the book in a thousand years, to be the one to lift Acenoth's curse... Sheikha, you cannot imagine what this will mean to Alika. Lifetimes of fear will be put to rest. And..." He stopped and swallowed. "And so much more." He picked up the map, rolling it up and out of her sight. He held it close to his chest.

Sybal's mind raced. What could she do? She couldn't enter the tomb herself; she didn't know where it lay, what might be protecting it. She didn't want to take the book into her own hands. Could it be destroyed? What kind of terror from the gods would that bring if they managed it? No, they still had to focus on Sharar. He was mortal, stoppable. For now.

"There are other ways to find the glory you seek," she started. "But Sharar? He knows he can control you."

"Knows he can control me?" Sokar barked back, disgusted. "Do you take me for a fool? A simpleton to be led by blind ambition?" The rage at her insult twisted his face.

In that moment, Sybal saw herself in the young Pharaoh. So sure of everything. Trusting in her own strength and determination. Being fed by the need to prove herself. All of that had nearly gotten Tzarik killed more than once. She'd almost dealt the killing blow. She understood.

"Your Eminence," she began gently, "I meant no disrespect. The reverence I have for your dynasty is unparalleled."

"So it would seem," the Pharaoh spat. "Are you here to stop Abigor? To have him killed?" At this, Sokar backed away from Sybal, suddenly afraid. "Are you here for me?"

"No!" Sybal shouted quickly.

The Mirage appeared from nowhere. Three of the lizard-like Masahk wavered into view and posed to pounce should their Pharaoh signal them. One, a male Masahk with red and yellow scales, glared at Sybal, almost daring her to strike. She took a step back, hands raised.

"Wise, sheikha," Sokar said softly. "I will show you the merciful Pharaoh I am and let you take this chance to leave."

"My king," Nasor whispered.

"Do not interrupt, jackal, unless you wish to be banished from the Dynast Palace," Sokar snapped. His eyes flashed back to Sybal. "I know who and what Abigor Sharar is, and what he wants. I understand. But I do not fear him."

Fool, Sybal thought.

The voice agreed in her mind. *He thinks he is safe so long as he stands by your sorcerer's side.*

More pressing would enrage the young Pharaoh even more, so Sybal bowed and turned to leave. Nasor did not follow her. He no doubt had to stay behind and placate the hotheaded Hawk King. She didn't judge the vizier for wanting to stay close to Sokar. It was the best place to be if he wanted to watch over his young charge.

Knowing she had to do something to occupy her mind and body, Sybal made her way back to the embassy. She changed into her black armor, armed herself, and went out into the smaller villages to look for a hunt.

Chapter 27

Ishmael's Heart

Makan Alu'Ekmet was not a large city, and Tarkan knew where to look for the Scriven bones of Elahel. After freeing himself from the Deep and the tangle of souls he'd used to soar over the god-land, he went directly to the Palace of Apostles. The square where he and Ashkan had first faced off looked strange in the sunlight. The glassy black structures and the blighted earth shone, cutting the sunbeams into refracted colors.

Beneath the Palace of Apostles lay the catacombs. Necromancers raised the dead, but not their own. Never their own... Tarkan thought about the hypocrisy as he walked the black underground, wondering in which grave Ashkan would have hidden his wife. Yes, other sentients could be raised, commanded. But not a tribal brother or sister. That would be obscene.

But using them and their remains to help him conquer the people who'd subjugated him? That was allowed, surely.

"You will be used for a great purpose," he whispered into the dark as he opened grave after grave. "Is that not a greater reward for your death than sleeping in the ground?"

None of the dead necromancers in Makan Alu'Ekmet had Scriven bones. Tarkan granted himself the choice to use another, should Elahel not be found. Or should he find another first? Using her had pushed Ashkan away. He knew that. But he'd had no other choice. The spell he would make would only work if he had the rare bones of such a necromancer. The Bone-Scriven were a noble sect. The time and agony it took to have the scriptures inlaid into the very bones was admirable. But it afforded them a much longer and safer life. With no sign on their outer bodies—lest they be Apostles with the emerald eyes—no sentient would know they were necromancers. It was how they lived so long within the cities. They were still a tribal people, gathering in family groups, but not wandering the desert sands and crossing the seas like him and the others.

Like Arne. The necromancer from Caerwren he'd met months ago on Al'Myrah came to mind every now and then. He wondered if Ishtar, Arne's lover, still lived, or if Arne had let her die. The illness Ishtar had carried with her had staggered Tarkan when he'd taken her wounds onto himself to dispel and banish the drekavak they'd brought into the world. He'd told Arne to make her Scriven to save her. Had he? The advice had come from a place of pride, of thinking he knew what would be best for Arne and Ishtar. But he'd been reluctant to take Zeva...

Thinking of Zeva sent a rage lancing through him. Tarkan growled and ripped a resting skeleton from its grave, throwing it to the ground. The ancient bones clattered and broke from the force of his sudden rage. He glared down at it. With a grunt, he stomped the skull, shattering it completely under his boot. In a wild flurry of sudden agony, he screamed, ripping a blade from the chest of a dead grave robber, and hacked at every body he'd pulled out so far. Swinging wildly, he hit stone and bones alike until the air was thick with dust and the echo of his agonized screams. He swung the blade until his shoulders ached and his throat was seared.

When he exhausted himself, he flung the sword and collapsed against an iron gate sectioning off two stone coffins inside an alcove. He gasped for air between sobs, his chest throbbing. Turning his face to the ceiling where more bones lined the crypt, he wailed one last time as loud as he could, forcing all the air from his lungs and filling the entire crypt with his sorrow. He doubled over, arms wrapped around himself as he imagined holding her close one last time. She had been everything. Had made him feel alive, surrounded by the dead. Over one hundred years on the map, and only those thirteen had meant anything to him.

Could he raise her? Beg for forgiveness?

No. Necromancers did not raise their own.

He should have never taken her to Caerwren. Should have never given in to her. Should have never offered to help Tzarik. Damn him. Damn both the Runers for forcing his hand and using Zeva against him in Northica.

Unsure how long he lay on the floor of the crypt, tears drying to his bone-thin face, Tarkan waited. If his heart had been flesh, it would have beat quickly. He waited long enough to believe it had slowed down, then pushed himself up. Gripping the iron gate, he pulled himself to his feet and looked in. This alcove had no cobwebs. The coffins—at least, the one on the left—were cleaner than the others.

Taking a deep breath to gain the last of his composure, Tarkan heaved the gate open and passed into the last grave site. Positioning himself, he pressed his palms onto the side of the lid and shoved it with all his might. To his surprise, it moved more easily than he'd thought. He shoved it until it clattered to the sandy floor between the two coffins. Looking in, he found what he'd sought.

Swathed in sheer black wrappings lay Elahel's familiar bones.

She had been tall for an Al'Myrahn woman, and her long body would do perfectly for his plan. He reached in, picking up one of her long leg bones, and turned it over in his thin fingers. The intricate work of the Nashira traitors was admirable. Beautiful, even. He ran his hand down the length of the bone, feeling the scriptures engraved there. What agony must that have been? All to be hidden and safe. He couldn't imagine doing such a thing to himself. Not even to hide.

Tarkan gathered her entire skeleton up, disassembling her from how Ashkan had lain her out, and wrapped her in the dressings he'd put over her. The Necro'Khan leapt up the stairs of the crypt and prepared to open the Deep once again to spirit himself to Porsh. One last time.

℞

THE SOULS that carried Tarkan shrieked and suddenly scattered, dropping him. With a grunt of pain, he landed hard against the familiar blighted ground of Porsh. He clutched Elahel's bones to his chest, not willing to drop any of them. The souls shrieked and dissipated into the fiery air of the Deep, leaving him alone. Tarkan sat up and looked around. Thousands of spirits moved before him. White, ghostly souls drifted in layers above and below. Some of them turned to look at him. When they did, he gasped with effort, throwing open a rift in the Deep and diving out.

He landed against the glassy earth of Porsh. As he stumbled to the side, he hit a familiar, great black entryway. Tarkan turned his face up and took in the ancient, decrepit facade of his father's manor. He stepped back, looking up at the elegant yet cruel ornate doors. Above them, on the arch, the spikes of the star Mirzam stabbed out.

Tarkan shoved the doors open, entering his family's home for the first time since killing Ishmael. Just inside the dark, expansive foyer, Tarkan touched the star on his forehead and traced the scriptures down his neck and over his heart. He whispered a quick prayer to Nephron, calling on him to hold Ishmael's no doubt vengeful spirit at bay. Then he marched through the manor to the hidden door that led to the family crypt below.

He knew the stairs well, the memory of them and their tight spiral coming back immediately as he trotted down below. His father's underground rooms were not entirely unlike Sharar's. Ishmael had been an ambitious necromancer. Diagrams on parchment, maps, glass bottles, and other mysterious and cruel instruments and paraphernalia lined the walls. To the side lay the two marble coffins that Ishmael had made for himself and his wife, Tarkan's mother, Isis. She had been a weak woman. He'd loved her, had tried to protect her, but she had done nothing for her sons, cowering under Ishmael's power. Like the entirety of Porsh had done. Except the damned Bone-Scriven.

The Runers had burned not only Ishmael and Isis, but his dead brother as well.

Tarkan moved from Isis's charred corpse to a chest near the coffins. This held his brother's bones. Ishmael had given him no proper burial. Tarkan flipped the lid open, looking in. His brother's bones showed the brokenness inflicted upon them before death. Tarkan slowly lowered his hand to the skull, running his fingers over the fractures.

"Ishan," he sighed, "you did not deserve Father's wrath. But he knew you were my weakness. We should have been able to stand up to him. I should have never trusted him. You were the sacrifice that earned me my scriptures." He ran his eyes over the rest of the skeleton. Nearly every bone bore a break. Ishmael had made sure Ishan couldn't run before he'd sacrificed him and made Tarkan an Apostle. An unnecessary and barbarous rite.

Tarkan merely glanced in at Isis as he passed, having no love for his mother anymore. He closed her marble coffin and placed

Elahel's bones atop it before turning to Ishmael's coffin. Tarkan grunted in effort, heaving the heavy lid off. It clattered to the side. Inside, Ishmael lay perfectly still. His flesh still clung to his bones, and his hair still shone black.

"Do we never fade?" Tarkan asked his father. "Burned, headless, heartless. And yet you will not turn to dust. Is this my fate, Father?" He waited, like he expected Ishmael to reply. "I've ascended," he told him. "I've taken your mantle and become stronger than you ever could have hoped to be. And I don't have the Mahit'O-nomicon." He shook his head.

Above him, the wind howled.

"I hope you have met Ishan in the afterlife," he went on. "I hope he's allowed to hurt you the way you hurt him. I plan to never make it there, so he must avenge himself. But you'll be with me, Father." He reached in, gripping the long hair atop Ishmael's head and lifting the preserved piece of the dead Necro'Khan out. He glared at Ishmael's closed eyes. "I took your heart. It seems that was the only way to kill you. But you're not quite gone. Father, your heart is my heart. Your blood, my blood. Watch me rise to power you never achieved. I will be the author of the blood, of new scriptures. You called yourself Necro'Khan, I will show them *I* am."

He tossed Ishmael's head back into the marble coffin and went to a large black chest under a table covered in blood, bones, and other remains. He unlocked the chest with keys from his satchel and tossed the lid open. Inside lay Ishmael's fleshy black box. Tarkan took it, opening it. Inside, among a necromancer's other instruments, lay a large flesh heart, perfectly preserved. A puncture mark showed where Tarkan had stabbed it once he'd removed the diamond heart from Ishmael's chest, turning it to flesh. Tarkan took it out and swore he felt it beat. He gripped it hard, imagining he could crush the thing in his fingers.

"The center of the blade that will drain the blood of millions," he whispered. "Scriven bones, heart of a Necro'Khan, held in my hand. I will fell nations with this blade." Taking up the ruby blade from within his father's box, he cut his wrist and clenched his fist. He hovered his wound over Ishmael's fleshy heart. Whispering a verse into the wind, he dribbled his blood over it. Where the blood touched it, the dead Necro'Khan's heart hardened once again into red diamond. "My blood will sustain you," he whispered. "You will serve me at last." Once it was entirely diamond, the heart glittered even in the dim light of the crypt.

A cold tendril touched Tarkan's cheek. The Necro'Khan stopped as he moved to ascend the steps. The cold touch slithered under his long hair to the back of his neck in a familiar, loathsome touch; a firm hand, gripping the nape of his neck.

"Show yourself," Tarkan hissed.

A soft, low laugh rose up from the barrier between the world and the afterlife. A white, ghostly figure materialized, starting from the claw-like hand that touched Tarkan. The louder the laugh grew, the more the figure appeared. Soon, standing before Tarkan was a hovering figure wrapped in decaying robes. The ghost wore a crown of five blades on his head over long, thin hair that fell into a skeletal face. Narrow lips curled into a cruel grin.

"Called myself Necro'Khan?" Ishmael's voice hissed. "I was Necro'Khan as a bearer of the Mahit'Onomicon. I was not even Scriven when I searched for the book, boy. I was more powerful as a mortal than you are as Necro'Khan."

"Father," Tarkan murmured, not sure if Ishmael's ghost really had appeared before him or if, in his grief, he'd imagined it.

"My son," Ishmael purred, gliding back to take in Tarkan. "The next Necro'Khan, the scourge of the map. You are nothing compared to me. You are still weak. You come for my heart because you know I am what you need."

"Torment me all you want with your words," Tarkan shot back. "But it was I, as an Apostle, who ended your immortal life. A thousand years snuffed out by your own son."

Ishmael hummed in thought. His blue eyes glowed in the ghostly face. "I knew the dangers of the lich king's sleep. I hoped one day to rise again, when Porsh needed me most. And in a sense, I shall." He gestured to the heart clutched in Tarkan's hand. "Still needing my aid, my son. I loved you, of course, and am proud to lend you my strength once again."

"I am taking it," Tarkan spat, shaking with rage. "Stealing your essence to use for my own means."

"Never waste a sentient," Ishmael agreed. "It is an old heart. A powerful one. One who fathered the author of the blood." He laughed at Tarkan's words.

"How?" Tarkan looked down into the coffin at the decapitated, dead Necro'Khan. "Were you Scriven when I was born?"

Ishmael chuckled darkly. "So much you do not know, Tarkan. A Scriven may plant his seed in a mortal womb."

Tarkan winced, disgusted. "How is that possible?"

Ishmael smiled. "For the one who holds and reads the Mahit'O-nomicon, not much is impossible. An Apostle may not create life. But a Scriven has the chance before he breaks his covenant with life and becomes an Apostle of death. A chance to create life one last time. Something you will never know. Something you have lost."

"Enough!" Tarkan shouted. "You will witness how strong I've become. Your hold over me has ended, Father. You will submit to me."

A low laugh emanated from Ishmael's throat. Tarkan blinked, ready to strike at the ghost if he needed to. But Ishmael was gone. Tarkan spun to look around the crypt, but no sign of the ghost remained.

"Damn you," Tarkan cursed softly. He fled the crypt, leaving behind his family for the last time.

Tarkan took a bag of small gems and gold from the family vault —untouched, since raiders did not come near Porsh—and re-entered the Deep to transport himself in a flash of souls to Ala'Nar.

SOMEHOW, Al'Myrah was more familiar than even his own home. Tarkan knew the scents, the warm wind, and the night bugs that sang loudly as he landed in an explosion of black ectoplasm and the sighs of the burnt-out souls. He walked for about an hour and melded with a thin line of caravaners entering Ala'Nar, and purchased a tall black horse off a merchant who was all too happy to part with the mount in exchange for an emerald.

Tarkan loaded Elahel's bones and his bags onto the horse and parted from the caravan to enter the big city the principality was named after. As he drew near to the eastern gate that protected the inner circle of the city, he took in the work that had been done since his last visit. Huge wooden frames and construction machines still lined parts of the wall and the inside. Some places had been abandoned, dark and empty.

He made sure to cover himself in the ample folds of his black cloak to hide the scriptures and his blue eyes.

There was a smith that forged orichalcum in the city on this side. It was late, but the tradesmen usually lived close by their forges. It would take some convincing, but Ishmael's gold and gems would do the trick. The common people liked money, and he had more than he'd ever need.

When he finally reached the street the smith was on, he checked the ends and allies quickly. Very few people were out besides some drunks, a few homeless people, and working men and women hanging out windows and leaning up against door frames of public houses. Inside the forge, Tarkan spotted a young man of Bahratt descent still working.

Tarkan covered his face and approached the man.

The smith looked up through long, sweaty bangs when he heard the horse slow in front of his forge. "I'm not working now, sira. I'm sorry," he said kindly.

"The fires are lit now," Tarkan mused, coming underneath the awning and looking at what the smith worked on. He was wrapping the handle of a short, straight blade in leather to make a grip. "What is your name?"

"Ari," the man replied simply.

Tarkan nodded. "You are the one I need, Ari."

Ari smiled meekly, flattered. "Thank you, sira, but I'm just finishing here. The fires are too small to forge anything now. Come back in the morning."

Tarkan pulled the bag of gems off his belt and dipped his fingers inside to pull out a sapphire. "I can pay. Anything you want. I need a sword by morning."

The young man looked up again, the fire reflecting in his large brown eyes. He thought a moment, biting the inside of his thin cheeks. "What do you want?"

The Necro'Khan smiled under his wrappings. "An orichalcum blade," he began.

Ari tilted his head, sighing. "I don't work on the Runer metal. My master does. He's due back in two or three days if you'd like to stay in town."

Tarkan silently shook his head, glaring death at the young man.

"I see." Ari eyed Tarkan in the dim, orange light of the forge. "Are you a Runer?"

"Does it matter?" Tarkan asked.

Considering the mysterious man before him, Ari bent his head back to his work. "I suppose not." He put the smaller sword down and looked into the flames. "Very well, sira, but it will cost. I..." He smiled shyly, rubbing the back of his neck. "I have a woman. She carries my child. I need money to take us away from the city. To start a new life in the country."

A dark mirth brought a smile to Tarkan's face. He dumped three more gems into his hand and offered them to Ari. "Double this when you hand me the completed blade."

Ari watched Tarkan's eyes as he slowly took the gems and pocketed them. "Very well. What kind of blade? Al'Myrahn scimitar? Xian straight blade?"

"Caerwren long sword," Tarkan cut in. He lifted the black bundle off the horse and dropped the bones with a clatter on Ari's table. "These must be forged into the center of the blade." Gently, he pulled out Ishmael's heart from his satchel. "And this is the center. Do not chip or break this ruby. If you do, I will know, and I will kill you."

Ari flipped open the wrappings and gasped, stumbling back in horror when he saw the Scriven bones. "By the lion's mane, what is this?" he cried.

"I will not answer questions, Ari," Tarkan said slowly. "Think of your woman and your child. Do this for them."

The smith shot a terrified look at Tarkan. "The bones will crack from the heat," he began.

"They won't," Tarkan promised him. "The magic from the metal will speak to the scriptures upon the bones. They will meld."

Ari swallowed hard, steadying his breath. "Very well, sira," he whispered. He gathered up the bones and the heart and re-ignited the forge. The heat shoved Tarkan's robes back in a hot wind. He stepped out of the forge, hitched the horse, and watched Ari begin his work.

As the night wore on, the streets emptied more. At some point, a public house finally kicked out the last of its patrons and a small herd filed past, drunk and singing, down the street. Tarkan's eyes traveled after them. A few streets away, the richer district lay. He'd been there once with Sharar. The scholar had slaughtered Sybal's family, then had him raise them to defend Sharar's retreat. The lady Runer had been furious, had thought he'd killed her family. Now, he wished he had.

Were the pair of them—Tzarik and Sybal—so heartless? To force Zeva to raise the army on the Northican mountain? And what had become of her body? He closed his eyes, trying to dispel the image of them burning her on a pyre like a Caerwren barbarian. They wouldn't, would they? Sybal, at the very least, followed her religion, knowing the burning of bodies was blasphemous. Was Zeva ash on the side of a frozen mountain in the west?

When he opened his eyes again, he saw Ari take the blade from the mold he'd poured and hammer it straight and into shape. The straight blade looked awkward to Tarkan, but wouldn't feel foreign in his hands, since he'd never wielded one. He watched the smith attach the cross piece and pommel, where Ishmael's heart gleamed. The smith's veins pulsed under his skin, showing the effect the metal had on him. Very few smiths forged with orichalcum, knowing the mutating effects it could have.

A few moments later, Ari lifted the sword and moved across the forge to the deep trough of water to cool the metal.

"Wait," Tarkan said, pushing himself up and approaching. "Let me."

Confused, Ari let Tarkan take the blade. He stepped back, wiping the sweat from his brow and leaning heavily against a wooden support beam. "I have a high tolerance for the stuff. It's utter agony, but Runers pay well. So long as I see a healer every now and then to purify my blood, it's not so bad. But once we're finished here, I might not have to forge such a blade ever again."

The hope in Ari's young voice would have turned Tarkan's heart once. Not now.

"The magic will come from blood," Tarkan said, admiring the

orange-hot, glimmering blade. It was well made. Finally crafted. A work of art, even.

"Sira?" Ari asked.

Tarkan nodded and turned to Ari. "It must be forged in blood."

Ari stood up, sensing danger. But too late.

With a shrill cry, Tarkan thrust the blade through Ari's middle with all his strength. The smith's eyes went wide and his mouth fell open in a mute gasp. Ari gripped the blade and pulled. Tarkan allowed him to shove the blade back out of his gut. The metal hissed and the smell of scorched, red blood filled the Necro'Khan's nostrils. Slowly, he pulled the blade out of the dying man the rest of the way. Ari groaned as the blade gradually made its way back out of him, sizzling the whole way. Tears dripped from his eyes.

"I am sorry," Tarkan whispered. He braced Ari with one hand as blood trickled from between his lips. He held up the massive blade, his arm shaking with the weight of it. The gem, Ishmael's heart, pulsed red as it soaked up the blood. Where he gripped the blade, Tarkan could feel the blood magic, faint though it was.

Ari made a rasping gag as he tried to breathe. Tarkan let go of him and he fell to the ground. Satisfied, seeing the pearlescent blade now tainted red, Tarkan gathered his things and loaded them onto the horse. He slid the blade into the saddle, lashing it there. Then he touched the heart.

"Your heart is my heart, Father. Your blood, my blood." He gripped the hilt and guard, putting the heart in the center of his hand. "You will watch, Father. You will see the Necro'Khan you created. Witness as I throw off every chain that has ever shackled me."

The heart pulsed, and Tarkan thought for a moment that the ghost of his father followed him and watched him now.

Chapter 28

---◇---

The Tomb of Acenoth

Sharar galloped on his white horse into the boundaries of the Dynast Palace, Amir just behind him. The guards at the bridge over the moat shouted, but didn't stop him when they recognized him. The scholar cut through the fields and mud pits where the slaves toiled, making them cry out and scatter before they were trampled. His horse snorted and panted angrily, tired of the push. When he pulled hard on the reins to stop it, it reared up, almost dislodging him. He slid off and marched towards the throne room.

Sokar was not there, nor was Nasor. A servant informed him that the Pharaoh and his court were out on the veranda overseeing some plans for the tomb.

"Which tomb?" he asked, catching his breath. He could mean Sokar's elaborate tomb or Acenoth's.

"Sira?" the servant asked, unsure.

"Never mind," the scholar snapped, shoving past the servant. He marched toward the ruby throne and the exit behind it.

"I'd rather stay behind, if I may," Amir said.

"I don't care what you'd rather do, Amir," Sharar replied. "You cannot show Nasor that his loathing of you has affected you." He glanced sideways at his Runer. "You will reap your revenge soon. I will see to it. But for now, defy him by standing before him."

His words had an effect on the Runer. He heard it in the more sure clop of his boots against the palace floor. But he still hung back, falling into step behind Sharar.

The sun dipped low in the east, making the slowly rising structures black silhouettes against an orange sky. Sokar, his architects, two priests, and Nasor stood around the table where they usually discussed the building and the slaves. Sokar wore his courtly raiments, complete with his golden hawk-like mask over his face. His long, feathery hair fanned out like a palm leaf. Sharar had learned long ago that Sokar donned the mask only when he had to; otherwise, he wore it when he didn't want others to see his face. It gave him a sense of protection.

"Abigor!" Sokar called when he spotted the scholar approaching. "Come and see what I've found. I had the scholars and scribes search the tunnels of tomes while you were away. We've found partial plans of Acenoth's tomb. They were not so complicated then as they are now. The problem was finding it. But I have two camps of excavators looking in the most probable locations now. When Acenoth's army went back on their word, the sands swallowed the tomb, you see. So we didn't even know where to look. Now, we have an idea."

Sharar joined the others at the table and looked down at the old, faded papyrus. The ancient Alikan language was farther from the modern Al'Myrahn they spoke, but he'd studied ancient tongues. The words—the ones he could make out—were poetic, describing mostly the battles Acenoth had won, his victories, his good works, and the romances he'd had.

"I trust your scholars and historians," Sharar said. "Well done. We can ride out tonight."

Sokar's head turned from Nasor to his priest, then back to Sharar. "So soon?"

The scholar bit back his first emotionally-driven reply. He leaned onto the table, pressing his palms into it hard. "Sokar, walk with me, will you?"

"Scholar, you will not take this boy out of my sight," Nasor cut in. His golden crook clinked against the floor.

Before Sharar could reply, Sokar squared up to Nasor, his fists clenched. "Boy?" he spat to his vizier. "I am your Pharaoh. Your *Dynast Pharaoh*. It is past time for you to show me the respect I deserve. I am my father's son. Do you need reminding, Nasor?"

Sharar bit the inside of his cheeks hard to stop the smirk that tried to give away his glee at seeing Sokar finally standing up to Nasor. He'd praise the boy king later, drawing him in one last time.

Nasor bowed his head. "Forgive me, Your Eminence." He kept his head bowed. "The rest of you, leave."

The priests and the architects bowed and quickly shuffled out.

"Amir, stay," Sharar ordered, turning with Sokar towards the fields. The Runer bowed his head and turned away from Nasor, leaving him behind. He felt the jackal's eyes on him until they turned a corner.

The fields of reeds, sugarcane, and other tall, dense, green plants would lend them some silence and privacy. Above them, the moon came out, bathing the crops in a cool, white light.

"Abigor," Sokar started with a sigh, "I'm sorry. I should have known you'd want to—"

Sharar faced Sokar, taking his shoulders in his hand and squeezing in what he hoped came across as affection. "Wait," he interrupted. He forced a smile onto his face. "I'm proud of you. For standing up to Nasor just now."

His words had the desired effect. Behind his gold mask, Sokar's large eyes glittered at his praise.

"It felt so wrong," Sokar argued back. "But..."

"No. No excuses." Sharar dropped his hand, clasping both behind his back. He gave a light laugh. "I cannot stand speaking to you when I cannot see your face."

Sokar pulled the golden ornament up and off his head. He tucked it under one arm as they continued their walk. The sound of the night creatures slowly rose as the clinking of chains and chisels died down.

"Never apologize to me," Sharar said. "And thank you for finding the maps and location of Acenoth's tomb. This brings us closer. But..." He sighed genuinely this time. "Things have happened that tell me we must act now, Sokar."

"What is it?" the boy asked.

Wondering how much he should tell Sokar, Sharar contemplated a moment before replying. If he told him everything, would it really matter? Or would it actually bring the boy closer to him?

"There is a threat close to you that I have not told you about," Sharar said, deciding. "Do you remember studying about the death cult that once nearly overthrew Alika? The one that wanted to bring back the worship of Nephron?"

Sokar nodded, brushing his long hair back over one shoulder. "Some years ago. They were spurred on by the Porshains. Long before my time. It's why we have so many slaves from Porsh."

"Yes. The cult was encouraged by the necromancers. But also by the one who led them. They called him Necro'Khan."

The young Pharaoh's face pinched just enough into a frown to tell Sharar he was trying to make the connection before Sharar spoke. He didn't wait for the boy to think it through. He needed to hurry. He stopped and faced Sokar.

"Another Necro'Khan has ascended," he said seriously. "A man I know personally. But he's not a good man. He's vindictive, and craves the power you and I will hold once we have the Mahit'O-nomicon. And he will come for me. For you and..." He cleared his throat and took Sokar's shoulder in his hand once again. "I was recently reminded of my son. And it made me realize I cannot put you in danger over a feud I have with this Necro'Khan."

"Abigor, no," Sokar said. "I will not stand down if a monster such as this is coming for you. We have been in this together ever since Father's death. Let me continue to stand with you."

"This touches me," he said. "But it means we must act quickly. First, we must dispatch the Runers you took hostage at the coliseum."

Sokar's lips parted and his eyes widened just a little as he paled.

"What happened?" Sharar asked. He hadn't moved his hand from Sokar's shoulder and had to stop himself from crushing him. "Where are they?"

The boy licked his lips and looked away into the field. He was afraid. "I-I'm sorry, Abigor. They got away."

Sharar dropped his hand, knowing he'd strangle the Pharaoh if he continued to touch him. He pressed his fist into his lips and turned away.

"I'm sorry, Abigor," Sokar pled. "We had them. I don't know how they escaped."

The scholar shot his gaze back to the veranda hidden behind the sugarcane. "I do. There are people in your court you cannot trust. They are working against you."

Stifling a scream of annoyance and rage, Sharar gritted his teeth and gripped his hair. He wanted to pull the small dagger from his boot and stab the stupid boy. This was what came from trusting others to do the simplest things. All Sokar had to do was lock up the two Runers, keep them shackled until his return.

"I'm..." Sokar stammered. "I'm so sorry. I didn't know they mattered so much."

Sharar took a deep breath. "The man, Tzarik, is the key to my research. In his veins is the answer to every question I have ever had." He swallowed a painful lump in his throat. "Are they in the embassy still?"

Sokar gulped. "No. Some noble woman is there now. She came to the palace not three days ago."

A long silence followed while he reined himself in. "You cannot trust Nasor, my king," Sharar whispered. "He is not loyal to you. Does not respect you. And now, with the Necro'Khan coming to Mysir, desiring the book…" He stopped. How could he convince the boy to act quickly? "Sokar," he turned to face him, plastering care and desperation on his face, "we must get it before the Necro'Khan. He will come for you and your kingdom. I have heard his plans. But we must trust one another. No one else. You wanted to leave your mark on your dynasty? Let me help you in protecting Alika from one of the most powerful sentients, one of the most feared."

Sokar gulped, but nodded. "We will go now. And we won't stop until I have placed the Mahit'Onomicon in your hands."

Ɀ

ONCE THEY RETURNED to the palace, Sokar ordered his men to prepare to march.

"Perfect timing, Your Eminence," one of the architects said after passing on the order. "We found it." He beamed.

"You found it?" Sharar gasped.

The architect nodded, pride swelling his chest. "It's south. Just on the banks of the second river. It's a beautiful work of art. Sadly, mostly destroyed, but we've found remnants as we've dug."

"Have you found the way in?" Sharar asked. His heart leapt into his throat.

"Better," the architect replied. "We've found the inner tomb. We found the One Thousand and One."

Sokar's face went slack in shock. "And Acenoth?"

The architect nodded. "His sarcophagus rests within a pyramid inside the tomb. We haven't touched them yet. The men are afraid of the curse."

"There is no curse on Acenoth," Sharar cut in. "The curse is on the One Thousand and One. Don't touch them. All we need is Acenoth."

Once provisions and the horses were ready, Sharar, Sokar, and a host of others—including Nasor and Amir—raced out into the desert to the tomb. Nasor protested, begging Sokar to stop and let them discuss, but the young Pharaoh stepped into his authority and commanded the vizier to follow if he must, but to be silent.

They galloped for some time before the rigs of excavation came into view over the horizon, outlined against the river. The architect led them around the valley they'd dug. The dunes of sand rose on either side of the tomb, and the facade faced the east and the river. The monotone chanting of a dozen priests inside the tomb cut through the night air.

"What are they doing?" Amir asked, sliding off his horse next to Sharar.

"They are afraid of the curse," Nasor replied flatly. "They are praying for protection. Some think we should offer sacrifice to Acenoth. Perhaps blood will placate him."

"Why?" the Runer pressed as the four of them marched to the entrance.

Nasor glared over at the Runer. "Once a pharaoh has acquired his glory, whatever that may be, he ascends to godhood. They are being cautious."

The Runer scoffed.

Nasor glared harder at him, gripping his staff. "I don't expect a common liar and a lowlife like a Runer to understand. Our pharaohs are gods incarnate, waiting to arise."

"Whatever you say," Amir mumbled, falling behind the other three.

Sharar put the bickering men out of his mind and took a torch from a slave standing near a brazier just outside the open door-way. Symbols, images, and small statues stood guard outside. Once he stepped in, he waited for his eyes to adjust. A few slaves had moved in a dozen or so braziers to light the tomb. Sharar blinked and finally beheld the cursed army. Laid out in rows before him, gold-leaf sarcophagi littered the space. The field of dead was so large, it faded into the darkness beyond.

"They are laid to rest just inside the opening," he mused, moving in amongst the one thousand and one sarcophagi. "They protect him at the very entrance." He raised his torch to take in the elaborate decor of the coffins. Each one was unique, perfectly depicting the man or Masahk inside. The stone faces had perhaps once been overlaid in gold, but that had faded considerably. Gems lined the sides where reliefs depicted their battle and their eventual curse.

He looked up, across the massive room where the army lay. Inside the huge tomb, a pyramid made of gold and rubies cut through the darkness into a sharp point. Even from below, he could see the opening at the top of the pyramid. Acenoth would be there. This was where the priests stood, shouting their prayers for protection to their gods.

After taking in the steps, Sharar marched into the massive graveyard of soldiers.

"Abigor!" Sokar called, not following him. "Wait."

"I do not have the luxury of fear, my king," he called back. Only Amir followed him through the field of dead soldiers.

The pair jogged through the dead and started up the many steps of the pyramid. They were smooth and slippery, and they both nearly tumbled back down the steps twice before reaching the top.

Amir panted when they finally met up with the priests. "How can it be this easy?" he asked.

"Easy?" Sharar snapped. He grabbed his Runer's arm, steadying himself while he caught his breath. "Amir, I have studied, hunted, explored, and experimented for twenty-two years. More than half my life. No one knew where the Mahit'Onomicon was buried. Or if it existed. Every country has its tale of how and why it came into being. I've read every scroll and tome I could find. Spent years in seminary. I had to hunt down a djinn and then learn how to bind it to me without bringing harm or repercussions onto myself." He straightened up. "There has been nothing easy about this.

"And now," he added in a murmur, "I may have to consider taking a curse upon myself."

Amir raised one brow. "So you do think there is a curse?"

"Undoubtedly." He passed by the priests and into the opening. "But I have to accept that and risk it. And once I have the book, it won't matter."

The inside of Acenoth's pyramid was modest. He expected more from such a feared and revered pharaoh. But then again, the monarchs built their own tombs. Acenoth must have been a humble man. Sharar walked around the small enclosure, lighting the three torches on the walls. Acenoth's sarcophagus shone in the firelight. The gold still clung to the outside, the blue marble bright as the three rivers of Alika. His hawkish likeness looked up from the ornate lid, bound in chains that kept the coffin closed. In the likeness's hands, Acenoth gripped a long-handled scythe. The curved blade was inlaid with gold, crackling out from a ruby near the top.

"For culling the invaders," Sharar noted, referencing a history he knew Amir was not familiar with.

"Black chains," Amir noted, pointing to but not touching the chains. "Painted over with ash and blood to keep his spirit inside."

"Break the lock," Sharar commanded, moving to put Amir closer to the sarcophagus.

"No," the Runer protested. "If I break these chains, the curse will fall on me."

"Don't be a fool, Amir," Sharar shot back.

The Runer shifted, frowning. "I thought you said there most likely was a curse."

"And there probably is. But once I am sorcerer, such things won't matter. No creature on the map will have as much magic and power as I. I will throw off curses, heal malignations, control the storms, and rain fire onto my enemies. You have nothing to fear."

Amir held his gaze a second too long, Sharar thought. But, as he always did, the Runer submitted to his command. He drew his scimitar, gripping the blunt edge with one hand and the hilt with the other. Using all his brutish strength, Amir brought the pommel down onto the lock that bound the chains. The metal cracked, but didn't sunder. Taking a breath, Amir hammered away again and again. On the fourth swing, he hissed and dropped his scimitar. His hand slipped, cutting his palm deep on the sharp edge. The blood spattered over Acenoth's likeness. Sharar shoved past him as the lock tumbled away.

"Help me," he grunted, shoving against the lid.

Amir joined him, and together, they shoved the sarcophagus open. The chains clattered loudly and the lid split as it hit the stone ground. The priests gasped and their prayers ceased, turning to frightened whispers. Everyone stood still. A small scuffle told Sharar that Sokar had arrived, shoving past the frightened priests. The young Pharaoh joined them in looking down on Acenoth.

Unsure what he had expected, Sharar lost his breath in awe. Inside, the ancient Masahk pharaoh lay, completely untouched by decay or time. His feathering glowed gold and blue. The curve of his majestic bird-like features made Sharar wish more Masahk looked like their ancestors. There was something imperial and imposing about the humanoid-animal combination that he knew would have struck awe into anyone looking upon such a king.

"He's beautiful," Sokar breathed. His hand unconsciously went to his far more human face.

The tomb seemed frighteningly quiet. Sharar ran his eyes down the supposed vindictive pharaoh to his chest. His lightly feathered arms clutched the object of Sharar's decades of desire: the Mahit'Onomicon, with one arm over the top and one over the bottom, letting the symbol forged onto the front show. The cover of the bound book was made of a now-familiar black, leathery skin pulled tight. Thick cords sewn through the spine held it together, looking like they'd once been dipped in blood.

"Is that a rune?" Amir asked, tilting his head to look at the symbol from the correct angle. "It almost looks like atan and buhkar. Or..." He frowned. "No, it's not."

"It does look like a rune," Sharar agreed. "But not one I've ever seen. Not even a sigil. The runes are very old. Chances are this symbol is written in the same language as the runes from long ago."

"That would be correct, wouldn't it?" Sokar asked. "If it is the Mahit'Onomicon from the creation story, it would be a rune we don't know. Or have lost. Like ancient languages."

But Sharar knew it. As he looked upon the strange symbol, he understood. A thrill shot through him, dousing any doubt he had. Yes, he'd forced the prophecy, making a wish to control the monsters and beasts of the map. But had that, in earnest, made him the Father of Monsters? Could he read the text? He took a shuddering breath, disbelief staying his hand.

"What's wrong?" Amir asked, ever attentive to the people around him. "Sharar?" He gently touched the scholar's shaking arm.

"I," he gasped. He moistened his lips, not taking his eyes off the book should he lose the translation. "I can read it. Not in words, but just in knowing. Like all the knowledge of the map has opened up to me." He couldn't stop the rise of his voice as joy filled his veins.

"What does it say?" Sokar asked, thrilled for his friend.

"I'm not sure how to translate it," Sharar confessed. He slowly moved his shaking hands to it. "It says so many things all at once. Like words with near the same meaning, but not the same. The closest I can think of is...Father of Monsters. But it means that the one who uses it shall be the Father of Monsters, and also that one who is the Father of Monsters shall use it. It's..." He swallowed. "It's incredible."

"It says all that?" Amir asked incredulously.

Sharar gave a dry laugh. "I knew you wouldn't understand."

He touched Acenoth's perfectly preserved hand and gently pried the dead pharaoh's fingers off the book. To his surprise, they held on like a vise, not stiff like the kind that came with death, but with pure, conscious strength. Once he had one of Acenoth's hands pried off, he stopped to check the pharaoh's face. He half expected to see the Masahk's eyes flash open and for the pharaoh to dive at him like a falcon. But the dead pharaoh did not move.

Finally, convinced he was meant to have it, Sharar pulled the book free. When he did, Acenoth's arms fell limp down at his sides. They landed without a thud, instead resting softly against his wings, hanging uselessly beneath him.

"Could the ancient Masahk fly?" Sokar asked. His own wings twitched slightly as he thought about them.

"There are images of them soaring above their armies," Sharar replied. "But that could just be an artistic rendering. We don't know for certain. Some strongly believe they did."

The young Pharaoh hummed sadly.

Sharar held the book firmly, gazing at the outside cover. "I... I could try to find a way, my friend."

Sokar smiled sadly, not meeting his eyes. "It would be a miracle."

From behind them, a deep voice asked, "What now, scholar?"

They turned to see Nasor appear in the doorway.

"Will you swallow your djinn? Consume his powers and take all that the demon is unto yourself?"

"Stay your words, Nasor," Sokar interjected. "Abigor is my friend. He's doing this for us. For Alika."

Sharar had had enough of the vizier. Locking eyes with the Masahk, he opened the Mahit'Onomicon. Nasor, Sokar, and Amir gasped, staggering back as a black wind pushed out from the pages. It was like a wind suddenly coming in an opened window.

A thousand voices filled Sharar's mind. A chill of fear shot up from his arms into his heart. Beneath his feet, the ground dropped away, making his stomach flip and pulling a cry from his throat. Against his will, his hands clenched the book harder. Joining the cacophony of voices, the roar of a thousand beasts rose up, deafening him. Then screams of the dead called out to him. First, he felt the urge to turn and run to them, to save them. Then, he wanted to possess them.

Behind him, a shadow moved. A colossus ran toward him. He screamed again, but it melted away. Above, millions of white glowing eyes looked down upon him. He sensed they wanted to tear him apart, so he ran. But the black ghosts pursued him. One shot toward him so fast, it ripped through him, going in through his back and ripping out the front of his chest. The pain blinded him. Then a monster, like a lion but black and shapeless, charged him down. It pounced, seizing his neck in its jaws, and ripped him to the ground where it tore at him.

This chasing, hunting, and tormenting went on for what felt like days, then weeks. Every creature he'd ever encountered chased him down and sank its claws or teeth into him, but he never died or fainted. He stayed alive and conscious to feel the pain, to be consumed by the fear.

"Enough!" he screamed as he lay in tatters in the darkness. "I have command over all of you, and I demand you cease your torment. You are mine!"

The last word had hardly left his mouth before everything went black. The pain disappeared.

"Abigor!" Sokar's scared voice called.

"I told you this was wrong," Nasor's voice chided.

Something heavy lay on top of Sharar. Something he couldn't buck off. Someone held his hands firmly in theirs. He was lying down. Finally getting a shuddering breath inside his lungs, Sharar opened his eyes. Amir was the one holding him down, straddling him, and gripping his head in his hands. His head throbbed, telling him he must have hit his skull against the ground before Amir had grappled him.

"Get off me," Sharar grunted, pushing against Amir.

"I had to," the Runer apologized, swinging himself off. He immediately offered Sharar a hand, pulling him to his feet.

"That was terrifying," Sokar added. He came to Sharar. "Are you all right?"

"Yes," the scholar breathed, looking around for the book. "In fact, I feel quite elated. What did you see?"

Sokar swallowed hard and didn't reply.

Amir said, "You attacked us. Went wild and started to scream that something was coming for you. I thought you'd been possessed, the way you moved."

Amir picked up the Mahit'Onomicon and handed it to Sharar. The scholar took the book, feeling a thrill shoot through him as he gripped it. He almost couldn't believe that he held it in his hands. At last.

"What will you do now, Al'Myrahn?" Nasor asked, leaning heavily on his crook. Desperation twisted the vizier's face.

Sharar clutched the book to his chest. "I have to go back to Gypsu."

"What? No," Sokar begged, grabbing his arm. "Not now. Not so soon."

"I have to," Sharar cut in. "I have one last wish to make. One last step." He faced Sokar, handing the book to Amir so he could take the Pharaoh's hands in his. "I swear to come right back." He leaned close to whisper into the Pharaoh's long, feathery ear. "Remember what I told you. Trust no one."

He pulled back, but Sokar leapt into his arms, wrapping his around Sharar's neck in an embrace. "Hurry, please."

Chapter 29

---◇---

Last of His Name

A thick, rancid smoke flowed over the all too familiar caldera that surrounded the road to the thronehall of Altevine. Tzarik tuned in to the nerves that bunched under his skin when he saw the clanland. The memories were from months ago, but throbbed fresh and painful in his mind. He stopped when they entered the first scattered farms and homesteads of the village.

"What is it?" Signar asked. His pale face stood out against the dark shadow of the cowl pulled over his yellow hair.

Behind them, the Runers, led by Tage, stopped as well. A few clansmen and women turned from their tasks to look at the band of Runers and single Altevine man. It must've been the first hours of a new morning. He couldn't tell because of the never-setting sun.

Tzarik ran his eyes over the peaks, the wide open green prairies, and noted how—despite it being the end of summer—the air still held a biting chill. He guessed it would never be warm on

Caerwren. Talismans and totems stood in every family plot. Sachets and other protective items hung from the eaves. In the center of this cluster of village homes, a pyre smoldered. They must've been burning their dead as they came.

Tzarik shook his head. "Memories, that's all. Being back makes me wonder if…" If he had done the right thing? He shook his head. "The time we spent on Caerwren was dark. Painful."

"Yes," Signar agreed. He took the lead, letting Tzarik follow. "The smells more than anything remind me of the days I lived outside my mother's hall."

Tzarik chided himself instantly. Of course Signar had bad memories of Altevine as well. He'd been selfish in his self-pity. "I'm sorry, Signar," he said. "That should never have happened to you."

"You know what it was like," Signar offered.

Tzarik frowned, glancing up at the tall boy. They'd never spoken about his past. They'd hardly spoken save in the last few weeks.

"You spoke about it when you bargained for me from Skarde," Signar said with a gentle smile.

"You remember that?"

Signar took a moment to reply, looking down to avoid tripping on the uneven earth. He led the Runers through the tiny smattering of homes to the larger city on the hill inside the caldera. "Yes, I do. I was not the imbecile they thought I was. I just couldn't find the words to speak. I couldn't make my mind stand still to piece together a phrase. I was too scared, too angry. I didn't know how to control the desires in my head and speak." He raised his head, glaring into the sun. "I used to speak. But mother wouldn't allow it. So I gave up. I let the wolf take over. It was simple, since it was so strong from the start. It was like a nightmare. I was trapped inside my own body, burning to speak, to beg for the torment to stop." He shook his head, stopping his story short.

Tzarik's heart broke a little more for the boy. He was more sure now than ever that he'd done the right thing in taking Signar.

"Reks," Tage whispered from behind. He nodded ahead.

Tzarik and Signar squinted into the sun and the hill before them. A small circle of people gathered, unmoving and staring down at them. The sulfates inside Tzarik did not rush, but he was sure the people were examining them closely. An old man stepped forward a little, his long white hair blowing in the icy wind. He raised a gnarl-knuckled hand and pointed at Signar.

"Kjarton?" he whispered. His gray eyes went wide. "It cannot be. The raven Reks?"

Tzarik took two steps to be right beside Signar. The way the man spoke did not indicate whether he was pleased or angry to see the resemblance.

"No," a woman with red hair whispered. "Not Kjarton." She ran a few steps towards them, hand over her mouth.

The Runers, led by Tage, came to surround Signar, just in case.

"Signar?" the woman gasped. "The son of the wolf?"

The people gasped in unison, hissing and whispering. "The last of his name," someone called from up the hill. "The lone wolf."

"The wildling!" another shouted, terrified.

"Peace," Tage shouted over the fear as Signar said, "Don't be afraid."

Tzarik moved closer to Signar should any of the fearful ones move to harm him or attack him.

Signar held his head high once more. "I am not the wildling that left your shores. I have found myself and tamed my wolf thanks to this man beside me."

A few people still cowered as Signar spoke, ready for him to jump at them. "How?" one asked.

"Through much trial," Signar answered honestly. "But I promise you, I am no longer wild. My wolf within has been tamed."

"A miracle," someone whispered.

"Have you come to remove Aras?" the old man asked, his chapped lips trembling. "Are you really Signar Wolf-tor?"

Slowly, Signar gripped the cowl of his cloak and pulled it off. Shaking his head like a wolf, he released his long, golden hair. "I have," he said as steadily as he could. "And I am."

Immediately, the people rushed their lost Reks. Tage's hand flew to his sword, but Tzarik gripped his wrist, shaking his head. He did not sense hostility from them now. The people reached up to touch the towering boy, crying thanks to Raudnir for bringing their lost wolf home. Some fell to their knees, tears spilling down their faces as they begged him to remove Aras. Some shouted that his mother had been the one to bring the malignation to Altevine and he should banish it. The voices called over each other until no discernible words could be made out.

Tage came forward, shoving a few people back to give Signar some room. "Is Aras in the thronehall?" he asked the people.

"Yes, always," the old man replied. "He is celebrating his last raid. His fleet just came back from Zealmor. Alasdair-Reks and Eibhlin-Reks cannot even defend their canton anymore. He's devastated them, captured some of the Albanacht—their warriors."

"Bastard," Tage spat. "He drives our alliance further away."

"And Northica?" Tzarik asked. "Skarde swore to watch over Altevine."

"He did," Tage replied. "Until Aras took Dain as a thrall. His army of Vilderkin are powerful."

Signar took a deep breath, then exhaled a huge cloud of steam. "Tage, go back into the main city. You and your men stay inside Aras's vision and defend the people from the malignation, should they need it."

"What do you mean?" Tage asked. "We must take you to Aras."

Tzarik stepped up between the young Runer and his ward.

"That sounds like you want a fight," he said. "What will happen when Signar goes to the thronehall?"

"They *will* fight," Tage said. "They must. He must show he is stronger than Aras."

A horrid vision filled Tzarik's mind: Signar and this Vilderkin in beastly, bloody combat. Him standing off to the side, unable to help. Dain, shackled and beaten near to death, surrounded by wild Vaeson guards. He shut his eyes tight.

"And I will," Signar said. "But first, I want my god to know I have returned. I heard him call me not two hours ago. Only with his blessing will I face Aras."

Tzarik had worried about this, since Skarde had mentioned the baptism a Vaeson must undergo once they returned to the shore. Had any Reks ever done such a thing? What did it mean?

The old man glanced at his fellow clansmen. His lips twisted in worry. "Strigganoct has battled Raudnir. There was a storm on the road from Altevine to Northica. Lightning set the forest there aflame. We fear Strigganoct is taking revenge on our god for the acts of Aras. The Volra say they read in the bones that the dragon is angry at the wolf for allowing Altevine to punish Dain."

"We heard he was a Vaeson shaped after Isodel, the hawk," Tzarik cut in. "Why would the Northican god attack Raudnir if Isodel is also a goddess of Northica?"

"The Vilderkin are not honored by our gods as the Reks are," Tage offered. "Because they do not worship or hunt in their name. They serve only themselves. After a time, a Vilderkin will lose their god-shape because of this. I cannot begin to know the reasons the gods do what they do. But Aras took Dain in the name of Altevine, which is blessed by Raudnir. That is enough."

"Damn the gods," Tzarik growled.

Signar shook his head. "You will understand, Tzarik." He flipped the hood back over his head and turned to the east. "I'll go now. Tage, stay and protect my people. Do not let word get back to Aras that I have returned."

Tage nodded. "Go east. It may take you a few days, but you will know when you have reached where Strigganoct and Raudnir battle."

THEY HAD to camp that night, but the next morning, Signar plowed through the shallow remnants of snow, over the hills and rocks, easily. He was eager to prove to his god that he deserved to take back his throne. Tzarik struggled, gasping, to try to stay even remotely close to Signar. The boy's long legs and lean muscles carried him easily over Caerwren's rough terrain. After only thirty minutes or so, Tzarik stopped, coughing and suffocating from the strain. He doubled over, hands on his knees.

His lungs burned as he tried to gasp, but the cold, dry air just made him cough more. He ran a few more paces to try to catch up, but dizziness made him sway. Focusing on Signar's huge frame ahead, he marched on.

They moved farther east and the sky grew darker. Lightning erupted from the clouds, striking the ground. A copse of trees loomed ahead of them. The trunks were black and charred, the branches brittle and leafless, having burned all away. Tzarik stopped when the muscles in his legs spasmed, forcing him to the ground. He went down hard and chose to remain there, gasping for air. Damn Signar and his long-legged strides.

"Tzarik," the boy called, rushing back. He reached down, gathering the Runer up in his arms and pulling him to his feet. "I believe we have reached the place."

Tzarik leaned on Signar but still couldn't get his legs to move. He offered a grunt in reply. The scar inside his leg on the muscle throbbed. He sucked in the cold air as the pain mounted. He couldn't stop himself from gripping his thigh and moaning.

"Wait here," Signar said, gently setting Tzarik down, putting his back against a large boulder that faced the burnt copse. He stood up and marched towards the smoldering earth.

"Signar," Tzarik called to him. The boy turned. "Be careful."

Regret at not being able to even stand fueled Tzarik's fear as Signar faced the place where the gods had battled. If they gave him a chance, he'd go with him. Even if he was sure to be rent apart, he would not let Signar face the vindictive dragon and wolf alone.

Signar marched up a rocky spear of earth overhanging the smitten ground, to the very end of an icy gray rock that stuck out from the hill. Tzarik watched the boy's muscles shift, how he clenched his left hand, then flexed his fingers.

"Raudnir!" Signar shouted into the air.

Tzarik realized the boy had no weapons. He'd have to trust his control over the wolf inside him.

"I am Signar Wolf-tor, last of my name, and I have returned to my home to take my canton back from Aras, the Vilderkin." The young Vaeson went still as stone, all shifting gone. His feet stood apart, firmly planted on the rock. When nothing happened, he added, "I will not stay, Raudnir. I must leave. I do not fear your wrath should I, a Vaeson, depart your shores once again."

Lightning flashed across the sky so quickly that Tzarik did not see where it started. It ended by striking the rock where Signar stood. Tzarik gave a shout of surprise, but Signar did not so much as flinch.

"I don't fear you, either, Strigganoct," Signar replied. "Why do you punish my god for the sins of a hawk? A hawk you share worship and revenge with. Dain is my ally. I have come to save him."

The sky rumbled with thunder as another bolt was prepared. Somewhere, sounding far away and muffled, a deep wolven howl rose up. Something, not the sulfates, tingled through Tzarik. It ran up his thighs to the top of his head. Too late, he realized what it was. He shoved against the ground, rolling to the side, but the lighting snapped up from the ground and struck him.

The world buzzed, his vision white. A perpetual cracking and snapping resounded in his skull.

"Face *me*, Strigganoct!" Signar screamed, raising his fist to the sky. He looked down at Tzarik. "Are you all right?"

Coughing again, Tzarik nodded. He pushed himself back up and panted against the rock. His heart thudded fast and hard, out of his control.

Another rumble of thunder rolled over the clouds. As it did, two great yellow eyes appeared in the sky over the trees. Tzarik froze, watching them. They moved closer, the earth shaking with every stride. The outline of sharp fur and long, pointed ears appeared. Then the huge chest and forelegs of what was clearly a mountain-sized wolf appeared in the smoke and mist. Terror surged through Tzarik. This wasn't like facing the obviously weak god Bolemesh. He looked up at Signar. The boy still stood his ground. Not a single quiver shook his frame.

"A lone wolf has come back to my shores?" Raudnir whispered in his god-like voice. His voice was soft and low, but still rattled the earth.

The wolf god drew closer through the clouds, making himself smaller the closer he got. His fur hung thick and matted. It was the same bright, fiery red Sjörna's had been. His bright yellow eyes had fire in them, burning and making waves of heat ripple around his fierce face. A scar ran over one eye. Even when Raudnir shrank down, he stood over the hill and rock Signar perched on. The wolf glared down at the boy, and Tzarik could not help but imagine him snapping Signar up into his mouth, devouring him easily.

"You do not shudder," Raudnir mused.

"I am not afraid of you," Signar shot back.

The smell of ash and sulfur filled Tzarik's nose.

"I have come to take or be given your blessing, since you are my god and it is you who gave me my wild shape," Signar went on.

"Take?" Raudnir barked. "You cannot take my blessing, insolent pup." His flaming eyes moved to the hand-shaped brand on Signar's shoulder. "Ah," he mused, "deals with demons of other gods. You are a busy boy, aren't you?"

"Let this be a testament to my courage," Signar offered. "Give me your blessing or I shall take it. Even without it, I will return to my clan and take my thronehall back from the Vilderkin who sits inside it, enslaving my allies and raiding Zealmor's people."

Raudnir growled, his lip snarling. His yellow eyes turned to Tzarik. "And this heathen?"

"My savior," Signar replied.

Tzarik struggled to his feet, still shaken and his legs still in pain. "I will go with him. Whatever he must do to earn your blessing so he may take his clan back—I will be with him."

The wolf god barked a laugh. "This heathen believes he may face me? In contest for my own creation?" He spat towards Signar.

"Listen to me, dog," Signar snapped.

Tzarik instantly saw the effect the insult had on Raudnir. The god slowly turned his head back to Signar, the scarred, fiery yellow eye igniting in rage. His ears pressed flat into his head. Tzarik worried Signar might think himself braver than he was. Or that his unbridled, wild courage would enrage the god.

"I will not rule alone," Signar went on. "That's not what a clan is. So I will not suffer this baptism alone."

"And if I refuse?" Raudnir smirked, the wind rippling through his red fur.

"Then I will not fight you," Signar replied.

"Then you will not be Reks!"

Signar scoffed. "Yes, I will. I will fight against you every day to keep my canton. I am Signar Wolf-tor, and I am Reks of Altevine whether you say so or not."

The boy's defiance in the face of his god was admirable, but Tzarik worried he'd be no help in this fight.

"Is that what is required?" Tzarik asked, struggling to stand. He didn't want to seem weak in the god's presence. "A battle? Signar against you?"

Raudnir turned his yellow eyes onto Tzarik. "I will be satisfied with a battle. Strigganoct has attacked me in a rage for the sins of Altevine, though Aras is not my child. I cannot forfeit a battle to a Vaeson who has left our shores. I must do my all to test him. To know he is worthy."

Tzarik waited. He felt the wolf had more to say. But Signar spoke first.

"I have heard Strigganoct is displeased with you," the boy said. "Was it he who gave you that scar on your eye? Bless me, Raudnir, and let me remove the Vilderkin."

"Kneel to a pup?" Raudnir guffawed. The god leaned down dangerously close to Signar with his fangs showing. "Your insults, your un-earned courage, have enraged me. Though I hate Aras and Isodel who blessed him, I will laugh as I tear your limbs from your body, should you submit to me."

"Enough talk, coward," Signar spat. "Come for me and spare no rage, for I, too, am a wolf."

Chapter 30

Wolven Rage

Raudnir roared at the final insult and snapped at Signar. The Vaeson boy rolled backward down the hill, avoiding the god's jaws. He shifted into his wolf just as Raudnir leapt onto him. Both snarled and their jaws locked together. The roaring from both wolves sounded to Tzarik like stone against metal. Their back legs scrambled against the earth, tearing it up and kicking clumps of earth up as they tussled.

Tzarik shoved himself up and took his runes from around his neck. If nothing else, he'd use halat to protect Signar from the god's maw. Limping, the wound in his leg throbbing still, he shuffled around the boulder he'd been leaning against and made his way up the rock to where Signar had been standing.

"You make a fine wolf," Raudnir praised him. Signar had flipped the god over his head and tossed him several yards.

Signar rolled back to his forepaws and shook his fur. He began a slow circle around Raudnir; the god did the same. Their eyes flashed at one another.

"It took me some time to control this wolf," Signar replied.

Tzarik swore the wolf god smirked. "Can you fight just as well as a man, Signar Wolf-tor?"

The golden wolf showed his teeth. "Would you deign to face me as a man, Raudnir?"

The red wolf hummed deep in his throat. "An interesting challenge, Wolf-tor. I accept."

Not sure what to expect, Tzarik held his rune hand up. Below, the red wolf god melted away like he'd seen Signar do so many times. In his place, a towering man stood. Raudnir made himself into a giant of a man. Bare chested, fiery veins pulsing over mountains of muscle, with a thick, wavy mane of red hair and matching ornate beard, Raudnir stood before them.

Tzarik found himself moving closer to the ledge. He didn't care how huge, imposing, or muscled the god made himself; he'd stand close to protect Signar.

Signar kept his eyes on Raudnir as he shifted back to his human form. "No weapons, god," he said with a smirk. "Only what you made us with."

"I accept," Raudnir replied. He dove at Signar and the two huge bodies collided into a sudden and fierce tussle.

Tzarik drew buhkar and dove from the ledge to land softly as a mist on the same level as the battle. Before he reformed, he took several steps back.

Raudnir, being taller, went for Signar's throat. He reached down and gripped the boy's neck with both hands. Then he lifted him and Signar choked once. Tzarik forced himself to stand back, even though his instincts told him to run in. The blood drained from his face as he watched Signar's legs kick in the air.

Signar didn't panic as the breath was choked out of him. He swung his feet up, planting them both on Raudnir's chest, and kicked as he arched his back. The god's hands fell away as Signar sprang free from his grip. Raudnir stumbled back a few paces, but then immediately charged at Signar. The Vaeson stood his ground, glaring at the charging god.

"Move!" Tzarik commanded, his voice cracking with worry.

Signar smiled slyly. Just as Raudnir raised his fist, the boy shifted into his wolf with a single leap. He gripped the god's arm in his mouth. When he landed, he swung his head around, drawing blood from the god's flesh. The ichor that released from Raudnir's veins was golden-red, but opalescent like the white blood, catching some of the sun's rays.

The gold wolf shook his head, thrashing back and forth. Tzarik knew what it felt like to be in those jaws like that. The scars on his middle twinged at the memory, as did the ones on his arm where Sjörna had gripped him just as Signar gripped Raudnir now.

The god roared and landed a punch to Signar's skull. The golden wolf let go with a yelp, but spun and lunged again.

"You Skelmir bastard—" Raudnir began.

He was cut off when Signar latched onto the god's human throat with his massive jaws. Raudnir thrashed, babbling incoherently before he finally shifted into his red wolf. Being the same size, Signar snapped down harder, grappling the god to the ground and holding him there. Raudnir struggled for just a moment, but the drawing of his blood made him cautious.

"Breaking your word, Wolf-tor?" Raudnir growled. "So be it."

Tzarik's sulfates rushed and he ran forward.

Raudnir quickly started to grow back to his original size. He flipped his head, tossing Signar far. The golden wolf yelped as he landed against the stones, rolling several yards. Tall enough to tower over the trees again, Raudnir lifted his forepaw to bring it down upon the dazed wolf. Tzarik shouted in effort as he drew halat and thrust his hands out to send the barrier to Signar.

It reached the boy just in time and lasted only a second. But it was long enough to stop the god's attack, his paw cracking the shield instead.

"Runer," Raudnir growled, "this is not your fight. Wolf-tor has already broken his own oath."

"Did I?" Signar asked, standing up in his human form. "I said no weapons. Only what you made us with." He tilted his head, smirking. "You made me a wolf."

Raudnir snarled, but in a way that told Tzarik the god had resigned himself to the trickster's words. "I see I must watch my words with you. A true Skelmir. Never have I had a mortal stand before me thus. I must confess, it impresses me."

"Then do you accept me?" Signar asked. "May I have your blessing and return to my thronehall?"

The red wolf sat, glaring down at the pair of them, considering. "I could destroy you now with a single thought, Skelmir," Raudnir reminded him. "I am a great god, not some weakling scurrying around the Deep."

"I understand," Signar said cautiously.

Raudnir's fiery eyes landed on Tzarik. He took a deep breath, exhaling smoke. "The dragon wishes to give you a gift as he greatly favors Dain Radjur-tor," he said, relaying a message neither of them could hear.

Signar frowned. "Strigganoct?"

"I do not like this." Raudnir's eyes flit back to Signar. "You are mine. You must give me sacrifices every Vasaras. From Northica. To atone for the hate I have endured from Strigganoct this last season."

Signar shook his head. "I want to do away with sacrifice."

"Ha!" Raudnir barked. "Then you are nothing to me."

Signar held his arms out to his sides and stepped forward. "Then destroy me, Raudnir."

"What are you doing?" Tzarik whispered, reaching to draw Signar back.

"Destroy me," Signar said again. "I am Signar Wolf-tor, last of my name. I am the lone wolf, Raudnir. Destroy me, and who will worship you?"

"I could make another," the god tried, but a certain reluctance made his voice soft.

"Yes," Signar agreed. "A blessed mortal, already breathing. But never again a god child, a natural born wolf, bearing your image."

Raudnir growled gently, his lip half snarling. "Damn you, Wolftor," he whispered.

Signar nodded. "So I might be. What I can promise you is worship," he went on. "Should we kill, it will be in your name and to the glory of the wolf."

The god leaned down, his yellow eyes smoldering. "You will take a wife and she will bear wolven Vaeson. And you will promise your children to me and my service."

"I will promise their service to the clan," Signar countered. "Which, in turn, is in service to you."

Raudnir eyed the boy cautiously, knowing this was once again some trick.

"If I do not lead your worship, wolf, no one will," Signar said with finality. "You may be a god, but I am your last hope of staying strong. Lest Strigganoct binds you beneath his mountain. That does not stop me from returning to Altevine and saving Dain." His eyes flicked around the smote land. "What gift does the dragon have for a wolf?"

"It is because of the radjur in Northica, blessed by the dragon, that I have no children among the Vaeson!" Raudnir barked, finally divulging his true animosity. "Why does Strigganoct bless the radjur when he is not made in his image? When Isodel gave them children in her likeness?"

Tzarik waited. In his time on Caerwren, he'd not seen a single dragon-shaped sentient. Just those who worshipped the dragon. Strigganoct had given Skarde and Dain the gift of lightning, but they did not bear his shape.

"Because he is proud," Signar said, almost soothingly, to the god. "Striggonoct would never deign to give mortals his shape. Thus, he gathers worship through fear of his kind. But you will be strong again. You have to bless me, though. Give me what is rightfully mine. And let Strigganoct bestow his gift so I may unite Northica and Altevine again. Raudnir, the malignation will destroy my clanlands before we may worship properly. I need all the strength I can gather."

The huge wolf god filled his lungs and gave a great sigh that pushed the trees around them in a cold, ashen wind. "Very well, little wolf. See the place above us, where you first challenged me?"

Signar and Tzarik both craned around to look at the rocky ledge.

"There you will find your blade." Raudnir stood, his ears slightly drooping. "Take it, as my gift to you. And little wolf?"

Signar looked back at his god.

"I will send a maiden to you," Raudnir went on. "You must take who I choose as your joining Reks. She must bear your children. They must serve your clan, as you have said."

"Aye," Signar agreed. "How will I know her?"

Raudnir turned, signaling they were finished speaking. "She will come on rivers of blood."

Before their eyes, the god phased away into the mist, turning to ash. The wind took the flakes away, leaving Tzarik and Signar alone. The Runer couldn't tear his eyes away from where the wolf had vanished. He held his tongue. Things on Caerwren were not like the culture and norms on Al'Myrah. What Signar had promised was barbaric, but that was the way of his people. And he understood: their gods were close. If Layth'asad appeared to him, walked the desert sands like the wolf did, he'd no doubt bend a knee to the white lion of Al'Myrah simply out of fear.

Tzarik didn't know what to say to Signar, but the boy turned to the crags, not expecting any words of advice.

"I see something," he said, looking up at the rock they'd stood on. "Tzarik, will you go see? If it is indeed my Vaeson blade, I want my first touch to be when I have summoned it."

The Runer nodded and marched up the hill. He used some of the rocks protruding from the grass to help steady his pace. As he crested the top, Signar's god-given blade came into view. He walked toward it, taking it in. It was an axe. With the haft, the weapon was as tall as him. He'd never be able to even lift it. But a giant like Signar could. And perhaps the Vaeson weapons did not feel as heavy to their bearers.

Raudnir had a Skelmir in him as well. The axe was nearly identical to the one that hung in Sjörna's thronehall above her throne. After hearing Skarde's tale, Tzarik realized it had been Irsa—Skarde's wife's—axe. Sjörna had taken it as a trophy, a prize for killing the lover of her husband's murderer. Knowing the blades came directly from the gods made the insult more obvious.

Signar's blade struck the stone at an angle, like Raudnir had swung the axe into the stone himself. A bright, golden gem with metallic strikes through it nestled between the heads of the axe. The gem was round and clear, like crystal in the shape of a wolf. A golden wolf. Tzarik reached out and stroked the gem. It reminded him of Azar's blade. His mentor's orichalcum scimitar had had a blue, cold gem in the center.

He dropped his hand. Was it the mark of a god?

Lightning sizzled between the axe and Tzarik's fingers. So Strigganoct had also blessed the blade. No doubt the god wanted one of his strongest worshiper's freed.

"Tzarik?" Signar called up. "Do you see it?"

"Yes," Tzarik called back down. "Summon it to yourself." He wanted to see the thing ripped from the stone.

He assumed Signar thrust his hand out, because the axe jerked suddenly. The stone cracked, spitting up dust and lightning. The axe gave a strange, metallic groan and shot out of the earth, down out of Tzarik's sight. He chased after it, looking down the small cliff. Below, Signar caught the thing as if it were no more than a pitchfork. Awe filled Tzarik as he looked down at the boy, now a man, gripping the colossal axe. Lightning kissed the earth from the head of the axe, then struck up into the sky. Tzarik swore he saw the outline of an antlered dragon behind the dark clouds. He'd seen that shape before.

Pride swelled Tzarik's heart, but then it burst, knowing he had to leave Signar now. His work with the wildling was done, and he had to pass his boy off to a wild, barbaric land to rule alone.

Chapter 31

Sorcerer Ascended

Sharar stood behind the table in his dungeon, slowly flipping through the pages of the sacred, ancient book. He stood across from the cell where Vicdan lay, still shackled. Amir had taken the precaution of binding his hands behind his back, and Sharar had fastened the bridle in his mouth and over his jaw.

The terror that had ripped through him when he'd first opened the book had not left entirely. The hairs on the back of his neck stood on end when his djinn slowly descended the stairs. In his human form, the djinn was an Al'Myrahn man with black hair and melancholy brown eyes.

"You struggle," the djinn mused, coming closer to the table. His eyes flitted to Vicdan, then to Amir. The Runer sat in a corner, his head tilted back against the wall, sleeping. "What stops you?"

Sharar stopped turning the pages, laying his hand against them. "I don't understand. I can control the beasts. Why can I not comprehend the text?"

Across the room, Vicdan shifted in his shackles, his green eyes focused on Sharar. The scholar didn't care if the necromancer heard him speak candidly. Not now. Vicdan couldn't escape.

The djinn walked around the table, putting it between himself and Sharar. "Because you are not that man. You are trying to cheat the laws and mores of the god's magic."

"Damn the gods," Sharar spat. "Their prophecy dictated that the one who could read the Mahit'Onomicon was a man who could control monsters, tame them. I made that wish. I am that man." He couldn't stop the anger rising in his throat. "Unless…" His eyes moved to his djinn. "I could make one more wish. But then, how do I know if the book will tell me how to take your essence?"

Vicdan made a strangled string of sounds that were clearly a question.

"Yes, I knew," the djinn replied, somehow understanding the unintelligible sounds.

"Know what?" Sharar quipped. He glared at Vicdan.

"He asked if I knew you were intending to destroy me, to take all that I am as your own." The djinn had no fear, meeting Sharar's eyes. "I knew." He looked back at Vicdan. "I desire it. No djinn will ever be set free by a mortal. Once we are unbound from our masters," he waved a hand to Sharar, "we are still prisoners to the artifact that holds us. If we are not tethered to the artifact, we are slaves to the gods who took us. There is no freedom apart from death."

Vicdan snapped three sharp syllables and regretted it immediately. He winced and whined as bloody saliva trickled down his chin.

"I'm afraid that is the truth, my friend," the djinn replied.

"Enough," Sharar barked. He closed the book and marched around to the cell. He took out his keys, waking Amir with a kick, and opened the door. Vicdan looked up with just enough trepidation to satisfy him. "While I contemplate how to go about ascending to sorcerer, you will entertain me. That's what you jongleurs do, correct?" He motioned for Amir to enter the cell. Once the Runer flanked him, he unlocked the bridle and Vicdan's wrists. "We are going to the desert. There have been enough battles on these sands that surely bodies lie in wait everywhere."

Vicdan spit a stream of blood from his mouth, wincing. He rubbed his wrists, aggravating the cuts from the shackles. "I won't raise, scholar. I won't be a pawn in your mad game."

Sharar laughed gently through his nose. He snatched Amir's dagger from the sheath on his thigh, gripped Vicdan quick as a jaguar, and slammed him into the bars. He pressed his body up against the jongleur's and the knife up against Vicdan's side.

"I have ways of making anyone do anything I say," Sharar whispered. "I'd love it if you forced me."

Vicdan tried to push back again, but couldn't jostle the enraged scholar off. "You're so rough, scholar," he said saucily. "You've yet to show me a really good time, but I expected a fine dinner first."

Sharar's glower faded. The damn necromancer was making a joke. Imprisoned, surrounded, a knife to his flesh, and he joked. Sharar gave in to the hysterics and laughed. Then he took a deep breath, pulled back his hand, and jammed the knife hard into Vicdan's side. The singer gasped and moaned, his hands scrambling at the bars to hold himself up as his knees weakened.

"Now," Sharar sighed, leaning close to Vicdan's ear, "I know how to kill you. I know this won't. But I also know you can feel it." He twisted the knife. "Necromancers need to breathe too, correct?" Sharar slowly slid his empty hand around Vicdan's throat. When he heard the younger man gasp, he smiled. "I think that's why I loved Tarkan. Nothing could kill him. Not when I removed his guts, not when I cut his throat. Not when I drowned him in a barrel of water."

A small shudder rippled through Sharar just remembering it.

"I'd love to experience that again. Will you give me that pleasure?"

Under his fingers, Sharar felt Vicdan swallow.

"No," the necromancer whispered, his voice rasping. "I'd rather raise my dead mother."

Sharar smiled.

WITH THE DJINN and Amir flanking him, Sharar forced Vicdan up the stairs and out into the cool desert night. They rode out a ways from the estate into some open desert. The dunes turned blue, bathed in the moonlight. The sand in Alika was white, unlike the golden, glittering sands of Al'Myrah. Sharar waited, standing between his two bodyguards.

"We've waited long enough," he called to Vicdan, who stood alone under the moon. "I warned you what stalling would mean. Raise me a single body, you whelp. One is all I'm asking. And I won't ask again."

When Vicdan only looked up from his hands where they hovered just an inch apart, Sharar saw defiance in his eyes. He motioned for Amir to approach the young man. When the Runer took two powerful steps forward, the black wind suddenly picked up. Sharar shook his head, smiling.

Only a moment later, though, the winds died down.

"What are you doing?" Sharar barked.

"I... I can't," Vicdan panted. "I don't have the strength."

Sharar had expected this. He snapped his fingers and his djinn brought Vicdan a waterskin filled with blood. "Drink."

The jongleur looked up from the skin despondently.

"Don't make me force you," Sharar reminded him.

Eyes watering, Vicdan drank the blood. He gagged and vomited up the whole swallow.

"Again," Sharar commanded.

Looking like he might weep, Vicdan did as he was told. He covered his mouth, handing the skin back to the djinn, and tried to swallow and keep it down. He retched a few times, but finally consumed it all.

"Raise me one body, Bone-Scriven," Sharar commanded.

Vicdan licked his bloody lips and put his hands together. He whispered, then his voice whipped away on the wind. Sand swirled around him. Sharar looked, wondering what Vicdan had found to raise. A small trickle of blood leaked from the young man's right eye. Whatever it was, it was big.

The ground shook and Sharar backed away, eyes flitting over the desert. Several yards to his right, the sands shifted. Then they kicked up in clouds. A long, sharp, onyx-colored spike appeared. It grew in girth closer to the ground, plunging out of the sand. Then, the spiny, familiar exoskeleton of an arachnid glinted in the moonlight.

"A creature of Rabazhi, the scorpion god," the djinn said.

Words left Sharar as the giant creature raised itself above the sands, shaking the granules from its armor. The creature gave a gentle, rhythmic moan that almost resembled the purring of a great cat. Its eight legs moved in a hypnotic motion, slowly crawling towards the group. Sharar stepped back and Amir placed himself between the advancing scorpion and the scholar.

"Well done," Sharar whispered, still in awe. "I knew you had it in you."

"Of course I do," Vicdan replied. His voice came raspy from the exertion, but he smiled. Vicdan blinked up at his risen. "You want to know something, scholar? They'll stop you, Tzarik and Sybal. Yes, they left me imprisoned on that icy rock with those utter barbarians—and I'll never forget how they treated me. But I trust them. They're made of sterner stuff than you can imagine."

Before Vicdan finished speaking, Sharar snapped his fingers at

Amir and pointed to Vicdan. The Runer acted quickly. He launched himself, fist cocked, at the jongleur. The blow landed on his face and bowled Vicdan over, and Amir proceeded to beat him once he had him grappled. Behind them, the scorpion fell, dead once again.

Sharar walked closer, looking down at the quickly bloodied necromancer. "Your faith is not unfounded, surely," he said simply, hands clasped behind his back. "I understand. I know Tzarik. And his half-breed woman is quite the riddle as well. But I've already won, my boy. I have the Mahit'Onomicon. I nearly have Tarkan at my side again, and even without him, I have you and no doubt Ashkan, for the right price. Your Runers have failed. All I need to do is make my final wish—"

Bloodied and mewling, Vicdan had managed to say the spell to raise another creature. A decaying dog leapt from the sands and crashed into Amir. The Runer spun off Vicdan and had to defend himself from the risen dog. Sharar ran at Vicdan, kicking the desperate man hard in the side of the head. The instant he did, Amir shoved the dog off and severed its head.

Vicdan rolled to the side, a strange, new vigor powering his frantic movements. He hissed, glaring through the blood smattered over his face. Sharar felt a chill rise up around them; the necromancer was calling on ghosts now. One appeared before him, a wild, deranged-looking man. It locked on to Sharar and shot towards him. Vicdan meant to force the spirit to possess the scholar. Sharar cried out and turned, ducking. But the icy presence of the ghost never filled him. He looked up to find Amir before him, legs wide, shielding him with halat. The white barrier glowed strong and unshattered in the dark night.

"Shackle him," Sharar barked to his djinn. The demon didn't even move, but the shackles appeared around Vicdan, binding his arms tightly behind his back. A length of chain hung off, which Amir grabbed quickly, pulling the necromancer toward them.

"Impressive, my boy," Sharar panted, dusting himself off. "I knew your ploy of weakness for what it was, but did not expect such vigor. Your long-sleeping scriptures are eager for work. You were brave to take on the three of us."

He stood up, safe now from most danger.

"But I think you assume I want Tzarik dead. That's quite the opposite. I want him alive. I *need* him alive. You see, necromancer, he's special. On Xia, a monster attacked Tzarik and a colleague of mine. That particular celestial being can only harm those who are guilty. The thing attacked Sybal, since she's a murderer. It attacked ShanBao, because there is no sin he's not committed. But Tzarik?"

Sharar sighed happily.

"I knew before, but that only confirmed it. I let slip a few things to ShanBao that perhaps I shouldn't have. I knew Tzarik was an innocent Runer. He has no crime."

Vicdan frowned from where he lay in the sand. His eyes unfocused as he thought back.

"Exactly," Sharar went on. "How? Why would the dark god of some of the blackest magic take an innocent soul? The Dohkma wants only tarnished souls. The runes should have rejected him. But they didn't."

"You've seen them reject an innocent," Vicdan said, more for himself than Sharar.

The scholar nodded. "But I don't care about that anymore. Like his birth, my son Enoch was a failed experiment."

Vicdan's eyes rounded.

"I hunted Tzarik even before he runed Sybal," Sharar went on. Pride at his arduous studies made the words spill from his mouth. "I knew about his innocence before. Or I had hoped what I'd heard was true. I tracked that little mouse across continents. He led me to Rhostrana, and I hate that snow-capped place of opulence and frivolity."

"But who could have known about Tzarik?" Vicdan asked, struggling to sit up. "Who told you?"

"I did," the djinn whispered so softly Sharar almost didn't hear him. "When he told me about Enoch, I told him about Tzarik."

Vicdan's breath rattled and he shook his head. "I don't understand. How did you know Tzarik was innocent?"

Sharar smiled slowly. "Because my djinn runed Tzarik when he was only a boy."

The scholar saw understanding whipping behind Vicdan's eyes. Even Amir's eyes dawned with some kind of understanding. The jongleur gasped. "You're... You're Azar?"

The djinn nodded. "Alas, I am."

"No," Vicdan gasped, his eyes turning glassy again. "How can you do this to him, then? Hand him over to this man?"

The djinn, Azar, looked away.

"You see, my dear boy?" Sharar asked, glee making his voice quiver. "I've had the upper hand all these years. Tarkan is the only man who has foiled me. I see his growing power. He is desperate to outrun my own. He takes the magic from Masahk blood, and he is forging a blade to control swarms of risen. Perhaps he even intends to make undead—sentient, risen soldiers."

Vicdan shifted a little. He looked away, contemplating. "He wants your blood. The blood of a sorcerer." He looked back at Sharar. "You're safer not ascended. Don't you see that?"

"And powerless," he shot back. "I have the book, you stupid boy. I will learn the Necro'khan's every weakness. To control him. To control *you*. But first, I must ascend." He turned to the djinn. "Shall I do it now? Make my final wish?"

"No!" Vicdan shouted, struggling to his feet, but Amir pulled him back hard, gripping him to hold him back. "You mad bastard!" he cried. "You're a sadistic monster." He glanced at the djinn. "Even if you ascended, you still won't be able to read the tome. Tzarik will stop you. Sybal will have your head for what you did to her family in Ala'Nar." Vicdan gave a dark grin. "She's changed since coming back from the Deep. I heard the story before I left those frozen shores. After what I saw on Caerwren, I don't doubt it."

This gave Sharar pause. "What has happened to our Lady Runer? She was dead. Tarkan brought her back."

Vicdan nodded.

"She came back from the Deep?" the djinn asked.

A moment of unsure silence passed between the four of them.

"Sharar," the djinn said, "you do not have to make your last wish. I…" He glanced at Amir, then Vicdan, then back at Sharar. "I will give myself—all that I am, every power I possess, every magical binding—to you. You do not need to wish."

The world tipped around Sharar. "What do you mean?" he stammered. "Why?"

"I will be undone either way, entering oblivion," the djinn said. "What happens after is no concern of mine. I had my fate decided long ago."

Amir had gone still, his eyes meeting Sharar's for a brief moment.

"There must be some trick, demon," Sharar quipped. He shot a look at Vicdan, but he looked just as confused. "She came back from the Deep?" Sharar said, repeating the djinn's question. "Why did that make you decide to give yourself up to me? Is it that you think she will be able to stand up to me? Demon, I will be second in power only to the gods. There is nothing Sybal or your precious Tzarik will be able to do to stop me. You know your own power; master of the elements, father of monsters, granter of miracles, bestower of curses, healer of mortal wounds. There is nothing you cannot do. I have no fear."

Was the djinn a fool? Why would he give himself up so easily? There had to be something the monster had not divulged. Did it matter? Anything the magic of the map threw at Sharar, he could battle. He would be a sorcerer and the possessor of the Mahit'O-nomicon, the book of knowledge. No, he had nothing to fear.

"Very well, demon," he said. "I accept you. Do as you wish."

Vicdan struggled to charge Sharar, but Amir stopped him. "Don't let him do this," Vicdan begged Amir. "You know he's vile. He'll kill you. He'll kill us all."

Amir ignored him, eyes fixed on Sharar.

The djinn raised his hand, his human facade melting away to reveal the white and icy blue demon underneath. "My wish is my command," he whispered.

He reached up and touched the center of Sharar's forehead. A chill shot through Sharar, then melted away. Whispers once again filled his mind. Spirits wavered and vanished in the peripheral of his vision.

Stay back, he shouted in his mind. "The book," he commanded Amir. The Runer retrieved it from the saddle and handed it to Sharar. Fingers trembling, he opened the Mahit'Onomicon to the very center. It read something about a deep sea monster that preyed on ships and cursed sailors as it passed.

"I understand," he whispered in awe. He looked up. Amir hid his emotions well, not showing anything on his scarred face. Vicdan pressed his lips together hard, trying to show bravery. "Demon," Sharar said, "will you give yourself to me now?"

"Don't," Vicdan whispered, beginning to shake.

"I have begun," the djinn replied. "All that I am will be you. But all other magics over you shall be destroyed."

The djinn, Azar, turned to smoldering ash where he stood. The ashes fell into a stream of ice and shot towards Sharar. The scholar forced himself to remain planted where he stood. The essence of the djinn shot into his nose, past his lips, and down his throat. The smoke and ash choked him and he coughed. The strange substance did not stop. It rushed down his throat and filled his chest and stomach with a scorching power. Sharar threw his head back as tears streamed from his eyes. The pain nearly made him black out. Every vein burned and his bones felt as if they splintered underneath. Deciding it would help to not hold his screams in, he shrieked in agony to the sky, falling to his knees.

The heat from the djinn's spirit melted the sand around his feet. Then, it was pulled up into waves around him, turning to white, clear glass. He arched his back, gripping his face as the last of him came undone inside. He thought the skin melted right from his body.

"Make it stop," he begged, and his voice sounded with the tone of demons. "I understand your power, your pain. Take it from me!"

In a flash, it left. The burning turned to a dull smolder and his vision burned red like an ember. He fell at last, gasping in the swirling cage of glass. Shakily, Sharar pushed himself up and stepped over the glass waves all around him. He cut his hand on it and fell, gasping. The smoke still filled his lungs, and puffs of it jetted out from his lips with every cough. He gasped and choked, thinking he'd never breathe easily again. Amir appeared by his side, supporting him as he tried to stand again.

Sharar let himself gag, sob, and choke. It was simpler than trying to hold back. "It hurts," he wheezed, pressing his hand into his chest.

"I know," Amir whispered. "I see it burning just beneath your skin."

"Will it stop?" Sharar moaned.

"I pray to the lion the pain never leaves you," Vicdan shot, his eyes red and voice scratchy.

No sooner had the necromancer spoken than the slow burning began to dissipate inside Sharar. His breathing turned less raged and the smoke cleared. But just as the fire went out, a familiar, biting, dark pain shot through his side. He doubled over into Amir's arms, gripping his old, malignant wound.

"Why?" he begged, feeling the blackness spread slowly over his middle.

Vicdan smiled. "An old wound has come back? Must have been magical. Azar said all the magic upon you would vanish, burned away by his essence. You fool."

Sharar moaned, his knees weakening as the pain flared up more. He drew his hand away to see black, malignant blood soaking through his robes and covering his palm. "No, please," he sobbed.

"You're just a man," Vicdan whispered with disdain. "A sad one at that. Pathetic."

A wave of fiery rage shot up through Sharar at the necromancer. He threw his hand out on instinct and a jet of flames burst from his palm. Amir jerked, jostling him, and threw a quickly drawn halat in front of Vicdan. The barrier flew from his fist, saving the singer.

"Why'd you save him?" Sharar growled, shoving Amir away from him.

"We need him," the Runer shot back. But he didn't go on, enraptured by Sharar's power.

Even Vicdan looked impressed, though terrified. "Well done, Runer," he whispered, eyes wide.

Slowly, Sharar turned his gaze up to the sky. He raised his arms, reaching for the clouds. He felt them in his grip. With just the slightest bit of will, the clouds roiled and lighting snapped behind them.

"Are you doing that?" Vicdan asked, quaking.

"Silence," Sharar whispered. He brought his hand down, ripping a bolt of lightning from the sky as he did so. The fulmination spidered down, directed by his hand.

Vicdan screamed and tried to scramble out of the way when he saw where Sharar directed the strike. The light hit Vicdan, shattering and scorching the earth around him. The singer gave a blood-curdling scream and fell limp, silenced instantly. Amir covered his ears with his hands, cringing away from the loud bang. The strike and sound resounded in Sharar's chest, making him stumble backwards. There would be more to that kind of magic, if only he could find out how to gather it to himself.

He couldn't stop the high, uncontrollable laugh that filled him once the lightning dissipated. He could command the storms and so much more. The sense of magic and power filled him like a maelstrom in his veins.

Vicdan wheezed and moaned, pushing himself up. Sharar knelt by him and pulled his tunic open, exposing the scar from where Ashkan had stabbed him.

"What more...can you possibly want from me?" Vicdan asked between breaths.

Sharar traced the wound, gently running his index finger over it. Vicdan shivered. Behind Sharar's touch, the wound vanished, leaving behind only the faintest scar. He did the same to the wound he'd inflicted on Vicdan's side. Then he reached for his own. He touched the malignant wound, willing it to heal.

Nothing changed.

"What the hell?" Sharar cursed. "Why?"

Amir answered, his voice coming soft and cautious. "A djinn cannot free themselves. Cannot heal themselves. Their magic does not work on them."

"Fool," Vicdan whispered.

"Gods damn it," Sharar croaked. He pounded the earth with his fist and took a breath. "Very well." He thought of Sokar, sitting sadly on his ruby throne, the mask hiding his too-human face, his long, beautiful, and useless wings. "I will do for others what I cannot do for myself."

Sharar imagined the Masahk pharaoh flying, using his wings like his ancestors had. "Give him a miracle," he whispered. "Give him the gift of his ancestors."

Chapter 32

---◇---

Signar-Reks

After camping in the swamps surrounding Altevine, Tzarik successfully used the utmost stealth and silence to get him and Signar up to the stone steps of the thronehall of Altevine without alerting the wild and uproarious Vilderkin. The outlander Vaeson shouted at the native Altevine clans people. Some fought, throwing fists and bloodying noses. Other Vilderkin lounged pompously in the streets, drinking and ordering their thralls to harass the people. Tzarik and Signar moved with their hoods low over their faces, trying to blend in.

As they reached the bottom of the steps that led up into the thronehall, Signar lifted his axe before ascending them. The guards outside the massive double doors stood in the opening, looking in, ignoring any approaching the hall from the outside. A ruckus and shouts came from within.

Tzarik took the lead, pushing Signar behind him. He knew there would be little he could do against a sentient like a Vilderkin, but rational thought left him when it came to Signar's protection.

They approached the open thronehall and the memories returned to Tzarik tenfold. The first time he'd come through those doors, Sjörna had lain before them, slaking her carnal lust with a captive Runer. The image had burned into his memory.

More bodies than he'd ever seen packed the thronehall this time. Tables and chairs were turned over, and even a brazier had spilled its hot coals out onto the dirt floor. Thralls and slave women alike, marked by the crude metal collars around their necks, ran back and forth, trying to keep safe while completing their tasks. Strange Vaeson, some suspended halfway through transformation, filled every corner. Hawks, radjur, white cougars, great owls, bears, a kind of enormous spotted cat, and falcons filled the hall. Despite the many bodies, only two voices spoke in the din.

"You disobeyed me!" someone shouted.

The voice of Tage replied, defiant, yet weak. "I did what was right," the young Runer replied.

Tzarik looked up and saw Signar could see over the crowd. Resigning himself, Tzarik climbed up onto a table to see over the massive horde of Caerwren sentients. The younger Runer stood before the throne on the elevated stone dais. His hair was tangled and his cloak hung askew on his shoulders. His one good eye had a bruise growing around it and his lip bled. Tzarik turned his eyes to the man on the throne.

Aras was a giant. Sjörna's throne was large, as had she been. But Aras dwarfed the antlered throne, his long legs bent and splayed out before him at the same time. The Vilderkin wore only a single wrap of animal leather around his hips. Aside from that, thick belts hung heavy from a blade at his side. A great bow rested against the right arm of the throne. Scars covered Aras's chest and arms. One ran down the side of his face to his shoulder. He had wild, stormy gray eyes and long, tangled, dusky hair. Aras glowered at the young Runer before him.

"What was right?" Aras asked, sitting up from where he lounged on the throne. "Is it right to allow this curse to leave our canton?"

"Those are our people," Tage begged. He ran his hand under his nose, wiping away white blood. "They should not be used like that."

Aras stood up and the other Vilderkin watched him. The Altevine natives bit their lips and their eyes wrinkled in worry. "Does one among you have a better idea?" he asked.

Tage turned to look into the thronehall, desperate. To Aras he said, "I've served you well. I've lost everything in your service."

Tzarik understood the pleading tone. "Has he sentenced Tage to death?" he asked, disgusted.

"So it seems," Signar replied. "Most likely sacrifice." The young Vaeson removed his hood and shouted, "Perhaps I could be of service to Altevine, Aras Hawk-tor."

All those around them murmured and backed away, leaving a great, empty circle around Signar and Tzarik. Some squinted up at him and a woman gasped, hand over her mouth.

"Signar?" someone whispered, and the name hissed through the onlookers. "The son of Sjörna-Reks? The wildling?"

Aras's hard eyes snapped to Signar. "No," he whispered. "How?"

"Yes," Signar said. He stepped forward, void of fear, and the people parted before him. "I am Signar Wolf-tor, and I will free my people from your grasp, Aras."

The Vilderkin stood up. He reached down and took a handful of Tage's hair, making the boy wince. "This Runer has defied me, Wolf-tor. If that is indeed who you are. You've been gone from our shores. Raudnir will not suffer you as Reks of his oldest people."

"I have spoken to my god," Signar shot back gently.

"Have you?" Aras said, a doubtful smirk pulling his lips up. He reached down, seizing Tage's arm and pulling him back. "Take this one away and put him with the thralls," he commanded an onlooking Vilderkin behind him.

"Wait," Tage pled. "I have been loyal, I've done all you asked." The guard grabbed him and struggled to haul him away. The young man put up a valiant fight.

"You cut down the totems," Aras snarled.

"You killed them!" Tage shouted back. "They were well-loved warriors, Volra, and clansmen. Are you killing any who might stand up to you? Like Korvoth!" he ended with a cry.

"Do not harm him further," Signar commanded. He strode to the center of the thronehall, facing Aras, and dropped his axe down behind him. It landed with a metallic clang against the dirt floor. "Test me if you will, Aras. But do not touch the Runer."

Aras held his hand up, stopping the guards. "Very well." He snapped his fingers and the Vilderkin holding Tage whipped the Runer down the back steps before lashing him to one of the twenty-four pillars. At least he was in eyesight. "Let's see if you are who you claim to be," Aras went on. "But know I have done what is best for this canton."

"Have you?" Signar barked. "You did not have to let them kill my people. Did you have to pillage Zealmore's shores?"

Aras smiled and lifted his great sword. He started to descend the steps to be on the same level as Signar. Tzarik's gut twisted in worry as the giant came closer to Signar. He was easily a head taller than Signar and far broader. His arms were thicker. But Signar did not even size up the man, choosing instead to lock his eyes onto Aras's. The wolf was fearless. He hoped that would not be his undoing.

"For the glory of Altevine," Aras replied. "We cannot show ourselves as weak right now. That's why I removed Northica, every last man and shieldmaiden."

"Where is Dain?" Signar asked. His voice was calm and

controlled,but his hands clenched, and he shifted his shoulders to relieve the tension.

"Waiting to be given," Aras replied. "I think now is the proper occasion. But before I offer sacrifice in your honor, you must prove to me and the people here that you are Signar Wolf-tor, last of his name, only son of the red wolf."

Signar nodded and stepped back to begin a slow circle around Aras. The Vilderkin shared Signar's courage and did not move. Signar made his way behind Aras and slowly marched up the stone steps to the throne. Aras turned and looked up at him, scoffing.

"We are waiting, little ma—"

Signar thrust his hand out, calling his massive axe to his left hand. The axe hit Aras on its way to its master's hand, bloodying him and knocking him over. Signar caught it, red blood flecking his cheek as it thudded into his hand.

Aras groaned and stood up. "Bastard," he growled. "That—"

Before he could speak again, Signar pounced. He leapt as a man but landed as the great golden wolf. Aras shouted in surprise, which turned to a scream of terror when Signar opened his maw and pressed his teeth against the man's throat.

"Wait!" Aras shouted. He gripped the wolf's fur, but couldn't dislodge the great monster.

All around them, people hissed, whispered, and shouted in fear. A flurry of motion shot through the other Vilderkin as they transformed into they wild shapes. Cawing, roaring, and bugling erupted from the others.

"Do not move," Signar warned them. He placed a huge paw on Aras's chest to prevent him from running. "I don't want to hurt anyone. Not my people, not our Vilderkin brothers and sisters. I was told I had to come back, to face Raudnir and take my throne, and I have. I fought hand-to-hand against my god, and I won. I promised to do what is right by Altevine and protect her. That means you as well. Perhaps Aras did what he thought was right. Perhaps he was fueled by greed and recognition."

Under the golden wolf, Aras regained his composure and pride. "I did," he grunted.

"You are not my enemy," Signar replied to him. "We cannot have enemies among our homes."

Aras swallowed. "Northica destroyed us. Skarde descended upon the wolven lands with a fury we did not deserve. He devastated the clans, sacrificed many to weaken us. I did what I had to when Altevine cried out for a savior."

Signar frowned. He pulled back, removing his paw from Aras's chest. The man dared not rise, but propped himself up on his elbows to look the wolf in the eye better.

"Is this true?" Signar asked.

Aras nodded, slowly pushing himself up to sit. "Skarde feared the malignation, what it might do. Our people became possessed, and no Runer could undo it. Monsters come from the rift in the bog that we cannot fight." He stopped and swallowed. His stormy eyes flit to Tage. "The Runers saved us, but..."

"But you wanted Altevine," Signar offered. "So you had to try to save her while removing any who might stand up against you." He looked to Tage and followed where the young Runer's eye ran.

Tzarik once again felt a wave of sorrow for the loss of Korvoth.

"What of Dain?" Signar asked.

Aras grunted in disgust. "The thunder hawk came after his father, to stay. He was my first prisoner."

Tzarik stepped forward. "Where is he?"

"I will have him brought," Aras said. He slowly pushed himself to his feet, keeping his eyes on Signar as he did so. "I..." He coughed. "I pledge my blade and my god-shape to you...Signar-Reks." He cautiously bowed his head low, exposing the back of his neck to the wolf.

The crowd repeated the name, whispering "Signar-Reks," over

and over until their voices grew. The Vilderkin and the people of Altevine shouted the name of their new ruler. The people began to ask Signar questions.

Tzarik slithered through the newly energetic horde to Tage and cut the ropes binding him.

"Thank you, brother," Tage sighed. He straightened out his cloak and wiped away the last of the blood on his face. "We must stay close to Signar. Aras has a silver tongue and will try to convince Signar-Reks to rule as he did: by blood alone. Even taking revenge on Skarde."

"You've done well, and are braver than most," Tzarik praised the boy. With Korvoth gone, Tage was alone to face the world. If he could give him any amount of encouragement now, he would.

"Did Skarde attack Altevine, as Aras claims?" Tzarik asked.

"Yes," Tage sighed sadly. "Out of fear. I cannot show you now, but the malignation is a haunt the likes of which I have never seen. I just wish Skarde had not responded in fear. But Dain did not capture Altevine like Skarde did. After the Reks left, Dain let us roam free, using the Runers to try to quell the malignation. We... have struggled."

Tzarik nodded. Skarde and Dain were both warriors, but Dain did not have the thoughtless, violent nature his father did.

"So he tried to heal Altevine?" Tzarik asked.

Tage nodded.

"Then let me take my place," Signar sighed. He motioned Tage and Tzarik to follow him to the edge of the dais and the throne.

Signar faced his people and a hush fell. Slowly, he lowered himself onto his mother's throne and looked out with a furrowed brow. He held out his left hand and his axe flew into it. He slammed the haft against the floor in a rhythm. Joining the tradition, the people began to clap and pound with him. Someone started a chorus and the others joined in, using the rhythm of the clatter. One voice started a verse of an ancient song and soon others joined in.

In moments, barrels of strong drink were cracked and the smell of roasting meat filled the thronehall.

"We are saved!" a woman shouted, raising a tankard sloppily before drinking with a crowd of men.

"Lead the pack, wolf!" someone else shouted.

The doors burst open and the revelries spilled out into the streets. Word of Signar's return spread faster than dragon fire. People began to arrive to bring him gifts, pledge their blades, offer thralls and their daughters as slaves or wives. Tzarik stood just behind Signar, reading his every twitch, the pulse of the vein in his neck, and how his flesh colored with the rush of blood from nerves.

"This is happening too fast," Signar whispered, looking up at Tzarik.

"So it has been since Dain was taken captive," Tage replied on his right.

Tzarik couldn't stop himself. He reached a hand down and clasped Signar's shoulder affectionately. The boy had done everything in his power to master his wolf. Perhaps that went deeper than Tzarik realized. It was innate, part of who the people of Caerwren were: part animal. Signar had done more than master his wildling side.

Signar reached up and clasped Tzarik's fingers in his own, thanking him. "I don't know what to do. I... I don't want to stay. Not yet."

The Runer had feared this as well. He didn't have a reply.

"Signar-Reks," Aras called, leaping up the steps. "I humbly ask that I remain near the throne, near you. I can be of use. I have been in Altevine since Skarde destroyed us. I can give you advice, council you."

"Thank you, Aras," Signar said, and Tzarik noted the caution.

But then, the boy's Skelmir emerged. "Perhaps you can find me the garments of a Vaeson. As you can see, I am terribly attired."

Aras raised his brows in honest confusion. "Find you... clothes?"

Signar nodded.

"Of course, my Reks." Aras vanished into the throng, looking embarrassed.

Tzarik didn't fight to hide his grin. "Keep your men humble." He nodded.

The three of them watched the revels for some time. Dancers came, Volra performed feats of illusion, and a few nearby tribes who were part of the canton came to offer sacrifice.

"I will not take sentient lives," Signar said to one chief, who brought him a pair of thralls captured from a tribe in Rom. "Give me your blades and your loyalty for now."

"And the Albanacht?" the chief asked. "We have two of the fiery blue warriors from Zealmor in chains."

"You captured two Albanacht warriors?" Signar asked in disbelief.

The chief nodded.

"Bring them," Signar ordered.

Tzarik glanced at Signar. "Albanacht?"

Tage supplied, "Warriors from Zealmor. They paint their skin blue. It used to be believed that they were born that way. They are quite wild and fierce."

The chief brought in the chained warriors. Like most on Caerwren, they wore very little. Their skin was painted a woad blue with black accents. It would make them blend into the dark crags of the mountain canton they came from. One was a white cougar Masahk with round, twitching ears. Her face and body were furless, showing her distance from her Masahk heritage. But her blue eyes had the slitted pupils of a cat. She glared at the three of them. The other was a man of tall stature.

Both had flaming red hair, brighter than even Sjörna's had been.

"Brave brother," Signar said. "I have a deal to make with you."

"Deals made in chains are weak," the Masahk woman spat. Her ears flattened against her head.

"Soon you will know we have no choice but to band together, keeping the Warpath alive," Signar replied. "I want you to go back to your canton and tell Alasdair-Reks and Eibhlin-Reks that there is danger on the map beyond our shores."

"What is beyond Caerwren doesn't matter," the man added.

"It will, I'm afraid," Signar said. "You must tell your Reks to come to Altevine to be informed."

The woman raised her chained arms. "We cannot leave if we wanted to."

Signar motioned for the chief to unlock their shackles. "Stay, and you will be fed and outfitted for your journey."

The man looked cautiously at the Masahk. "We will not stay close," he said.

"As you wish," Signar said with finality. "All I ask is you bring word to your Reks."

Tzarik watched the strange warriors slip out of the thronehall. Signar wanted to gather allies, knowing what brewed on Alika. He appreciated the boy's effort.

"Signar-Reks!" Aras's voice rang out over the din. "I have brought you a kingly sacrifice."

The crowd parted to allow Aras and his captive through. He held a short, ceremonial bone sword in his right hand and chains in his left, attached to shackles on the potential sacrifice. Aras shoved the man down onto his knees so his back showed. Crisscrossing marks of repeated floggings etched over the man's back, shoulders, and even the back of his thighs. Some looked fresh. Aras gripped the man's ashen hair and lifted his face.

Tzarik started the same time Signar did.

"Dain!" Signar cried, throwing himself up from the throne. The songs and chants quieted.

"Yes, my Reks," Aras crowed proudly. "A kingly gift for you to give to Raudnir to show your worship. To retaliate against Skarde-Reks. For your people."

Dain's bloodied face ignited in recognition once he saw Signar's face. "Skelmir?" he whispered. "Signar?" Wonder at seeing the wildling on the throne filled Dain's face. "Signar, is that you?"

"It is," Signar replied.

Tzarik could not help but feel the connection between the two young men. Signar clearly admired Dain, perhaps even loved him for the kindness he must have shown while Signar was a prisoner in Northica.

"Aras," Signar said sternly. "Release Dain now."

To Tzarik's surprise, the others in the hall murmured at this. Signar immediately shrank, worried he'd said the wrong thing.

"Reks," Aras began, using the chains to pull Dain up to kneeling. "This is the son of the man who descended upon us in a force so violent I had no choice but to intervene. I came to Altevine when it was almost too late. I saved your canton from Northica." He firmly pressed the ceremonial blade against Dain's throat. "Let his blood cleanse the blight his father left."

Signar glanced around at the people present. All of them looked either in agreement with Aras, or showed only the slightest trepidation. The Reks turned to Tzarik and Tage.

Tage tilted his head sadly. "Skarde did come. And he did threaten Altevine, but he did it out of fear of the malignation. But it was Aras who sacrificed Korvoth."

"I didn't know who the man was," Aras cut in. "I killed many. Those who refused to strike back at Northica made us weaker still."

Tage blinked, a tear falling onto his cheek. He turned away to hide his silent weeping.

"The more I hear, the more you anger me, Aras," Signar said dangerously.

"My Reks," the Vilderkin started again.

"Signar-Reks," a Volra spoke up. He raised his hand and came forward. "Sacrifice is our way. Skarde has already taken another wife who is filled with child. The bones say she may bear three sons at once." He shook his head. "Dain is of no consequence. And this will prove to Strigganoct that the Wolf is strong still."

At this, Signar ground his teeth. "He means something to me." He faced his people, head held high. "When Skarde took me from where the mountain buried me, and locked me in a cage made of the blades of my mother's warriors, only Dain showed me compassion. Treated me like a sentient creature. He came to me in the nights, spoke to me like a man, gave me food and water." He looked down at the captive prince with burning friendship in his green eyes. "He began my long quest to finding my sanity. Without him, I would not be the Vaeson I am now. In a way, he saved Altevine long before I even left these shores."

Great regard for Dain touched Tzarik's heart as well. So it had been Dain. The Northican prince had started what Tzarik had finished. Treating Signar like a living, valuable Vaeson life was all it had taken to start his journey to conquer his wolf.

"Aras," Signar said. His tone turned stony. "Release Dain now or take his place on the altar of sacrifice." He raised his head, much like his mother used to do. "What is your shape, Aras? What creature would I be sacrificing to Raudnir?"

"I am made in the image of Isodel, like Dain," Aras replied.

"So it would make little difference." Signar's voice turned to ice. "Then let us…" The boy's voice faltered and he studied Aras hard. A softness overcame Signar.

Tzarik took in the man below them. If Aras was a Vilderkin, it meant he could shift, but was not a Reks. But he hadn't shifted when Signar had clamped his wolven jaws around the man's neck.

Had he lost his god-shape? That was the way of Vilderkin. Eventually, their blessing faded away. Signar realized this, but had just shown mercy in stopping himself from saying it out loud. Despite Aras showing his vile nature, Signar had not exposed his lack of god-shape in front of half the clan.

Signar would be a courageous and merciful Reks.

The fear and trepidation on Aras's face shown when he noticed what Signar was about to say as well. He gulped when the golden Reks did not go on.

Signar marched down the steps, making Aras stumble back, dropping Dain's chains. Then he swiped the keys from Aras and knelt before Dain. He took the Northican man's face in his hands and pressed his forehead to his.

"Thank you, Dain," he whispered. "For your mercy toward me all those months ago."

Dain smiled weakly. "You're a whole new man now." He glanced up, meeting Tzarik's eyes. "He really did it."

Signar smiled once more and stood, unshackling Dain. He bent and helped the wounded man to stand straight in the presence of his people.

"Dain, I want you to rest in my rooms. I'll have the healers and Volra come to you."

"No, not yet," Dain interjected. "Let me come speak with you."

Signar studied Dain's face for a moment before nodding. "Tage, Tzarik, you as well." He looked at the Volra, who still looked stunned. "Bring me the chief of the Volra and all who claim to be warlords." He stopped and faced Aras. "Can I trust you to stand by me in this time? I do not wish to leave behind strength if I can help it."

Aras swallowed hard, eyes downcast. "Yes, my Reks."

Chapter 33

---◇---

Rakthar Reborn

The souls surrounding Tarkan screamed as he landed hard in the now familiar tunnels near Ala'Nar. The black cloud dissipated in a long, sad moan of destroyed eternal life. As the Deep vanished and he reappeared on the mortal side of the barrier, he gathered himself with a steadying breath. Ari's blood had almost drained from the sword, so he had stopped along the way to slaughter a dozen other souls to refill the blade. But he still felt a little pull just from using the magic. It wanted *his* blood, but he had to force it to take it from the blade.

He looked around and found a few bones, which he wrapped in the decaying cloth of the skeleton's garments. An abandoned camp of bandits supplied oil, flint, and steel to make a torch. Within an hour, he traversed the tunnels, reliving his memories of the place until he found what he sought.

Rakthar's bones and what little was left of his flesh and sinews lay old and rotting just before him. Tarkan approached the long-dead dragon and ran his hand up and down one of the long bones in his winged foreleg.

"We saw many years together, old friend," he sighed. He remembered the black egg Ishmael had given him. Remembered how he'd watched over it and the night it had hatched. "We shall fly together in life once more."

Pulling the sword from his back, he stabbed it into the earth before Rakthar's decaying nose.

"It will take much blood," he whispered. "But I am prepared." Whispering words of his own in the necrotic tongue, spoken out loud for strength, he hovered his hands around Ishmael's heart and called on the blood to weave Rakthar whole again. The eye of Nephron latched onto him, wings and tendrils twitching in rage as he spun his own verses, but Tarkan didn't care.

The blood flowed in rivulets from the blade to the dragon and around its body. The magic pulled hard on Tarkan himself, searching for life to take. He'd consumed, but not much, and soon the weakness started to fill him. This was a harder task than Sharar's son had been. Harder than raising the One Thousand and One would be. They had bodies of flesh already preserved. Rakthar had to be woven from the blood magic. If he could do this, he could raise the army.

Opening his blue eyes, Tarkan took in his work some minutes later. Black, leathery flesh crawled from where it remained over the rest of the dragon's body. He'd need more blood to sustain it eventually, but so far, the sword still pulsed with living blood. More and more flesh spidered out, weaving together over the bones until Rakthar was solid black once again.

"Now wake," Tarkan asked his dragon. "Rise again, my friend."

With one final tug, the magic pulled on his heart like a blade slipping out. He gasped as life was syphoned from him and into the dragon. Rakthar's blazing eyes flashed open, his cat-like pupils focusing into the darkness. A soft, purring trill emanated from his throat as he lifted his head slowly. His curved horns wove anew and the little spines along his back stood up as he inspected the tunnels. The flaring of his nostrils told Tarkan he sniffed the air. Then he turned his face to Tarkan.

The big, terrifying black face with yellow eyes struck fear into others. Tarkan smiled up at the beast, recognizing the familiar glint in his eyes. Rakthar gave a small sniff and then rose up onto his legs. Looking down at Tarkan, he gave a soft rumble.

"So you do remember me," Tarkan said, a wave of relief washing over him. He held his hand out, palm facing the dragon.

Rakthar growled gently, flicking the tip of his large snout into Tarkan's palm. With that gesture, nearly a century of memories and emotions flooded Tarkan. He hadn't realized how much he'd missed his dragon.

"Well done," he praised Rakthar. "But we have much to do. And you must learn to journey through the Deep. You are undead. It shouldn't hurt you like it might a living mount." He turned and began to walk out of the cave, Rakthar following with a rumbling gait behind him.

The two made their way out so that the dragon could stretch his wings and take a deep breath of the fresh air. And he did. Once they were outside, Rakthar spread his wings in a mighty stretch and threw his head back to arch his long neck. The curved horns on his head gleamed like black ivory.

Tarkan whistled and the dragon obeyed like it always had, crouching to let him mount. "We are going to Makan Alu'Ekmet through the Deep. We have Apostles to meet, my friend."

SHARAR STOOD ON HIS BALCONY, looking up into the sun. Behind him, his servants finished gathering his things. He'd be off to the Dynast Palace in mere minutes, but there was one more thing he wanted to do. By now, Sokar would have learned his wings could carry him far and wide. He'd felt the magic take effect the minute he'd willed it. But now, he wanted the rest of Alika to know he'd ascended.

"Forgive me, Krah," he whispered, raising his left hand high into the air, "but today, it is you I defy."

The snapping of the magic coursed through him and up to the tips of his fingers as he called on a darkness. Above him, the sky grew dark. The sun turned dark yellow and then began to fade to an orange behind a black shadow.

"What's happening?" Amir asked, appearing behind him. "What are you doing, scholar?"

"Sorcerer," Sharar reminded him. He didn't explain himself to the Runer. It was Amir's job to witness his power, not question it. "Alikans worship Krah, the god of the sun. They will know who to fear once the ball of fire is hidden from their eyes."

Amir turned his blue eyes up into the darkening sky. More and more, the sun vanished. Sharar heard his breathing pick up. "Why?" the Runer asked. "Just to instill fear?"

"What else?" Sharar asked. His hand shook as the magic coursed through him, increasing the longer he held the intent.

Soon, the entire sky went black. The sun had not moved, it had not faded; a darkness had simply engulfed the sky, making every celestial light go out. No stars shone, nor the moon. Complete and total darkness overtook the city.

"Is this happening in Mysir as well?" Amir asked.

"Over all Alika," Sharar replied. "Fitting for opening the tomb of Acenoth IV."

Amir waited and Sharar sensed the Runer expected him to go on, as he so often did. So he obliged.

"Krah promised Acenoth victory a thousand years ago," he explained. "You see, Krah—one of only two Masahk gods of Alika on the map, that I know of—is a lion Masahk. Since the pharaohs have all been Masahk, they love Krah more than most. They think they are gods incarnate. So when Krah promised Acenoth victory before the sun rose, he forced his men to continue the fight, staving off the invading Al'Myrahns. The sun did not shine for three days."

Amir raised his head, brow gently furrowed. "And so you will reenact that miracle. To let the people know Acenoth's tomb is opening."

"And that I am in control," he added. "What are the signs of the coming of the Father of Monsters? Miracles: Sokar may use his wings like his ancestors now. Controlling the beasts: they have seen me accomplish that feat. And a natural phenomenon: the darkness."

"You did all these things?" Amir asked.

Sharar smiled. "I did. Because I have the power to." He looked up at the black sky. No light emitted at all. "So long as they know who I am, I don't care that I fulfilled the revelation myself. Perhaps that's how all revelations come to pass. Someone simply sets about fulfilling the signs by their own will."

"I've never been one for prophecies, revelations, and other such magi magic," Amir grunted.

"You Runers never are. Too bitter, perhaps."

"The monsters we slay are products of the gods," Amir reminded Sharar. "We can't possibly love them."

"So be it," Sharar sighed. "We must hurry to Mysir. We will take the river caravans to speed our visit to Sokar. Bring the necromancer."

※

RAKTHAR BRAVED the Deep so boldly, Tarkan thought he must have been born to it. But he was a western dragon. Perhaps such places ran deep in his blood. Propelled by the speed of devouring the souls and the flight of his dragon, he arrived back in Makan Alu'Ekmet in mere days. The hurried travel spun his stomach, but he bore it for the haste.

He and Rakthar appeared in a splattering of the black ecto-plasm in the city square. Rakthar roared as he skidded to a stop, wings splayed out. Tarkan held on tightly as his eyes beheld a mass of Apostles just outside the temple. All their blue eyes turned up to him atop his undead dragon. The red blade glowed on his back as he looked down on his small army.

Waiting until Rakthar calmed, he spotted Ashkan. He stood with a particularly tall Apostle with the black skin of Yenka. The man had arms thick as young trees and a gleaming bald head. His blue eyes looked particularly fierce in his face. Tarkan slid from Rakthar's back and approached, taking in the reverent eyes of the Apostles around him.

"You have done well, Ashkan," he said. "Together, we are enough to take the Dynast Palace. And soon, we will have an army of undead and Acenoth himself."

"So it is true?" the bald necromancer asked. He bowed quickly to Tarkan. "I am called Faraji. I come from a tribe in Yenka who reveres House Mirzam. I have personally torn the arms from men of Nashira and beaten them to death." He inclined his head to Ashkan. "But I join with fealty with those who will follow our Necro'Khan."

Tarkan had never met a necromancer with such physical strength. "I count you as an asset," he replied to Faraji.

He turned and scanned his Apostles. This was what he wanted, what he needed. A flock of necromancers at his side, willing to follow him. To worship him. Overhead, the sky turned unnaturally dark.

"My brothers and sisters," Tarkan said to the dozen or so Apos-tles waiting. "We are not on a noble quest to free our Porshain brothers from Alika. We are not holy men on a pilgrimage to the

Dynast Pharaoh. Do not seek revenge for how the map has feared and destroyed us. I am not seeking to complete what my father, the last Necro'Khan, set out to do. No. Find your own purpose. Do what you will, but follow me."

Beside him, Faraji smiled darkly.

"This darkness is a sign that the sorcerer has ascended," he went on. "That is who we are up against. That is who will supply the last of the magic we need to be stronger than any being upon the map. We will kneel to no one. Ever. We are beyond death, my brothers and sisters. We are eternal, and the sorcerer seeks to make us his prisoners, taking the one power he does not possess."

"I will rend him limb from limb," Faraji growled with a twisted smile.

"Prepare for travel," Tarkan finished. "Find a mount. We do not need our risen with us as the tombs of Mysir will provide. You need not consume as I will sustain every risen with the magic I have created. All I need is your loyalty. For you to follow me."

He glanced sideways at Ashkan. The Apostle looked defeated, resigned. Tarkan didn't care. He'd gotten what he needed from Ashkan, and the man knew he had nothing left to defend.

"We are going to the tomb of Acenoth IV," he said with finality. "It is open, and I will raise the One Thousand and One. The first army of truly undead shall walk into the Dynast Palace at my command."

Chapter 34

The Sigiled Blades

The mead hall was similar to the one Tzarik had been in with Sybal and Zeva when they'd first arrived in Northica to speak with Skarde. This one boasted carvings and engravings of wolves, the Valravn, and intricate green knots. Already the people inside had scrambled to make way for Signar. By the time Tzarik, Signar, Dain, and Tage arrived, the Volra had cleared a long rectangular table and set up salted pork, strong drink, and a few strange root vegetables.

Signar sat at the head, placing Dain and Tzarik on his right and left. Tage sat at Tzarik's side. Thralls moved to serve them. Tzarik admired Signar's restraint as he waited for warriors, Volra, and a few others to arrive. They all had the same trepidation and curiosity bending their brows.

The boy leaned close to Tzarik. "Will you help me?" he asked softly.

"Of course," Tzarik replied. "Just tell me what you are doing." He didn't mention how his job here was done now, as much as it pained him. But it would be better to leave the boy quickly and quietly. To avoid sloppy, emotional goodbyes. To slip out before Signar knew he was gone. But first, he needed to hunt down the blades.

"I'm going back with you," Signar said suddenly. His eyes sparkled at the surprise on Tzarik's face. "I can smell your worry," he said. "Something in your sulfates changes and I can smell it coming from your scalp."

He'd forgotten the boy's wolven attributes blended into his human form. He'd have to find a way to control himself, to stop the scent of fear and worry.

Tage glared at Aras when he sat across from him, near Dain. The Northican prince did not so much as flinch. "How can you allow him to sit next to you after what he's done?" Tage asked Dain.

A bit of lightning snapped behind Dain's blue eyes. "I don't fear him," he replied with a good-hearted smile. "And he did nothing I might not have done in his stead. He didn't kill me." His tone lifted, amused. "A mistake on his part, perhaps. Now he is at my mercy."

Tzarik enjoyed Dain making light of a situation that might have ended with him dismembered and burned on pyres all across Altevine. He liked that about the young man. But Tage had been wounded by Aras's brief reign. The boy Runer's face twisted in a melancholic rage.

"Dain is too kind," Tage said to Aras, his eye shining with unshed tears. "I will hate you forever for ordering my master's death."

Signar's keen green eyes studied Tage and Aras in turn. "I must leave someone in my place when I return to Alika for a time."

"Leaving?" Tage asked, his voice cracking. "Stay. You are Reks now. Altevine is yours to protect. The malignation is growing stronger. Soon the sun will set and we will be set upon by the darkness that comes with night."

"I know," Signar whispered. "And it was my mother's doing. But I have something I must finish. People I must protect."

Tzarik shot him a look. His eyes were drawn away from his young ward when the doors opened and a Volra covered in more ornaments than others entered. His stern face had a few lines, but his stride was strong. Unlike the other men of Caerwren, his chin grew no beard. Black ceremonial paint covered his eyes, with a line down his chin.

"Viggo," Aras called to the Volra.

"One loyal to you?" Tage spat.

Tzarik gave the hotheaded boy a warning stare. He didn't have time to explain to Tage why he needed to find a way to mourn Korvoth that did not hinder Signar. His hate would hurt Altevine. He also understood. Aras may not have been the one to kill Korvoth, but he had given the order.

"We were loyal," Tage snarled to Tzarik, seeing his look. "Korvoth stayed close to the thronehall for Altevine. That put him first in line for the savagery the Vilderkin unleashed."

The Volra, Viggo, bowed to Signar. "I heard the wolf had returned," he whispered in awe. His bare arms, like the others, were firm with muscle. He glanced at Aras.

"I am Reks now," Signar assured the servant of the gods. "You need not fear Aras any longer. But he will remain."

Viggo's eyes looked out from behind the white animal-skin fringe of his headdress. "As you wish, my Reks."

"I need him," Signar added, seeing how most in Altevine felt about the invading Vilderkin. "We have much to do, and I cannot spare a single man. Please, sit."

Viggo sat next to Aras and turned to face the door. "As requested, warlords have been summoned. The closest are on their way." He stopped but clearly wanted to ask why.

"You will be my council," Signar said to Tage, Aras, Dain, and

Viggo. "Dain, I pray to Raudnir your father will see fit to listen to us."

"If he doesn't, I'll have his ears," Dain replied jovially.

"Good." Signar motioned to Tage. "While I am gone, Tage will sit in my stead."

"What?" Aras barked, balling his fist on the table.

The boy Runer paled, blue eye widening.

"You will be his closest council," Signar added. "Dain must return to Northica and bring them all the news we are about to discuss."

"Understood," Dain replied.

"Signar-Reks," Viggo asked. "What draws you away from your shores so soon? Have you not seen or heard of the curse that has risen up in this land since the red wolf opened the Deep? Far worse things are to come. I fear for Altevine. If we cannot contain it, stop it, all of Caerwren may be swallowed up in this malignation. We have plenty of Runers, almost an army, but the things that are coming from the Deep are a challenge even for the most seasoned of Runers."

"This is why we must bind the malignation with the totems," Aras cut in. "Marking a boundary worked for much of the season."

"Killing our own?" Tage shot at Aras.

Aras glared at the young Runer. "No. The Masahk from the east, who came through two moons ago, cleared away more of the curse than any of us have. He said he'd return soon."

Viggo hummed and shook his head. "I did not like that Masahk. He spoke too little. And the power he had over the malignation should have made any of you suspicious of him."

"What Masahk?" Signar and Tzarik asked together.

Viggo shifted uncomfortably and looked to Aras, but Tage replied.

"Two months ago," the young Runer began, "a Masahk came to

our shores from the north. From Rhostrana, I believe, by the looks of his garments. But he was not Rhostranan. Couldn't be, since they enslave every Masahk that crosses their borders. I wish he had stayed. He banished much of the malignation using a strange-colored blade. It was straight, had one edge, and was covered in sigils I've never seen. He..." Tage struggled to find the right words. "I don't know. He captured the haunts in that blade. When we showed him the place the malignation came from, he sent the slain spirits into it. Into the blade."

Familiarity shot through Tzarik. "He bound the malignation behind sigils?"

Aras nodded. "He wanted us to make a structure around the place of origin, where Sjörna first opened the Deep, and to lock the land away behind such sigils. But he left."

"Like a crypt?" Tzarik asked.

"I suppose," Aras replied. "I didn't understand. He was too silent."

Taking a risk, Tzarik asked, "Was this Masahk Xian?"

Tage nodded. "A fox, I think."

Tzarik unconsciously gripped the white dragon symbol hanging around his neck. "It has to be him. I let him live. I thought he bled out."

"Who?" Signar asked.

The older Runer turned his eyes to the east, out one of the few windows in the mead hall. "Yasuke. A Wushito warrior, a general in their creed. We crossed ways and swords more than once on Xia." He stopped, his mind suddenly reeling. "Xia. Get me a map," Tzarik ordered, suddenly standing.

Aras ran to fetch one.

"The Wushito?" Viggo asked, almost breathless. "Devourers of demons. So he was."

"What do you mean?" Tzarik asked.

He'd watched the Wushito slay monsters without the sulfates. He believed their power came from those sigiled blades, but he couldn't explain how. But the Wushito did not kill the monsters like Runers. He'd assumed they bound them, locking them away in the crypt.

"Viggo," Tzarik said before the Volra could reply, "where is this Masahk now? We must find him. And those blades. I had three on my horse before Sjörna killed him and turned him into a nithing pole to attack Skarde."

The image of Mamun's skin and head atop the gruesome pole still turned his stomach. He should have never named that horse.

"Were you here?" he finished.

"I was," Viggo replied. "I know of what you speak. The Masahk took one before he vanished. The blade he used to aid us."

"Which one did he take?" Tzarik asked. "Where are they?"

"In the treasure hold," Viggo said quickly. "I warned our clansmen not to touch them."

Before Tzarik could bark a command, Signar snapped his fingers, ordering one of the thralls nearby to go to the hold and bring the swords.

"He took a blade that looked red," Viggo replied, a little shaken by the sudden energy coming from the stoic Runer. "They are terrible things. Whispers come from the blades, and horror fills the air around them."

"I understand," Tzarik mused. Every time one of the blades got close to him—and the time ShanBao had stabbed him with one—his sulfates reacted in utter repulsion, making his skin crawl. "I thought perhaps they gathered the souls of their hunts in the blades. Or in these sigiled talismans made of parchment. Then... they put them in the crypt?" He ended by asking himself, unsure.

"The map," Aras said, laying a huge canvas down on the table. He, Tage, and Viggo unrolled it, holding it down.

Tzarik leaned over it. He still could not read Caerwren as well as he could speak it, but he knew the map well. He tapped Xia on the map, then traced a line to Caerwren, then to Alika. "That puts

Al'Myrah in the center," he mused, tapping his home country next. "Sharar knew about the crypt. He must have done research on it before even going to Xia. Which means Tarkan knew about it."

He leaned back, eyes tracing the invisible triangle he'd drawn again.

"He will open the Deep on Alika. He's surrounding Al'Myrah."

"Who?" Aras asked.

"The Necro'Khan," Tzarik said offhandedly, knowing at least Viggo would understand. And he did. The Volra gasped and drew a circle over his heart before turning his eyes skywards.

"Do we return to Al'Myrah?" Signar asked.

"No," Tzarik said quickly. "Alika is where he is. Looking for that book. As is Sharar." He rubbed his chin and frowned. "They wouldn't be working with one another. Tarkan wouldn't."

"Perhaps they are competing for the book," Signar suggested. "In a race with one another."

"That has to be it," Tzarik replied. "They hate each other, and don't want one or the other to have the Mahit'Onomicon. We must stop them both. I've run from Sharar long enough." He looked up. "Where are the swords?"

Just then, a servant woman fell through the massive doors, slamming them open with her entire body.

"My Reks!" the servant woman panted, clutching her chest and wheezing. "We went to the hold as instructed and he's here. He's returned. He wants to take the other blades. Our men locked the doors, capturing him inside."

"Who?" Signar asked.

"The Xian Masahk," she gasped. "I ran as fast as I could. But you must hurry. I was afraid he would slaughter everyone near the hold."

Tzarik leapt up. Suddenly, the memory of the fiery, dashing figure they'd first seen when they'd arrived came back to him. "Yasuke is here now? Where is the treasure hold?"

She nodded. "Behind the thronehall, opposite the garrison."

Leaving the others, Tzarik sprang up and dashed out of the mead hall. Never had he run so fast in all his life. He slipped on the mud and some still icy patches, but at least no snow covered the ground now. He shivered, having left his cloak behind from the heat of the mead hall. He spotted the familiar garrison where he'd spent ample time on his first trip to Caerwren. To the left of it, a small, circular hut stood. The door to it was closed, with five men leaning up against it.

"He's quiet," one said as they approached.

"Open it." Tzarik raced to the door to find it only covered a set of stone, spiral stairs. He caught his breath, knowing Yasuke, a man he'd tried to kill, most likely waited at the bottom. Not only was the Wushito a formidable warrior, but he was Masahk and used his magical gift often. Tzarik touched the white dragon pendent on his neck again.

Thank you, he thought to the god of Xia. *Give him peace of mind. Let him hear me.*

Slowly, he descended the steps into a room full of artifacts, statues, chests, and crates of weapons and gems. A familiar, tall, muscled frame stood before an open chest upon a rickety table, a sword in his hand. Yasuke's fox-like ears twitched in Tzarik's direction. His long, reddish-brown hair spilled over the fur hood of a thick cloak.

"These are here because of you," the Masahk said in a monotone. "You've traveled far and wide, I see." He turned to face the Runer. His face gave away no emotion, the yellow eyes scanning him and Signar, who had followed Tzarik down.

Just above the clasp of Yasuke's cloak, Tzarik spotted the top of what was no doubt a long, deep scar that ran down his neck and over his chest. He'd given Yasuke that scar, but had spared his life. He could have killed the Reaver, but in that moment, something had stayed his hand, even though Yasuke had asked Tzarik to end him.

"How did you know I came to Caerwren?" Tzarik asked.

"I sought out that monk you knew on Xia," Yasuke said simply.

"TaoShin," Tzarik offered, remembering the old monk fondly.

Yasuke nodded. "He told me the council he gave you; to come to Caerwren. So I followed you. But you weren't here yet."

The Runer nodded, letting Yasuke know he wasn't entirely wrong. "I had to go to Al'Myrah... Sybal was dead. Killed by Wu-Zhiang."

To Tzarik's surprise, the Wushito sighed sadly, his face crumbling into sympathy. "I am sorry, Runer. She was worth a hundred warriors."

"Is," Tzarik said. "We...brought her back from the Deep."

Yasuke straightened his back slowly, but didn't reply. He held his tongue. Tzarik understood the Wushito warrior knew the severity of what that meant. "So this is your doing," he said after a moment. "The malignation. The haunts."

"I'm afraid so," Tzarik replied. The weight of what they'd done crushed him. "I handed this power to Tarkan, practically forced him to take it. The Necro'Khan," he added when Yasuke tilted his head slightly. He quickly explained his past with Tarkan and Sharar before ending with, "They're racing for the book. The Xai'de Jing, as you call it. They found it in Alika."

"In the tomb," Yasuke offered. "So I've thought for some time, as have many scholars. It should have been protected by the pharaoh's curse."

"And it may be," Tzarik said. "But that won't stop a sorcerer or a Necro'Khan." He looked up at Yasuke. "What happened after I left you?"

Seeing the Runer wouldn't let him leave with the blades until he was satisfied, the Wushito sighed and gave in. "After I came here, looking for you and my blade, I was caught on the Black Road. They took me to Volograd."

"Rhostrana?" Signar asked. "You were taken as a slave?"

Yasuke nodded. "They have ways of taming Masahk in Volograd. But I escaped. Eventually." He waited a beat before going on. "I came back and took my blade and went on a quest to find my path, as we Wushito are taught to do. To seek out violence for good. After some time, I realized I needed to take the other blades. They should not be here among these people. They don't understand them."

"I'm not sure even I do," Tzarik confessed.

"They are not yours to understand," Yasuke said sternly. "They don't belong here; I must take them back to Xia."

"Are you still with Wushito?" Tzarik asked.

The fox Masahk slowly shook his head. "You should have killed me that day. Instead, I fled in disgrace. It was best that I paid for my cowardice on Rhostrana as a slave."

Tzarik doubted anyone deserved to be a slave. Having been one for most of his younger life, he'd not wish it on almost anyone.

"But now I must go back. If only for the swords." Yasuke reached to his back and pulled his long sigiled blade free of its unique scabbard.

The metal rang in Tzarik's ears and his sulfates whinged at being so close. "Tell me about the blades," he said.

The Masahk narrowed his sharp yellow eyes at the Runer. "They are Wushito secrets, Runer."

"They are powerful," he countered. "I know Reavers hunt Runers, but we are past that now. Especially us, Yasuke."

The Wushito gently laid the blade in his palm, holding it toward Tzarik. "You want to use them on your enemies? This sorcerer and Necro'Khan? Why not use your own orichalcum blade? Sharp edges all cut the same."

Tzarik shifted, getting fed up with how Yasuke avoided his

request. "Tell me what they do and I'll know if they will be stronger against my enemies, as you call them. I came all this way to find them, for the chance to know if they can help me stop Sharar and Tarkan."

Yasuke gave a long, resigned sigh. "Take the blade, Runer," he said at length.

Touching the sigiled blade was the last thing Tzarik wanted to do, but if it would get Yasuke to speak, he'd suffer just long enough to get the information he needed. Slowly, he picked up the blade from Yasuke's hand. His sulfates started to boil under his skin, exhausting his muscles and bringing a horrid pain. It felt like a thousand evil spirits swarmed around him. The sulfates were not trying to harm him; they were warning him. It was too much.

He gasped and dropped the blade, stumbling backward. Signar rushed to his side, steadying him. Tzarik realized had been right to wrap them in black and not touch them while he had them in his possession.

"Now you, Reks," Yasuke said. He quickly snatched up the blade and held it out to Signar.

"No," Tzarik protested. "Enough games, Yasuke."

"Watch, Runer," the Masahk ordered. He flicked the handle to Signar.

Tentatively, the young Vaeson took the handle. Tzarik waited for a reaction, but Signar only frowned slightly, turning the blade with his wrist. "I feel nothing," he replied.

"With study and meditation, you can open yourself up to the power inside the blade," Yasuke said. He took the sword back and held it up into the white sunlight. It glinted a pearlescent red.

"Orichalcum?" Tzarik sputtered.

"Yes," Yasuke said. "The sigils take the souls of sentients, including the likes of haunts, demons, guardians, and celestials. And they slay the monsters, just as you do, Runer."

"How?" Tzarik asked. "The metal will kill you within years. Months, for some."

Yasuke ran his long, lithe finger over the sigils. "With souls trapped inside the blade, taken by the sigils, the orichalcum feasts on them, not the one who wields it. So we slay with these blades, taking souls to protect ourselves. But we open ourselves up to possession of anything inside. They are dangerous to wield. But we train ourselves to use the demonic and spiritual power inside rather than let it take us. Some time ago, Wushito discovered orichalcum likes the taste of Runer blood. And so we specialized in training against Runers.

"These sigils also turn their spirits into power, if we open ourselves up to the souls within, giving us the strength we have to fight. Fast enough and strong enough to take down Runers. But the risk is why we train as Wushito. Not just any sentient can wield a sigiled blade.

"And when we are close to our Runer prey..." He brought the sigiled blade not half an inch from Tzarik's face and the Runer's heart immediately hammered in warning and fear. "The unknown panic slows their minds. Like being enveloped in constant danger. They quickly become overwhelmed."

Tzarik smacked the blade away. He glared at Yasuke, remembering how vile the Wushito generals had been all that time ago. "The necrotic scriptures are much like my sulfites. The blade may aid in battling Tarkan, should it come to that. And if the sigils take their souls within, it will stop them from haunting the map once they are dead, should they be rejected from the afterlife." He glared at Yasuke, disgusted. "But that's the difference between Wushito and Runers: we don't kill sentients unless we have to. You do so to protect yourselves and to grow in strength."

"I have to," Yasuke argued.

"To protect yourself from a blade you should not wield," Tzarik snapped. "Orichalcum is magic from the black god in the north,

the very one you protect your shores from. It is not yours to use."
In his mind, he cursed Wushito once again. "I will take ShanBoa's
blade. Even if I cannot wield it—"

"I can," Signar interjected.

Signar in close combat with Sharar or Tarkan was the last thing
Tzarik wanted. Let alone being open to the possession the sword
offered. If what Yasuke said was true, the Wushito willingly
opened themselves to the danger of possession just to take the
power of the souls inside the blade.

"Then what?" Yasuke cut in. "You slay your sorcerer or your
Necro'Khan with this blade, trapping their spirits inside. Then?"

Tzarik squared up to Yasuke. "There are now three openings on
the map to the Deep—or soon will be."

Yasuke's smooth face quickly flashed a confused frown before
it vanished, hidden behind his impassive mask.

"The Crypt on Xia," Tzarik went on, knowing he had the
Wushito's attention now. "The scar on Caerwren, letting out the
malignation. And he will open one on Alika soon. There is only
one who can open the Deep: a Necro'Khan. Once Sharar is dead,
we can lock Tarkan in the Deep, killing him on this side with a
sigiled blade. That way, we know we have his spirit trapped."

"We kill Sharar first?" Signar murmured, thinking.

"Not necessarily," Tzarik replied. He eyed Yasuke. "We will
need someone to close or bind these scars to the Deep. And empty
the sigiled blade of Sharar's soul so he cannot haunt this side."

"Not all scars can be healed." Yasuke sheathed his blade. "Are
you asking me to join your fight, Runer?"

"I think you'll have to," Tzarik said. "Tarkan will come to break
the sigils on the crypt in the Hallow City. He wants all three open.
Once he gets the scar open on Alika, he will come for Xia. You
won't have a choice, Yasuke. Is it not Wushito's oath to protect Xia
from the supernatural?"

Yasuke nodded stiffly. "It is. I understand. If I must return to

Xia, I must. I do not know how I will be received. Even if I did not wish to face Hiro and the Wushito, I must return the blades."

Without another word, Tzarik slipped the dragon medallion off his neck. He offered it to Yasuke. "Hiro gave me this. It will at least get you into the Royal City to speak to him."

"He must trust you entirely," Yasuke mused, taking the pendent and holding it up to let the sun catch the jade. "I won't thank you, Runer, for you have endangered us all. But I will give you my word to try my utmost to aid you. You spared my life. You do not know the disgrace it has brought me, but I know you saw it as an act of mercy. And so I will repay you with this."

He held up the long red blade. "ShanBao's blade. It is powerful, harboring years of demonic souls. Whoever you give it to to wield must be strong of will. The allure of the demon's power is formidable, and you do not have our training."

Tzarik took the wrapped blade and handed it to Signar. "Thank you, Yasuke. And please, warn Xia. Speak to Hiro. We must get back to Alika. Sharar and Tarkan are on the move, and Sybal is alone."

Yasuke gave them a deep bow. "I wish you the best of luck, Runer, and may the White Dragon smile on you."

Tzarik nodded and Yasuke turned on his heel, marching up the steps into the cold air. The door of the treasure hold closed, cutting off their vision of him and the light from above.

"You are not to wield that blade," Tzarik warned Signar. "We will find someone who can. But first, we must get back to Alika. We've been gone too long."

Chapter 35

Fate-Bound

The night bugs sang softly as Sybal stepped off the riverboat and took in Gypsu. The city that gave the province its name glittered even in the moonlight, like a spike of gold amidst the white sand. Firelight lit the streets, and a few Alikan priests rushed past her, following an overseer from the temple of Krah.

"It cannot be," the overseer of the temple moaned to his priests. "First the blood moon and now this. We must have read the signs wrong."

Sybal watched them run, then looked back at Krah's temple. The lion Masahk god looked to the east, his hand outstretched as if to guide the sun. His crown, made of sun beams, shot out from behind his head in magnificent spears of light. Like Bahratt and a few other countries, Alika had many gods. But their prime god was Ashmalia, goddess of the moon.

"What have you done?" she asked Krah lightly. "Are you bringing a hot winter? Killing their crops with a burning sun?"

Regret at her words suddenly filled her and she bowed her head. "I beg your forgiveness," she said with a gentle smile. "I assumed you might be a jealous god, since they revere Ashmalia so much more."

She moved through the outer streets, looking for an opulent neighborhood. Somewhere a wealthy scholar who thought highly of himself might live. She was tired of waiting for Tzarik to return, and staying at the embassy kept her up at night. She couldn't sleep knowing Sharar knew where they had been. Her nerves burned with worry. Now, she wanted to find Sharar's house in Gypsu. It might not help, but knowing where the scholar laid his head would give her some peace of mind. Somehow.

Deciding to ask just one person, she looked at first for another Runer. Someone who might know Sharar's paid Runer bodyguard. But, like on Al'Myrah, Runers were rare on Alika. So she opted to climb high and look out over the huge city. She hitched her horse and then ascended a tall courthouse using the ladder that ran up the side. She panted by the time she reached the top, carefully climbing over the domed roof. She went up to the spire, gripping it tight, and looked out. It was the dead of night, but the wealthy houses stuck out of the city like pyres.

"Ah," she mused, seeing what she looked for. "That's you." Her eyes found a tall manor in the Shamir district, just two streets down. The home was dark, with only a few windows lit with candlelight. But a massive observatory topped the home. The glass ceiling made it sparkle in the moonlight.

That's when she noticed it: no moon hung in the sky. No stars shone. She whispered a small curse. Perhaps the clouds simply covered the sky. Cautiously watching the heavens, she descended the courthouse and slithered through the streets towards Sharar's home.

Finding her way there in a matter of minutes, she waited, watching the front. Then she took a quick circle of the front half. The back opened up into extensive land and gardens. Even an old cemetery. The house was ancient. She crept to the back, wondering if the gardens would supply her with the necessary cover to get close. Not sure what she looked for, she slinked to the back and kept her eyes alert. Above the back gardens, a balcony stuck out. Silken veils covered the wide open entry to the room beyond. She inspected the wall, but saw no easy or obvious way to scale the outside and get to the balcony.

I shouldn't go in, she told herself. *There's no reason to. Unless...*

Unless the artifact was here? Where was Sharar? He could be at home. He could be at the palace. She'd been gone from the embassy for a couple of days at that point.

Something clinked and clattered in front of her. She gasped and dropped down behind the fountain. The nearest cover was a line of ferns about ten feet behind her. She'd gotten too close. Raising her head, she peeked over to look at the servant's entrance at the back of the manor. She held her breath.

A Runer—Amir, she remembered his name to be—had appeared, his weapons and gear strapped to his hips giving him away. She couldn't help but notice how tall he was. His long, dirty hair reminded her of Tzarik. He stood at the back, unlocking the door. He pushed it open, then stopped. She gasped, but stayed still. He hadn't turned around. Amir partially tilted his head toward her, but didn't turn.

"Amir. Back from the hunt?" a servant inside asked. "Will you be staying, or joining Master Sharar in Mysir?"

"Quiet," Amir snapped at the servant. He waited a moment, then said, "Leave. Tell the others to go now."

A few sputtered lines of protest came back, but the Runer quickly dismissed the servants. Sybal waited as Amir went into the house, leaving the back door entirely ajar. A trap, perhaps? Overcome with curiosity, and having seen the small trail of servants hurrying out, boldness pushed her to rise and approach the door. It was only one Runer. She'd overpowered Tzarik many times.

I will watch over you, the voice whispered.

The inside lay dark. Only a single oil lamp on a small table near a lounge burned bright. Clattering came from her left and she followed it. Staying low, she moved like a shadow, drawing buhkar slowly to turn to mist. She passed soundlessly over the floor until she followed the noises to a thick, steel-enforced door. It hung open, leading to a dark set of stairs. Amir had gone down.

Sybal leaned against the frame, pressing herself into the wall to hide, and craned her neck to look down. No light came, but she could see well enough. A few items gave the basement away as a garrison came into view. Chains on the walls and even a scold's bridle just at the edge of her vision showed themselves.

Monster, she thought. *He has a dungeon under his home. Just like Tarkan told us.* She wondered for a moment if this, or his home in Hatal, was where Sharar had tortured Zeva, scarring her for life. Perhaps both. A loathing for the scholar rose like bile in her throat.

Behind her, deeper in the manor, something opened and closed. Gasping, she crouched and hurried into the dungeon to hide on the stairs. She'd thought Amir had gone into the basement, but she must have been wrong. As she came to the bottom of the stairs, something caught her eyes. She snapped her head back into the darkness of the dungeon. Something fastened to the wall glowed a pale blue.

Curious, she stood and walked to it. The dungeon was cold and damp, and smelled like blood the deeper she went into it. Her foot slipped once and she looked down. A streak of dark red—almost black—blood smeared its way out of one cell and across the room. Some poor soul had been tortured and had most likely bled out. She turned and followed the blood trail with her eyes. It faded, showing where the bleeding body must have been picked up.

Turning back to the wall, she found what glowed.

"Gods," she whispered. The thing glowing, hanging from the wall, was a long scimitar. The blade was straighter than her scimitar, but still bore the unique look of Al'Myrahn swords. The orichalcum blade was practically white, and the golden handle held an icy blue gem in the center. An inscription on the blade swooped and swirled from the hilt to the tip. "I know this sword," she said to herself. Tzarik had told her what Azar's blade looked like, and she recognized the gem in the center, which he'd told Tzarik was ice from the Frozen Nation. Seeing it, she believed that story. She could almost feel the cold emanating from it.

Yi ahd oh'a Dohkma, the inscription on the blade read. It was ancient Al'Myrahn, but she knew it.

"The hand of the Dohkma," she whispered.

A good servant, the voice whispered to her. *He brought me many souls.* Despite her knowing the voice belonged to the runes' dark god, it still spoke with Freja's voice to her.

"Azar was your prisoner," she mused. "Did you take him, as you will me someday?"

The voice gave a light chuckle. *I did. I'd all but forgotten about him. I gave him a fine blade. Perhaps you should wield it.*

Sybal hovered her hand over the scimitar, afraid to touch the sword. So the Dohkma had cursed Azar, as Tzarik had said. Had taken him, made him a djinn. Her heart leapt into her throat, choking her. "It's him! Holy Krishvu, it's him. Azar is Sharar's djinn!"

As you see clearly before you, stupid woman, the voice said darkly. *I loved this blade. I made it myself. Gave it to Azar so he could bring me every soul I asked for. I guided him well.*

Above her, the floor creaked. She gasped, wiping away the tears that had spilled down her cheeks. She quickly lifted the artifact. Removing her black cloak, she wrapped it around the blade.

You will take Azar's blade? the voiced asked in disbelief.

"It's the artifact," she reasoned. "If he's the djinn—"

"You're too late."

Sybal turned. Amir stood at the end of the stairs, watching her.

He had a set of keys on his belt. She drew her own scimitar in her right hand, her left prepared to jump to her runes.

Amir slowly walked away from the stairs, circling around the garrison and the wall of cells. He didn't come close to her. In fact, Sybal sensed he wanted to stay away from her, didn't want to engage. Something else lurked behind his large blue eyes that she couldn't place. Whatever it was, it didn't make her sulfates run.

"Too late?" she asked.

Amir nodded. He looked so much like Tzarik, though a handful of years younger, that it made her heart hurt. She missed him. Wanted him back. To hold him and touch him. To know he was alive. What if he came back and she wasn't there? She shouldn't have left Mysir. She'd take the river boats, as they could make the journey in two days.

"Sharar has already consumed the djinn," Amir clarified.

Sybal noted how cautiously he moved around her. She had hardly no fear of him, but he was wary of her. "Did he… Are you certain?" She wasn't sure how to talk to this Runer. Sharar's Runer.

"Yes," he replied. He stopped his circling now, as far from her as she was from the steps that would take her out. "He displayed only a fraction of his power. I am afraid there is no stopping him now, Runer. Not even the Dynast Pharaoh will be able to stop him once he truly begins to wield his power. We haven't begun to witness what he will be able to do." He furrowed his brow. "Do you know what a fate-binding is?"

Sybal shook her head. What was the Runer's game?

"Perhaps now is not the time to tell you," he mumbled, rubbing his unshaven chin. "You're not ready to hear it. Not yet." He had more to say, but didn't go on.

Sybal glared at Amir. "What do you want to tell me?"

"Sharar has taken the djinn's power. Even the necrotic scriptures will bend to him soon, I think. He took the necromancer he'd caught and left."

"Necromancer?" she asked, her heart stumbling in her chest. "Tarkan?"

"No," Amir replied. "Some imbecile he had me capture in the port. A man named Vicdan."

She choked. Vicdan, a necromancer? "How was he...? What did...?" She couldn't get any fully-formed thoughts out.

"Bone-Scriven," Amir offered. "He's Porshain, a part of House Nashira. Sharar said it was the only tribe of necromancers who stood up to the last Necro'Khan."

"He's brave," she said, trying to wrap her head around what Amir told her. Could it possibly be true? And he was Sharar's captive?

"He is brave," Amir agreed. "I think Sharar is foolish to keep him. But, I'm probably wrong."

Sybal looked up from her blade to Amir. "He makes you feel foolish, doesn't he? Makes you doubt your own intelligence. That's how he controls you. He hates Runers just as much as everyone else, if not more. Trust your gut."

Amir's face was impossible to read. "Your Vicdan isn't the only necromancer he's taken under his sway. There is another."

Sybal's head spun, consumed by the information Amir was offering.

"Sharar spoke with an Apostle of your Necro'Khan," Amir went on. "We think this Apostle, Ashkan, is looking for a way to turn on Tarkan."

"Stop," Sybal snapped, raising her blade. "Why are you telling me this?"

This question stopped Amir and turned his face to stone. "Go," he snarled. "Get out."

Something wasn't right. Why was the Runer being so open with her? Had he left the doors open on purpose? Yes, but not as a trap. Sybal frowned, frightened and unsure. Slowly, she moved across the room, focusing on Amir's weight balanced on his feet.

He didn't shift, didn't come after her. He was indeed letting her go, though his eyes tracked her every movement. She ran halfway up the stairs, then turned to look at him one last time.

"Thank you, Amir," she said. She clutched Azar's sword to her middle.

"Go!" he shouted.

She ran.

SYBAL PUSHED her horse and hurried the riverboat driver, making it back to Mysir and the embassy in just two days. A light flickered in the window of the library. Sybal's heart leapt. Signar and Tzarik must have come back. She forced her horse to run and slid out of the saddle before it came to a complete stop. The doors banged open as she hit them. Her smile melted away.

Tzarik did not stand in the entryway studying a letter. A woman, tall, dark-skinned, with black hair and veiled entirely in red and gold, did: Nefiri.

"So, you are a Sheikha?" the magi asked simply, dropping the letter. The sound of keys in an envelope clanged against the wood. "Your man in Ala'Nar confirms it. Inside is the deed to your land and the keys. Congratulations, I suppose. Were you always a wealthy lady, or is this the man you killed to earn your runes?"

"Give me the letter," Sybal snapped, holding her hand out. She wasn't afraid of the magi. If she had to, she'd make her bleed to get her letter. She wanted to cut Nefiri anyway for her lifetime of disgusting prophesying.

"You should be thanking me," Nefiri scoffed. "I heard through gossip that the scholar knows two Runers were staying in the embassy. I told them you'd gone days ago."

"Give me the letter, magi," Sybal growled.

"Come and take it," Nefiri purred, motioning to where she dropped it on a small table.

Sweating, covered in sand, and no doubt smelling, Sybal shoved past Nefiri and took the letter, the seal broken. She didn't dare read it and take her eyes off the magi. She didn't trust Nefiri at all.

"What's wrong?" the magi asked, gracefully sitting down on a red lounge. She rang a brass bell and waited for a servant to come. "Something in your aura is...considerably agitated." She motioned to the lounge opposite her. "Sit. Speak with me. Woman to woman."

Sybal hesitated, but after listening and realizing Tzarik and Signar were not in the manor, she resigned herself. She'd stay, too, until they returned, then leave with them both.

"I saw a vision four nights ago," Nefiri went on. She picked a yellow flower from a nearby potted plant and slowly tore the petals off with her long, clean fingers. "I saw the sun sink into a river of blood. It hissed as it was doused, and a creature rose up from a grave followed by a thousand and one stars. But these stars did not light the night, and the monster slayed the moon. So much darkness."

Sybal laughed dryly. "You prophets are always seeing such pleasant things. Do you get a thrill out of it?"

Nefiri glared at Sybal over her red veil. "It was about Acenoth, Runer. You should know. Or have you not had your ear to the ground while you were here? I was trying to help you by giving you this place so near the palace."

The magi stopped. Her eyes flashed to Sybal's hands where she held the wrapped scimitar. Nefiri sat up, red mouth dropping open. Her eyes immediately shone.

"Sybal," she whispered, "what do you have there?" She stood.

Sybal looked around, then down at her lap where she'd lain Azar's scimitar when Nefiri had asked her to sit. "An old blade," she answered easily. Then she remembered the horrible story

Nefiri had told her; Nefiri knew Azar. She'd know the blade. "I need it," she said darkly. "I will not give it up."

Nefiri sprang to her feet. "Do you know what that is?" she cried, pointing dramatically. "Where did you find it?" Her voice cracked like she might burst into weeping.

Confused by the magi's sudden emotion, she said, "I broke into Sharar's home in Gypsu. For good reason, magi, so don't—"

Nefiri gave a great cry and clamped her hands over her mouth, tears spilling over her fingers. She turned from Sybal. "No, gods, please, no!" she cried. She paced, almost running back and forth as moans and wales broke from her lips.

"Calm yourself," Sybal ordered, standing. "I know what this means."

"You do not know," Nefiri growled, sniffling. "I should have killed Tzarik when I had the chance."

Sybal glared, mouth agape. "You bitch. After what you did to him?"

"Don't pretend to be righteous, Runer," the magi shot back at her. "Damn you, and damn Tzarik."

"I've had enough of you," Sybal spat. She turned to leave.

"No, please!" Nefiri cried, reaching out and seizing the back of her cloak to stop her. "I must tell you. You must know. There's a way to stop the scholar."

Ice shot through Sybal. Slowly, she turned to face the magi. "What do you know about Sharar?"

"More than I would like," she whispered. Her eyes were rimmed with red as she calmed herself. "He's been a staple in Sokar'Xenoteph's life for most of it. I believe he had something to do with the Hawk King's father's death, but Nasor and I could never prove it. And his djinn..." Her eyes fell onto Azar's blade. "This was his djinn? He's gone now?" she asked, looking up at Sybal. Fresh tears filled her brown eyes. Her hand shook as it reached out to Azar's blade. "I don't sense him. He's gone. Truly gone. Sybal," she took a deep breath, "you must prepare yourself for what is to come next."

"I know," Sybal confessed. "Amir, Sharar's Runer, said Sharar was powerful. That we couldn't stop him."

"You can," Nefiri sighed. Her arms hung limp at her side. "If you have the strength. The courage."

At last, Sybal understood that Nefiri was dancing around an answer that she wanted Sybal to ask about. This was what Tzarik hated; the cryptic talk to get them to ask. It infuriated her while no doubt making Nefiri feel superior. So she did what she thought Tzarik might do.

"Tell me, witch," she said, adding the insulting lower title. "Stop playing games. I won't beg you. And if it is as important as you are making it out to be, you will simply tell me."

The magi turned to look at Sybal over her shoulder, shocked at the lady Runer's boldness. "You speak like him, you know? You stand like him. So much of him is in you now. I saw you in him as well."

"You try my patience, magi," Sybal growled. She unwrapped Azar's blade and gripped the handle.

Nefiri nodded and finally squared up to Sybal. "You can stop Sharar before he harms anyone. Before he discovers more of his power."

"I can't get close to him," Sybal started.

"You don't have to," Nefiri cut in. "You are as close as you can possibly be to the one person who can kill him. Sharar might not even know it."

Sybal did not have to think long before she realized Nefiri meant Tzarik. "How can Tzarik kill Sharar? I won't send him in alone."

"You need not even live without him," the magi pressed.

Sybal blinked, frowning.

"If you take his life."

"Enough!" Sybal barked, taking a menacing step toward the magi. "Speak plainly!"

Nefiri gasped and tripped on the lounge, falling onto it when she leapt back from Sybal. Seeing the vile woman cower gave Sybal a sense of justice for her past evil.

"When we performed the rite on Bahratt," Nefiri said, forcing her voice to be steady, "Azar got into a rage. He was livid at what I'd done to his boy."

"Good," Sybal growled. She wished Azar would have cut Nefiri's head off then and there.

The magi shook her head. "He made an oath while Tzarik was on that altar," she went on, voice quivering. "He swore to never break the Trial of Two. That Tzarik's fate would be bound to his forever, and his to Tzarik's. He thought that oath would protect Tzarik and give him an outlet to death." She frowned. "Azar's essence is alive in the sorcerer. Tzarik must still live."

She couldn't say why yet, but the pit of Sybal's stomach dropped. Like she half comprehended what the magi was saying.

"Do you see?" Nefiri whispered, taking in the way Sybal's face paled. "Fate-bound."

"What is that?" Sybal shot. "Amir mentioned it as well, but he wouldn't tell me. Said I wasn't ready."

"Destiny is one's purpose in life. Fate is the end to destiny. Even though Azar turned into a djinn in the end, that oath will hold. Fate cannot be changed. Sybal?" Nefiri asked when the Runer did not speak. "Do you understand? So long as Azar lives within Sharar, Tzarik will live. As long as Tzarik lives, Sharar will draw breath. You can stop Sharar by taking Tzarik's life." She stood again, looking into the Runer's vacant eyes. "Do it yourself. Kill Tzarik and end yourself, breaking your oath to the runes. You can go together."

"You're lying," Sybal spat on instinct. Her voice shook and tears drowned her eyes. No. Tzarik couldn't die. She wouldn't allow it. Not for the sake of whole map.

Nefiri's wide brown eyes quivered in her face. "I wouldn't lie about this. I know my prophecy was about Sharar and his Necro'Khan. They will flood the map in blood. He's already a sorcerer. It's only a matter of time before he comes to his full strength." She sniffled and swallowed. "Please, Lady Runer. It can be you."

Feeling and breath finally filled Sybal as she scoffed. Her nose tingled and hot tears filled her eyes. "I've died as many times as I'm allowed," she said. She sniffled, looking down at Azar's blade. "What I believe to have been death itself told me I could not cross over again. I've died many times, magi. Even if I did find a way…"

She stopped and called upon the voice. She heard the ice forming and crackling over her skin as the power of the Dohkma filled her, showing the familiar touch to the magi.

"I'd end up just like Azar," Sybal whispered. Steam puffed from her mouth as she spoke.

The horrified look on Nefiri's face was worth divulging her secret. The magi cringed away from her.

"There is no simple answer," Sybal whispered, feeling the touch recede. "I am damned to eternity. And you ask me to endure it alone? Without him?"

"I do," Nefiri whispered, quivering. "Sybal, you cannot be selfish now. A sorcerer is a monster of untold magic and power. As that Runer said, you have not witnessed even a fraction of Sharar's might. Once he learns what he can do, there will be no stopping him. Do you know where he is now?"

Sybal shook her head. "In the Dynast Palace, perhaps. But even if I could get close enough to hold his hand, I wouldn't strike him down. Not now."

"Sybal," Nefiri begged, reaching out to her.

"No!" Sybal shot back, jerking out of Nefiri's grasp. "I won't harm Tzarik. I can't. He's fought for his life, fought to protect it even from himself. I won't take that away from him."

The magi's eyes dropped in melancholy. "Then you'll sacrifice the entire map for your love."

Sybal looked away. "Sharar doesn't know yet. I have to move with that advantage. I will find a way to stop him and let Tzarik live."

Chapter 36

---◈---

The One Thousand and One

Tarkan stood on the western bank of the east side of The Cradle, looking up at the magnificent structure through the thick green forest. In the darkness of the moonless night, no one spotted the black-clad necromancers. He and Ashkan waited far off, looking for the signal from the other Apostles that they were in place.

"You are sure you could not find more?" Tarkan asked. "Are Apostles so rare?"

Ashkan waited a beat, no doubt choosing his words cautiously, before he answered. "Since Ala'Nar, they are hidden more than before. I have checked the Makans here and on Al'Myrah, since they were closest. Our brothers and sisters hide well. I fear not many are taking new apprentices, and even fewer are birthing their own before breaking their covenant script and making themselves infertile."

"A risk," Tarkan murmured, knowing most wouldn't try to bear living children, even if only Scriven. It had worked for Ishmael and his mother Isis, but even he wouldn't have risked it had he had the chance. "We must give our tribes a chance to make their own followers," he went on. "But not these twelve."

Ashkan looked over at Tarkan, one brow raised.

"Seven must die," the Necro'Khan went on. "We will need, at the very least, six more. I require twelve Apostles to follow me."

Ashkan whipped his head out into the darkness where the unsuspecting twelve necromancers prepared to raise their dead and invade The Cradle. "You will sacrifice them?"

"In a way," Tarkan replied. He turned back to his own black-painted wagon and risen mount. "Their blood must mix within the golden orb of the Cradle, where the salt spring rises."

"Why?" Ashkan asked. Tarkan was shocked to find a little disgust in his Apostle's tone.

"The salts within the waters of Alika," Tarkan began, "have a unique attribute that means little to those unable to wield magic."

He pulled the ruby blade from his thigh and slid the sharp edge over the palm of his own hand, drawing some of his black-red blood. He squeezed his fingers so it dropped through his knuckles onto the ground. The drops of blood hit a small purple flower growing there. It withered almost instantly.

"When something magic, black or otherwise, touches the salt water," he went on, "the magic in the salts enhances it. And with my spell..." He faced Ashkan. "Hold out your hand."

The Apostle lifted his hand.

Tarkan took a glass bottle from his saddlebag. "This water was stolen from within the Cradle by an obliging thief. It is not purified like the water in the Three Rivers." He popped The cork out and tipped some into Ashkan's hand. Hissing a single sentence that quickly vanished into the wind, he put drops of his blood into the tiny pool of water in the Apostle's palm. "This is no longer tainted water. It *is* blood." He motioned to the ground.

Ashkan slowly tipped his hand, letting the liquid fall to the ground. When it hit the small patches of moss and greenery that grew near The Cradle, they shriveled up, dead, like the flower before, killed by the necrotic blood.

Ashkan's eyes fixed on the ground.

Tarkan's scriptures stirred, telling him the twelve Apostles were ready. "Father chose my mother because of her knowledge. She was a servant of The Cradle."

Ashkan shook his head and turned to face the west, joining the other necromancers in surrounding The Cradle at a distance. "Ishmael was wise and cunning. Do you ever wonder why he slept for so long?"

Tarkan drew the massive, blood-red orichalcum blade. He ran his thumb over his father's heart. "No," he whispered. "I will let his foolishness go undiscovered and surpass him in every way. And he will know of it where he sleeps in our hell."

Tarkan easily raised the corpses in his wagon, commanding them to shamble toward The Cradle. Like a temple, The Cradle was guarded by a few kehann, but was filled mostly with what Alikans called servants of The Cradle—priest-like sentients who prayed over the salt water, oversaw the purification, and made sure The Cradle ran as it should, making the water clean and safe for the sentients of Alika. They also moved glass bottles of the blue salt, taking them to select traders and merchants to sell. The rest of the magic salt was destroyed in fire in a great brass furnace. Without The Cradle, Alika would not exist as a nation. The water, being filled with salt that could mutate a sentient if consumed, had killed any who had come before the first pharaoh who'd discovered how to purify the water. Thus, the first Alikans had been tribal, traveling from pure spring to pure spring.

Ashkan raised his corpses as well. Tarkan felt his eye on the sword he carried. He knew Ashkan might betray him at any moment, enraged at his desecration of Elahel's bones. But for now, he had been loyal.

"What are you waiting for?" Ashkan asked when Tarkan didn't start the march to The Cradle.

The Necro'Khan had faith in Sharar. Surely the man had ascended and taken the powers of the djinn by now. The scholar would have been spurred into action when Tarkan left. Sharar loved pomp and big shows of power. Surely...

"What time of day do you think it is?" Tarkan asked. His blue eyes flitted to the sky above. No stars shone. Not even the moon. The only light came from The Cradle.

Ashkan sighed a light hum, looking around. "The sun should have started to rise. I did not want to doubt you, but was hesitant when you said we'd attack during the day. But it seems the sun has forgotten to rise. It's been held back, like in the story of Acenoth and the Three Suns."

"When Acenoth fought off the invaders from Al'Myrah." Tarkan nodded, remembering the godtale everyone on Alika and Al'Myrah knew. "Ashmalia promised him he'd achieve victory before the sun set. And so she wed Krah, and asked him, as a favor to her, to hold the sun still for three days while Acenoth battled."

"I know the tale," Ashkan said.

The Necro'Khan stopped, realizing he had indeed picked up a little of Sharar's personality, explaining things as if only he knew them. He stopped there.

"I knew Sharar would not be able to withhold the temptation," he went on. "I needed the sky dark for the spell. He has held the sun back, disrespecting their god Krah and showing his power over the gods' dominion."

"And you knew he would do this?" Ashkan asked. "Wasn't that a risk?"

Tarkan scoffed, smirking. "No. I bloodied the moon of Ashmalia without the powers of a sorcerer. Sharar had to prove to me he was just as strong." He looked up into the black sky. "He will hold the sun for three days at least. This also means the door to Acenoth's tomb is open."

He raised his hands, shoving his risen forward. The corpses hissed and shambled into the forest. The familiar hissing and growling of the other twelve sending in their hordes joined his. Ashkan did the same. Tarkan stood back, not needing to sustain the spell like the Apostles did. He watched Ashkan whisper into the black howling wind that kicked up the sand and rustled the foliage around him. He did not miss standing so still. So vulnerable.

He lifted his sword and placed it hard on his shoulder, commanding his risen horse to follow him. Ashkan, eyes red, took slow steps to keep up with him. The risen hordes breached The Cradle. Cries from the unsuspecting kehann rose and the weeping of the servants cut through the din of battle. The people of The Cradle could not hope to win. The risen could not be killed. Every battle with a necromancer was a futile one.

"With the tomb open," Tarkan went on as they advanced, "it may be flooded. I will command the newly turned rivers of blood and fill the tomb. Opening the Deep, I will call upon the souls of the One Thousand and One and Acenoth himself. Their souls will be placed back into their bodies to fulfill their oath."

Beside him, Ashkan blinked rapidly, gasping. "Not risen. Undead. Sentient risen." He swore, understanding Tarkan's plan to the fullest now. "True heresy, Necro'Khan. True damnation. How could you do something so vile? Placing living souls into dead bodies…"

"They will be sustained," Tarkan assured him with a malicious grin. "With this blade, filled with the blood of the river—the blood of necromancers—imbued by the bones of a Bone-Scriven, and given the power of the heart of a Necro'Khan, they will live forever."

"And Acenoth will command his army for you?" Disdain and doubt oozed from Ashkan's throat.

"Yes," Tarkan purred back. "Because he has an oath to fulfill. To protect Alika from the invaders of Al'Myrah."

Ashkan understood then. Tarkan saw his shoulders drop and all fight leave his face. "You have...planned well, my khan," he whispered, resigned to his fate.

The pair broke through the jungle and beheld the massive golden sphere of The Cradle. Servants ran, trying to raise an alarm, but were cut down too quickly. Kehanns fought valiantly, but also fell to the risen. One of the Apostles had risen griffins and half a dozen of the scorpion monsters Ashkan had risen before. The monsters and sentients flooded The Cradle.

"Khan!" Faraji shouted from far away, hardly visible through the throng. "Stop the runner. He's going for the beacon!"

Tarkan turned to see one young, brave kehann in his holy armor dashing to a tower with a torch in hand. Reaching behind him, Tarkan called up something he'd been saving. He flung his arm in an arch over his head and felt the pull such a monster took on his own blood as he raised it. He marched to the kehann, his enormous red sword hefted onto his shoulder. Imbued by the flesh he'd consumed before, he could wield the blade, if only for a short time. He only needed a moment to frighten the young man.

The kehann turned to see him bearing down on him and cried out, breaking into a sprint.

"Run, boy," Tarkan jeered. "It will do you no good."

The thing he'd summoned bolted overhead. Rakthar shot a blast of pure energy at the beacon tower, shattering it from the top down. The rubble fell, raining down around the young kehann, stopping him in his flight. He turned and faced the Necro'Khan, blade at the ready, feet apart. Tarkan stopped, admiring the young man's spirit.

"It is a pity, but perhaps the strength of your soul will feed the Deep," he said. He waved his arm and Rakthar landed with a crash behind him, stretching his newly flesh and blood wings and giving a haunting roar. With a simple prodding from his mind, the risen flanked the young man, overpowering him and taking him hostage.

Tarkan leapt up onto Rakthar's foreclaw and climbed onto his body. He kicked the dragon's side and it lifted off with a powerful beat of its wings. "Take three prisoners," he shouted down to his Apostles. "We will use them to open the Deep."

He looked down from Rakthar's back, watching as The Cradle swarmed with risen.

"Don't let any escape!" he shouted, seeing one servant of The Cradle break away and dash. The small figure raced to the river. "Don't destroy the boats. We need one to return to Mysir."

Two of his Apostles arced their arms and turned to face the fleeing servant of The Cradle. Instantly, two dozen or more risen swarmed them, taking them down. His own risen moved without his command. It was an unfair battle. Coming in the dark of the sunless day to face the no doubt confused guardians and servants of The Cradle, the necromancers overtook the peaceful land with ease.

It reminded Tarkan of his second attack on Ala'Nar, when he'd returned to reap revenge on the Runers for desecrating his family's crypt. He remembered how terrified the people had been of him. How much the Runers had feared him in that moment. The gap in power at the time had made him feel unstoppable. Then Sharar had reminded him he was a prisoner. He'd bent a knee to the likes of Sjörna-Reks to remind himself of what he was trying to escape, so that moments like this would feel sweeter.

And he'd outwitted Sharar. Or had, at the very least, predicted the prideful scholar's moves. When Sharar learned his spell over the sun had helped Tarkan raise Acenoth and the One Thousand

and One, the scholar would be furious, knowing his prisoner had outwitted him. Used him.

Several minutes later, Ashkan waved a torch up at Tarkan, signaling him. Tarkan guided Rakthar down to the top balcony of The Cradle. The risen dragon landed hard, then stilled, dead once again as Tarkan took his concentration away from it.

"The prisoners," Faraji said with a dark grin. He waved his hand as a dozen of his own risen dragged four kehann, including the brave one from the beacon, into the space.

Tarkan led his followers into the golden sphere. The doorways to The Cradle were all wide, perfect circles, tall enough for creatures as big as Rakthar to walk through. A level spanned the entire sphere, making a huge, circular walkway half a mile in diameter. Below, the spring roared, kicking up mist and salty air, making it almost impossible to see the other side from where they stood. The three rivers flowed out from the enormous spring below, through the golden and crystal machines that drew out the salt. Three colossal glass orbs hung in the center, gathering the salt before it slid down brass pipes and out into the distribution tunnels they could not see.

"Magnificent," Ashkan mused.

"Pure, earth-given power," Tarkan added. He moved close to Ashkan. "Find seven and bring them here. Summon your risen; I want no fight from the sacrifices."

Ashkan bowed wordlessly and turned to gather the Apostles. When they arrived, he had them take the captive kehanns and slaughter them, lining them up for the Blood Path inside The Cradle. The sounds of their screams echoed long inside the golden sphere.

"Ashkan, when I open the Deep, cut their throats and spill their blood into The Cradle," he commanded.

"I will do it," Faraji offered, a manic glint glittering in his eye.

"You will help," Tarkan ordered. "They will fight."

He moved to the head of the Blood Path and hovered his hands close together, speaking the words. Almost instantly, having done it so many times now, he felt the rift between his fingers. He ripped opened the Deep, the rivulets of blood flowing up from the corpses and into the blade at his side. Once he felt the corpses were drained of their blood, he unsheathed the blade and cut open the rift.

Acenoth, he called into the Deep, *I, Tarkan of Porsh, Necro'Khan and master of the dead, summon you. A man from Al' Myrah threatens Alika. Come and fulfill your oath, pharaoh. Fight for me. I will return your soul to your body. You shall be strong, sustained by the blood.*

Tarkan did not expect to see the ancient pharaoh. When a dark blue and gold ghost solidified before his eyes, he gasped and stumbled back. A tall, pure hawk Masahk stood before him in spirit form. Acenoth held a strange partizan in his left hand. The long tip jutted out to the sky, but from the side of the base where the tip and haft met, a long, curved blade like a scythe arched out. Unlike the modern Masahk, Acenoth's wings folded against his back, high over his hawk-like head. He was clad in golden, gleaming armor and robed in a dark blue cloak.

"Summon me, master of death?" he asked in a deep, calm voice. "How long has it been since I've walked the dunes of the map, since I've sung the praises and bent a knee in worship to death?"

Tarkan found his voice and said, "Over a thousand years, pharaoh. I am Tarkan, son of Ishmael, and I have come to give you a second life, if only for a time. But your men must follow you."

"A son of slaves calls me," Acenoth replied, raising his hawk-shaped head.

"Son of Ishmael," Tarkan repeated. "The man who gave you the power of the dead. Who wrote the words of your gods upon his skin and gave you victory over Al'Myrah."

Acenoth took a long-legged step to turn and face Tarkan square on. To Tarkan's surprise, a small shiver ran down his back.

"A good servant," Acenoth replied steadily. "I remember him with honor." He took a deep, slow breath. "You summon me and my One Thousand and One soldiers to ride with you and fight a sorcerer again?"

Tarkan felt compelled to bow his head to the great pharaoh, but denied it, facing him. "I do."

"And they shall," Acenoth replied. His keen golden eyes scanned Tarkan. "It matters not who has called me. I yearn to fight." He turned and raised his strange partizan behind him. A river of souls washed up, rushing toward them. "Where is the battle, master of death?"

"The blood," Tarkan said. "Through this rift is a river of blood that will lead you to Mysir and your tomb. As you are buried there, you will rise a grave-born. The blood will feed your bodies, your souls will enter, and you shall be the first true undead to be risen by a necromancer of Porsh."

"An honor," Acenoth replied. He pounded his fist over his chest and bowed to Tarkan. "But promise me this."

Tarkan waited. He'd not expected another promise from an oath-bound undead.

"Do not send us back to the Deep," Acenoth asked. "Let our spirits go where they will. If Krah has forgiven us, we will away to Ahryu as was intended and see the field of the reeds."

"So be it," Tarkan promised, not caring where the ancient pharaoh's spirit came to rest, even if that meant it haunted this side of the barrier. "I will not force you back into the Deep. You have my word."

Acenoth gave a hawkish grin and raised his partizan again to his host of ghostly warriors. "Through the rift and to the river of blood, my men. We will fight again!" He faced Tarkan. "We away to Mysir, the home of the ruby throne."

Tarkan couldn't stop the dark smirk that took his face now. "Yes. *My* ruby throne."

Chapter 37

Onslaught

"Scholar! Thank Krah you're here!"

One of the Mirage tore herself away from a gaggle of servants and palace guards and ran to Sharar. She took his hand in her scaly one and pulled him down the golden halls of the Dynast Palace.

"What has happened?" Sharar asked. "It must be truly terrible. My Runer hasn't even returned from taking my things to my room and you're hysterical."

"It's the Pharaoh," she shot back. "He's mad. The whole map is mad, no doubt. The sun has not shown yet today."

Sharar smiled. "It is not madness that has taken the Hawk King. It is no doubt a thousand years of joy rising within him."

The Mirage eyed Sharar, a cautious glare hidden behind her narrowing pupils. "So you've done it? What you always said you would." She didn't sound pleased.

He knew not everyone in the palace found him as agreeable as Sokar did. But it didn't matter. All he needed was Sokar.

"Why?" she asked. "Why withhold the sun—"

"It is of no matter to you," he cut in. "What is this madness you speak of?"

A ruckus reached his ears then. Someone shouted outside the council chamber, no doubt standing on the balcony that stuck out from the glorious war room. He heard Nasor and a few other familiar voices, including one that belonged to the overseer and another to a priest. Amir dashed up behind him before he entered, panting.

"The necromancer is secure," he whispered as they marched in sync toward the council chamber doors.

"Well done," Sharar said.

The three of them burst through the door to hear the three men shouting at Sokar, who stood on the rail of the balcony.

Sokar stood on the alabaster railing, magnificent, emerald green wings spread out on either side of him. He raised his arms to the sunless sky and Sharar wished for a moment he had not with-held the sun so that the rays might shine on the poor youth, warming his joy. But he had to show his power, his dominion, over something as strong as the sun.

"Sokar, please!" Nasor shouted, banging the end of his golden crook against the floor. "This is madness. You will fall to your death."

"It's a miracle, Nasor," Sokar called back, his voice high with joy.

"It is indeed," Sharar shouted over the din. The others turned to face him.

"I should have known," Nasor growled. He almost turned to face Sharar, but Sokar moved to leap. Nasor whirled back around, hooked the young Pharaoh with the crook of his staff, and pulled him roughly to the ground. "Enough, Sokar!" he shouted. "You will fall to your death."

"Don't hold him back," Sharar said. He marched up to the jackal and shoved him hard, away from Sokar. Then he offered the boy his hand, pulling him up. "I did this." He pointed to the folded, powerful wings on Sokar's back. "I took the djinn and his powers. I have held the sun this last day to prove my power to you."

Nasor's brows fell. "You defy Krah and stop his sun from rising?"

"I gave Sokar, a boy I care very much about, the power of flight. Like his ancestors."

The vizier stammered, looking from the overseer to the priest to Amir. Sharar expected him to say something derogatory to Amir, perhaps beat him again, but Nasor stayed his hand. The vizier's attitude toward Runers had changed quite suddenly.

So it was you, he thought bitterly. *You let my prized hunt get away.*

"If you must test your wings," Nasor said at length, "then try somewhere lower to the ground, Your Eminence."

"Is your faith in me so weak?" Sharar spat at the vizier.

"No," Nasor said softly. "But I distrust powerful magic from demons. From foreigners. I distrust sorcerers. Such magic is outlawed in your land, yes?"

Nasor may have to die sooner than expected, Sharar mused. *He is vexing me greatly.* He glanced at Amir, remembering his promise to let the Runer dispatch the Masahk who had abused him so much. He hoped to keep that promise.

Sokar gave a growl of frustration and marched to a large table in the middle of the council chamber. "Am I Dynast Pharaoh or not? You will not heed my words, Nasor, and you are trying my patience."

"Yes, Your Eminence," Nasor mumbled, fist over his heart and bowing his head.

Sokar stood on the table. "I trust you, Sharar. Don't let me look like a fool." He smiled cautiously.

"I would never, my friend." He watched the boy. He trusted his own power.

Sokar spread his wings like no Masahk in over a thousand had done and gave them one great beat. The wind shoved Sharar's robes and long hair back, forcing him to step back with the others. Sokar strained, giving another beat until he found a rhythm. Fortunately, the council chamber was large. The ceiling, painted to match a blue sky, towered overhead. Slowly, Sokar rose with the graceful dip and rising motion of his wings. Sharar let himself be taken in by the magnificence of the Masahk Pharaoh. A thousand years ago, such a Masahk would have commanded armies by this act alone, driving all who saw him into reverence.

A wind pushed through the huge archway from the balcony and Sokar leveled out his wings, angling them to catch it by instinct alone. He hovered without the beat of his wings and slowly bent them to return to the ground. When he landed, he gasped, laughing and panting. Sharar caught him as he fell forward, not used to the weight of the wings being folded high above him.

"Magnificent, my boy," he whispered. He took Sokar's face in his hands and beamed down at him. Then he embraced him, with Sokar eagerly returning the gesture.

"You did this," Sokar gasped, emotion overtaking him. "I will shine like a jewel on the crown of this dynasty! And it's all thanks to you. But I fear Krah may reap his revenge for what you've done to the sun."

Sharar smiled, helping the Pharaoh up to his avian feet. "I don't fear Krah, and neither should you," he said. "See what I've done to his greatest creation? You have nothing to fear, my boy."

Sokar smiled down at Sharar. "You may be right. I—" He stopped, eyes locking on something outside the balcony's archway. "What in the name of Ashmalia?" he whispered. "Nasor, look."

All the others turned to look out over the balcony to the river a few miles off. The beautiful blue water turned to a darker shade of blue, then purple, at last flowing a bright, bloody red as it streamed out from the Cradle. The blood gushed quickly, turning the whole river a bright crimson. Sharar watched its progress down the river and out of sight as it reached Acenoth's tomb. His stomach dropped out from under him.

"It's him, isn't it?" Amir whispered at his side. "What's he doing?"

Something Sharar had never felt before filled him. It reminded him of rage, but also of the embarrassment he might feel if he mispronounced a word during a lecture, which he'd only done once in his life. Had he made a mistake? Or had Tarkan outwitted him? No, neither of those things could be true. Perhaps the rivers were not blood. Perhaps it was a side effect of the sun not rising. Yes, it must have been algae in the water.

Against the white sands of Alika, the rivers looked even redder than blood.

"Sharar?" Sokar asked, lightly touching his arm, eyes fixed on the river. "What is that? Has something happened to the Cradle?"

The scholar resigned himself. He sighed deeply. "Blood. It's the Necro'Khan."

"We have to leave," Amir said, a tinge of fear in his voice.

"Leave?" Sharar quipped. "Does this scare you, Runer?"

Amir shifted his weight from one foot to the other. "It is beyond me, sorcerer. I know my place in the magical order. You possess all the power you can ever need." He swallowed. "You don't...need me anymore. Let me go."

Sharar smiled and laughed lightly. "That is nonsense. I do not plan on altering myself with my magic. I still need your brute strength. Your strong will." He glared at the Runer. "Don't turn on me now."

Amir shook his head a fraction in each direction. "I wasn't going to."

Liar, Sharar mused. His wording told Sharar he was trying to lie without breaking his runic oath. Was he to always be surrounded by traitors? Runers really were an emotional, fickle bunch. "What worries you? Is it your former apprentice? I can have him sent for. In fact, it might do me well to have more than one Runer by my side."

"Leave him alone," Amir said. It almost sounded like begging.

Sharar sighed, tired of the growing weakness in his Runer. "I cannot discuss this now, Amir. Either you stay or you run. Do you really want to run from me?"

Outside, far away, something made of stone cracked. The boom shook the entire palace, making everyone shout and tossing a few of them to the floor. Sharar braced himself against the table and looked out. He had no idea what Tarkan was doing, but he had to find out.

"Amir, with me," he ordered, dashing out of the palace.

TZARIK HIT the floor of the embassy hard. With the wind knocked out of him, he strained, vomiting onto the ground before he could really push himself up. He shivered from the stress of taking the djinn's portal and quivered from the regurgitation. Then he sniffed and ran his hand over his lips. Beside him, Signar stood up, seemingly fine.

"I will try to remember how much taking a portal does not agree with you," Signar said, smiling and helping Tzarik up.

Tzarik grunted a reply and let Signar lead him to a table where a crystal carafe of water waited. This was why Tzarik hated most places that were not Al'Myrah. He couldn't swim, so he hated taking boats. Beasts like dragons took him too high and made his mind go black with irrational fear. And now he knew portals made him ill. It would be better to go home to Al'Myrah, its familiar architecture, its warm, orange sand, and never leave. Better to stay somewhere, so he would never have to take a boat, dragon, or portal ever again. To stop hunting.

"I've never thought about retiring," he mused after taking a long drink. "I don't know if Runers can. But I'd like to." He sighed, one hand on his hip while his brain slowly stopped spinning in his skull. "So I never have to travel like that again."

"Retire?" Signar asked.

Tzarik nodded, taking a drink. "Quit. Stop hunting. Maybe keep bees."

Signar laughed out loud. "You only have to hunt every so often, yes? Perhaps you could keep jackalopes at bay."

"They don't have those on Al'Myrah."

"Then fight off some household spirits. Something small and simple."

Tzarik nodded. "I'd like that."

The door burst open as a flurry that was Sybal rammed through it. She held her scimitar at the ready. "You're back!" she squealed, dashing in once she saw it was them and not an intruder. She dropped her blade and ran to Tzarik, wrapping him in her long arms. Her strength squeezed the breath out of him, but he didn't have time to gather it before she was kissing him over and over, gripping his face.

Constricting one arm around Tzarik, she reached out to Signar with the other, waving him in. The boy smiled shyly and let Sybal crush him with her newfound affection as well. Tzarik felt Sybal's heart hammering against the side of his head as she hugged them both.

When she finally released them, he said, "We have a lot to tell you. Do we have time?"

Sybal's eyes went to the axe on Signar's back. "You did it? You're Signar-Reks?"

He nodded.

"I hope you will tell me," she said. Her eyes shot to the windows, doors, and back again. "I am afraid…"

Tzarik frowned. It didn't sound like she would go on.

Sybal cleared her throat. "I'm afraid I have terrible news. I don't know what can be done. Nefiri was here, but she ran," Sybal said.

"Ran?" Tzarik asked.

Sybal nodded. "The sun has not shown itself in almost two days."

Signar looked out the window, a small frown creasing his brow.

Sybal gathered herself. "It's Sharar. He's… He's done it. He's a sorcerer now."

"How do you know? Were you hurt?" Tzarik asked.

Sybal shook her head. "I…went to his manor. He was gone," she added when his face paled and an angry glower preceded the tirade about safety he was about to give her. "I couldn't stay here, knowing he knew where we were. I ran into Amir, that Runer he has working for him."

Tzarik bit his tongue. She was alive. She had no bandages. She spoke calmly. Everything would be all right.

"He told me." She shook her head, going over the conversation she must have had with the Runer. "I can't say why he was so open with me, but he told me."

Tzarik whipped around to look out the window that faced north toward Gypsu. "He's been here a long while if you had time to travel up and back."

"Four days at least," she said. "What's he waiting for?"

"He's showing his power," Signar suggested, but he spoke with assurance. "Hiding the sun? It will drive fear into the entire country."

Sybal frowned. "It rose on Caerwren?"

Signar nodded. "It never sets this time of year. His power did not reach us. As if his magic only touched Alika."

Pride at how far Signar had come since being the wildling that had shaken him like a dead rabbit filled Tzarik. Signar was putting himself in a place of power, pulling on thoughts that must have been filling his head since he sat on his mother's throne. He knew the taste of power. He must have had similar thoughts. In that moment, the sorrow of losing him again to the barbarous continent gripped Tzarik's heart. If he had his way, he'd never let the boy go.

"That sounds like Sharar," Tzarik confessed. "Amir is a brave man if he does not fear Sharar. When I confronted him with Tarkan, I was terrified of the power he hid. I had seen the power of a djinn once. I was right to be afraid of him."

Sybal gulped, brows knitting.

"What is it?" he asked.

"Tzarik," she began, looking lost, scared.

Outside, a scream rent the air. Something shattered, and a dozen panicked footsteps rushed through the halls of the embassy and outside. Utter chaos broke out.

"What's happened?" Sybal shouted at a servant running past.

"It's the curse! It must be Acenoth's curse!" the servant girl screamed. "Blood! It's all blood!"

Tzarik ran out the front of the embassy that faced one of the three rivers, Signar and Sybal flanking him. He skidded to a stop, taking in the water that ran through the artificial rills. The water glittered red and opaque. The smell alone told him it was blood. The sharp iron scent pierced his nose.

"What the hell?" he whispered. He looked over the embassy walls to the Dynast Palace. Was this Sharar? Was he inside the palace now? "Follow me," he ordered the other two.

He led them out of the embassy to the stables. Already the servants were in a full panic, fleeing the grounds. Just as they reached the stable doors, a voice called out to them.

"Tzarik, wait!"

They turned to see Nefiri charging at them on a great white horse, covered in her red and gold silks and veils. Her horse whinnied and reared up in pure fright as lightning cracked across the sky.

"Nefiri?" Tzarik asked. "I thought you'd run."

She spun her horse, trying to calm it, but the thing was too wild. "I went to the palace," she explained. "But it's overrun with undead. Your Necro'Khan has struck."

The Runers exchanged quick glances.

"Don't," Nefiri warned, seeing the looks in their eyes. "Do not go to the Dynast Palace. It will be folly. I have seen it. Trust me, Sybal," she urged, locking eyes with his apprentice. "You must go. You cannot save Alika tonight."

"We won't flee," Tzarik barked.

"Tarkan has an army of undead," Nefiri reasoned, begging soaking her tone and filling her eyes with tears. "He's clashed with the sorcerer within the palace. Please, Tzarik, go! It's you they want."

At this, Sybal gripped his arm and pulled him away from Nefiri. "There's something I have to tell you," she whispered.

"Not here," Nefiri added. "Go to the rivers. Flee. You will have your chance to face the sorcerer and Necro'Khan another day. But for now, go, please!"

TARKAN STOOD on a sandstone mountain overlooking Mysir and the palace. Rakthar and Acenoth flanked him now. Acenoth hadn't stopped admiring his flesh since Tarkan had placed his soul back into his decaying body. With the river of blood, Tarkan wove them bodies again, making them whole and strong. The ancient pharaoh held his hand up in the torchlight, turning it to look at his long, strong fingers.

"We once worshiped death," Acenoth said in his deep, brassy voice. "We were right to do so. Death was my god. I thought that in dying, I would ascend to godhood. But I see now it is in life we conquer death. I have been given a second chance to drive the foreign sorcerer from my shores."

Tarkan hardly listened to the ancient pharaoh's ramblings, his eyes tracking his Apostles. The One Thousand and One already marched into Mysir. From here, he could spot tiny fires, hear their screams, and watched as the temples' kehanns scrambled to gather the military.

"He will know I am here," Tarkan said. "Your men cannot die. I need them with me when I go into the palace."

"We are your servants," Acenoth replied.

Tarkan nodded. "Take this." He handed him a mori blade; the glass was empty, waiting to be filled with blood. "I will tell you when to use it. For now, command your men from above. Let Mysir see you. When you see Rakthar land behind the palace on that balcony, come to me."

"Yes, my khan," Acenoth said, bowing his head, fist over his heart.

The ancient Masahk spread his wings and lifted himself into the air, flying majestically over the carnage below. He shot like a falcon in a dive into the fray, shouting commands to his undead soldiers. Tarkan watched, admiring every fluttering feather, every elegant flap of the wings he had pieced back together.

"My friend," he whispered to Rakthar. "Bear me once again into battle."

Rakthar gave a deep, trilling purr when Tarkan ran his bony hand up and down the dragon's long snout. At his side, the blood blade glowed and Ishmael's heart pulsed. Not even half the blood had drained from the metal. It didn't matter when he could command the red rivers of life now flowing through the entire continent. He climbed up Rakthar's front leg and slung his own over where Rakthar's neck met his shoulders. He petted the dragon, the black scales glittering in the firelight that consumed Mysir.

"Onward," he whispered. Giving him a soft kick, he held on as Rakthar leapt up, diving almost straight off from the mountain peak. Tarkan clutched him tightly, utterly unafraid.

He circled the battle, taking in the brutality of the risen and undead slaughtering all who stood in their path. They carved an easy line into the palace, overtaking even invisible guards Tarkan could not see. He touched the heart of the sword. "We are all one blood," he whispered. "My Apostles. Acenoth. Speak through our blood," he commanded. "What do you see?"

Pulling some of the blood from the orichalcum into his pores, Tarkan heard Acenoth's voice.

"We are inside the palace," the ancient pharaoh replied. "They fall like sickly cows in plague."

"Sokar? Where is the Pharaoh?"

Acenoth laughed. "Cowering behind his sorcerer. Come, my kahn. He is near!"

Tarkan shot through the smoke and flame. "Don't let him out of your sight."

"He does not fight with the strength of a sorcerer," Acenoth replied. "His attention is divided. Should he drop his hold over the sun, he may try to kill us all."

"No fear," Tarkan replied. "I will sustain you with the blood. He will not be able to destroy you. Not yet. Your oath to not rest until Alika is safe will fight against his demonic magic."

The balcony he'd mentioned came into view. He had swept the palace grounds and knew this was the Pharaoh's war room. If an attack happened, they'd barricade him inside and have guards on the openings. As he spun around, he found he was right. Twelve guards stood watch on the balcony. Tarkan smirked, laughing darkly.

"Destroy them, Rakthar."

The black dragon arched his neck back, then flung it forward, blasting the guards with his dark breath. One shattered entirely, spraying the others with his red blood. They tried to rally and shoot, but Rakthar made quick work of them. Tarkan guided the dragon down, summoning Acenoth, some of his soldiers, and his risen to him. He felt the horde swarm to him.

Inside the war room, many voices cried out.

Chapter 38

Fall of the Pharaoh

"Get the necromancer!" Sharar ordered Amir.

Dust filled the air from the blast outside the walls. The Runer pushed himself up from underneath a few pieces of rubble and shook his head, the wind knocked out of him.

"We need to leave," Amir pleaded.

"Not now. He's here." Sharar turned to look out the newly blasted wall. "Go, Amir. Bring the necromancer."

Groaning and holding his ribs, Amir did as he was told. A cry behind Sharar alerted him to the others. Sokar lay on the floor, one of his long, beautiful wings trapped under rubble. Outside, undead soldiers swarmed in. In the sky, Sharar caught the familiar black streak of a dragon he'd not seen in some years.

"Tarkan," Sharar growled.

"Sharar, help me!" Sokar cried.

Outside the war room doors, guards shrieked and cried out as the onslaught came closer. Sharar ran to the piece of rubble holding Sokar down and called for Nasor to help. Together, the two of them shoved hard against the rubble until it finally turned. Sokar cried out as the jagged sides crushed and cut his wings. When he was free, Sharar dipped and wrapped his arm around his middle to help him up.

"Where are the Mirage?" Nasor shouted, tossing his jackal head to and fro.

"Fighting," Sharar groaned. "Take Sokar. Get him away from here."

Nasor reached for the Pharaoh, but the door burst open and fell down. Sand and dust converged into the room, making them all cough and cover their eyes. Outlined in the doorway was the unmistakable form of Acenoth IV. His great wings splayed out behind him in feathery arches.

Sharar roared and called on his fire. Tossing it toward the undead pharaoh, he thought he'd have him. But one of the soldiers ran in front of Acenoth, holding up a great golden shield to block the flow of fire. Sharar panted, slowly backing away.

"You have your tricks, sorcerer," Acenoth said, stepping over the corpses of the palace guards and some of the Mirage. More than a dozen undead soldiers flanked Acenoth as he entered the room. The other entrances were blocked by more undead.

"I am your descendent," Sokar tried, his one wounded wing quivering from pain and fear. "Why are you—"

Acenoth shouted, throwing his hands forward to signal his men.

Nasor dropped the Pharaoh and entered combat with his golden crook, engaging two of the undead to defend Sokar. A few remaining palace guards joined the fray, but Acenoth eyed Sharar, who slowly backed away.

"Every river has its end, sorcerer," Acenoth said, spinning his weapon in his hand. "You are no different."

Sharar's mind reeled as he tried to think of a spell. The ones that came naturally wouldn't do much against Acenoth. He had to back away and get a moment to think. He'd never been a warrior, a soldier. He was strong, yes, but not a fighter. That was why he always hired the brutish Runers.

"Sharar!" Amir's voice rang out.

A flood of risen swarmed the undead. Acenoth turned and Sharar looked around the massive Masahk to see Vicdan and Amir appear. Vicdan had a host of risen at his command and put them into action.

"Keep back!" Sharar called to Vicdan. "Don't let them near you. Amir!" he added, ordering the Runer to protect the necromancer.

The Runer guided Vicdan to a distance and fended off two undead who'd noticed their approach. The risen clashed with the undead in a sudden and terrifying tumult.

"Can't think on your feet, sorcerer?" Acenoth guffawed. Then he lunged forward, slashing at Sharar as he turned and ran, slinging a fist of fire at the Pharaoh.

While true, Sharar didn't reply. He'd never been in a battle before. The confusion, noise, and aggression made it impossible to think. He sent a bolt of lightning at Acenoth, hitting him and giving Sharar just a moment to see an undead aiming a bow at Vicdan. Grunting, he slung another bolt, striking the undead to the ground and saving the necromancer.

As he did, the wound on his side tingled.

Not now! Sharar begged. But the infection didn't heed his pleas. The pain shot through him, but he had to ignore it. Holding himself high, he thrust his hands out at an oncoming undead, sending it hurtling backwards into two more. By then, Acenoth stood up again.

"You can knock me down all you want, sorcerer," Acenoth said, "but I cannot be killed."

As he said this, Sharar saw a thin rivulet of red shoot into Acenoth from outside, giving him strength. The ancient pharaoh groaned in pleasure, rolling his shoulders.

"Let's go again, mortal," the undead Masahk jeered.

Realizing that if he stayed he'd be killed, Sharar turned to flee out the blasted wall. But the way was blocked. A giant black dragon with arching horns landed hard, shaking the palace. Atop the neck, near the skull, stood Tarkan. In his hand, a massive, straight-bladed sword glowed. The rivulets of blood came from the sword, feeding and strengthening the undead army.

Tarkan's icy eyes landed on Sharar. The Necro'Khan smiled.

ॐ

TARKAN MARCHED TOWARD SHARAR, his sanguine blade held tight in his left hand.

"Return to dust!" Sharar shouted, making a motion like he was throwing something at Acenoth.

Tarkan's heart would have skipped a beat were it still flesh and blood. Acenoth faded into gray before his eyes. Cinders wafted off his feathers and flesh until he succumbed, falling into a pile of ash. Sharar's wild, leering grin grew.

"You cannot stand up to a sorcerer, Tarkan," Sharar said, laughing.

Tarkan stood his ground, though his nerves wanted to quake. "You cannot raise the dead, Sharar. Your spells mean nothing to us."

Unclenching his fist quickly, he focused on the ashes. Blood flew in graceful arches from his blade to Acenoth, weaving him anew. Tarkan saw Sharar move to attack him. He hissed the simplest spell: one of the five original spells. He wavered, vanishing as he stepped where once blood had been spilled. Sharar cursed and spun on the spot.

Tarkan watched the battle around him, safe in his invisibility. The Runer, Amir, fought valiantly against the undead and risen alike. With him stood Vicdan, using his own risen to try to stem the flow. Amir protected Vicdan as he moved to keep away from the physical battle. The pair maneuvered ever closer to the second exit, looking as if they intended to run.

"Ashkan," Tarkan ordered through the blood, "attack the Bone-Scriven. Stop him."

Once Acenoth was risen again, he charged Sharar, engaging him in close combat. This forced him to stop slinging spells and fight like a mortal man. Tarkan spoke to Faraji through the blood.

"Get the boy king."

Faraji appeared almost immediately, no longer controlling his risen, opting for a blade. His veins pulsed under his black skin and blood smeared all down his robes. With a small horde of undead, Faraji attacked the posse surrounding the Pharaoh.

"Get me the sorcerer's blood," Tarkan commanded Acenoth.

With the sheer amount of undead and risen, the Pharaoh's guard, the kehanns, and others were overwhelmed.

Tarkan slithered up behind Sharar. "Now, Acenoth."

Acenoth parried one of Sharar's attacks, ducked under a quick ball of fire, and attempted to stab his chest with the mori blade. The sorcerer panicked and, in a flash of red sparks, vanished only to appear a few yards away, stumbling out of what Tarkan could only describe as a portal. Sharar looked just as shocked.

Sharar made the spell again, appearing beside a stunned Tarkan. Sharar spun, slashing at where he heard Tarkan's voice come from. Tarkan ducked and ran out of the way. He'd missed his chance––for now––to get Sharar's blood.

"I have him!" Faraji shouted.

Tarkan turned to find the young Pharaoh grappled in Faraji's great arms. Looking back at where Ashkan moved in on Vicdan, he found his Apostle using half a dozen risen to attack the Runer.

"Kill him, you fool," Tarkan growled.

Acenoth commanded one of his undead and the soldier fired at the Runer and the necromancer. Vicdan gasped as the bolt lodged itself into his left shoulder with a thud. He stumbled and fell backwards, out of Tarkan's sight. Amir soon became overwhelmed and fell to fighting on one knee.

"Ashkan!" Tarkan shouted. "Take the sorcerer's Runer." He turned back to see Sharar fleeing. "Stay, Sharar," Tarkan commanded. "Or I'll rip the boy's wings from his body."

Sokar screamed as Faraji slammed him hard onto his belly. The Apostle put one foot into the small of the Masahk's back to stop him from squirming. With one hand, he pressed Sokar's face against the ground. His wings flapped and flailed desperately. Faraji's other hand gripped the base of Sokar's wounded wing tightly. The boy yowled, begging Sharar to save him.

Tarkan waited, expecting Sharar to at least hesitate. But Sharar took the chance, fleeing with no one to stop him.

"Abigor!" Sokar screamed, thrashing against his captor.

"Break him!" Tarkan screamed.

The strong Apostle growled as he pulled and twisted his wrist hard. Sokar's screams covered every other sound as blood and sinew spilled and snapped. Just as Faraji cracked the bone and pulled the wing free, Sokar's cries stopped. He passed out from the pain and went limp.

"A disgrace of a pharaoh," Acenoth growled, kicking the other Masahk over onto his back to look at his tear-stained face.

In the silence, Tarkan snapped his head around the room. Sharar had fled. Rage, the adrenaline from the battle, and the thrill of Faraji's bloody display drove Tarkan into madness.

"Take the Runer," he snarled.

Faraji dove at Amir; the Runer was so exhausted and wounded that he went down easily. Faraji slapped his hand over Amir's mouth and nose, jerking his head back hard. He pulled his ruby blade and moved to cut Amir's throat. The Runer thrashed, clawing for breath and freedom.

"Don't," Tarkan ordered his Apostle. Faraji stopped, frowning.

Tarkan looked around at the carnage. It had been some time since he'd participated in a battle and won. He let his eyes rove over the bodies, the blood, the risen, and the undead.

Dazed and enthralled, Tarkan motioned Acenoth to give his undead orders. "We take the palace," he panted, the shuddering and breathlessness finally catching up with him. "Don't go out into the city. Yet. Soon enough."

"But the Al'Myrahn sorcerer escaped," Acenoth said.

Tarkan's eyes flitted to Amir. "We have an Al'Myrahn. And he'll tell us everything we want to know."

Amir glared at him over Faraji's massive hand. He thrashed once but stopped when the powerful Apostle started to strangle him.

"The Bone-Scriven?" Tarkan asked. He looked around, but Vicdan was gone. He was wounded somewhere. If the jongleur had gotten away and managed to leave the palace grounds, he'd flee. Maybe even try to track down Tzarik and Sybal. This gave Tarkan an idea.

They had Amir. The Runer knew Sharar. He could give them a lead, at the very least. He glanced down at the knife in his hand, where Sharar's blood should have been floating in the glass. Yes, Vicdan would go to Tzarik and Sybal. They were the only ones who would piece together exactly what had happened at the Dynast Palace. And he needed to reap his revenge on them, to send them back to where he'd rescued them from.

"Acenoth," Tarkan ordered finally, "Where is the vizier?"

"Wounded, but perhaps not dead," Acenoth replied, gesturing to somewhere behind him. "He fell soon after the onslaught. He lies within the palace."

Tarkan nodded. "Take the pharaoh and his jackal to the dungeon. Make sure they cannot escape. I'll deal with them later."

He left the war room and his men behind, wandering out into the empty, devastated palace.

He turned a corner and found himself in the throne room. Bodies littered the floor, and the decorative plants were hewn and scattered. Blackened pillars from fire lined the room. Slowly, he walked down the throne room, imagining it full of sentients while the boy king was in court.

When he reached the bottom step of the dais, he looked up at the ruby throne.

He placed one foot on the first step. Then the other on the second.

He ascended until the throne waited just before him. Turning, he faced the huge, dead-filled throne room. Then he took a deep breath and sat. The back of the throne pressed into his spine. The arms, smooth and clear, felt cool under his palms. He propped the blood blade up against the side of the throne, Ishmael's heart still pulsing.

"Father," he whispered, "I have surpassed you tenfold."

Chapter 39

---◆---

The Scholar's Runer

A day and a half later, Tarkan stood in the palace's dungeon and watched the Runer come back to consciousness. He noted the rapid rising and falling of his chest before his eyes fluttered open. Sweat gave his throat a light sheen. His fear smelled almost intoxicating. With the help of Faraji, he'd lashed the half-conscious Runer to the familiar torture table. He'd had the Apostles raid Sharar's home only to find it empty of the scholar but filled with his old torture devices and instruments.

Never in his life had Tarkan thought he'd be looking down at someone bound where he had been bound. As he watched Amir squirm, a thrill shot through him. Having power over another being, one strong and fearless like a Runer, thrilled him. A blood-lust like he'd never felt boiled up in his veins. Amir's dark, healthy flesh begged to be cut, rent open so his blood flowed. But Runer blood was foul. He could see the white veins pulsing in the Runer's honey skin.

"Do you know where we are?" Tarkan asked softly, his eyes never leaving Amir's.

Amir swallowed and strained to look around. "A prison." He looked back at Tarkan. "What happened at the palace? Why have you brought me here?"

Ashkan appeared on the other side, descending the stone steps. He carried something in his arms.

"To make you talk," Tarkan whispered. "This is the dungeon under the Dynast Palace. I know well what Sharar's torture chamber looked like, so I it replicated it as best I could. Why I have you is rather simple, Runer. You were Sharar's Runer for years, no doubt. You know him, his plans, where he'd run to. He's left these shores. You will tell me where he went."

Amir jerked against the restraints, testing them one last time. "You resort to torture?"

Tarkan smiled darkly. "I had the best teacher." He signaled Ashkan and walked to the head of the table so Amir could not see him. Ashkan moved closer. He laid down the bundle and unwrapped it. Something long, thin, and glass-like glittered within.

"You don't have to do this," Amir called to Tarkan. "I'll tell you whatever you want to know. Sharar is no friend of mine. Hasn't been for some time. I was loyal to the coin, not him."

Tarkan remained quiet, not answering, out of sight. Ashkan pulled out one of the glassy things, handling it delicately. Tarkan recognized it as an ancient Al'Myrahn torture device, a long, thin, sharp spear of glass. Made for slipping between the ribs and into the lungs, making tiny, painful punctures. If the victim struggled or breathed too hard, the thin needle would break, doing far more damage internally. The victims would often suffocate from holding their own breath.

"Necro'Khan, listen to me," Amir protested. "He wanted to go to Al'Myrah. He intends to threaten the sultana. He doesn't want her throne; he wants to stand behind her. To control her from the shadows."

Tarkan took note, but still did not speak. He didn't care if Amir spilled every single one of his life's secrets before Ashkan even started. That wasn't what he really wanted. For once, he was not the one on the table.

Ashkan waited, holding the glass spike. Beside him, another table was filled with all manner of waiting, cruel instruments. Ashkan waited for a command. Tarkan sighed, nodding.

"Don't," Amir begged.

Ashkan, face stony and impassive, gently touched the end of the glass to Amir's ribs. He waited just a moment before slowly pressing on the blunt end. The glass slipped into the Runer's skin like a fiery arrow through snow. At first Amir didn't make a sound. Then, when it found its mark, he gasped and groaned. He clenched his eyes tight and suddenly fought for breath. His right hand shook violently in the restraints.

"Why are you doing as he commands?" Amir asked Ashkan, his breath rasping.

Ashkan glared at Amir, eyes empty.

"Raise a ghost," Tarkan instructed Ashkan. "Take command of it, have it possess him." As he walked past, he gripped Amir's leather string of runes and ripped them from his neck. "I want to hear his screams from above."

"Necro'Khan," Amir moaned, almost begging, but he still had too much defiance in his tone for Tarkan to heed his plea. "Tell me what you want to know."

Tarkan wasn't going to let Sharar's pet off that easily. If he couldn't have the scholar now, his Runer would do. He marched to the steps, taking them two at a time, and slammed the door behind him.

AT FIRST, no sound came up from the dungeon below. Tarkan knew the floors had been built to hold noise in, but with the right prodding, a true scream of pain could penetrate them. He waited, the clicking of some celestial mechanism passing the time. Tarkan pressed his back into the door and closed his eyes. The door was a hidden entrance inside a study of the palace. In another prison, Sokar lay in a bloody heap, most likely dying.

Tarkan thought he should move now. He was delaying his victory, all for the satisfaction of doling out the punishment he'd endured. He'd taken Mysir, had taken the ruby throne. Sokar was his battered and dying prisoner. The palace was under his control. The Apostles flocked to him, knowing a Necro'Khan had risen and sat on the Pharaoh's throne, thanks to the testament of the Apostles he'd let live. It all overwhelmed him.

But he wasn't satisfied. Sharar and the Runers still walked the map. When Ishmael had destroyed Porsh, he'd gone on a pilgrimage to the north to find a sacred temple to Nephron and give him thanks for his necrotic gifts. Ishmael had revered their gods, and perhaps he should, too.

But what more can I give you? Tarkan wondered to his god. *I gave you everything. And you took her.*

Suddenly, Amir's scream tore up from the ground below. Tarkan leaned against the door harder, finding he had not moved from it. He clenched his eyes shut tight, remembering his own screams.

Zeva's screams.

Amir's cries of pain turned to ones of fear, then to yowling sobs. Tarkan pressed his palms over his ears hard, trying to cut out the piteous screams. Ashkan was quick and merciless. Tarkan appreciated how quick he was to show his loyalty. Quick to do his bidding, to stay in his good graces. Ashkan was a good Apostle. Ashkan would bring the utmost torment to this Runer on his behalf while he cowered away above them.

Cowered? No. He couldn't hide from what he'd forced Ashkan to do. He would go down and watch. He had to.

He took two quick steps away from the door, then turned, marching back. He gripped the handle. *No. I cannot watch,* he told himself. Was he this much of coward? *I must look upon him. I must witness what I do.*

Resigning himself, Tarkan threw the door open and marched down. Amir had quieted down. Only strained, wheezing gasps came out of him now. The sooner he got the torture over, the sooner he could return to the throne. And Acenoth and his One Thousand and One needed to be dealt with as well as the boy king and his loyal vizier. But they could wait.

Tarkan looked upon the Runer. Amir shivered from the possession that had just left his body, but sweat shone over the surface of his flesh. Ashkan dripped the familiar acid slowly over his torso from above. Tarkan's skin crawled.

"Go on," he whispered when his Apostle stopped. A long, thin sword stabbed through the Runer's left shoulder, pinning him to the table. His left wrist hung free, showing he must have broken it loose, or Ashkan had unshackled him when he was possessed.

"And if he tells me what you want to know?" Ashkan asked.

Tarkan steeled his dead heart. "Hurt him anyway. He's Sharar's pet. I want to hear him scream."

Another small drop of the green acid landed on Amir's chest, hissing as it ate away at the top layer of his skin before fizzling out. "I told you. He's going to Hatal. To the sultana," Amir said through clenched teeth.

"I heard you," Tarkan whispered, eyes fixed on his victim. "That's not what I want to hear. Ashkan...take his eyes."

Amir growled and shouted in protest. He struggled but stopped when his shoulder bled more. Tarkan spotted the glass blades, white with blood, on the side of the table.

Ashkan picked up a thin orichalcum blade and bent over Amir. The Runer steeled himself, not begging for mercy this time.

Tarkan turned away, eyes closed. His body recoiled when Amir screamed so high and loud that he knew half the country had to have heard him. It must have taken longer than he'd imagined to pull an eye from a man's socket, because Amir didn't stop screaming for some time. It went on and on until Tarkan thought he couldn't bear it any longer.

You became what you always hated, a sweet, soft, innocent voice said right in his ear.

"Zeva?" Tarkan shouted, eyes flying open. He spun on the spot, looking all around. "Zeva!" he cried. Nothing appeared. Not a ghost, not a wisp of her long, beautiful black hair, or the white veil she wore to cover her face.

Tarkan stopped, feeling foolish. He angrily wiped a single tear away from his sunken cheek. Ashkan had stopped, watching Tarkan. A bloody scar ran from Amir's brow to his cheek. The blade, white with blood, was held in Ashkan's hand. The Runer moaned, half conscious, face turned toward him. He winced, but still had his eye. Tarkan couldn't give the command again, his stomach twisting.

Amir gasped, unable to speak for a moment. Another drop of acid splashed over him, making him wheeze and gasp. Tarkan saw bone appear.

"Enough," he said suddenly. "Stop, Ashkan." He marched to his captive and shoved the acid away, spinning a brass handle to shut off the glass contraption. The movement placed him over Amir. He looked down at the mangled man.

Amir choked, trying to speak. "You think...you can stand up t-to Sharar?" he stammered. "He's craved this power s-so long. Once he understands all h-he can do, you are a dead man."

"Still loyal to Sharar?" Tarkan asked, honestly dumbfounded.

Amir shook his head as best he could. "I'm not a b-bitter Runer. Someone taught me to love this world. Monsters like you deserve to be h-hunted." His voice shook so badly he could barely go on. "Sharar's a vile man, a monster just like you. Murder was not m-my crime. I can kill you. And I will—it's my job."

"Alone?" Tarkan asked, amused. "I've never met a Runer like you, Amir. It would be a shame to snuff out a light like yours."

"Not a-alone," Amir went on. His body began to shake, his white blood leaking out of wounds that would not clot.

Tarkan glanced around. Sharar no doubt had vials of Runer blood somewhere. He could replenish Amir, make him heal with his rune, and then rip him open all over again.

"I'll find the others if I have to," Amir whispered. He turned his face up to the ceiling. "They'll help me."

"Tzarik and Sybal?" Tarkan asked.

To Tarkan's shock, Amir smiled. He tried to laugh, gasping. "Fate-bound," he whispered, his good eye growing heavy. "We can take away the last piece of magic you desire: Sharar's blood."

Tarkan snapped his fingers at Ashkan, who immediately turned and went to Sharar's shelves, looking for sulfates. The Runer was fading and needed to be given strength.

"Fate-bound?" the Necro'Khan asked. "That's djinn magic. Who —" He stopped. "Sharar's djinn? To which one? How?"

"The djinn was a man named Azar," Amir moaned. "Sybal didn't know." The Runer fought to draw his breath, wheezing and strug-gling, drowning in his own blood, but he smiled when he said her name.

"How do you know?" Tarkan asked, suspicious of the informa-tion. Would the Runer lie after all the pain he'd endured?

Amir took a shuddering breath. "The djinn told me some months ago."

"Why?" Tarkan growled.

"He told me how much I reminded him of—" he stopped to cough and clear his throat before going on. "I reminded him of his apprentice. I didn't know who that was, though. Just Sharar's mark. The djinn is not like others of his ilk. He was a sorrowful creature. I never liked Sharar much. I wanted to leave him, but the coin was too good." He lost his breath then and stopped talking.

Ashkan appeared, stabbing the needle into Amir's arm and hanging up the glass and corked bottle. Tarkan pulled Amir's runes from his robes. He cut the cord and placed artiah in Amir's palm.

"Heal yourself," he ordered. "Tell me more about the djinn. What else can you tell me?"

Amir tried to raise his left arm, but moaned and dropped it. Tarkan gripped the blade that pinned him to the table and pulled it out. The Runer didn't move. His breath came ragged and shallow. Tarkan watched the white blood run down the rubbery tube to the large needle, then to the Runer's arm.

"Leave him a moment," he whispered to Ashkan. He turned, leading his Apostle up the steps, away from the vile smell of the Runer's sulfates.

"If he heals enough, he will escape," Ashkan said once they were above ground.

"I know," Tarkan replied. "I'm counting on it. Assuming he has any fight in him left."

Ashkan fell into step with the Necro'Khan. "You want him to escape?"

Tarkan nodded. "We will follow him to Tzarik and Sybal. If what he said is true—" he couldn't stop the manic smile that took over his face, "—then Tzarik and Sharar are fate-bound. Tzarik's fate will be Sharar's fate. Sharar will indeed be hard to corner once he comes into his demonic powers. But Tzarik is still just a Runer. If we have him, we as good as have Sharar. I wonder if the sorcerer knew?"

"And you think Amir will find them? Look for them?"

Tarkan nodded. "He's not like his brethren, or how Tzarik was when I first met him. He's not apathetic to his fellow sentients. He has a code of honor, of righteousness. He will do what he can to aid those who would stop Sharar."

"What are your orders then, my khan?" Ashkan asked flatly.

Tarkan looked back at the dungeon door. He'd heard Zeva; he had no doubt about that. Why, he couldn't guess, nor how. Had it really been her, or had he imagined her voice in a time of weakness?

"We must find as many Apostles as we can," he said. "They will follow me if they are true to the scriptures. We must find them before Sharar does. Our powers are the one magic of this map a djinn does not possess. This is why I must create as many spells as I can. To grow more power that he does not possess. To find ways to bend the blood and death to my will. With all the world against me, I have only that."

Ashkan nodded, giving a small bow. "If he had even a single necromancer, what would that mean?"

Tarkan glared at Ashkan. "Do not leave me now, Apostle," he warned darkly.

"I will not. But I cannot speak for my brothers."

"This is why we must work now," Tarkan observed. "Our race for one another has begun. I will destroy Sharar before he reaches the pinnacle of his power. It is all in that book. If he reads the Mahit'Onomicon, he will unlock his strength. And learn his limits."

Ashkan nodded, frowning. "Find the fate-bound Runer. Find the Mahit'Onomicon." He took a breath. "We do need more men. I will find all I can. And you?"

"I must return to the palace." Tarkan glared south, in the direction of the throne room. "My reign as author of the blood starts now."

Chapter 40

---◆---

Convergence

Sybal snaked her way through the quickly moving citizens of Alika. Most were fleeing, clogging the rivers, the ports, the streets. She pulled the hood of a crimson cloak she'd purchased up over her easily spotted yellow hair. She and Tzarik covered themselves to hide the black of their Runer garb.

They'd almost run to the palace the night before, but Nefiri's warning had stayed them. Instead, the three of them fled to the river, but every other sentient had had the same idea. But Tzarik wouldn't run yet, leaving Alika's shores. So they'd hidden in the city, trying to discover what had happened. A few hours after the attack, it took no time at all for word to travel over the city and the evacuation to begin. They knew immediately that Nefiri had spoken truth and that Sharar and Tarkan had clashed in the palace. The sudden stop of the battle made them realize the Necro'Khan and the sorcerer had come to a stalemate.

"The undead still fill the palace," Tzarik had said, after being informed by a fleeing Alikan. "Sharar must have fled."

But he wasn't dead. He couldn't be. Sybal knew this. They needed to hide from Sharar—and perhaps Tarkan, if he'd found out about the fate-binding—and make a plan. Getting to Al'Myrah and warning the hot-headed sultana was Sybal's idea. *The fight is beyond us for now,* she thought. But they weren't going to give up. They just had to keep moving.

She slipped around the river's edge, looking for an abandoned boat. There weren't many, but a few were in such poor condition that no one wanted to steal them. They needed someone who knew a little about boats to tell them which ones might get them to Gypsu. From there, they'd sail back to Al'Myrah. And perhaps prepare for a war against a sorcerer.

But she had other things burning on her mind. She and Tzarik had not had a moment to catch one another up on their quests. Or to catch up on another long overdue activity she craved. Perhaps it was for the best, though. She didn't know how to tell him.

A purple riverboat stuck out to her. It reminded her of the nomadic Masahk tribes that traveled as entertainers. She rushed to it, shoving away a teenage boy who tried to hop the side and board.

"This is mine," she snarled. "Back off."

The boy made a rude gesture then ran into the throng of fleeing Alikans. Sybal stood up on the boat and waved her arms. She wasn't sure Tzarik could see her, but knew Signar would. While she waited for them to make it to the boat, she had to fend off three more groups of people. Then she went aboard to find it was a two room boat with a camp-like kitchen on the back deck. It was perfect.

She claimed one room for her and Tzarik, leaving the other for Signar. It wouldn't be very private for her and Tzarik once it came to the nightly activities she craved, but she'd leave that to Tzarik to explain.

Yes. She would make love to him and then tell him.

A sob made her gasp before she realized emotion had taken her over. She bit her lower lip hard, willing the tears not to fall.

Above her on the deck, two sets of strides she knew all too well walked across the top.

⚡

"WE CAN'T STAY HERE," Tzarik said once they were all three onboard. "The hull is sagging too deeply."

"We should have gone to the palace," Signar called, climbing up from below. "I don't think we tried hard enough."

Sybal met Tzarik's eyes. "We weren't prepared. It would have been a fool's fight. That undead army would have slaughtered us." She turned her eyes in the direction of the Dynast Palace. "It might be better to let them fight and kill each other off. But we will find a way to confront them."

"It feels like cowardice," Signar argued. He tapped the haft of his Vaeson axe, eyes piercing the sky above.

"That's something I will never understand about your kind," Tzarik said, sighing in good humor. "You and Sybal. So brash, charging into fights you cannot hope to win."

"It's the ice in our blood," Signar supplied with a similar smile. "But what can we do?"

Sybal eyed the long, thin, wrapped item on Tzarik's back. "You found the sigiled blade?"

Tzarik took it from his back and handed it to Signar. Sybal was confused at first, but when the boy unwrapped the long red blade and her sulfates boiled, she understood. She cringed away from it, wincing.

"What is that?" she asked. Tzarik moved away from the blade, too.

"Orichalcum," Signar supplied. "I can wield it safely because of the sigils. They trap the souls of the sentients killed, and the essence of demons and monsters, feeding the cursed metal. The spirits within set your sulfates aflame, he said."

"Who said?" Sybal asked, her head spinning. She pointed to the black wrappings, begging Signar to cover it once again behind the protective black. He did as she asked. "You met someone?"

Tzarik took a deep breath. "Yasuke."

"Yasuke?" Sybal gasped. She remembered the Masahk general. He'd been a frightening warrior, loyal to Wushito. But he had also helped them more than once before her death. "He was on Caerwren?"

"Yes," Tzarik said. "He's had quite a journey, by the sound of it. He followed TaoShin's advice and tracked me to Caerwren, but arrived before me. Then he found the blades and went on some sort of Wushito quest to find his direction. He came back for the blades after freeing himself from Rhostrana."

"Oh, gods," Sybal whispered. "He'd been taken as a slave? And he let you take this blade?"

"ShanBao's blade," Tzarik said. "I remember it from our fight. He stabbed me with it." His hand went to his torso, where no doubt the scar remained. "The sulfates protected me from supernatural damage, leaving only a scar. That's why my soul was not taken like the other sentients. The sigils could not fight the sulfates."

Now Sybal understood. She reached out to Signar, who handed over the blade cautiously. Carefully, using only two fingers, she lifted the black wrappings to look at the metal. The blade did indeed have a pearlescent red shine to it. Now that she knew, she recognized the orichalcum.

"The colors must come from the essence within," she mused. "The red must mean there are many."

"Or many demons," Tzarik suggested. "ShanBao used a parchment demon sigil when we fought, taking the thing inside himself and using its strength to try to overpower me."

Sybal smiled at her mentor. "You were a match for demon essence." Then her face fell and her heart sank. She had to tell him what Nefiri had said. She prayed to Layth'asad he was a match for higher demons. That he'd have an idea of how to save himself.

She cleared her throat and swallowed. She'd let him finish telling their tale first.

"And you?" She smiled at Signar, gently touching his face affectionately. "I see a Vaeson blade at your side. Tell me."

Signar launched into his own story, how they'd come to Caerwren, met Tage, and the sadness of Korvoth's fate.

"Oh." Sybal sighed sadly. "He was a good man, and a good Runer. He saved my life when we met him by chance on Al'Myrah, and he told us of the Runer's Death."

"Without him, we would not have made it long on Caerwren," Tzarik added. "He fought like a lion against the mori and the nolreith. I think perhaps it was his bravery that led to his death."

"This Aras killed him?" Sybal asked.

"No," Signar said with conviction. "Not directly. His strength is an asset to Altevine, though."

Sybal winced in disgust. Signar hadn't known Korvoth like they had, so he wouldn't understand. "But you saved Dain," she said, pushing past her sorrow. "Signar, was he kind to you when you were a prisoner in Northica?"

Signar nodded. "It was he who called me Skelmir. We understood one another somehow. The wild hawk in him spoke to the wolf in me. I remember the first night…" He trailed off.

"Tell us," Sybal said softly, taking this hand.

The young Vaeson licked his lips and looked away. "They were cruel to me. But you cannot hate them for it," he warned them.

Sybal exchanged a glance with Tzarik. His face said he'd be willing to cleave their heads from their shoulders if they hurt Signar again. She agreed.

"But not Dain." Signar smiled wistfully, remembering. "He

brought me food, and..." He lifted his left arm to show a terrible scar on the underside of his forearm. "When I was bleeding from this wound, he put his hands into my cage after ordering the others away. I was afraid of him. But he whispered to me, told me to not be afraid. I was, but I knew I'd lost too much blood. I wouldn't put my arm through the bars, which were made of swords, so he put his hand in. He took my arm and cleaned the wound." Signar swallowed. "I remember weeping, but not why I wept. Then he wrapped it. I tore it off the next day. I didn't understand. But I remember him."

"A fierce warrior with a kind heart." Sybal sighed.

Around them, another wave of evacuees started to fill the shores. The Runers looked up, curious. Some people were wounded while others ran in sheer panic.

"We should move," Sybal started. "We probably shouldn't stay here. Let's—"

Tzarik grabbed her arm, silencing her. His eyes shot into the moving swarm. Confused, she scanned the people with him. Following his piercing gaze, she saw what had staggered him.

A young man stumbled through the crowd, hand pressed to a wound on his left shoulder. He looked exhausted, tired, and thirsty. His long, deep brown hair still shone under the grime and desert dust.

"Vicdan?" Sybal whispered, her heart leaping into her throat. "Vicdan!" she screamed, waving her arms wildly. She leapt down, Tzarik calling her back, and plowed her way through the people. She heard Tzarik bark at Signar to stay and then the sound of his feet dashing after her.

The jongleur looked up from his sad trudge, eyes watering. His mouth fell open in a sob of relief. "Hello, Sybal," he said as genially as ever, despite his wound and beaten appearance.

"You're alive," she called, colliding hard with him and wrapping him in a tight hug. "We thought Skarde had killed you, until he said you were taken by pirates." She squeezed him hard, letting him know they'd try harder to keep him safe next time. "What happened?"

Vicdan pulled back, wiping his eyes with the palm of his hand hard. "You mean when Sharar had his brute of a Runer hunt me down and take me captive? Or when the bastard ate up the djinn like a hearty stew?"

"What do you mean?" Sybal looked into Vicdan's honey-colored face and her heart skipped a beat again. His eyes were a startlingly bright, almost glowing, green. Like a Runer's eyes.

Like a necromancer's eyes...

"You escaped?" Sybal asked.

Vicdan took a deep breath. "With help from someone I didn't expect. I figured you'd be here. I'm glad I was right."

Tzarik caught up with her, panting. He caught Vicdan's eyes as well. "What's happened to you?" he asked gruffly, grabbing Vicdan's shoulder.

"That would be an arrow," he said, wincing as the Runer's fingers set his wound aflame. "Oh, you mean the eyes." His face fell. "I'm... I'm so sorry, Tzarik, Sybal. I never told you."

"I don't understand," Sybal whispered.

Tzarik pulled Vicdan closer to them and started back toward Signar, but the boy had left the boat and followed. Tzarik glared at the Vaeson and told him to fetch the horses before someone stole them.

"What do you mean, you're sorry?" Sybal asked. "Vicdan, what is that?"

Vicdan stopped and faced them both. His eyes shone again as fear took over his handsome features. "Don't be mad at me, you two. There was no reason to tell you."

"Spit it out, singer," Tzarik growled. He'd not let go of Vicdan's arm yet.

"I'm... My tribe was Nashira," the young man whispered,

defeated. "The tribe that stood against house Mirzam—Tarkan's tribe. I come from a long line of Bone-Scriven Porshains."

Sybal couldn't stop her eyes from examining every part of him. "I don't see—"

"*Bone-Scriven*," Vicdan repeated. "The scriptures are on my very bones. Don't ask."

Tzarik shared a look with Sybal, then glared at the jongleur.

"I'm so sorry, Tzarik," Vicdan said. "I was too frightened to tell you when I met you, and after that, there was no point. I liked you two, and—"

"Does Sharar know?" Tzarik cut in.

"He made me an Apostle," Vicdan answered sadly, weakly motioning to his eyes. "Now I can't plow sentients with abandon." He tried to smile like his old self, but worry at the Runers' reaction kept his joviality at bay still.

"He made you an Apostle for a reason, no doubt," Sybal added. "Did he hurt you?"

Vicdan waved his hand, scoffing. "I can cope with pain. It's you two I was worried about. He wants to use me against Tarkan. I'm... I'm just so sorry I didn't tell you."

"No matter," Tzarik said, waving him off. He leaned in and embraced Vicdan with both arms. "You're alive and escaped him."

Sybal smiled at Vicdan's wide, shocked eyes over Tzarik's shoulder.

The Runer quickly ended the embrace. "We cannot talk more here. Let's find a safer place."

The four of them, Signar reappearing with the horses, slipped through the mass exodus back into the city. Life half went on as normal, with the peasantry unable to stop their way of life just because the palace had been attacked. A few homes reinforced had their windows, hired militia, or outfitted themselves before going about their daily lives. Others had packed wagons to leave the city, afraid of the unknown danger.

Sybal spotted a public house still open, fighting off a pair of raiders, and pointed it out to Tzarik. He nodded, then stopped. Sybal felt it, too, her sulfates telling her eyes were on them. She stopped, positioning herself between Signar, Vicdan, and the danger. Tzarik put his hand to his scimitar handle.

"I smell Runer blood," Sybal whispered. "I've only ever smelled it when I'm bleeding."

"I do as well," Tzarik confirmed. His eyes swept the crowd faster than hers. He grabbed her hand. Cautiously, he tilted his head to the west.

Sybal looked and spotted their follower. A man, far taller than Tzarik and wearing a Runer cloak and black tunic, shambled in their direction. He stumbled and put a hand out to grip the brick wall of the alley he trudged up. His hand was snow white, covered in Runer sulfates.

"Amir?" Vicdan whispered. "He helped me escape. He must have followed me."

"Helped you?" Sybal asked. "He aided me as well. Tzarik?"

Her mentor nodded wordlessly.

Sybal moved through the street to Amir. When he saw her, he moaned in relief. He reached his blood-covered hand out to her. Seeing the extreme pain in his gait, she ran to catch him before he fell. She could see under his hood now and spotted a river of sulfates leaking from his left eye. His lid was closed tight over it. She slipped her hand around his middle and he gasped and moaned.

"I've got you," she whispered, pulling him up with another gasp of pain. "Forgive me," she mumbled. She reached for his tunic—he didn't have his Runer armor on— and lifted the fabric. "Gods," she whispered when she saw the fresh wounds.

His entire torso was cut, slashed, and burned. His left eye was severely wounded. In a few places, it looked like he'd had a chance to draw the healing rune, but the stones didn't hang around his neck.

"What happened?" she gasped, lifting him. Despite his tall frame, he was thin and light, easy to carry.

"T-Tarkan," he moaned.

"Tarkan did this to you?" she said with a gasp.

Amir didn't answer, his head lolling back in complete, painful exhaustion.

"I'll get healing supplies," Vicdan volunteered. "I'll meet you inside."

Chapter 41

---◆---

Split

The public house they found had a fairly full tavern. Rather than the quiet din that usually filled the dining area of such places, a loud rumbling rolled over the people inside. Every sentient discussed what might have happened, some told stories as if they had been at the palace, and others were making plans to flee in case of another mysterious attack. A warrior or two shouted that they would go to the palace and were looking for brave fighters to go with them to investigate what had happened and find the Pharaoh. Groups of Masahk and Porshain slaves already dotted the streets, having fled the palace. They brought tales of magic, necromancy, and horror.

Tzarik shoved his way to the front and paid for three rooms, putting a large dent in his Al'Myrahn coin. Once he had it, the five of them quickly moved up the stairs, taking their saddlebags and other things into the middle room for privacy. Sybal laid the half-conscious Amir on the bed and drew artiah over his entire body a few times to get the healing started, then stepped back so Vicdan could begin his own healing.

"Oy, Sybal," Vicdan said with a wicked grin while he cleaned Amir's wounds with the supplies he'd picked up. "You're just about the only woman on the map I can shag now without dire consequences. It's been a while for me. Why not a pity shag?"

"I'll kill you, that's why," Tzarik growled, despite knowing the young man was in jest.

"You haven't changed at all," Sybal said, smiling and pouring some hot water into the basin from the brass pot beside the fire.

"I find change repugnant," Vicdan replied, still smiling. His gentle fingers worked their magic, cleaning and binding Amir's wounds while Sybal helped, drawing the healing rune over the worst wounds once more.

Tzarik moved to the window and looked out, taking in the flowing streets below. The sun should have been high, but had still not risen. The dust in the darkness obscured a lot of his vision. He closed the shutters and motioned for Signar to keep a look out. "I've been giving it some thought," he began, leaning up against the far wall and crossing his arms. "We should go after Tarkan first."

Amir moaned and turned to look at Tzarik. "No," he countered. "Tarkan is not at the height of his power. Not according to him."

Tzarik frowned at the stranger. "Explain," he quipped.

The other Runer gathered his strength and turned his head to face Tzarik. He looked half dead with the wrapping around his head and eye.

"Tarkan takes the blood of sentients," Amir said. "He gains that power. He went hunting for Masahk to test his theory some time ago. He bent fire to his will almost like a sorcerer." He stopped, panting in pain.

For a moment, Tzarik didn't understand why that meant they should not go after Tarkan first. Didn't that make him more powerful? "He wants blood," Tzarik mused when he saw what Amir tried to say. "Sharar's? The blood of a sorcerer?"

Amir nodded, wincing. Tzarik moved his gaze to Sybal. She now stood exactly as he did: leaning up against the opposite wall, arms crossed. Her fists were balled under her arms, though, and her brow was furrowed deeply. She didn't look at him.

"What is it?" he asked her.

Her blue orbs danced back and forth in her pretty face as she fought to find the words to answer him. "I... I don't want to tell you. I'm so scared, Tzarik."

He pushed himself up and crossed the room. Ignoring the others and their eyes, he cupped her face gently and bowed her forehead to his.

"There's nothing you cannot face," he whispered before kissing her gently.

She hissed in a sob and a tear ran down her cheek. Her face twisted in sadness and she shook her head. "No," she replied to something Tzarik could not hear. "I won't tell him."

"Sybal," he murmured, unmoving. "Tell me."

The sulfates warned Tzarik of Signar's changing body heat from where he stood by the window. The boy was worried now, too.

Sybal sighed. "Very well." She gently shoved Tzarik away and moved to her bags. She pulled a long, gently curved, wrapped thing he had only vaguely noticed before from the side of the leather cargo. Then she faced him, holding it like a sword. "Tzarik, do nothing. I mean it."

Confused, he nodded and shrugged. Behind him, Vicdan waited, not breathing. Amir tensed, his own sulfates no doubt rushing.

Tzarik had no idea what to expect. But when Sybal unwrapped an orichalcum blade, his confusion mounted as his fear dissipated.

"I don't understand," he began. Then his voice cut off.

Sybal unwrapped the pommel and hilt. Familiar engravings under gold leaf came into view. The scimitar was straighter than most. In the center of the cross guard, a blue, icy gem lay embedded. Tzarik knew that sword as well as his own. His heart stopped and all the breath vanished from his lungs. But something wasn't right about it. The gem used to almost glow, almost emanate a gentle light. Now, it loomed dark and dull. Like the life in it had gone out.

"Where…" he stammered before swallowing hard. "Where did you get that blade?"

His apprentice sighed, a fresh wave of sorrow devouring her. "From Sharar's estate."

Tzarik whipped around to look at Amir. The Runer nodded in accord.

"Why did he have it?" Tzarik asked. "Sybal, I don't understand. Just speak plainly."

She gasped at his harsh tone, but nodded, still holding the blade. "Azar vanished that day from you—as you told me—because he was god-touched."

Of course. Tzarik knew that. Azar had been touched Tzarik's entire life, ever since the man had found him as a small boy about to be executed in Ala'Nar.

"The god took him," he said, trying to meet Sybal at what she implied. "He became a djinn. That's why he vanished. I left everything of his in that shambled house we were hiding in. A sandstorm had come in and we needed to find shelter. I don't know where we were. I was dying."

Sybal sucked in more in air. "Nefiri told me," she said.

She didn't move to hand Tzarik Azar's blade. Even the strange writing on the side of the blade looked dull compared to the last time he'd seen it.

"Told you what?" Tzarik cut in. "How she…" He stopped.

Sybal nodded. "Yes. And how, to save you for a moment, Azar fate-bound himself to you."

Vicdan and Amir shared a quick glance.

Signar made the closest thing to a whimper a human could make. "What does that mean?"

Tzarik finally found his breath and inhaled sharply. How could that be true? Azar would have known that, with the state Tzarik was in at the time, being fate-bound wouldn't save him. No... It would have killed him. Azar had bound himself to Tzarik in the hope of dying.

"He must have known his god was about to take him," Tzarik mumbled, remembering his master's face. He'd loved Azar, and had thought Azar had loved him.

Or had he? Tzarik thought back to that night and spoke out loud to hear his own thoughts as he tried to sort them out. "No, he did. I was half dead from the ritual. He runed me to keep me alive. To ensure I lived, he..." His heart broke a little more. "He succumbed on my behalf. Let the touch take him at last. Became a djinn and bound himself to me so I would live."

He turned his face to Azar's blade, his chest tightening.

"A man worthy of a ballad," Vicdan mused soberly.

"Sharar took the djinn," Amir offered.

"He must have known you were on the hunt," Vicdan said to Tzarik. "But then..." The last of the joviality left Vicdan's face. "Oh, no, no." He dropped the last of the bandages he held in his hand. "Oh, gods, no."

Sybal nodded, eyes swimming in tears.

"What is it?" Signar asked.

Tzarik lost all feeling in his fingers, toes, and then arms and legs until it reached his heart, freezing him. He glanced at the wrapped, sigiled blade attached the saddlebags on the floor. "To kill Sharar...I must die."

No one spoke for a moment.

Amir groaned, pushing himself up. "He wants you alive. He's always wanted you alive. No doubt he'll want to keep you safe once he finds out. We must find him before the Necro'Khan does. He wants Sharar alive as well, for as long as he can stand. To drink his blood."

"Isn't he a sorcerer now?" Vicdan asked. "I was there, too."

"You were?" Sybal asked.

Vicdan nodded. "Necromancy is the one thing a sorcerer cannot do. That and whatever other parameters the gods put on them in that book."

"The book?" Tzarik asked, his throat dry. His mind still spun, but he had to gain control.

Vicdan nodded. "Sharar doesn't know what powers he has, doesn't know what tethers the gods have placed on such beings."

"What are they?" Tzarik asked.

Vicdan shrugged. "They'll be in the Mahit'Onomicon. As will every other magical secret."

"But there are limits to a sorcerer's power?" Amir asked, hopeful for the first time.

"There has to be," Vicdan explained. "They are the ones who have taken the powers of demons, not gods. But..." He rubbed his chest and winced. "Even as a man who doesn't know what he can and cannot do, he's powerful. More powerful than any being on the map. There is no magic like sorcery. No being like a sorcerer. No one has a harness on magic like them. And they cannot be bound like djinns, which makes them seem limitless."

"I've seen a small taste of it," Sybal mused. "We bound a djinn earlier this year. The fight was terrifying. Were I not... Well, he almost killed me."

The jongleur moved his sad green eyes to Tzarik. "I know how this sounds to you, old friend. I remember who you were when I first found you sulking in Ala'Nar." He stood up and almost walked toward Tzarik, but then thought better and held his ground. "I beg you, don't return to those thoughts. Not now. There has to be a way to stop him without death."

Tzarik didn't believe Vicdan. Not now. The dark recesses of his mind where he used to dwell, smoking and drinking, hoping consciousness would leave him, came back strong. It was a familiar place in his head to be. A place he knew and could control. Yes, he could slip back there. To the man he was before Sybal.

Sybal. He looked up and met her eyes. Only love, hope, and fear shone in her bright, blue eyes. He wanted to take her in his arms and hold her. Forever, if he could. She had forever. He'd thought at first that she'd vanish before him. Now, it looked like he would be leaving life behind first.

He had almost no time at all now. She'd have to endure forever without him.

"I'll go back to him," Vicdan said suddenly into the cold silence.

"What do you mean?" Tzarik asked. "Why?"

Vicdan took up a cloth and wiped Amir's white blood from his hands. He'd taken some sulfates from Tzarik's bag at some point and had replenished the Runer's blood.

"The Apostles, every last one on the map, will flock to their Necro'Khan," Vicdan answered in a scholarly tone. "There's not many tribe members of Nashira left, but that is of little consequence. Sharar wants a necromancer to study, to have by his side. He will read that damned book and try to find a way to take the necrotic powers for himself. So long as it's me he studies...he won't take another. He won't kill me, as I've said, because the others are more likely to be loyal to their Khan."

Amir said, "Sharar won't just take you back. Let me deliver you."

"Where?" Sybal asked.

"He was going to head back to Al'Myrah," Amir said, "once he was sorcerer. I know his routs well, as I've traveled with him for some years. He'll go to his home in Hatal. Vicdan, let me chain you once we're there. I'll leave you in the city's garrison and a letter for Sharar at the banks he frequents. He'll come for you, and with any luck will believe I am still loyal to some degree. I'll return once I'm more healed."

Vicdan hummed, a little annoyed. "Very well. But wait to leave me all trussed up until you know he's coming. I'm not sitting in prison for days with that bridle on."

A bit of pity for the talkative young man took Tzarik at this. Being unable to speak surely was the real torture for Vicdan.

"Before we leave," Amir added, "Tzarik, go into the city and buy a pair of messenger hawks. The ones trained on scent."

Tzarik knew the birds. Unlike regular messenger birds, who flew only between two places, messenger hawks were trained to fly to a certain place based on a smell they were presented with. Trained to fly to Ala'nar, for example, based on the smell of a yellow spice they sold there. Trained to fly to Rhostrana based on the scent of the salty meats they sold in the icy country.

"That way," Amir finished, "we can communicate with one another."

Tzarik felt Sybal's eyes on him. He couldn't delay, allowing her to wallow in sadness. "I'll go immediately," he said.

He ordered them to wait to leave the room until he returned.

The Runer jogged down the stairs and out the front door, rounding to the stables where his horse waited. When he reached it, he stopped, gasping. The emotion was getting the better of him. He pressed his hand into his chest and coughed. More than anything, he didn't want to return to the man he had been before Sybal. He leaned his arm on the side of the stable and pressed his head against it, collapsing against the wall. Something else halted him. Something he couldn't put into words.

Chapter 42

---◆---

Return to Al'Myrah

Sharar waited days before making his next move. He hid, at first, in his own home, waiting out the panic from Mysir. He watched, worried Tarkan might find him. But the days passed with no sign of the Necro'Khan leaving Mysir. Sharar traveled by the river back to Gypsu where he waited several more days, contemplating his next step. With the djinn gone and Amir missing, he had no one to speak of his plans with. He found himself speaking out loud, but no replies came. Realizing his fear was unfounded with his new found power, he made up his mind to travel back to Al'Myrah. By the time he worked up the courage to try a portal, it had been two weeks since the attack on the palace. By now, the others surely would have moved.

Sharar stumbled from the portal. The fiery, spinning circle had appeared a few feet above the golden sand of Al'Myrah and he tumbled out, landing hard. His mount, a black Al'Myrahn race horse, whined as it leapt through, kicking up sand as its hooves made contact. Taking the portal had not sat well with him, but he had to shove his nausea aside. Pushing himself up, he found himself only a mile from where he'd tried to drop through. Behind him, the portal snapped shut. He dusted off his robes and took in his homeland.

He stood atop the orange mountains of southern Al'Myrah, overlooking Hatal and the glorious aureate domes of the sultana's palace. He took in a deep breath and held it, loving the burning air of his homeland. The spices filled the air and the sun seemed to have a gentler warmth. Salt filled the air on Alika, and the sun shone harshly, glaring off the white sands. He'd decided to hide the sun almost purely out of spite for the white sands and their blinding refraction. Here on Al'Myrah, it shone.

The sorcerer glared up at the orb, bringing his spell to Al'Myrah now. The magic came almost like an instinct to him. He could feel what he wanted to do. Slowly, the circular orange orb began to vanish. It never set; he'd just hidden it. He watched, forcing his eyes to latch onto the burning sun even as they watered. Slowly, a shadow passed over the sun, blotting it out. The sky turned a dark, burnt orange. A few stars flickered into life as the greater light vanished. Slowly, those vanished into darkness as well, blackening the sky.

Satisfied, he looked out over the borders of the principality of Hatal.

"I love you," he whispered to Al'Myrah. "And I've missed you." He knelt and pushed his long fingers into the orange and gold sand, feeling the soft, dust-like quality of it. He glanced to his left and right, missing having a companion.

Forcing aside his emotion and the longing for hearth and home, he took the reins of his horse and ventured farther into the mountains. He couldn't go to Hatal, not yet. He needed to arrive in such a way that fear would strike into the heart of the woman who sat upon Al'Myrah's golden throne. Moving cautiously over the crags and sharp mountain spines, he journeyed up to where he knew a red dragon roosted.

The dragons, for near on a hundred years, avoided civilization. Not only Runers, but some human and Masahk sentients alike, had turned to dragon hunting fifty years ago, slaughtering many. The market for dragon hide, teeth, and claws had nearly capsized due to the glutting of it. For several seasons, the people of Al'Myrah had thought they had hunted dragons to extinction. They nearly had. Now the beasts stayed in the mountains, hardly ever coming out to the cities.

Fearless, knowing he could control the beasts, Sharar marched into a large, rocky clearing atop the lonely mountain nearest Hatal. He spotted signs of the red dragon everywhere: claw marks, animals bones, scorch marks, and even a large pile of dragon dung.

"Where are you now?" he murmured to himself, scanning the openings to three dens. He missed having Amir by his side to speak with about the creatures. If the Runer still lived, he'd like to find him one day, as well as his necromancer. Sharar had a sense Amir had grown less and less fond of him and their alliance over the recent weeks, but he didn't care. He liked the Runer and knew how to keep him on a short leash.

A deep, roiling rumble came from the left den. Sharar spun to look into the darkness.

He stepped into the shadow of the cave. "Let me see as a Runer sees," he whispered. As his eyes slowly adjusted, a splitting pain shot through them, making them water. He blinked, keeping focused inside. Vaguely outlined against the darkness, he spotted a red beast with a spiny back and a twisted set of black horns looking his way. The dragon hunkered down like a cat, slitted yellow eyes watching him.

"You think you can pounce on me?" he called to the monster. "I will take your mind as my own." He reached out to the dragon's mind and found it easily. Dragons were fierce, loyal, but stupid beasts. With perhaps the intelligence of a lion, he found the mind of the fire-breather simple to take under his command. "Walk to me," he ordered it.

Trembling, shaking its head, trying to throw off the tether it no doubt felt, the red beast rose up and slowly marched out to Sharar. Despite knowing he held it fast, Sharar backed up a few steps as the beast emerged. Its softer underbelly glimmered gold and its scales shone like rubies. Black claws and horns made it look fierce. It walked on all fours, like a horse, its wings folded on its side, unlike the western dragons whose wings elegantly sloped from their spines to the bend of their forelegs. Like Rakthar, that damned black dragon Tarkan loved so much. Sharar had been jealous of the dragon for years. How Tarkan had tamed the thing, he'd never know. But he didn't need to know now.

"Roar for me," he commanded the beast.

The red dragon threw its head back and gave a thunderous shout to the dark sky above.

Satisfied, though still wary, Sharar commanded, "Kneel. Let me mount you."

It bent down, offering a front leg as a stepping stool. It lowered its head, commanded by Sharar's will, and allowed him to climb up. He couldn't stop a gasp of timidity as he did. He'd never mounted anything greater than a draft horse. Being up upon the dragon's shoulders sent a shocking thrill through his limbs. He watched the ground push away as the beast stood up.

"Well done, you," he praised. He cautiously patted the dragon's scales, finding them hard and smooth. He inspected where his thighs met the scales and realized he no doubt would rub himself raw during the flight. But he tossed the thought aside, knowing he could heal himself.

"I will learn my other powers soon enough," he told the dragon. "For now, our power is fear. To the palace then, beast. Tanyin," he added after a second. "That's what I'll call you. It means dragon in the old tongue." Laughing at his own unimaginative name, he directed it into the sky and toward the sultana's palace.

⚡

SYBAL HELD her tears in as the great ship sailed into port on Hatal's shores, glad to be home again. They had been to Moshav, but only for a short time. Crossing Al'Myrah with Signar in the cage seemed a lifetime ago. Now, the boy walked beside her, tall and strong. Behind her, Tzarik led the pack of horses up from the hanging stables below. Amir came down first, leading his great black horse that reminded her of Mamun. His blue eyes took in Hatal's port city, which was called Mazahara, and was rivaled in the buzz and noise only by Singad. Being the capital province, more people, merchants, traders, dignitaries, and other such people flowed through.

"Do you miss it?" Amir asked at Sybal's side.

She looked up at him. "Don't you?"

"Terribly," he mumbled.

She offered him a gentle smile. Somehow, knowing the Runer she had assumed would be an enemy missed his home as much as her made her put aside her prejudice. There were few Runers on Al'Myrah, and all of them hated the people, but they loved their country.

"I wish I didn't have to come back under such circumstances," Amir finished.

Sybal looked ahead, being able to see over most of the people and mounts clogging the immediate area. "You are sure Sharar came back to Al'Myrah?"

Amir nodded. "That was his plan. To return here. Vicdan and I must move quickly."

"Perhaps he misses home as well," Sybal tried, but she doubted it.

"Where will we go?" Signar asked, joining her in looking for a way out of the docks. He began to lead the way, cutting through the people easily.

"I have a place. Tzarik?" she asked. Her mentor had been quieter than usual, speaking perhaps only two words to her and Signar the entire voyage from Alika. He was dwelling on what she'd said. That could be dangerous for him. She made sure to not leave him alone, to keep him in her sights. "What's our first move?"

The older Runer's blue eyes had dulled. He took a long breath. "I don't know," he mumbled.

Sybal groaned inwardly. In the last year, he had become a new man. And now he was changing back to the silent, sullen Runer he had been when she'd first met him.

Won't you seek my council? the voice asked sweetly. *After all, it is my demon within the sorcerer.*

Won't you smite him, then? she snapped.

The voice laughed lightly. *I give you my strength, my power, and my council. What more do you want, woman? The map is your domain. Fight your own battles.*

"We know Sharar won't kill Tzarik," Sybal began.

"Does he know?" Signar asked. "About the fate-binding?"

Amir shook his head. "That's not why he initially hunted Tzarik. Sharar...had a son. A young boy who was runed."

Sybal started at this.

"A son?" she asked, wondering what woman would lie with such a slimy snake.

"Yes," Amir said. "A man who hated Sharar runed him out of spite. The runes did not take to him, mutating him, making him very ill. Sharar thought the runes rejected him because he was innocent. Blameless."

Sybal glanced at Tzarik. "I see. He believes some answer lies within Tzarik." She glanced around. "Let's not talk here. I have a place for us to stay."

"You do?" Amir asked.

She nodded. "Before I was a Runer, I was Lady Sybal El'Freja. And now, with my family dead, I am the only heir. I am Sheikha now. My family had a small house in Hatal, as well as our estate in Ala'Nar. But I doubt that's standing anymore. I wrote ahead to our Keeper of the Keys to see if he was still enjoying my fathers pay. He was. I had him work with a quadi to get me the keys to my land. We can stay as long as we need."

Amir grinned and scoffed lightly. "A home? A roof? You are fortunate."

Vicdan moaned sadly. "And I'm off to prison."

"I've had a home my whole life," Sybal said. "Until I was runed. I had to grow accustomed to your way. Amir..." She stalled a moment, testing her instincts. She felt nothing warn her against him. "You are welcome to come back to us. If you will help."

"I plan to," the other Runer replied with assurance. "My former apprentice, Ashar, resides in Al'Myrah, though this is not his home. He runs a forge with his own apprentice, Ari, when he's not hunting. He will be a good ally for us."

"I remember Ashar," she said, recalling the nightmare that was the coliseum and their hunt for the pishaca. "He was extraordinarily brave."

"He is." Amir grinned proudly. "Also a much better man than I. I fear Sharar knew my..." He trailed off, clearing his throat.

"Affection for him?" Sybal offered with a smile. "It's all right to like another human being, Amir. I've been telling Tzarik that for years." She quickly glanced at Tzarik, but he remained stony.

Amir's face paled as his blood flushed his cheeks. He averted his eyes from Sybal. "So I've found out recently. Ashar made me a better person. He's courageous, good. Once we're together again, we will aid you in any way we can. He has connections on Bahratt, which may be of use."

"They will," Sybal promised. "Especially since mine have long since expired." She stopped and turned to take the reins of her horse from Tzarik, who was still quiet. "We'll stay at my family's home in Hatal where we can speak in private. Vicdan..."

She faced the sullen singer and offered him a tight hug.

"You know you're brave for doing this, right?"

"I'm aware of my heroism," he said with a smirk. "But I do expect rescuing."

Sybal released him and reached out, touching Amir's arm. "Be careful. Both of you."

"You as well," Amir replied.

Vicdan and Amir turned, vanishing into the city to head to a place Sharar would be sure to look. Sybal sighed deeply, wishing her friends—people she cared about—didn't have to be put in such danger.

I wish a lot of things right now, she sighed inwardly. *A great many things.*

Tzarik followed her in silence.

Chapter 43

A Cure For Fate

The palace came into Sharar's view, and just as it did, the people of the main city of Hatal screamed and scattered like ants. He'd healed himself only once during the flight, and now the sun began to shine over the dunes once again. He could have used the portal, but that seemed far less dramatic.

"What the hell?" he mumbled, wondering if the magic had somehow worn off. He willed the sun to shadow itself once more. "Why?" he growled.

Angered now, he directed Tanyin down into the walls of the palace and directly to the floating veranda where the harem was located. Guards screamed, but he directed Tanyin to belch a jet of fire at them, scattering them. Making sure the Mahit'Onomicon was still lashed securely to his hip, he dismounted and marched inside the harem. The men inside panicked, dropping everything and running.

"Do not run," Sharar ordered, brazenly striding inside. He pointed to a guard who strode toward him and Tanyin snapped him up in his jaws. The man screamed as his bones crunched and his blood leaked down between the massive teeth.

Sharar scanned the strange harem of men before him.

"Where is Kalil?" he asked. "The first husband. That is his name, is it not?"

A few of the men in the harem nodded and some looked around.

"What do you want?" a high, strong voice asked from his left.

Sharar turned and the small mass parted to show one man, perhaps ten years younger than himself, standing defiantly with his gilded fists clenched. He wore white and gold wrapped around his lithe frame and had shiny, combed hair. He looked surprisingly brave for a man facing a dragon. His golden eyes flashed defiance and courage.

"Everyone saw this beast come here," the younger man went on, glaring and not trembling. "You have only moments before the guards descend."

"Tell them to stay back," Sharar ordered, squaring up to Kalil, the sultana's first husband. "Boy," he growled, when the man didn't move, "I will burn this palace to the ground with everyone inside before you can stop me. I have hidden Alika's sun for days. I am the Father of Monsters. I am not a man to try."

Kalil gulped and his wide amber eyes turned from defiance to fearful consideration.

"I will not harm another," Sharar promised, "but do not force my hand." He raised his left hand, calling on the sky above. Thunder rumbled overhead.

Kalil gasped and his eyes flitted up for just a moment. "Stay," he commanded the other men. "I will return," he promised Sharar.

"You stay," Sharar ordered. "Send another."

Kalil turned his head to a much younger member of the harem. "Bagoas, go. Tell everyone on this level to leave. Have them pass the word on."

"Yes, sira," Bagoas whispered, his voice trembling. He stood and ran on bare feet down the hall. He called to everyone to leave, his voice growing fainter for a minute.

Sharar kept his eyes trained on Kalil. The sultana's husband did not shudder in his presence.

Bagoas reappeared. "They are all gone."

"Now," Kalil said, forcing his voice to not tremble. "What do you want?"

"Where is the sultana?" Sharar asked.

"I won't let you harm her," Kalil said as bravely as he could.

"And I won't," Sharar said. "I am not here to kill her. I am here to speak with her." He smiled charmingly. "She will want to be on the side of the first sorcerer to walk the map in a thousand years."

Kalil's face twitched with a tinge of fear now. "So you are," he confirmed. "Leave the rest of the men be," he bargained. "Don't harm Hatal."

"Take me to the sultana," Sharar ordered.

Kalil nodded. Unsure what powers the sorcerer might wield, the man said, "I will take you to her. If you swear not to harm her."

Sharar sighed. "I am not here to hurt her. I am here to bargain. Keep the guards off me and you have a deal."

The man turned and marched back to the door. Sharar followed, constantly calling on his magic to keep in touch with the roiling clouds above, should he need to call down a strike of lightning on the gilded young man.

It had been some time since he'd been inside the palace. The tapestries on the golden walls still told stories in bright weaves, the statues still watched over the halls with glaring, fierce eyes. Like the palace in Alika, small man-made streams flowed inside, and a few patches where trees sprouted up kept nature alive within the halls of pillars and opulence.

"She's in her chamber," Kalil said nervously. "She went there to pray when the sun vanished. Now I see her prayers were in vain."

Sharar smiled.

Kalil stopped outside two massive golden doors inlaid with gems. "She is alone. I will not leave her with you."

The sorcerer smiled again. "I'd hope not."

The man pushed in the doors and entered. The sultana's room glittered with every trapping a woman of her standing could want. She stood alone on a balcony, all swathed in white and gold, with ample amounts of her honey skin showing. Her black hair hung loose as Sharar had never seen it before, waving in the gentle desert air.

"Kalil?" she whispered.

When her husband did not reply, she turned and gasped, one hand gathering her sheer skirts. "Who are you?"

"Abigor Sharar," he answered, coming close to her. "I once was a scholar in your court."

The gilded woman scanned him carefully. Her beautiful dark eyes narrowed. "I think I remember you. What do you want? Are you here to tell me why the sun vanished? Just now I thought it would shine again, but it has gone dark." She took a deep breath. "I said once that it was the end of days, when the dead walked my sands, killing my people in Ala'Nar. A damned Runer told me to stay my hand. Now..."

Beside Sharar, Kalil lowered his head.

"Tell me about that," Sharar asked, interested. "I am something of an expert when it comes to Runers. And the risen dead."

The sultana glared cautiously at Sharar as he joined her at the small balcony's edge. "I was full of fear." She motioned for Kalil to join them and he did. She took his hand. "I was going to sacrifice the love of my life to start a war I could not hope to win."

Gently, she raised Kalil's palm to her lips and kissed it before placing it against her face with a sigh. She nuzzled her cheek into his soft hand.

"I forgave you," Kalil whispered.

"I don't deserve you," she replied. She lowered his hand, but still held it. "I thought it best for Al'Myrah to die in battle. But the Runer stopped me. Said he'd take care of it."

"And did he?" Sharar asked, knowing full well this upstart of a Runer had to have been Tzarik.

The sultana half shrugged. "The dead have not been risen in some time on Al'Myrah."

Sharar smiled, his joy bubbling over inside. "Sabi, that necromancer acted on my orders," he said with a grin. "He was my slave at the time. But I was weaker than he."

The sultana pulled away, horror striking her face. Her pink lips twitched, not finding the words to express herself.

"Yes," Sharar mused. "But that necromancer got away from me. He's the Necro'Khan now. And I am afraid he will come to Al'Myrah. But you have no need to fear if you do as I say."

"Why would I?" the woman snapped. "You attacked Al'Myrah!"

"And I will again if you do not do as I say," he growled back. Overhead, the thunder rumbled as he summoned up a strike of lightning. When she did not flinch, he cast around in his mind for another spell. He wasn't sure what else he could do. He'd not had time to pore over the Mahit'Onomicon yet. He needed time. Time to study. He thought about making Kalil burst into flames, but nothing came to mind. So he reached to conjure fiery hail.

The sky turned black with clouds and whistling orbs started to fall from the sky.

"What are you doing?" the sultana cried.

A small piece of fire fell into Hatal, crashing hard into a city street. Another fell, breaking through a courthouse roof and setting it aflame. The sultana screamed and Kalil shouted about him breaking his word. But Sharar didn't hear them. As he called the hail, he felt the sun once again slip from his control. Behind the black clouds, it began to shine.

What the hell? he growled to himself again. He still held Tanyin and the hail. Two. He held two spells. Like the two wishes he'd made.

Cursing the Mahit'Onomicon, he released the fiery hail and the lightning. The sultana and Kalil stopped shouting when he did and the weather cleared. They clung to one another, terrified as Hatal started to smolder.

"I swear!" the sultana said, finishing whatever tirade she had been screaming at him. "I see your power. Please, stop."

Not having heard her at all, Sharar smiled simply. "I don't want to take your palace, your throne. I want you to remain in power."

"But you will control her," Kalil spat. At some point, he'd placed himself between Sharar and his wife.

Oddly brave for the foppish man, Sharar thought. "Exactly," he said, smiling at Kalil. "And don't think you're safe if she does as she's told. I can kill you and all of Hatal as easily as I hid the sun."

But he wasn't sure now. He'd have to read the damned book and find what limits had been placed on his sorcery. And the book held more spells, but it seemed he couldn't cast them until he'd read them. It mattered little, surely. Reading and learning was what he did best. There had to be one to set a man ablaze. That would be the simplest way to take out Tarkan. Burning a lich often did the trick.

Annoyed, he gripped the book. "Do we have an accord then, your majesty?" He glared at the woman.

"What do you want me to do?" she asked, afraid. Her hands went to her stomach, rounding over the top and bottom.

She was with child.

"For now? Nothing," Sharar instructed. "I have some research to do. You have seen my power. Do not set one gilded finger out of line, or Hatal burns. Do you understand me? I am here to save you from the Necro'Khan."

"Of course." She nodded. For a moment, he thought about

taking Kalil as prisoner, but decided against it. She'd know he could have, and perhaps would be thankful he did not.

"I won't have time to ask if you have betrayed me," Sharar warned her, preparing to leave. "So do not test me."

"I swear," she said, gasping. He suspected she was grateful he was leaving.

Smiling, Sharar turned, his silken robes billowing around him, and marched back to Tanyin. He needed to return home. Somewhere he could read the book in silence and try to understand. He wasn't powerless, but he didn't have limitless power, either. He'd known from the start the book was the key, but he'd abandoned it too early.

Taking his dragon, Sharar made his way to his old home in Hatal.

෫

AFTER LETTING Tanyin hide in the mountains, still under his will, Sharar went to his most trusted keeper at the bank of Hatal to retrieve his keys and make sure the affairs of his estate were still in order. He never let anything go to his groundskeeper at home while he was away. It had been months, and he knew there would be at least something that needed attending to.

"Ah, sira," the banker said, recognizing Sharar. "Back from your travels, are you?"

"As you see," Sharar said, smiling. "They went well, though I could have done with more studying, it seems."

"As you wish," the banker said with a laugh. "I don't have a head for such book learning. Speaking of which, that Runer of yours came by."

"Amir?" Sharar asked.

The banker nodded. "Left a letter and a key." The man turned around to the wall of little wooden slots and scanned it until he found a sealed parchment with a key slipped inside. The banker took it down and handed it to Sharar after he signed for it.

"That's all?" Sharar asked.

The banker nodded. "Been a quiet year for traveling parcels. Your groundskeeper did stop by, but I had nothing for the estate."

Curious, Sharar tore open the letter.

SHARAR,

I realize now you no longer have to pay me and, should you so choose, you could strike me down where I stand. I would rather stand with you than against you, since the result of such opposition would no doubt be my death. I am a Runer, sorcerer, and my loyalty is to survival. I have gone to hunt and gather my pay from Sheikh Sahir. As an offering, I have left a gift for you at the central prison. Take him with my fealty. I will return and find you, bringing news that is of the utmost importance for you to hear. Be wary, the Necro'Khan hunts you.

Signed,

Amir Al-Saiid

SHARAR STARED at the Runer's signature. Amir was fearless and had a will of iron. Hiding like this wasn't like him. Unless he feared he might lead someone to Sharar. He was loyal like that. Unsure, Sharar took the key and walked the few blocks to the smaller prison house in the legal district. A man and a few guards at the front recognized the key and led him in.

"Strange Runer," the warden said as he led Sharar into the prison and down a long line of cells. "Brought in a man all trussed up, with a torture device on his head."

A necromancer? Sharar thought. "Thank you, sira. For your silence." He handed him a few gold coins when they stopped at a dark section of the prison.

The man pointed into the cell. Sitting with his back against the stone wall, jaw bound behind the familiar bridle and arms bound behind him, was Vicdan. Half of his face had turned purple from a beating.

"Gods damn me," Sharar mused. "It is you. Well done, Amir."

Vicdan glared up at Sharar through his one un-swollen eye. He didn't try to even move around the cruel device.

Sharar handed the man the key and waited as he unlocked the cell. "I'm so happy to see you again, my boy." He smiled. "We have a lot of work to do."

SYBAL'S FAMILY'S home in Hatal was just as she remembered it. The Keeper of the Keys had followed through on their correspondence and had prepared the place for her arrival some weeks before. He greeted them at the gate, recognizing Sybal and looking nervous. She shooed him away after he called for servants to take their horses to the stable.

The home sat outside the larger city amidst other farms and vineyards. Itself a vineyard, a few servants moved about, seeing to the grapes and the storehouses. She ordered they be left alone, but noted the curious and shocked looks of the workers and servants as she, now a Runer, entered with a pale man from the west and two other Runers. It must indeed be strange for them to see three Runers in what had been their home for almost four years.

"Basari," she called once they entered the main portion of the house, "you have done well taking care of my family's estate. Thank you."

"O-of course, Lady Sybal," the older man stammered. He fiddled with the end of his long white beard. "It was Dorsa. The man who ran your mines."

"Dorsa?" she asked, remembering the man well. "Where is he?"

"At the main estate in Ala'Nar," Basari replied. "Shall I send for him?"

"No," she said, smiling. "No need." She turned to Tzarik and Signar. "You may choose whichever room you wish. But you must be clean. Both of you."

Signar rolled his eyes and departed, wandering off to explore the elaborate structure. He'd spent his time on Alika in the embassy, but buildings like this still brought awe to him. Sybal smiled, watching him roam down the hall, his head tilted up to take in the ornate ceilings with their paintings and golden rafters.

She moved to Tzarik, taking his hand and guiding him up the steps to the largest bedroom. Once there, she removed her own armor, watching him. He stood with his back to her, looking out the window over the vineyard.

"Please, say something," she said softly. "I don't like this silence. Especially without knowing what you're thinking." He didn't move. "Tzarik," she called a little more forcefully, but still kindly.

Annoyed, she pulled her boots off, then moved toward him, coming around to face him. Gently, she unlaced his armor and slid her fingers underneath, removing it. She set it down, then ran the back of her hand down his cheek.

He took a long, deep breath. "You would have to lose me at some point, anyway," he said with a ragged sigh. "What's sooner rather than later?"

An icy bolt shot through her. "What are you saying?"

His sad eyes turned down, avoiding her gaze. "You're immortal, as far as we can tell. I'm not."

Realizing she hadn't thought of that, and rather shocked she had not, she dropped her hands from his shoulders. "Or the touch takes me first. Can't we wait for that instead?"

Unable to stop herself from touching him, she ran both her hands through his grimy hair, holding him tight. She kissed him and hugged him, squeezing his hard, muscled body against hers.

An urgency filled her then and she pulled him to the bed. She lay first, pulling him on top of her. Finally, he met her eyes. She smiled, blinking slowly as his hand ran down her face. He gently rubbed his thumb over her lips.

"I couldn't bear to lose you," he said. "But you—"

"I couldn't either," she quipped, cutting him off. "I'm not as strong as you think I am."

"Sybal," he said, stopping her with a kiss. "You were someone before me." His eyes ran over the room, acknowledging her family and her status. "I was no one. I was not even human before you. You are everything to me. You saved me, made me whole."

A light giggle brought a smile to her lips. "I practically had to force you."

"But you understand, don't you?" he begged. "We can't let Sharar and Tarkan fight one another all across the map. And Tarkan had Amir as his prisoner. We have to assume he knows about me and... Sharar. He'll hunt me down, and you. Sharar has hunted me for years. I have faith in you to finish the fight."

She sat up, shoving him back a little. "Are you suggesting we take your life? And I face Tarkan alone?"

"Not alone," he said. He took her face in his hand firmly. "We have made friends, allies. And you..."

She shook her head. "Not without you. We will find a way. Let Tarkan and Sharar battle each other. We will find a cure for this fate you have been bound with."

"And let them rampage over our home?" Tzarik spat, suddenly showing anger. "Signar's throne is in the midst of this..." He fought to find a word for it. "Deep Rift," he finally spat out. "He is in danger as well. Tarkan went to Caerwren for a purpose, and I helped him destroy Altevine."

Bitterness, guilt, and fear twisted Tzarik's face and voice.

"Please," Sybal begged, tears spilling down her cheeks. "Don't think like that. Don't talk about ending your own life, not again. You fought so hard to pull yourself out of that dark place."

"I don't want to go back there," he argued, desperate. "But what else can we do? We don't know how to stop a sorcerer. We don't know what he is capable of. We have a chance to stop him now."

"We'll find a way!" Sybal shouted, shoving him from her. He flailed backwards, falling from the bed. She regretted her violent action, but forced herself not to run to him.

He stayed where he fell, not willing to get up. She turned away to face the open wall that looked out over the vineyard. She sniffled and fiercely wiped at her eyes. He wouldn't rise without her.

"Come here," she whispered sadly, holding her hand out.

Slowly, Tzarik stood and rejoined her on the bed. She laid down, pulling him with her.

Sybal's long, elegant fingers wrapped around his middle. She didn't speak, but pulled him into an embrace. Her long arms enveloped him, crushing him against her. She still didn't speak, just held him. Her hand caressed the back of his head gently, fingers tangling in his long hair.

He shifted, straddling her, and slowly bent to kiss her neck. She lifted her head, inviting his kisses and presenting herself to him. Unconsciously, she reached her arms above her head and arched into his touches. His hand slipped under her tunic and found every soft, sensitive spot, making her gasp and move in pleasure. To her, every time felt like the first time.

She reciprocated when he pulled her tunic off and soon they wrapped around one another, naked, flesh to flesh. He devoured her in touches and with his lips. Holding him tightly as they began a rhythmic pulse wasn't enough. She threw her legs around him, pulling him deeper as she methodically bucked her hips to him. A sudden bolt of lightning shot through her as his roving hand saw to her every need.

In an instant, everything exploded. She cried out, tossing her head back, digging her nails into his back. At the same time, he groaned, biting the soft spot between her neck and shoulder. Time slowed as a wave of heat washed over them together. Tzarik collapsed onto her. She caught his face, pressing their lips together and parting his with her tongue.

After several more minutes, the storm quelled and they lay together, limbs entangled around one another. Tzarik lay behind her, his arm wrapped around her middle. He gently ran his fingers down her back, over her scars. She didn't want to break the spell, but they had to speak. To continue the conversation.

Sybal turned, breaking his gentle caresses, and faced him. "We will find a way," she whispered, petting his hair. "The mihals say the cure for fate is patience. I swear, I will save you. Like you saved me."

Tzarik cast his eyes down. The paleness from his rushing sulfates faded from his cheeks. He pulled away, fighting to find the right words.

"Sybal," he choked, finally realizing what had stopped him. He'd found the words, but didn't want to say them. Not to her.

"I," he whispered, fear at the confession strangling his words. "I don't want to die. Not now."

℞

The hunt ends in *Season of the Runer Book V: A Cure for Fate*

The Runes

Artiah: The rune of healing. Drawing artiah will mend minor abrasions and heal larger wounds enough to allow escape. Artiah will also take away a small amount of pain.

Atan: The rune of light. Drawing atan will create an orb of light for all eyes to see by. Atan also reveals hidden spirits and can show disguised monsters in their true form.

Buhkar: The rune of mist. When buhkar is drawn, the Runer dissolves into a black, smokey mist able to slip between tight spaces, evade a grip, and blend into shadows easily to be undetected.

Halat: The rune of protection. When halat is drawn, the caster is safe inside a circle of protection. Anything that wishes the caster harm cannot pass the boundaries of the protective circle.

Jiun: The fury rune. Jiun—the most dangerous of the runes—turns the Runer into a berserker. Cutting off all feeling to wounds and ailments, the rune pushes the caster beyond their inhibitions. Jiun also lends temporary strength and heightened senses.

For more information about the world of the Runers, please visit www.abigaillinhardt.com/sotr

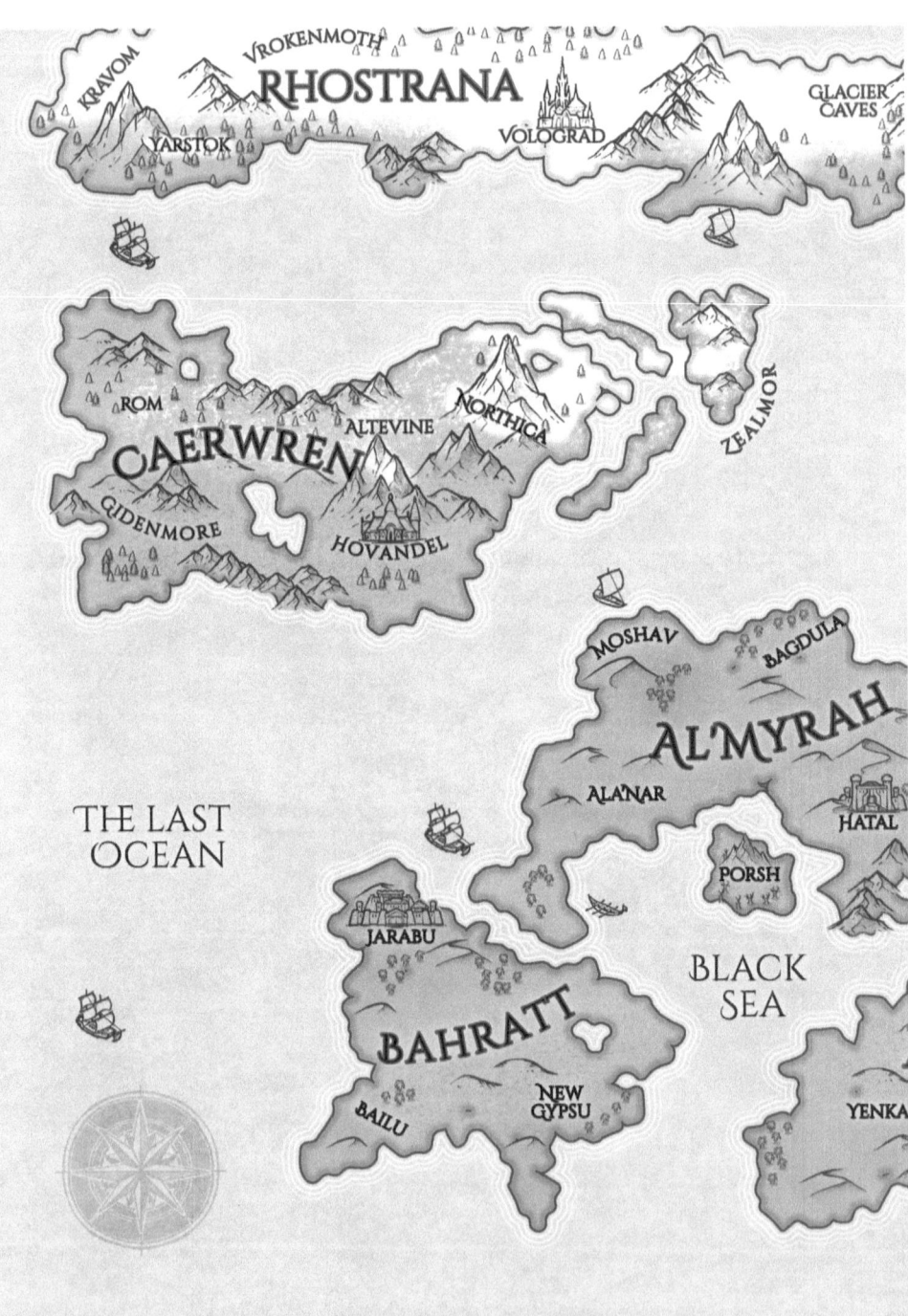